Smartly dressed, resourceful, and discreet, **David Gunn** has undertaken assignments in Central America, North Africa and Russia (among numerous other places). Coming from a service family, he is happiest when on the move and tends not to stay in one place for very long, but if he calls anywhere home, it's the UK. His first two novels, *Death's Head* and *Death's Head: Maximum Offence*, are published in Bantam paperback.

D1471743

DEATH'S HEAD

DAY OF THE DAMNED

David Gunn

BANTAM PRESS

LONDON · TORONTO · SYDNEY · AUCKLAND · JOHANNESBURG

TRANSWORLD PUBLISHERS
61–63 Uxbridge Road, London W5 5SA
a division of The Random House Group Ltd
www.booksattransworld.co.uk

First published in Great Britain
in 2009 by Bantam Press
a division of Transworld Publishers

A CIP catalogue record for this book
is available from the British Library.

ISBN 9780593058732

Addresses for Random House Group Ltd companies outside the UK
can be found at: www.randomhouse.co.uk
The Random House Group Ltd Reg. No. 954009

The Random House Group Limited supports The Forest Stewardship
Council (FSC), the leading international forest-certification organization. All our
titles that are printed on Greenpeace-approved FSC-certified paper carry the FSC logo.
Our paper procurement policy can be found at
www.rbooks.co.uk/environment

Typeset in 12.5/15pt Bembo by
Falcon Oast Graphic Art Ltd.
Printed and bound in Great Britain by
CPI Mackays, Chatham, ME5 8TD

2 4 6 8 10 9 7 5 3 1

For –
Do unto others as they would do unto you.
Only do it faster and harder.

Prologue

GENERAL JAXX APPROACHES A WALL AND SPINS ON HIS HEEL, HIS
timing perfect as his left boot stamps on marble, his step
echoing like a rifle shot off the walls of the emperor's audience
chamber.

Twenty paces later, he turns and heads back. He marches
with the iron determination of a man who remembers being
whipped for marching out of step. In that memory he's eight,
his first year at the Academy.

A fire burns in the great fireplace. OctoV likes to be warm. Or
maybe he just likes his generals to be uncomfortable. The
emperor wears full dress, and expects his officers to do the same.

The difference is he wears his lightly.

On the wall OctoV takes salute from his victorious troops.
One of them is the general's great-grandfather. He stands
behind a major in the Wolf Brigade, whose fur cloak must be
vile in that heat.

General Indigo Jaxx is both younger and older than his
emperor. OctoV was fourteen when the general was born.
He was fourteen the year the general's father was born. He's
been that age for as long as anyone can remember.

The general runs a hand through his cropped hair.

It comes away wet.

OctoV, the glorious and victorious, the undefeated and ruler of more worlds than any man can count, whose sweat is perfume to his subjects . . .

Some generals vomit before an audience. Others kill themselves. One gave his ADC his own rank badges and told him to pretend. Both died the death that act deserved.

'Meeting him is like having your brains extracted, liquidized and returned by someone using a mallet and a blunt spoon.' The officer who wrote that left his own brains across the note on which it was written.

But Indigo Jaxx is not just general of the Death's Head, the emperor's elite force. He is Duke of Farlight, the most powerful man in the empire after OctoV. And since OctoV is not strictly a man at all . . .

Aware his marching could be seen as nerves, General Jaxx stamps to a halt, pivots on his heel and stares out of a window. His heartbeat is steadying and his pulse slowing. When he sweeps his fingers through his hair they come away dry.

His body knows what his mind has yet to accept.

It has stood down its defences, untied the knot in his gut, dried the sweat on his ribs and replaced all three with a cold certainty that makes no sense but accepts no refusal.

OctoV is not going to show.

This afternoon's audience between the emperor and his empire's most loyal subject, General Indigo Jaxx, has been cancelled.

Taking a look around the audience chamber, the general nods grimly. His staff wait beyond the door, and under no circumstances must they discover the meeting never took place.

'Sir,' says Jaxx loudly.

This is what he always calls the emperor. The only one of OctoV's subjects allowed that latitude.

'Yes, sir,' he says. 'Certainly, sir.'

Having counted to a hundred, he bows himself out.

'Back to HQ,' he growls.

As General Jaxx leaves the palace without noticing a Wolf Brigade general's amusement, he considers what the emperor's decision to cancel the meeting might mean, and knows it is not good.

Chapter 1

THE LIZARD'S MISTAKE IS TO MOVE. THE MOMENT IT SWAPS granite for red dirt and the temptation of food, it's dead. Because my blade hisses through the air to open its spine from skull to tail.

It's a small lizard.

All the big ones are eaten.

Picking it up with metal fingers, I hold it over the fire until its flesh crisps and the skin peels. The man I offer to share with doesn't want to. So I bite off its head, chewing happily.

'Sven,' Anton says. 'That's disgusting.'

It's not disgusting at all. It's hot and salty from the grass and the saline bugs filling its stomach. Believe me, I've tasted worse.

'He only does it to annoy you,' says a voice.

My side arm has been sulking since we landed yesterday. It wants battle. It wants slaughter. It wants glory and another chip upgrade. The SIG's got a wolf hunt instead. Pulling the gun from my holster, I toggle it into silence.

'Can I look?' Anton asks.

He takes the SIG-37 carefully. The piece has that effect on

people. Full AI side arms are rare. Not to mention illegal. 'Pretty,' he says, handing it back.

Not sure that's the word I'd use . . .

'Yeah, I know,' Anton says. 'Never ask a man if he's Legion. He'll tell you if he is. If not, there's no need to embarrass him.'

In my case telling people is compulsory. That's because I was once busted back from sergeant, and the law wants trouble-makers identified early, particularly dangerous ones.

We're near the edge of the rift, hidden in scrub.

A fire burns behind us. Dry kindling and dry wood so it makes no smoke. A freshly killed rabbit roasts above it. The spit is made from thorn and I trapped the animal two minutes ago. Anton's hungry and still refusing to eat lizard.

'You know,' he says, 'it's good to see you.'

I'm waiting for the *but*.

'But we thought . . .'

'OctoV suggested it,' I say, cutting him short. 'And a suggestion from our glorious leader . . .'

'So the general had no option?'

'None.'

Anton is shocked. As well he might be. I'm here on leave at OctoV's suggestion. The idea that our glorious leader should bother with the welfare of a junior lieutenant, even a useful one, is so absurd I'm wondering about his real reasons. So is Anton, from the look of things.

'It's strange,' he says, 'how little Debro and I know about you.'

'What's to know? I'm a Death's Head lieutenant.'

'That's it?'

'Before that, a prisoner on Paradise.'

'And before that,' he says, 'the Légion Etrangère . . . Sven, that's not really an answer.'

Sounds like one to me.

He tells me most people, if you ask them who they are, tell

12

you about their family or their childhood, where they grew up, what they wanted to be. 'Come on,' he says. 'What is your earliest memory? Debro was wondering.'

Killing a dog. I'm five, maybe six. The dog is bigger than me. But old and toothless. The dog has only one canine. I have a brick.

I win.

Before I can drag the dog into hiding, older boys take it.

One of them uses the brick I used on the dog. When I wake, they're gone and so is my food for the week. The smell of meat leads me to their fire. From their surprise, they weren't expecting me to get up again. But I mend fast. How much faster than others I don't know back then.

And I fight dirty.

Kicking embers at one, I knee another between his legs. He's old enough for it to matter. A third turns to run and I kill him with my brick. They should have taken it with them.

No one argues when I go through the dead boy's pack and take his blade.

The dog is too hot to carry. So I use my new knife to cut free a half-cooked leg and spend the next two days throwing my guts up.

Anton wishes he hadn't asked. 'You know,' he says, 'maybe you shouldn't tell Debro after all . . .'

Three hours to darkness. To be honest, I'd rather be here on my own. But it's his hunt. I'm only here because Debro, his ex-wife, thinks I'll keep him safe. Although the sour smile on their daughter's face when we leave says she believes the opposite.

'Something wrong?'

'Why?'

Anton glances at me. He's been doing that lately. Mostly when he thinks I'm not looking. 'You're grinding your teeth.'

'Thinking about Apt.'

That's Lady Aptitude Tezuka Wildeside, all of sixteen.

He decides teeth-grinding makes sense.

★

People keep to themselves in the high plains. Few families live here from choice. Most have fled debts or are running from conscription in the army of our glorious emperor. A few like Anton are in exile.

Some are in hiding . . .

I'm on extended leave. It's the same thing.

The ground is hard, the grass sparse. Water is rare as hen's teeth. Sixty miles from where we sit it pisses oil instead of rain. A pall of smoke hangs to the north of us and drifts from the roiling flames that rise from the rift floor. A hundred fires, a thousand fires. No one knows or cares. The rift is just somewhere to avoid if you have sense.

A geoforming malfunction, Debro says.

No idea what that means.

There is a deadly beauty to the hills around us. The heat will bake you, and the cloudless nights freeze your flesh to your bones. False paths wait to tip you down ravines. Sour water poisons those who drink unwisely. And that's before you meet the snakes, wild dogs and mountain cats. And wolves.

Anton is an ex-captain of the palace guard, ex-husband to Senator Debro Wildeside, one of the richest women in the empire, and an ex-inmate on Paradise, a prison planet on the other edge of the spiral arm.

Me, I'm ex-Legion.

Think I might have mentioned that.

He's told Debro we're here to shoot a rogue wolf.

I know better. Anton wants to talk. You'd think, out in the desert, that he's trying to avoid the spies of our glorious leader. But since our glorious leader hears everything, I assume he wants to avoid being heard by Debro.

Anton grins when I say this. 'You've changed.'

'*Adaptive*,' I tell him. 'That's me.'

His eyes widen. Adaptive isn't a word I use.

14

'Said so in my last psych report.'

'The one they shredded?'

Yeah, that one.

'So,' I ask, 'what's this about?'

The last time Anton and I talked was on Paradise. I was keeping him and Debro alive. Times change. I get the feeling he's trying to repay his debt.

'Sven,' he says, 'if you need money . . .'

'I don't.'

Anton sighs. 'We know you're in trouble.'

That is one way of putting it. Dig two friends out of prison. Blow up an enemy mother ship. Protect some snot-nosed colonel from his own stupidity. Get my general promoted. Win praises from our glorious leader. And end up with a list of enemies longer than I can count, starting with General Jaxx himself.

Welcome to the Octovian Empire.

Anton won't let me shake off his thanks.

That tells me how things have changed. In prison I'd simply punch him into silence. Now we're on his ex-wife's land, with his buggy parked behind us, and he owns the hunting rifle I'm using. It's a beauty, too. Perfect balance, a custom stock and a telescopic sight so true that looking through it feels like being there. The round's 7.62, full metal jacket. Anton's old-fashioned like that.

'We couldn't believe it,' he says.

He hesitates.

'No.' The man corrects himself. '*I* couldn't believe it. Debro always said you'd come through. But when the guards arrived . . .'

Memory chokes his voice.

'Leave it.'

Being freed isn't the first thing on anybody's mind when the guards turn up. Being taken for questioning. Being shot. But freed?

Time to change this conversation.

'You really think a wolf's out there?'

Anton squints towards the goat we've tethered to a post. The animal has sunk into an exhausted silence. Its tugs against the rope are weaker than they were an hour ago.

'Yes,' he says.

'Then we'll give it another five minutes.'

'After that?'

'We go looking.'

His laugh is a bark. 'Believe you would.'

What's to believe? Temperature's dropping and night's coming in. There are tacos and cold beers waiting for us at Wildeside. The sooner the wolf is dead, the sooner I get a drink.

'*Sven . . .*'

Seems I won't have to go looking after all.

The wolf is huge. Grizzled and grey around its muzzle. It's also limping, and has a gash on its haunches that looks fresh. As it crests a boulder, the beast stops to look back. Neck out, head held awkwardly.

'Clear shot,' Anton says.

I can see that. Hell, I've rarely had an easier target. The animal's backlit by twilight. My line of sight is clear. And the animal so close the scope is a luxury.

So what stops me?

That gut feeling I get before shit goes bad.

'*Sven . . .*'

'Not yet.'

Anton scowls, but he waits in silence. So does the wolf. The goat, however, goes berserk. All the more so because the wolf is ignoring it. When the SIG-37 shivers out of standby, I know we're in trouble.

'Arid wastes,' it says. 'Pitiless sun. Poisonous water. A million miles from the nearest decent bar. Remember how you said we'd be safe here?'

Not sure I put it like that.

'Guess what? You were wrong.'

Very slowly, I hand Anton back his rifle.

'Go,' I tell him. 'Get back to the buggy.'

The idiot shakes his head.

'Listen,' I say. 'I didn't bring you back to get you killed. Leave. I'll keep you covered.'

'Sven,' he says, 'I can't—'

'Just do it.'

'Guys,' my gun says. 'Focus on what's out there.'

Chapter 2

I CAN PUT A NAME TO THE DANGER. SERGEANT HORSE HITO, killer by appointment to Indigo Jaxx, general of the Death's Head. Now Hito is a man I regard with respect; I just didn't expect him to find me so fast.

Torn between its prey and the person coming up behind, the wolf hesitates. Probably thinks Sergeant Hito wants its supper.

'Just Hito?' I ask.

My SIG does that whirring thing. 'No,' it says. 'Two . . .' It hesitates, flicks a few diodes. 'Three . . . Four,' it confirms finally. 'The first has broken away. He's heading towards us.'

Doesn't sound right to me. 'Stealth camouflage?'

'No . . . Yes.' The SIG sounds puzzled. 'Maybe.'

'Fucking great.'

'Not my fault,' it says. 'It's—' I ignore whatever else my gun wants to say. Because the trouble is here.

'Sven,' Anton says.

Yeah. Seen it.

Fuck knows what it is. But it's not General Jaxx's assassin. Even Horse Hito at his ugliest doesn't look this rough.

Triangular face, sunken red eyes, needle-like teeth. When the

18

wind changes direction we smell its stink. Like vinegar. The weirdest thing is its skin. Silver and leathery.

Anton fires.

Picking itself up, the creature gazes towards us and then turns to the wolf, which finally breaks its silence with a long low growl.

'It's a fury,' Anton says.

I'll take his word for it. 'Hollow-point,' I tell my gun.

Flechette's too specialized and I don't plan to light the night sky with incendiary, which would simply advertise my position to anyone else out there. Like the real Horse Hito.

Hollow-points spread. That's why I use them. These slugs keep 99.8 per cent of their mass and achieve a 300 per cent spread on a typical torso shot, and I fire three in quick succession. Turns out to be as pointless as shooting holes in a wet paper bag.

'Wait,' Anton shouts.

So I hold off going after it with a knife.

As the fury advances, the wolf tips back on its haunches. And then it springs. That's when something strange happens. Instead of dodging, the fury slams its fist into the wolf's ribs.

We hear bones break.

Gripping the wolf's scruff with one hand, the creature rams the fingers of its other hand into the animal's chest. The wolf howls. Obviously. Blood runs down the fury's wrist, but it also drips from the wounds we punched in its gut.

'Fuck,' I say.

Anton nods. 'Drinks through its fingers.'

'Blood?'

'Only blood.'

I can see why he's worried.

Now the wolf's dead there's no prize for guessing the next target. Unless we were the target all along. Mind you, there's always the goat. Ripping free my knife, I flip it round and throw.

19

Bleating turns to a scream of pain.

And the fury racing towards Anton hesitates. Twitching sideways, it heads for the goat instead. Grabbing the animal, the fury sinks its fingers through muscle and fresh blood begins to trickle from its gut.

The bastard has skeletal arms and legs, a sack-like gut and a focus so tight it can't do more than one thing at once. Fight or feed, not both.

That's its weakness.

Maybe it's used to people backing away. Or maybe I just imagine something flicker behind those eyes.

'Sven,' Anton says.

'I know what I'm doing.'

'Hey,' says my gun. 'Always a first time.'

We're circling, the fury and I.

It lunges and I block its wrist. Like being hit with a steel bar. Next time I'm going to use my combat arm. I step sideways and it steps sideways. Not sure this thing is alive in a sense I understand. But it mimics my steps perfectly.

And it's going to be a bastard to kill.

It lunges, I block.

When it makes its fifth or sixth lunge, I step into it. And feel the creature's fist crack open my chest. Bones break and ribs are forced apart as it reaches inside.

Hurts like hell.

That is where the fury comes unstuck. Its skeleton might be metal. But so is my combat arm, which is piston driven and twisted with braided hose. Plus I kill on instinct. Now I might have learnt to keep that under control . . .

. . . But everyone's allowed a day off.

Gripping its wrist, to stop it reaching my heart, makes the fury raise its head and hiss at me. So I tighten my own fingers and twist. Bones break somewhere under that leathery skin.

'Earth to Anton,' the SIG says.

I'm getting there.

Ramming my gun against the creature's throat, I pull the trigger and watch bits of steel spine, wire and withered flesh exit through the back of its neck. Hollow-point, got to love it.

'Throat?' Anton says.

Obviously. I doubt if it has a brain worth shooting.

Man down. Anton kneels at my side as blood pools in a fuzzy-edged circle round me. Darkness is here and the night goggles he's slipped over my eyes make my blood look almost fluorescent.

'Sven . . .'

'I'm fine.'

He stares at me.

'Go get the buggy,' I tell him.

Flicking up his own goggles, he examines my face. Not sure what he expects to see without night vision. 'OK,' he says. He wants to say something more. Goodbye, probably . . . Idiot thinks I'm dying.

He's right, of course. Only my metabolism isn't that simple. Already I can feel flesh closing and bones beginning to heal.

'Sven,' he says.

'Yeah,' I say. 'It hurts. Now fuck off.'

He leaves without looking back. Sir Anton Tezuka, armiger and trade lord . . . Walks away, with his head up and shoulders back. Losing himself in the darkness to give his friend space to die with dignity.

Shit, you've got to love the Tezuka-Wildeside.

They're screwed to hell. But they know how to behave.

Reaching into the gash in my chest, I find a cracked rib and pull it straight. The broken ones are trickier.

There are three of these. Two have simply snapped, but the third is smashed in two places so I deal with it first. Feeling for

21

the sharpness of broken bone, I slot the section into place. Hurts like fuck, again.

Always does. Every single time.

That's why I sent Anton away. Don't like showing pain, and sometimes, like now, it's impossible not to. Blood from a bitten lip drips on my jacket. When the ribs are done, I settle myself against a rock and wait.

Anton isn't getting the buggy. He's gone to fetch a burial party.

Dumb bastard.

It's almost daylight before I hear a vehicle in the valley below. It's not the buggy. An ex-militia scout car to judge from its camouflage. Painted-out numbers are just visible on the turret. A whip antenna flicks in the breeze.

Gears shift and the scout car begins its climb.

Fat-wheels lurch as it bounces over rock and slams down again. The reconnaissance vehicle isn't fast, but it's powerful enough to grind its way up this slope.

I can hear it change gear, the wild dog that has been watching me can hear it change gear, and so can the buzzards circling high in the pink sky overhead. Guess Anton reckons that if Horse Hito is out there he'd have attacked already.

First out of the cab is a blonde-haired girl, who runs towards me, loses her nerve and slides to a halt, face twisted with misery. About a year back, the first fifteen years of Aptitude's well-ordered life crashed into mine.

The stiffness to her shoulders tells me she's crying.

'Hey,' I say. 'It's OK.'

'*Sven* . . . ?'

I'm almost on my feet, when she flings herself into my arms and almost knocks me over. I'm a foot taller, twice her weight and twice as broad. You need to see us together to realize how absurd that is.

'Dad said . . .'

Aptitude stops. Realizes she's clinging to me.

She steps back. Probably just as well. Because I'm realizing all the wrong things. Like she smells good and her breasts are firm and her lips are close. She's sixteen, for all she's a widow. I'm twenty-nine, maybe thirty.

That's too wide a gap for either of us.

Of course, her husband was three times my age. But that's the Octovian Empire for you. 'Don't get rid of me that easily,' I say.

We're halfway back to Wildeside when my SIG wakes. Its faint shiver has me scanning the horizon for Horse Hito. Looks clear to me. Although I squint out of the window into the sun for a few seconds, because that's where he'll be coming from.

Well. It's where I'd be coming from.

'What?' I demand.

'Sven,' it says. 'The good news? Or the bad?'

'The good,' Aptitude says.

Anton suggests we start with the bad.

I sit it out. The SIG–37's locked to my DNA. So mine is the answer it's waiting for. Plus it wants to tell me anyway. 'Don't forget the other furies out there.'

'That's the bad bit, right?'

'No,' it says. 'That's the good. Most died.'

'What's the bad?'

'Debro owns the ship they died in.'

'OK,' I agree. 'That's not good.'

'Oh,' my SIG says. 'That's not the bad bit . . .' It hesitates. 'Well, not the *really* bad bit. The ship was travelling on a false certificate.'

'Oh shit,' Anton says.

But the SIG's got more. '*And* its journey wasn't logged. You know what that means . . .'

All trading journeys in the Octovian Empire must be logged in advance, with cargo given and routes outlined. Once chosen, routes must be adhered to. Failure to log an upcoming journey is treason. The penalty for treason is death.

Round here, that's the penalty for everything.

Chapter 3

IT'S ALMOST NOON WHEN WE CREST A SLOPE TO SEE A shattered cargo carrier on the high plain in front of us. Imagine a giant silver fish, and then smash its spine with a metal bar and that's how it looks.

Make that a fish with no markings.

'Poetic,' says my gun.

Slapping the SIG into silence, I tell Aptitude to stay where she is and Anton to cover me and kill anything that moves. Neither looks happy.

Too bad.

Gun held combat-style across my body, I head down a slope, giving myself cover where I can. That's most of the time, because the bits of slope not littered with rock have fragments of cargo carrier as big as our scout car.

Of course, that means anyone down there has cover too. Only the gun says the sole life sign inside the cruiser is on the edge of flickering out.

A section of tail fin lies in the dirt. A name stencilled beneath a number, both crudely painted out. The angle of the sun makes the name visible.

Olber's Paradox.

No idea who Olber was. Not too sure what a paradox is either.

The first casualty lies a hundred and fifty paces from the wreck. The cargo loader's guts make a pattern in the dirt, what's left of them. The arrangement looks accidental. His head rests twenty paces beyond.

Blowflies rise, furious at being disturbed. Only to resettle. There's a stink to the air. The heat isn't being kind to the corpses.

This is nasty.

A crew member stares at the sky. Her eyes poached white by the sun. Her pistol is in its holster. The handle of a dagger juts from her boot. Although her neck is broken and the back of her head pulped, the blood on a rock behind her says her death is an accident.

'Still getting life signs?'

'They're fading,' the SIG says.

It directs me towards a middle section. This obviously flipped on impact and came to rest upside down. A wide scar in the dirt shows where it spun before hitting a massive boulder that brought it to an abrupt halt.

I'm surprised anything is alive in there at all.

'Hollow-point,' I say.

The SIG swaps clips.

Stepping up to a wall of ripped metal, I swing myself round its edge and sweep the inside. A dozen bodies lie at my feet. They're even ranker than those outside. Eight chairs and a table are bolted to the floor over my head.

Broken beer bottles. Dried blood.

A naked girl no bigger than a kitten whirls six inches from a cracked holo watch belonging to one of the bodies. Every time she reaches between her thighs, she vanishes in a crackle of static, only to reappear and start again.

Seems I've found the crew quarters.

One of the beds is occupied.

Its owner hangs limp from the fat strap that kept him locked down and alive when *Olber's Paradox* crashed. A hard habit to break. Buckling yourself in. Speaks to me of a life spent planet-hopping. Since the man can't release his belt without smashing everything left unbroken in his body, I have to go to him.

'Make it fast,' the SIG says.

Punching a hole in the wall gives me my first foothold and lets me stretch for a handhold above. It would sever the fingers of anyone normal. But I'm using my prosthetic arm and aiming for a safer hold above that.

My arm's combat issue. No idea how many people have used it before me.

The real problem comes when I reach the top. Eight beds are bolted in a row. The one I want is in the middle. The bolts securing the nearest bed hold when I reach for it and swing free. After that, I swing myself from one metal bed frame to another. Takes me a couple of minutes to reach the last person alive in this ship.

'You in there?'

Something flutters behind his eyes.

'Wake up . . .'

He doesn't.

'Sven,' the SIG says. 'Bad choice.'

OK, I'm not going to slap him awake. In the end I work my way to the side of his bed and reach for the buckle of his safety belt. It's jammed, obviously. So I'm hanging from an upside-down bed, trying to free someone who's bent double like a piece of wet washing.

'Admit it. You're enjoying yourself.'

Reaching between my shoulder blades, I find my throwing knife and half cut the strap. There's a story to that blade. But now's not the right time for it. Dropping the blade to find later, I reach forward and yank at the weakened strap.

He falls as the strap snaps. And so do I, almost.

At the last second, I tense my arm, and the bar, the bolts and my bones are strong enough to stop us hitting the floor.

Leaving my survivor in the shade, I search the rest of his ship.

Another dozen crew members are in various states of corruption. A small cage is full of those creatures that attacked earlier. Another cage is ripped open. The ceiling above the first one did a good job of introducing itself to the floor, and it looks like a dead monster sandwich.

Sheet metal. Smashed creature. Sheet metal.

Works for me.

A quick trawl of the rest produces nothing useful. I had in mind gold, diamonds, body armour or at least some interesting weapons. The things legionnaires dream about, when they're not dreaming about beautiful young tribal women willing to remove their clothes.

Used to live in the desert. Probably shows.

And the only tribeswomen willing to take off their clothes did it for money, and were neither young nor beautiful. They were sullen and silent, and regarded us with something between fear, hatred and contempt.

Aptitude comes running. Only to stop when she sees me scowl.

'What?' she demands, chin up and eyes narrowing.

She really is ridiculously beautiful. Even wearing her father's old combat jacket and desert boots. I wonder about the jacket, before realizing it has a temperature-controlled lining and she's been baking up there in the truck.

'You didn't know it was safe to come down.'

'The gun said there was only one thing left alive in there. You're holding him. How can it not be safe?'

28

She's angry at being told to wait.

Probably angrier still at working herself into a state because she thought I was dead. Then discovering I wasn't. Several women who know me would get angry about that.

'Aptitude—'

She glares at me.

'Let's get him deeper into the shade.'

Taking his legs, she helps me up the hill, although I take most of the weight. We dump him in the shadow of the truck and Aptitude goes to find a first-aid kit. She does it without being told. She's not the kid I think.

That's half the problem.

'Morphine,' Anton tells her.

Aptitude's already on it. She hands me a hypodermic with a tiny needle and a tube that needs squeezing. Might be old-fashioned. But battlefield morphine works and it's cheap and you can buy it anywhere.

Much like Kemzin 19s. The cookie-cutter SLR of choice for skinflint dictators everywhere. Anonymous, efficient, near impossible to break. Our glorious leader loves the Kemzin 19. Not that I'm suggesting for one minute that our leader . . .

The crew carried Kemzins.

Now why would the crew of a cargo carrier be armed? Leaning close to the injured man, I take a better look and swear.

'What?' Aptitude demands.

I ignore her.

Pumping a second syringe into his neck, I watch the crewman's eyes roll back and his breathing steady. He's luckier than he deserves. A handful of smashed ribs, from where the strap compressed his chest on impact. A dislocated leg and cracked hip. A broken arm. Some ugly bruising. Could be worse.

The dehydration is killing him.

And we can deal with that.

'Let me,' Aptitude says, dropping to a crouch. She has a bag of saline solution in her hand. As we watch, she slides a needle into his wrist, lets the blood flow back to rid it of air bubbles and attaches a plastic tube, turning a petcock to let the liquid flow.

'Where did you learn to do that?'

'School,' she says.

Anton's watching with amusement.

'So,' Aptitude says, when her father disappears to fetch a splint. 'Who is he?'

His name is Carl and he's a cargo skipper. The last time we met I swapped my coat, ex-Death's Head, ballistic-lined, for passage into Farlight from an off-world orbit. I didn't know it then but I was on my way to kill her.

Aptitude . . .

Anton's only daughter.

The one who's wondering what my scowl means this time. No idea what Carl's second name is. Probably doesn't have one. Most people I know don't. I do only because Debro gave me one.

Sliding my hand into his jacket I find his ID.

Same face, false name. Unless it was false last time round. Makes me wonder if the whole crew signed on with false papers. This makes me wonder something else . . .

'SIG,' I say. 'Check the black box.'

'There isn't one.'

Of course there is. It's bad enough not logging the journey. But no black box? My gun will tell me *Olber's Paradox* isn't carrying an emergency beacon next.

'Hey,' the SIG says. 'Guess what . . .'

The U/Free, who own three quarters of the galaxy, don't approve of unregistered ships. Being on the United Free's non-approved list is a bad place to be. Of course, the U/Free

30

don't *own* anything. As they'll be the first to tell you. They are a Commonwealth of Free Peoples united in their wish for peace.

The fact we still use money amuses them.

On their planets, houses build themselves, the weather does what it's told and everything is free. Our habit of killing each other amuses them less. So they provide observers to ensure we slaughter each other according to the rules.

Break the rules and bad things happen.

Planets find themselves in different orbits. Whole sun systems disappear. Galactic maps get redrawn. The U/Free talk quietly. But they carry a very big stick.

OctoV doesn't approve of unregistered ships either. Of course, his list of capital crimes would fill a book. Probably does. But we're talking serious here. Death for the captain. Death for his crew. Quite possibly death for the owner.

Our glorious leader and his ministers don't object to smuggling as such. They just want to make damn sure they get their cut.

'I mean it,' the SIG says. 'No recorder.'

Either this is black ops, or the captain came from so far out-system he didn't know the rules. We can skip that because Carl would have told him. So that means we're dealing with black ops.

Not good, given Anton promised OctoV to stay out of trouble.

'Where are you going?' he asks me.

'Forgotten something.'

'What?'

'My coat.'

Same flies, same headless cargo loader, same stench on entering the crew quarters. A woman lies on top of my coat, and her guts are rotted to the softness of jam. So I scrape the worst off with my knife, then take the thing outside and scrub it with handfuls of dirt.

'He had your coat?' Anton's looking at me strangely.

'Yeah. It's a long story.'

'We've got time.'

'He hasn't.'

Anton helps me load Carl into the scout car.

Using back roads, we loop round to approach Wildeside from the opposite direction, arriving as the sun is starting to set. Not sure it's going to make any difference. If OctoV is lensing us from high orbit, he'll have been tracking us the whole trip anyway.

Debro's not sure if she's delighted to see me alive, furious we're so late back, or prepared to wait to find out what happened. Being her, she decides to wait. And her anger fades when she sees Carl. Peeling back his shirt without wincing at the stink, she checks his broken ribs and Aptitude's handiwork.

She's impressive, Debro.

Aptitude is going to be like her when she grows up. Aptitude just doesn't know that yet. 'Get him inside,' Debro says.

Anton and I carry him between us.

The room she chooses is down three flights, and in the far corner of the palazzo. We're underground. I'm wondering if there's any significance in that when Debro's next question tells me, *yes* . . .

'You plan to tell me where you found him?'

I shake my head.

'*Sven* . . .'

'You don't want to know.'

'But Aptitude and Anton know already.'

'Then you'd better make sure you're the one who replies if anyone comes knocking. Hadn't you?'

She's smart enough to know that's an answer in itself.

Chapter 4

WHEN I'M TWELVE A LEGION LIEUTENANT PUTS A PISTOL TO MY head.

It misfires. Maybe he can't be bothered to try again. Maybe he decides the goddess luck, that whore whose favour soldiers need, has decreed I should live. Alternatively, he's so drunk he forgets why he was going to shoot me.

All of these are possible.

A week later he marches me into the desert.

That's me, him and two dozen volunteers who've just completed three weeks' basic training, max ... He carries a camelback water carrier, dried meat and his Colt automatic. I carry a camelback, his spare clips, a compass and a sliver of mirror for signalling when the radio doesn't work.

This is most of the time.

At first, I think he's taking me out to finish off what he began five days earlier on another planet. But why take two dozen others with him? And why bother to swap one shit hole for another?

We march for a week.

After two days our camelbacks are empty.

The water hole we find on the third day is brackish.

That's the term he uses. He means it's almost black and stinks of death and tastes of corruption and salt. Vomiting and the bubbleshits keep us busy for the next two days. Between the vomiting and soiling ourselves we march south, headed for a horizon that always stays just out of reach.

The sun is hot.

But it's the nights that kill.

The temperature drops so fast it seems impossible the heat in the sand beneath our boots can be squandered so easily. Blue skies turn black. And birds swirl briefly in the scarlet gap between the two and then disappear.

We don't know where.

On the seventh day, Lieutenant Bonafont makes a joke about resting that no one else understands. He tells us that over the next dune is our fort. The furthest south of any fort the Légion Etrangère has ever held on this planet. He was here more years ago than he wants to remember.

He's right, there is a fort.

If you can call a mud-brick ruin, with cracked corner turrets and a broken double-pillared gate a fort. It needs rebuilding, Lieutenant Bonafont tells us. He's sure we can see that for ourselves. To rebuild it, we'll need bricks.

Does anyone know how to make bricks in the desert?

'Piss,' he says.

So we do. He has me work the sand with a shovel until the mix is wet enough to be slopped into a wooden form and tamped down. *Shovel, form* and *tamp* are not words I've heard before.

One form makes twelve bricks.

We have five forms but not enough piss.

We'll make more tomorrow, he tells me. He's wrong, of course. There is no tomorrow for most of us. As the moon crests a dune far to our east, a wailing cry breaks the silence.

A boom follows.

Our new bricks blow inwards, and damp sand scatters across our tiny parade ground. A grenade comes to rest in the open doorway of the stores. Our sergeant, wall-eyed and bald, grabs the grenade, tosses it inside and slams the door.

The quartermaster screams his fury but dies anyway.

As does Sergeant Nero, who falls back with a spike of door jutting from his belly. It's the second splinter, the one through his eye, that kills him.

I see him die by the light of a flare our corporal desperately tries to stamp out. His boots spread phosphorus. Until the whole parade ground around him is lit with a sullen glow.

'Where's your fucking rifle?' he screams.

Seems little point saying no one gave me one.

Anyway, a Kemzin lies at my feet, its owner killed when the wall blew in. So I grab it, and work its lever as I watched the corporal do that afternoon.

My first shot kills a tribal.

And has the corporal screaming treason.

Apparently, firing before the order is given is punishable by death. As he heads in my direction, I work the lever again and point the Kemzin at his gut.

He decides not to bother.

An army pours into our fort.

They wear black robes and have their faces hidden.

All wail that unearthly cry. Doesn't matter that they're badly armed, and used up their explosives in the first few minutes of the attack. There are more of them than there are of us, and they've fought before.

Most of those around me haven't.

Swords slash; daggers find their way into guts. Every tribal we shoot is replaced by another, until they're clambering over their own dead to get through our walls. And we're being backed into a corner of the parade ground.

For raw recruits, we die well. When our clips are empty, our blades come out. In the end only two of us remain. I'm one. My Kemzin is empty, but its cheap plastic stock is slick with blood and brains.

The man next to me, the man who put his gun to my head, still holds that gun. The tribal leader opposite is trying to guess if it's loaded. This matters, because this time round, the lieutenant has it pointed at his head. Their chief offers us a quick death in return for surrender.

My lieutenant refuses.

The sun is rising, its colour splashing the dunes beyond our wall. *Looks pretty*, I think. No idea why. I'm not the kind to notice things like that. It just does.

Their leader says something.

Everyone stops looking at the lieutenant's gun.

They look at me instead.

A small man, who unwraps a layer of his cloak to reveal swirls tattooed onto his face, steps forward to translate a question.

'Why are you smiling?'

I shrug, what else am I supposed to do?

When the tribal leader speaks again it's into perfect silence. His words are deep and guttural, paced slowly and with gaps.

'You are facing death,' his translator tells me.

My grin surprises him. As if I need telling. Of course I'm facing death. I've faced it every day of my life. It's what keeps me alive.

He translates my reply slowly.

Beside me, Lieutenant Bonafont nods. Sweat beads his face, dark patches disfigure his uniform. The heat rises with every fraction of an inch the sun climbs in the sky. And the lieutenant's been holding his gun to their chief's head for five minutes. But if he stinks of sweat and alcohol, he doesn't stink of fear.

Their leader unwraps his face.

He has tattoos, like his translator, although their ink is fading. His beard has gone grey in places. Half of his teeth are missing when he grins. Those that remain are yellow enough to be old bones, and his breath smells sour.

'How old?' he demands.

The gun my lieutenant holds on him might as well not exist.

His translator relays the question. Just as he relays my answer. I tell their leader his world is prettier than mine. He says that's why he wants it back.

'What happened then?' Aptitude asks.

'We leave at noon with a single camelback of water between us. It takes eight days to reach Fort Libidad, which was where we started. For the last three of those I'm supporting my lieutenant. For the last, I carry him on my back.'

'Fuck,' she says.

'*Aptitude.*' Debro's voice is sharp.

'Yeah,' she says. 'I know. All the same . . .'

Anton reaches for his wine. Lunch hasn't begun and his glass is almost empty. He's soaking up the alcohol in his gut with hunks of bread torn from a fat loaf the size and shape of a small rock. Aptitude's contribution to the meal.

'This is good,' Anton says.

Aptitude scowls.

We're supposed to know it's good. She made it.

A waft of garlic hits us the moment the door opens. An old woman whose name I don't know carries in a serving dish, four plates and a bowl of water with petals floating in it.

'Gathered these myself,' she says, placing the dish on the table.

'Aptitude,' Debro says, 'how many?'

The girl's good manners fight her wish to say *none*.

'What are they?' I ask.

I mean, I know what they look like. But I'm assuming this

is a bluff and the snail shells are stuffed with pine nuts or something fancy. It's not a bluff, they really are snails.

Won't be my first, of course.

But the last time I was starving and my sister told me if I didn't eat them I'd die of hunger anyway.

'Sven?' Debro says.

I hold out my plate. She has that effect on me.

I can kill without thinking. Run until my ankles are raw and my boots full of blood. And I can smash any barrier that pain tries to put in my way. But have Debro offer me snails . . .

'What?' Aptitude asks.

Anton's grinning.

We're halfway through the first course when the old woman returns to whisper in Debro's ear. Debro glances at Anton, who follows both women out of the room.

'Subtle,' Aptitude says.

Her smile fades when they return. Must be the man behind them.

Tall and bearded, he's older than Anton, who's older than me. A scar runs down his right cheek. Since it would cost little to remove, choice obviously keeps it there. He's wearing uniform with the purple flashes of a staff officer. The flashes are edged with pewter thread. A wolf skin is draped over one shoulder.

'Shadow's here in his official capacity.'

'Although it's always a pleasure . . .' The words drawl from his lips. This man is high clan. One of the oldest families. People like him talk only to their own. I might as well be furniture.

'He's been asking about smugglers,' Debro adds. 'Apparently they might have crashed near here. Don't suppose you've heard about it?'

'No one's said a thing,' Aptitude says firmly.

Anton ignores the question. 'General Luc,' he says, 'may I introduce Lieutenant Sven Tveskoeg, Obsidian Cross, Second Class.'

The man stares at me.

And I remember why his brigade is called *the Grey-Eyed Boys*.

They have their irises decoloured on joining. But it's not the grey eyes, pewter buttons or the pelt across his shoulder that tells me who this is. It's the bullet round his neck, where most officers wear an obsidian cross.

This is the Wolf.

Commander of the emperor's guards.

That round is live, though dull with age. Letters and numbers are engraved up one side. SHADOW LUC, Z193XX79.

As a cadet, General Luc bought a .72 slug with his own name on it as a joke. When his luck held through the first of the Doubter riots and an attack on OctoV's palace, he decided his charm worked.

So did his enemies, which was more important.

'Death's Head?' he barks.

The Grey-Eyed Boys don't like the Black Machine. That's fine, we don't like them either. Over-privileged and over-paid. Most of them have never faced a proper battle in their lives.

'General Jaxx's ADC,' Anton says.

The Wolf sneers. As if he expects no better. Then he looks me up and down. Very obviously and very slowly. So I do the same, and he doesn't like that.

Dumb insolence, you can't beat it.

Well you can. A lead implant to the back of the skull tops dumb insolence any day.

We're of equal height. But I've got a combat arm, minus its spikes. My hair's cropped. My skull a little wider than most. Even out of uniform, in combats and singlet, it must be obvious what I do for a living.

Kill things.

He has thick hair, swept back in a grey mane, and grey-flecked eyes that examine me without blinking. The Wolf radiates privilege, money and power. He thinks he was born to rule. I think a strategically thrown grenade can improve most chains of command with the pull of a pin.

This is a man with little need of show.

An officer whose reputation for savagery is so extreme no one could have done even half the things he's accused of doing. His anger is growing. Debro must feel it too, because she frowns.

And General Luc smiles.

'Garlic snails,' he says. 'Always my favourite.'

Anton shoots his ex-wife a look and it's hard to know what it is meant to say, except that it's not kind. The woman who brought the finger bowl lays an extra place at the table. I ask Aptitude her name. It's Katie, she's the cook. Before that she was Aptitude's nurse.

'And then you got Sophie?'

Sophie was Aptitude's bodyguard. She died the day I burnt Villa Thomassi to the ground and shot Aptitude's husband.

When I look up, General Luc is staring at me.

I stare back and he refuses to look away. He doesn't like my grin. But then I don't like being stared at.

'So,' he says. 'Tveskoeg.'

'It's an old Earth name.'

I'm only saying what Debro told me.

Until I met her I was *Sven*, nothing else. She gave me the other name. One day she'll tell me what it means. The tightness that crosses his face is matched by a tightness in her own. Seems I've wandered into another minefield.

'You believe in Earth Perfect?'

I shrug. Politics is dangerous enough without adding religion. Our enemies, the Uplifted, believe Earth never existed. It's a myth, used by fools to explain why so many people in the galaxy look the same.

We believe it exists, however.

Well, most of us do. It's still out there, perfect and waiting.

A few people, the *doubters*, believe it was destroyed. Earth existed, right enough. Just doesn't any longer. It's Earth's memory we should keep perfect.

Debro's one. Doubters live simpler lives than most. In Farlight there's a community that still uses donkey carts rather than trucks or hovers. Not because they're poor, but from choice. Sounds weird to me.

'Never gave it much thought, sir.'

'Maybe you should.'

I don't like it when other people make Debro unhappy. And Debro's sitting there, with a tight smile on her face and her fingers gripping her fork so tightly her knuckles must hurt. She doesn't like it when people talk about Earth.

Aptitude's noticed it too.

'Snails,' I say. 'Did you develop your taste for them on Rogate, sir?'

Anton chokes on his wine.

The story's famous. As a captain, trapped on a planet where winter lasts eighteen months, Shadow Luc and his troop survive without rations when their supply line is broken. A surprising number survive. The same isn't true of civilians in the area. His report mentions a diet of roots dug from the frozen earth.

No one believes it.

Eating human flesh is one thing. Being reminded of it is another. At least where the high clans are concerned. And the Wolf heads one of the richest in the empire, shippers of spices and weapons to the planets along this edge of the spiral.

Also, suppliers of leaders to the imperial senate. And commanders to the Wolf Brigade. Only death can wipe my rudeness clean.

He glares. I smile. Earth is forgotten.

Leaning forward, Aptitude asks about his trip over.

She listens carefully as he replies, and spends the next five minutes asking questions that need answers. It's like watching a child calm a dangerous animal.

The snails are replaced by rabbit. When that's gone, Katie brings goat's cheese and hard biscuits, which General Luc offers Aptitude, before loading five onto his own plate. Another high plains delicacy, obviously.

I'm not the only one noticing how much attention he pays her.

Anton and Debro keep glancing at each other. It's not a cheerful glance. Since I can't ask Debro what is wrong while he's there, I wait until she begins to clear the table and then offer to help. An event so unlikely Aptitude pauses to watch me go.

'Why's he here?' I ask, the moment we're on the stairs.

'Why do you think?' Her voice is flat.

'*Aptitude?*'

'It's complicated,' she says. 'I knew Shadow when I was a child.' Hesitating on the edge of saying more, she decides to say it anyway. 'My mother adored him. He and my father hunted together. We were engaged for a while.'

'What happened?'

'I broke it off.'

'Why?'

Debro blushes. 'His tastes are *interesting*. Unfortunately, we own adjoining estates, and he's lieutenant governor of this province, so our meeting occasionally is inevitable.' She hesitates. 'Sven, he's dangerous.'

'I'm not afraid.'

'But I am. And you're making matters worse.'

Catching herself, Debro sighs. 'Look at those eyes,' she says. 'It's like being watched by a rabid dog. He's a killer.'

'Debro—'

'*No,*' she says. 'You're not the same.'

42

I wonder which one of us she's trying to reassure. She's sweet, Debro. But she's also wrong. The Sven she sees isn't the one I take into battle.

Chapter 5

'SO,' SAYS DEBRO. 'WHAT DO YOU THINK?' SHE MEANS WHAT DO I think of her roof terrace, with its red tiles and low white wall and its view of a road that twists through the village towards the gates to her compound.

'Good place for a belt-fed.'

Anton laughs. 'She's talking about the view.'

'So am I.'

It would take two belt-feds. With a mortar behind them.

That would be enough to hold Wildeside for a while. In the long run, you want a place badly enough you can take it. Might be nothing left to take. That's not the point. The owners don't have it either.

'Sven,' Anton says. 'Your lips are moving.'

'He's thinking,' my gun says.

Maybe a couple of belt-feds. A mortar. A sniper behind the wall, firing through one of the squat drains that jut beyond the roof. Although God knows when it last rained around here. Some ground-to-airs to take out enemy batwings.

I know the sniper I'd choose. She's three days from here. With the rest of my troop. There isn't a single one of the Death's Head auxiliaries who wouldn't die at my order.

Give me the right battle and I'll sacrifice the lot. Only, my quarrel with General Jaxx isn't the right battle. So they're in Farlight, keeping their heads down. And I'm out here on the high plains.

My attempt to keep them alive.

For later.

General Luc sits with Aptitude, under the shade of a striped awning, on one of those double seats that swings backwards and forwards from chains hooked to a bar overhead. He's keeping the seat swinging with the lazy kick of one boot.

One arm is draped over the back of the seat.

The fact he's watching to see if I've noticed doesn't help. Although it's the fact his other hand rests lightly on Aptitude's wrist, and she's sitting very still indeed, and pretending not to mind, that makes me want to wring his neck.

Only he is Debro's guest. She'd object. People like Debro always do.

'Going for a walk,' I tell them. 'See you in a minute.'

Pushing back a rattan chair, I check my pockets for cigars and sling my holster over my shoulder rather than belt it round my waist. The SIG stays silent. But you can bet it's got an opinion on everything that's happened so far.

'I'll join you,' the Wolf says.

Anton and Debro look at each other.

'It's a free world. Sir.'

Actually, it isn't. But to point that out is treason. So I smile, while he pretends to take my comment at face value. And I stand back; to show the steps down to the gardens are his.

A quick push and we'd have the problem solved.

'Sven . . .' says Debro.

Yes, I know.

Behave.

Luc takes a cigar and my offer of flame without comment. Leaning against the back of a bench, in the shadow of a twisted cork tree, he manages to look both relaxed and dangerous. He has the confidence of someone who's never lost a fight.

I have.

I'd like to say I learn from mistakes. It's probably bullshit. The only thing I learn is to repeat them more inventively next time. Turns out the Wolf wants to talk about my losing my arm.

At least, that's how he starts our conversation.

'What happened?'

'A ferox, sir.'

General Luc checks I'm not mocking him. 'You escaped from the clutches of a ferox?'

'Killed it.'

Now he's really looking.

'It was old,' I say. 'Almost dead. It took my arm and I took its head. Carried the damn thing back with me through the desert. Needed proof I hadn't injured myself intentionally.' Self-inflicted injuries are a capital offence in the Legion.

'You were a sergeant?'

That tells me he knew who I was before Anton introduced us.

'Ex-sergeant, sir. I got busted for punching an officer.'

Another capital offence. So now he knows there's more to the story than I'm saying. Otherwise I wouldn't still be alive.

'Out there,' the Wolf says, 'is a crashed cargo carrier.'

'So you said.'

'Unlicensed. You know the penalty?'

'Death, I imagine. That's the penalty for everything round here.'

General Luc scowls. 'Exactly. Could you protect a family who found themselves charged with such a crime?'

'Without question.'

'How?' he demands.

'Kill the man who accuses them.'

On our way back, he stops to point to the horizon. 'That's where my land starts,' he says, indicating a low line of hills. 'A thousand square miles of high plain, canyon and scrubland. Five towns, one city and a hundred villages. Lady Aptitude will inherit eight hundred square miles of—'

General Luc pauses.

'You know,' he says, 'Debro never said how you met.'

He's right. She didn't.

'We met on Paradise, sir. That's—'

'I know what it is.'

Yeah, he would know. I had to be sent there to discover it's a prison planet.

'I heard you traded OctoV's gratitude for their freedom. What did they do, save your life?'

It was the other way round.

Three dozen exiles, dissidents and failed revolutionaries meet a common criminal. Who turns out to be the only thing keeping them alive. And then he's a common criminal they need. That's liberals for you.

'Well?' General Luc demands.

'Something like that, sir.'

It's the answer he expects. 'So you only met Lady Aptitude recently?'

'I arrived here yesterday.'

'Avoiding General Jaxx.' The Wolf bares his yellow teeth. As if he's just said something clever. But you'd have to be an idiot not to realize General Jaxx is unhappy with me. I don't know what makes Jaxx hate Anton or Anton hate him.

Anton will tell me if he wants me to know.

And General Jaxx? Indigo Jaxx isn't the kind of man you ask personal questions. He isn't the kind you ask any questions at all.

'I hear you saved his son.'

I don't answer.

'That's what they're saying. You're the real hero of Hekati.'

He names a campaign that got more publicity than it deserves. Hekati was a minor ring world. It got destroyed. As did an Uplift mother ship. I had something to do with its destruction. Colonel Vijay Jaxx was the ranking officer so he took the credit.

'Supposed to be the only thing keeping you alive.'

I can see the hills over the Wolf's shoulder. A long streak of purple that edges the horizon. They're as impressive as ever. But I no longer feel the same about them. Now I know who they belong to.

'Don't you have anything to say?'

'No, sir.'

His laugh is sour. 'Silence,' he says. 'A good quality in a staff officer.'

And here I am thinking the qualities needed are cowardice and self-interest. Must just be the ones I've met.

The Wolf pretends to reconsider something.

I'm not fooled for a minute.

'You're an interesting man, Sven. Someone who could go a long way in the right company. Or have a very short career indeed. If his choices are wrong. You understand what I'm saying?'

I could say yes. But that would be a lie.

So I hold my tongue. Something that comes easily to me.

'Jaxx has no family.'

Yes, he has, I think, before realizing what the Wolf means.

General Indigo Jaxx is not high clan. I didn't know that. The Wolf must see the surprise in my eyes, because he smiles darkly. 'What he has,' he says, 'is OctoV's favour. This can be . . .'

He doesn't bother completing that sentence.

People like me are so used to thinking of Indigo Jaxx as

all-powerful, the idea he might be vulnerable to the emperor's whims comes as a shock. The Wolf is waiting to see how I've taken his suggestion.

Unfortunately, I'm not quite sure what it is.

Grinding his cigar under his heel, General Luc turns to go. I think our talk is over until he turns back. 'Interested?'

'In what, sir?'

'Didn't you listen to anything I said?'

Yeah. Doesn't mean I understood it, though.

'Jaxx is overreaching himself,' he says. 'And Debro's a doubter. As for Anton . . . he married money. Then was stupid enough to divorce it. What Anton thinks is irrelevant.'

He sighs heavily.

'They saved your life. You had them freed. You're quits. Find yourself a better patron.'

'Debro's a friend.'

Loyal to the point of stupidity. That's from my shredded psych report.

'Sven,' the Wolf says. 'Don't make mistakes you'll regret.'

'Is that a threat?'

Wrong question.

He's offered me his patronage. To piss General Jaxx off probably. I've just rejected it. A part of him wants to say he doesn't need to threaten scum like me. The bigger part wants to take out my throat.

It shows in his eyes, which narrow when I smile.

'We'll meet again,' he tells me.

'I'm counting on it.'

Anger locks his shoulders as he stamps up the stairs ahead of me and kicks open the door. It's obvious to Debro and Anton that something is badly wrong. Bowing stiffly, General Luc tells them he's taking his leave. When he turns to Aptitude, it's to discover she's not even listening.

'I'm off,' he says.

Aptitude nods, absent-mindedly.

The Wolf's scowl turns into something darker. He's just realized that he could abandon the roof terrace and she'd never even notice. The girl is staring across the tiled roofs of the village to the road beyond. There is something hungry and naked about her gaze.

Chapter 6

'EXPECTING SOMEONE?' THE GENERAL'S VOICE IS MILD.

Way too mild.

And Aptitude has her back to him. So she misses the anger in his eyes. 'There's a gyrobike,' she says. 'Coming through the hills.'

In three steps the general stands beside her.

'An Icefeld 38.'

The Wolf's eyes must be augmented to see that distance. He glances back. 'Your regiment uses Icefelds,' he says, looking at me. 'Don't they?'

'Most regiments use Icefelds.'

'Perhaps your general wants a word.'

Aptitude opens her mouth to disagree. It's all Debro can do not to tell her to keep it shut. But she doesn't want to draw General Luc's attention. Mind you, there's no need. He's seen for himself.

'Or are you expecting someone?' he asks, voice silky.

Aptitude blushes.

About the worst thing she can do.

Six months she lived in Farlight at Golden Memories. That's

my bar below Calinda Gap. Yet every street smart we taught her vanishes the moment she finds herself home. Even now, she can't smell trouble brewing.

'Who are you expecting?'

'Vijay Jaxx,' Aptitude says. 'Well, not Vijay himself. He's off-planet. But he said he'd be sending—'

'A message?'

Aptitude's blushing again.

'A little present? Some love token?'

General Luc is grinning. Like this is the funniest thing he's heard.

'Your beloved is the son of the man who wants to kill Sven?'

'*Wants to*—?' Aptitude is so busy being shocked by the bit about General Jaxx wanting me dead that she misses his reference to Vijay as her beloved. I don't. The Wolf and I are unequal in rank, birth and wealth. But we share one habit. We use words sparingly.

When Aptitude doesn't deny it, something goes flat behind the general's grey eyes. 'So,' he says. 'This is what your mother didn't mention. Your heart belongs to Colonel Vijay Jaxx, hero of the battle for Hekati?'

Aptitude stares at the tiles.

'Well?'

She nods.

'And his heart belongs to you?'

This time she looks up. 'Yes,' she says, walking straight into his trap. 'My heart is his. And his is mine.' She sounds about twelve, and in need of a good slap.

Debro puts her head in her hands.

'*Mine is his and his is mine . . .*' Sweeping Debro's daughter a low bow, General Luc says, 'In that case, it would be my pleasure to deliver it to you . . . On a plate.'

A second later, he disappears.

★

I'm out of my seat when Anton grabs me. Breaking his grip, I flip him round and slam him into a wall.

'*Sven.*'

'Sorry . . .'

Debro nods towards Anton. She's right; he's the one I should be apologizing to. Hauling him up from the tiles, I check he's steady on his feet.

'That was a pretty good block.'

Anton smiles ruefully. When he puts a hand to his mouth his fingers come away bloody. 'Not good enough,' he says.

Debro is looking between me, Anton's split lip and her daughter's face which is frozen in shock as she finally realizes what General Luc intends.

Her look is one I will never forget.

Debro's a liberal. People like her believe everything can be made right if only you talk nicely or understand what the other person wants.

People like me know that's shit.

You make the rules. If someone doesn't like them, you break that person or they break you. I saw the darkness in the Wolf's eyes. He's going to do exactly what he promised. Deliver Vijay's heart to Aptitude.

Unless one of us stops him. And that has to be me.

'Sven,' says Debro, when I yank the gun from my belt.

For once I ignore her.

My SIG-37 wakes instantly. This just proves it can when it wants.

Beneath us, doors grind open as General Luc's combat car exits from Palazzo Wildeside. Damn thing's wolf grey. A long hood and short trunk, a turret like an upturned cup.

Looks like someone smashed the cup and glued it back with the missing pieces replaced by bombproof glass. Seems no logic to what shape or where the windows are. It's probably coincidence the vehicle looks like a wolf's skull on wheels. Then again, maybe not.

'What's with that turret?'

'Better deflection of pressure waves.' The SIG obviously regards this as a personal insult.

'OK. Where's its weakness?'

'Blast bucket design, post-blast roll-back, high-protection crew capsule. Apart from that shitty colour scheme, you tell me.'

'How good's the roll-back?'

My SIG admits that might be a weak point.

We're planning to explode an airburst at ground level in front of the car, and use the lift to explode a second airburst a quarter of a second later, with a third a quarter of a second after that.

If I can flip the vehicle . . .

'More to the point,' the SIG says, 'if you can keep it flipped.'

Yeah, then I can shoot General Luc when he crawls from the wreckage. Alternatively, we can build a huge bonfire round his car if he refuses to come out.

The SIG and I are good at improvising.

'*Sven . . .*'

I'm sighting when Debro puts her hand on my wrist. Very slowly she pushes my hand towards the ground and I let her.

'Thank you,' she says.

'Debro—'

'Etiquette won't allow it. The general was our guest.'

'And he's lieutenant governor. Commander of the Wolf Brigade. While you're on remand and liable to be sent back to Paradise . . . ?'

'That too,' she says.

Anton is promising his daughter that the Wolf doesn't mean it. Aptitude knows it's a lie. There's no way General Luc will *see*

54

reason when he calms down. The Wolf made a promise. It's a promise he will keep.

'Sven,' my gun says. 'You might want to check this out.'

'*What?*'

It tells me to take a look at what the Wolf's doing now.

Seems that vowing to deliver Colonel Vijay's heart to Aptitude on a plate isn't enough. The Wolf intends to stop her getting Vijay's message as well.

His scout car parks across our entrance.

The gyrobike is going to find its way blocked. Its rider will have other problems. A ragged crowd is filling the dusty square that squats in front of Debro's compound. Provincial militia, village police, guards from the local jail, even a pair who look like bailiffs. The Wolf is calling up cannon fodder.

Must mean he has a plan. Otherwise, all he need do is shoot the Icefeld's rider when he enters the square. A second later I hear a whine of gyros, and four police bikes enter the square from one direction, stop to talk to a police sergeant, and then peel away from the crowd to head out of the village.

The bikes are as ragged as their riders.

The sergeant strides across to the Wolf's vehicle and I see a hatch drop on the turret. Don't know what General Luc says but the sergeant nods. A second later, he talks to a couple of other officers.

They begin erecting a roadblock where the main street, such as it is, enters the square. 'What are the odds of him involving himself?' I ask Anton.

'Luc?'

'Yeah.'

Anton sucks his teeth. 'Slight.'

More is the pity . . . General Luc won't get his hands dirty. He's going to watch while others do it for him. Although you can bet he'll kill Vijay Jaxx himself. That's different, clearly.

The police bikes are ex-combat issue, painted dirt grey and almost invisible against the scrub and withered groves beyond the village.

'Recognize their riders?' I say, handing Anton my field-glasses.

He shakes his head.

'Not friends of yours?'

'No,' he says sharply.

'You're sure?'

'*Sven!*'

'Just checking.'

'No,' says Anton. 'Not friends.'

'And not recent guests either?' the SIG says.

He grins, seeing where this conversation is going. 'No,' he says. 'Definitely not recent guests.'

'So Debro's not going to object if I kill them?'

Anton shrugs, as if to say, who knows what Debro will object to . . . And follows me down the stairs before she has time to notice we're gone.

Chapter 7

HIGH–PITCHED AND WHINING. CHEAP GYROS AND WORSE maintenance. That's the militia for you. Probably the same everywhere.

Combat comes with its own set of rules.

These are put into books and made into rhymes. So even idiots like me can remember them. But basically they come down to: *Kill early, kill often.* (That's our motto in the Aux.) And about as true a saying as any I know. Along with *Make every bullet count, because I'm going to be counting them.* This lot, however, are strictly *Spray and pray.*

'Guard the doors,' I tell Anton.

'No guns,' he says. 'If you can avoid it.'

Can't believe he wants me to keep the noise down.

'Sven,' he says.

I turn back, a scowl still on my face.

'Thought you could use this . . .' He unhooks something from the wall and tosses it in my direction. I catch it from instinct, although it's so light I can barely see it against the arch beyond. Turns out to be a length of clear monofilament, carefully wound into a loop. You could drag a broken scout car from Wildeside to Farlight with this stuff. It has other uses too . . . My scowl becomes a grin.

'Rat bike incoming,' the SIG announces.

Diodes flicker along its side.

'Make that two. Trash heaps on wheels. And those are just the riders. Can't begin to describe the machines.'

This is getting interesting.

'Keep me covered.'

Anton nods.

Reaching behind him, he produces a hunting rifle. Makes me wonder if he always keeps one by the palazzo door, or if he knew something like this might happen.

Racing towards the Wolf's vehicle, I roll myself over its hood and land on the far side, just as Vijay's messenger skids to a halt. The man thinks I'm his enemy. Reasonable guess. He's already reaching for a side arm.

'Behind you,' I say.

Contempt shows in his eyes. *You expect me to——?*

And then he hears the whine of a police bike and turns. He's too late. As the new bike makes a skid turn, its rider flicks a sling and something shatters the messenger's helmet.

A steel ball bearing.

Simple, cheap, and, flung from a bike, horribly effective.

The U/Free, those guardians of decency and keepers of the peace between lesser races, like us, have weapons that can turn you to dust. Or cook you from the inside out. Bombs that suck oxygen from the air and leave whole armies choking to death with every breath.

But most people on this edge of the spiral arm get knifed, hit over the head, or shot with a simple projectile. Our glorious leader is determined to win his war against the metalheads.

He's not keen on it costing a lot.

Look at the state of that gyrobike for a start. What I'm trying to say is, local police and militia come cheap. They exist to give the rest of us bodies to pile up and walk over. And splitting people's skulls with ball bearings comes cheaper than sucking oxygen out of the atmosphere.

'Back away,' the officer tells me.

'Fuckwit,' the SIG says. 'Does he look like—?'

It doesn't bother to finish. Because, by then, I've reached the man.

Kicking out his single wheel, I hear cold cast steel shatter. We're too close for his sling to be of use and his bike's already falling. So I make do with punching him. His visor shatters like the wheel.

When I kick him in the gut, someone in the crowd yells in outrage. No one's told him about Anton's keep-the-noise-down rule obviously.

The bike's still whining. Only now it's on its side. Should have broken the man and kept the bike, I realize. Still, there's always the next bike or the one after that.

My SIG–37 clears a path through the crowd.

It does this with much whirring, flashing of little lights and a running commentary on the parentage, dress sense and body odour of the people around me. And it rotates clips at least four times just for the hell of it. Telling me loudly what each one contains.

'Hollow-point, explosive, incendiary, flechette.'

An idiot tries to grab the SIG from my hand. Slamming its handle into one side of his face breaks his jaw, so I smash the other side to keep things even and step over him.

The crowd stays back.

Reaching the entrance to the square, I tie one end of Anton's monofilament to the window bars of a house and fix the other to a window opposite.

'Show time,' the SIG says.

'Yeah.'

'You just going to stand there?'

'Yep.' Let's give these bastards something to aim at.

As a bike races up the main street, its rider sees I'm holding a gun. He can't work out why I don't raise it. He's still gunning his accelerator and scrabbling for the shotgun in a holster hung from his tank when he discovers the answer.

Taking him across the throat, the wire hangs him there for a second and then drops him in a bloody heap. Blood pisses into the dirt. A new mouth gapes where his neck used to be.

The rider behind drops his machine rather than hit the wire. It's a good choice but a bad landing. His spine snaps when the bike flips and comes down on top of him. He's screaming with fear rather than pain. I doubt he's got much feeling in his arms or legs.

'*Sven . . .*'

Yeah, I know.

Although since when did the SIG get fussy about such things?

Stamping across to the man, I put a bullet through his head. Hollow-point. Seems a pity to waste anything fancier.

That leaves another two bikes.

Time to take this fight outside the square.

At least that's what I'm thinking as I go back to take Vijay's message from his dead messenger. Before someone in the crowd has that bright idea for himself. Only Vijay's messenger isn't dead.

That complicates things.

Grabbing his collar, I drag him across the dirt towards the palazzo door. Since General Luc shows no signs of moving his vehicle, I toss my burden onto its hood, and vault over it myself, dragging him after me.

Debro stands next to Anton. 'Help me get him inside,' she says.

I look at her.

'Please.'

Give me the Aux and a real battle any day. If there's ground to take, we'll take it. If we can, we'll keep it. If we can't, we're happy to die trying.

That's what we do. In the silence that follows – if silence follows, if we're lucky enough to be alive to say prayers – we'll say the soldier's prayer over our oppos. *Sleep well and a better life next time.*

Walking away from a fight doesn't sit easy.

Even if it's Debro who asks.

I'm in a filthy temper when Aptitude finds me on a balcony, scowling at the smudges of smoke that drift from the distant rift. In front of me is the SIG–37, field-stripped to its chassis, barrel, clips, slide and springs. I've got the bloody gun on silent, so it doesn't bitch about me pulling its chip.

'Sorry,' Aptitude says. 'Didn't mean to interrupt.'

Fifty seconds later the SIG's reassembled and swearing hard enough to make Aptitude blush. Unless that's about something else. She's dressed in a robe that makes her look taller than she is. And it does nothing to hide her hips or the swell of her breasts.

'Sven,' she says, 'you're staring.'

'I don't belong here.'

'You know—' She fumbles to catch her sentence. 'I mean, I know you don't really feel at home here. So I'm wondering . . .' This time her words do fade away.

'Why I'm here?'

'Yes.'

'Might as well waste my leave here as anywhere.'

Aptitude turns to hide the hurt in her eyes. And then she swings back and her chin goes up and she opens her mouth . . . And halts, when she sees me grinning.

'That's better,' I say.

Guess my grin gets wider. Because she spins on her heel.

'*Aptitude . . .*'

She hesitates in the doorway.

'Does your mother know that I shot your husband and burnt his house? That I was supposed to kill you?'

'But you didn't,' says Aptitude, 'did you?'

No, I simply disobeyed a general's orders, slaughtered half the guests at a wedding party, kidnapped the bride and hid her in a brothel. Paying good money to make sure she worked behind the bar and not on her back. Of course, I stole the money from the guests at the party in the first place.

So it wasn't that big a deal.

Only I still haven't got round to telling Anton or Debro.

They think I hunted down their daughter out of the goodness of my heart and hid her away. Sometime or other they're going to start putting facts together and work out what really happened.

'I think you need to tell them,' Aptitude says.

'No,' I say. 'You do.'

'It wasn't as if I liked Senator Thomassi anyway,' she says, then flushes at my smile. 'You know what I mean.'

She's right, I do.

Part of my problem is I'm not cut out for families. I don't remember my parents. The woman who took me in, and told everyone I was her brother, was slaughtered by Lieutenant Bonafont, the closest thing to a father I've ever had.

See what I mean?

Never met a family that wasn't more trouble than it was worth.

In a moment, Aptitude is going to drop the politeness she's using to hold herself upright, and ask me the question that made her come to find me. I know what it is. Just as I know the answer she wants is not one I'll give.

'Dad wondered if you'd come upstairs.'

Obviously enough, that's not the question.

We climb in silence. There are elevators on every floor of the compound. Brass-framed and panelled in dark wood. Never seen anyone use them. At the door of the roof terrace, I stop to let her catch up.

She's ready with her question.

'He didn't mean it, did he? General Luc. When he said that about—'

'Yes,' I say, 'he did.'

She turns away and I grab her wrist.

That's how Debro finds us. So I guess she heard me on the stairs. For once, I ignore her. There are things I need to say. 'Doesn't mean I'm going to let it happen,' I tell Aptitude.

She has tears in her eyes.

Putting my fist to my heart, I promise to protect Vijay Jaxx from General Luc. This oath will bind me until I die. When I look up, Debro's staring. She's remembering the vow I made on Paradise to protect her daughter.

It's a Legion vow. Not made lightly.

Life in the Legion was simpler. You protect your own. And everyone wears uniform so you know who they are.

'Catch,' Anton says. Something arcs through the air and drops into my hand. The bottle is cold enough to have water dribbling down its side. 'You look like a man who needs a beer.'

He smiles as I drain the bottle in one go.

Catching my empty, he tosses me another. This one takes two gulps. Debro and Aptitude look at each other. Beers gone, I notice there's a fourth person on the terrace. Seeing me, she tries to stand.

Debro catches her before she hits the tiles.

A few seconds later, the trooper's back in her chair and Debro's glaring as if this is somehow my fault.

'Tell her to stand easy,' Anton mutters.

Her name is Leona. She's a sergeant in the militia.

What I think is a sticky finish to her outrider jacket is droplets of oil from the smoke drifting over the rift. She came the long way round so as not to be seen. She says her mistake was radioing for permission to enter Debro's estate. Someone in the local police obviously owns a band scanner.

She's wrong, of course. The mistake isn't hers.

Aptitude looks guilty.

'Sorry, sir,' Leona says.

I tell her it doesn't matter.

Fair hair, slightly round face. She's got that floppy fringe some NCOs wear to look more like officers. And she's compact, rather than small. With a gaze that falters, before making itself hold mine.

Green, with splinters of slate. Her eyes are unusual enough to make me look again. And there's enough bulk to her shoulders to say she works out.

The sergeant looks like she might be useful in a fight.

I file that information for later.

'Sir,' she says. 'I have a delivery for you.'

'From the general?'

When talking to anyone from Farlight there's only one general. Indigo Jaxx, newly created duke of that city.

'From his son, sir.'

My parcel is the size of a small bomb. Seeing me scowl, Debro takes the envelope from my fingers.

'It's OK,' I say. 'I can read.'

She looks slightly surprised. 'So what . . . ?'

Then she gets it. Raising her eyebrows, she passes the envelope to Anton, who nods approvingly.

'Clever,' he says.

The address looks odd because Vijay uses a machine that strikes one letter after another onto the label.

'No trail,' Debro says. 'No electronic traces.'

Anton nods. After a second, it occurs to me he's asking about the note inside. So I hand him Colonel Vijay's message.

'Want to take a guess who'd like you dead?'

I shrug. 'Could be the Enlightened. I killed one of their generals, and blew up his mother ship. Could be the U/Free. Ms Osamu didn't like how things worked out between us. And then, of course . . .'

Shouldn't be saying this.

Not sure I care.

'. . . there's always Jaxx. Less public to have me murdered than fix a court martial or send me somewhere dangerous.'

Debro's laugh sounds strained.

'Only you could have all three sides wanting to kill you at once.'

All three . . . I run that again. Never thought of the U/Free as a side before. They're the observers. Strictly neutral. God knows, they tell us often enough.

'Sven? You OK?'

'Neurons firing,' the SIG tells Aptitude. 'Blood vessels tightening. He's thinking. Can't you tell?'

My parcel is wrapped with tamper tape and sealed. It has a military frank mark, but no return address and feels heavy enough to contain a fistful of shrapnel if that is what someone has in mind. 'Just taking this outside.'

Anton has the sense to nod.

No trigger and no shrapnel wrapped round an explosive core. The SIG told me it was safe. All the same . . .

One end has a black glass cap. The other a quick-release carabiner clasp. So it can be clipped to a belt. Pointing the cap at a bush, I push what looks like a trigger button. Nothing happens.

So I push again.

When that doesn't work, I decide Vijay's present is broken.

I'm heading back to the roof terrace when the handle suddenly drags, and then comes free. A smoking gash scars the stair wall behind me.

A prod at the wall creates a smouldering hole. I make another before deciding Debro won't thank me for messing with her plaster. But the temptation is strong, and the wooden rail looks old and in need of replacing anyway.

My first blow severs it. My second sends a section clattering down the stairs.

There are three controls on the sabre's handle.

A silver button turns the blade on. A wheel adjusts for colour and visibility. A smaller wheel below that produces a low humming.

'You're grinning,' Anton says.

Yeah, quite possibly. I have a laser dagger that's saved my life. But this, I didn't even know laser blades this big existed. If I'd had one when I met the ferox I'd probably still have both arms.

Anton sees the handle hanging from my belt.

As if by telepathy, Debro looks where he's looking. Her face drops. 'That's your present from Vijay?'

'Smart, isn't it?'

'You realize it's illegal?'

My grin must widen, because she sighs.

Neither Debro nor Anton is paying attention to Aptitude. She's standing at the edge of the terrace, blushing deeply, re-reading a letter in her hand for what is obviously the fifth or sixth time.

'Printed on that machine?' I ask Anton.

'The envelope certainly was.'

Could be Colonel Vijay's careful by nature. Could be his father's spies intercept his messages. General Jaxx is capable of that. There's another option, of course. The Colonel's trying to avoid the attention of our glorious leader.

OctoV, the glorious and undefeated.

Makes me wonder why.

That thought vanishes when knocking begins at the front door. Someone wants our attention. Wants it badly, by the sound of it. Anton and I are halfway down the stairs when the knocking is replaced by the sound of a sledgehammer.

Chapter 8

THE MEN CROWDING DEBRO'S STEPS WEAR RAGS. THEY HAVE the faces of those who fight the land for food and lose. Their hair is lank, their scowls weathered to the roughness of new leather. Dirt pocks their skin like powder burn.

I grew up around people like these.

That was on another planet.

General Luc's scout car is now parked across the square, its gull-wing doors wide open. The Wolf is leaning against the hood, looking amused. He smokes a cigar with a lazy arrogance that probably took years to achieve.

Unless he was born with it.

'Lock Wildeside down,' Anton says.

Not sure what took him so long.

As steel bars fall into place behind us, blocking all access to the compound, the man holding the sledgehammer steps back. Maybe he wasn't expecting someone holding a gun to answer the door.

'What?' I demand.

He mutters something.

Just not loud enough to be heard.

So I start shutting the door and his scowl gets darker.

A man raises an ancient rifle. A few brandish cheap cavalry swords, stamped from sheet metal and sharpened on a wheel. Only one man worries me, and even he doesn't worry me that much. He holds a distress pistol.

When he raises it, I can see the orange point of a flare.

'Lower your weapon,' Anton tells him.

The man doesn't. 'Give us the heretic.'

'The *what?*'

'We know he's a doubter.'

It's a long time since I've heard that word in public. I've known troopers who believed life was once simpler, that there was only one kind of human. Personally, I believe there are as many types of human as there are star systems.

I'm just not sure why it matters.

'Who said he was a doubter?' Anton demands.

'They did.' The man jerks his thumb towards the village police, who are watching from a distance. Behind them, the Wolf lights another cigar.

He smiles when he sees me notice.

'Look . . .' Anton says.

Wrong approach. He shouldn't be arguing. He should be telling that man to lower his pistol or die. Situations like this need to be kept simple.

'You have to give him up.'

'Why?'

Gesturing at his companions, the man makes them stand back so we can see the three silent gyrobikes and two dead riders lying in the dirt.

'See,' he says. 'That's a crime.'

When Anton opens his mouth to reply it occurs to me that it's time to end this conversation. 'The messenger didn't kill them. I did.'

The man looks at me.

'And I'll kill you if you don't lower that pistol.'

'*Dangerous words.*'

General Luc is flanked by his ADC and his driver. Both wear full combat gear, with their visors down. Maybe the Wolf thinks he's bullet-proof. Our eyes lock, and he doesn't like it when I grin.

Why does he think I do it?

'So,' I say. 'Getting others to do your fighting?'

The Wolf's face tightens.

As if on cue, two more bikes roll into the dusty square and the crowd decides to fall back some more. Slowly, the riders climb from their bikes. What they don't do is unholster their shotguns.

That tells me they're amateurs.

A bunch of dirt farmers wearing what was once uniform.

Don't get me wrong. Where I came from dirt farmers are aristocracy. And I've worn enough rags in my time. I'm just saying I wouldn't want this lot guarding my back. For a start, their bikes block each other. So it's impossible for them to move out swiftly.

See what I mean?

Anton's holding his hunting rifle with one hand. He's holding it lightly. So lightly it looks as if it might slip from his fingers at any moment.

No one's fooled.

That rifle is expensive. Made by a famous maker. The Wolf undoubtedly has one like it. He knows who'll be taking the first bullet.

'Your call,' Anton says.

Anton began in the palace guard. He married a senator, one of the richest women in Farlight. She might be a doubter, and he might be in exile and newly released from prison; but still . . .

The stab of jealousy surprises me.

Never knew I was ambitious.

I discover I am now. The empire's bigger than I knew and more complicated than I expected. Dying here would be a really shitty move.

'Tezuka,' General Luc says, 'let's keep this civil.'

This time it's Anton's face that tightens. He doesn't like being patronized. It took Aptitude to tell me what that means. Before that, I just thought it was people being rude.

'What do you want?' he says.

Glad to see he's ignoring the bit about being civil.

Twisting slightly, the Wolf nods to the bodies in the square. 'They're police,' he says. 'Killing police is a capital crime. Even village ones. What do you think I want? I want Vijay Jaxx's messenger.'

'The messenger didn't kill those men.'

'No,' says General Luc. 'He didn't, did he? But he did refuse an order to stop. That's a crime in itself . . .'

The Wolf smiles.

'Don't worry,' he says. 'I only want to ask a few questions.'

Anton nods thoughtfully.

Now, I haven't forgiven General Luc for upsetting Aptitude. And I'm not interested in Anton's respect for the law complicating things. Besides, I need to ask Sergeant Leona some questions of my own. And I don't rate my chances of getting her back once the Wolf has her. At least, getting her back unbroken.

'Not going to happen. Want to know why?'

I take his silence as a yes.

'This is a Death's Head matter. You have a problem with Colonel Vijay's messenger take it up with HQ. The day I get an order telling me to hand the messenger over is the day it happens. Until then . . .'

The Wolf looks me up and down.

'You'll remember me,' I say. 'How many seven-foot

ex-Legion sergeants with one metal arm are you likely to meet?'

Anton laughs.

General Luc doesn't like that.

As his pistol comes up, we hear a click as Anton works the slide on his hunting rifle. Seems like leaving it late to me. In my hand the SIG-37 shivers, runs a rapid diagnostic and chooses explosive. Since we've got metal bars behind us, stone walls both sides and doors ahead, I'm not too sure about its choice.

But I needn't have worried.

Luc is staring at the automatic in my hand. He's opening and shutting his mouth like a dying fish. Could be the fact it's pointing at his gut. Although he seems too outraged for it to be just that.

'Yeah,' says my gun. 'Right first time.'

The lights on his side arm are switching off one after another.

This is what usually happens when a semi AI weapon comes up against something fully AI. 'That's illegal,' the Wolf says.

The SIG-37 sighs.

The general is right, of course.

It's illegal almost everywhere.

In fact, owning a fully AI weapon is not just illegal, it's a capital offence. I watch the Wolf remember that. See calculation enter his face as he wonders how he can use this to his advantage.

'General Jaxx knows I have it.'

'Does he now?' the Wolf says.

'Yeah. And so does our glorious leader.'

General Luc goes still. OctoV's name has that effect on most people.

'You realize,' Anton says, 'that Sven has met the emperor?' He's talking to the Wolf, obviously. 'On more than one occasion?'

'More than—?' The Wolf knows about my meeting OctoV the day General Jaxx was made Duke of Farlight. Everybody knows about that. It was the emperor's first public appearance in a hundred years.

'Haven't you?' Anton says to me. 'Met him, more than once?'

'Three times,' I say. 'Unless it's four.'

The general is scowling at me. The look of a predator denied its prey.

I'm nobody's prey. But it impresses me General Luc thinks I might be. The Wolf is a man with no cut-off. Someone who doesn't like to be denied.

Lowering his pistol, he holsters it as if I'm not there.

'Change is coming,' he tells Anton. 'Decide where your loyalties lie.'

'They lie with the emperor.' Anton says this firmly.

'In that case,' General Luc says, 'maybe you need to consider where the emperor's loyalties lie.'

Chapter 9

'SVEN,' ANTON SAYS.

Yeah, I know. *If you can't fix it with a hammer, you've got an electrical problem.* Doesn't stop him saying it.

Takes me a day to rebuild Sergeant Leona's gyrobike. Having removed its fairing, I unbolt its saddle, side boxes and shotgun holster. Inside all this is a single fusion unit, matched to a cheap gyro that will keep the bike upright in most conditions short of a direct hit.

Stripped to her singlet and combats, the sergeant sandblasts paint from its fairing on my orders. Sweat darkens Leona's spine, and stains the singlet under her arms, finally sticking cotton to her breasts and gut.

'Nipples like bullets,' Anton mutters.

I'm supposed to be the one who says stuff like that.

Debro thinks the sergeant needs to take it easy. I think the fairing plates need to be able to flex properly. It's obviously been years since they could do that.

Leona cuts back five coats of paint.

As she does, I take the fusion unit apart. It's old, obviously enough. But the ceramic shielding is sound and the fuel rod good for several half-lives longer than all of ours added together. After the unit is back in one piece, I balance the wheel and take the Icefeld for a spin.

It brakes well enough, turns on the spot and lets me slide down a gravel slope without losing its grip. Getting back up again is tougher. But only because the engine isn't really built for someone my size.

The next bike is quicker.

Sergeant Leona sandblasts the fairing as I rebuild the unit, balance its wheel and repair one set of brakes. As an after-thought, I check for bugs and find two.

My first thought is to crush them.

Instead, I put them on a shelf. If anyone bothers to check, I hope it will look as though the bike is sitting in a garage for the next few days. It's when I cut the badges and braid and medal ribbons off my uniform that Debro decides I'm not just amusing myself and asks what's going on.

'I'm going to Farlight.'

'You'd be an idiot to try.'

'Debro—'

'A complete idiot.'

'Not true,' the SIG says. 'There are bits missing.' You can always rely on it to help matters.

'Vijay needs to know about General Luc.'

'So send a message,' Debro says. 'It will be simpler. Probably quicker. And . . .' She shrugs. 'Safer all round, I imagine.'

Anton catches up with me as I'm adjusting the pair of coils that act as electric brakes on the Icefeld. It's a simple enough system. Something about his scowl suggests Debro sent him. 'Not much hope of arguing you out of this?'

'None.'

'Didn't think so,' he says.

Five minutes later he's back with the other police bike we

75

downed. When he reaches into his pocket for a hex set, I know Debro isn't going to like this. Dropping to a crouch, he traces a wire to the bars and adjusts the brake lever. Then he follows a fibre optic from a switch under the lever down to the inside of the fairing.

'Interesting,' he says.

He says nothing for the next few minutes because he's busy unscrewing the fairing. This done, he traces his optic to behind the wheel and removes the fender as well.

Gun mounts.

One at the rear matches another at the front. Both are activated by ribbons of optic. These bikes were designed to run S&Ps. Short-barrelled weapons that blip clips in seconds but fire fast enough to scare what's out there.

'Remove your fender,' Anton tells Leona.

She looks at me.

I nod.

The sergeant goes to work.

When Anton returns he has an armful of pulse pistols, more optic and enough clips to start a small war. Stripping a barrel from its chassis, he unclips the chassis from its handle, removes a trigger guard, rips free a tiny panel and plugs optic into place.

Thumbing the button on the Icefeld's handlebars produces a sharp click. Ignition not pin fire. Caseless not cartridges. We're talking weight-reduction here.

Grinning, Anton slides a clip into place.

'Better try it on single,' he says.

A touch of a button and half the garage door disappears with a bang loud enough to bring Debro running. There's a fist-sized chunk out of the wall beyond.

'Just helping Sven,' Anton says.

A look passes between them. No idea what it says. But Debro nods and disappears. A few minutes later Aptitude turns

76

up with a plate of fried peppers and three beers. Anton takes his, I take mine, and Leona shakes her head.

'Don't waste it,' I tell her.

The sergeant looks worried. There are rules against non-coms drinking with officers. Equally, there are rules against disobeying orders. And Aptitude is watching with a strange expression on her face.

She wants to know how I'll handle this.

'It's OK,' I say. 'We're off-duty.'

Leona drinks.

Anton, meanwhile, strips back another pistol and sets about bolting its breech, barrel and clip box into position. There's a dogged determination about him I recognize. Most days I see it in myself. Not since Hekati, though.

That thought halts the beer bottle halfway to my lips.

'You OK?' Aptitude asks.

'Just thinking.'

My gun snorts. So I turn it off.

'If you want to talk . . .?' Aptitude says quietly.

Must shake my head too firmly, because she tells me she's needed in the kitchens and shuts the stair door behind her with a bang.

The restlessness that brought me here is going to take me back to Farlight. There's a chance I'll die there. It's better than evens. But better to meet death face on than sit around waiting for it to find you.

'Going for a walk,' I tell Anton.

Picking up my beer, I discover it's already empty. Mind you, they're small bottles.

It's cooler outside than in the garage.

Well, provided you keep to the shade. Taking a track out of the village, I skirt the edge of the hill that Debro's compound commands, and head for open country. It's blisteringly hot and tar from the road sticks to my boots. There's no one around to see me take off my shirt.

The flesh where my stump slides under the edge of my combat arm is raw. So I remove the arm to give the flesh some air. The scar tissue looks like tortoiseshell, with an open wound where metal has worn it away.

It used to look a lot worse until I met Colonel Madeleine.

Not only did she tidy up the stump, she liked the result so much she cut her initials into her handiwork. She also made me another arm.

Unfortunately I lost that on Hekati.

So now I have this one.

Old and crude, with a mess of overlapping plates and braided hoses.

A socket in the elbow takes a spike. A collection of ceramic blades slot into the forearm. I don't wear these around Debro. Although a noise behind me makes me wish I did and that the arm was back on my shoulder where it belongs.

'Sven . . .'

It's Aptitude, carrying a fresh bottle.

'Thought you might want . . .' Her voice fades as she sees the state of my shoulder, although it's already beginning to heal.

As my old lieutenant used to say, you need to be a fast healer or a fast learner. Since I wasn't the second it was as well I was the first. And then she sees a scar on my side and walks around me, like she's walking round a tree.

I make myself stand there.

'Fuck,' she says, and then blushes. 'Was that the ferox . . . ?'

'No,' I say. 'That was people.'

'You were tortured?'

'Whipped,' I tell her. 'In the Legion. Usually it kills.'

Aptitude digests this. Handing me the beer, she sits herself on a rock and stares into the distance. Takes me a moment to realize it's because my chest is bare. Since she's just taken a good look at the scars on my back that doesn't make any sense at all. But then I'm not a sixteen-year-old girl and I'm not high clan.

Refitting my arm, I tighten the grips that hold it in place. Pistons hiss and braided hoses flex as my fingers come back to life. The fighting arm is a work of art. It's just a work of art made to fit someone else.

'Our house medical AI—'

'*Aptitude.*'

She stops talking.

'It's like that because I want it like that. Some lessons you need to remember.' I'm pretty sure we've had this conversation before.

Not sure why we're having it again.

'But you remember it anyway.'

'Without the scars I'd forget.'

We both know we're not here to talk about my scars. And I'm pretty certain Aptitude didn't leave Wildeside's air-conditioning just to bring me a beer.

'Come on,' I say. 'Spit it out.'

She flushes. Takes another long look at the horizon.

Smoke drifting from the rift at one edge and the line of hills that form the boundary to the Wolf's estates at the other. Not much out there she'd want to look at. So I figure she's taking care not to look at me.

But I don't need to see her face to know she's desperate. That's obvious from the way she clenches her fists.

'Sven . . .'

'I don't break my promises.'

She laughs, unhappily. 'You think I don't know that? If anyone can protect Vijay from General Luc—'

'So what's this about?'

'I want to go too.'

'You can't.'

Flipping round, she starts to protest and shuts up when I

scowl. She looks as if she's about to cry. And Aptitude doesn't.

Not usually.

'You're taking Leona,' she protests.

'So?'

'She's a woman.'

'No, she's a sergeant in the Farlight militia. A combat-hardened, fully trained specialist with two tours of duty behind her.' This has nothing to do with gender. Although I know Aptitude won't believe that.

'I'm scared,' she says.

'Of course you are . . .'

A nicely brought up girl like her. How could she not be?

Aptitude shakes her head crossly. 'You don't understand. I'm going to get you both killed.'

'Me and Leona?'

'No! You and Vijay. The two men I—'

Wisely, Aptitude doesn't finish that sentence.

'Sven,' she says, 'I've already got Vijay in trouble. And now . . .'

I don't realize I'm gripping her shoulders until she whimpers. Then I step back and make myself step back again. Telling her she's a stupid little idiot isn't the answer. So that means I've got to apologize.

'You stay at Wildeside.'

She still wants to object, so I give her reasons. 'If the Wolf captures you, Vijay's dead. You think he wouldn't give himself up?'

The tears come.

Ignoring them, I take another look at the horizon. I have a better idea than Aptitude what's out there. 'Your dad told you about the furies? *We* need sex and food. Some of us need to fight . . .'

She's looking at me strangely.

Maybe I shouldn't have mentioned sex.

'Furies need to kill. All their instincts are sewn up in one primal urge.'

'They're human?'

Maybe once, I think.

The definition of human is wide these days. Wide enough to include me, Anton and Debro, all three. But I'm not sure it can be pushed that far.

'No,' I say.

Better if Aptitude thinks of them as machines.

Unbuckling my gun belt, I wrap it around Aptitude's waist.

'Open the holster,' I say.

Her fingers fumble with the catch.

'And again. This time make it smoother.'

Aptitude's second go is better. Her third better still. Slow healer, quick learner. Works for some people.

'Now give me the gun,' I say.

The correct term is a side arm or piece.

Actually, the correct term is SIG-37, with added Colt combat AI, up-rated memory chip and pulse-rifle capacity. Battle planning, forward projection, combat probabilities and one-minute certain. In U/Free territories the SIG would have voting rights.

One-minute certain means the SIG can tell you with 99.2 per cent accuracy what is going to happen in the next sixty seconds. (Combat situations only.) It's a useful edge to have in battle.

Although it burns battery like nothing else.

I'll take five minutes' high probability, with some power left, over certainty any day. The other thing it does is tactics, targeting and three-level-deep identity.

If your enemy is running black flag it will tell you who they really are. And if that second identity is a lie, the SIG digs one level deeper.

I don't bother Aptitude with any of this.

'Keep it turned on,' I tell her. 'Keep it close. And do what it suggests, unless you have good reasons for thinking it's wrong. Even then, check it's not the other way round.'

'You think the furies will attack?'

'You've got food, you've got power. They can sense things like that. And the furies aren't your only problem.'

She looks at me.

'You heard the crowd. "Kill the doubter."'

'They were talking about Sergeant Leona.'

Aptitude's right. But it won't take the village long to transfer their hatred to Debro. She threw several families out of the compound when she reclaimed it. I know it's hers. But they're likely to look at it differently.

Chapter 10

HAVING WOKEN, THE SIG NOTICES APTITUDE IS WEARING ITS holster and lets fly with a string of insults about my character, parentage and cheap sexual habits. Most of which are true. Luckily it swears in machine code.

A language she doesn't know.

'Shut it.'

When the SIG ignores me, I walk it to the edge of a promontory and offer to let it take a close look at the valley floor.

'You wouldn't.'

'Try me.'

We waste a full minute discussing which is worse: being owned by me or rusting at the foot of a hill being shat on by goats, the SIG insisting that rust and goat shit could only be an improvement.

And then we get back to what matters.

'Right,' I say. 'You saw that crashed ship. How many furies were in there originally?'

The SIG doesn't reply. All the same it's listening.

'That was Mum's ship,' Aptitude says. 'With the markings painted out.'

'So,' I say. 'How many?'

'Lots,' the SIG says. 'Lots plus. Your guess is as good as mine.'

This time when I hold it over the edge I use only two fingers. Diodes flash along the gun's side. 'Thirty-eight,' it says finally.

'You're certain?'

'No. Of course not. I just picked the first fucking—' It stops. 'Yeah,' it says. 'Ninety-three degrees. High probable.' The SIG's just realized why its holster hangs from Aptitude's hip.

Doesn't mean it likes it. But it's beginning to understand.

There are still a dozen furies out there.

One can take down twenty militia in a concerted attack. Working on those sorts of figures, that means—

The SIG's there already. 'Serious shit.'

The sun is low and the horizon starting to go dark. We're an hour from sunset, which is when I need to leave for Farlight. Two days' ride, at least. Maybe three. And I have a couple of arguments to have first.

Starting with the SIG.

Only the SIG doesn't want to argue.

It's so reasonable I'm suspicious. Until I remember I took it from Aptitude's bodyguard. So just maybe there's Tezuka-Wildeside loyalty coded into its make-up somewhere.

'You'll do it?'

'Yeah,' it says. 'For her.'

Walking across, I fold Aptitude's fingers round its handle and hold them tight before the SIG has time to change its mind.

'Ouch . . .'

The SIG's already logging her genotype. Unravelling enough of Aptitude's DNA to lock down her identity. 'Human/Post human,' it says. 'High Clan 3, tailored for trade. Interesting mix . . .'

'It's yours until I take it back.'

She must know what parting with the SIG–37 is costing me. Doesn't mean I'm going to let it show. 'Keep the battery pack charged. Sleep with it under your pillow. And if you feel it shiver get yourself somewhere safe.'

'What about you?'

'I'll be fine.'

'Sven,' says the gun. 'Tell me you're not going to rely on . . .' It's dissing my sabre. The one Colonel Vijay sent. At least, I think so.

'Why wouldn't I?'

'Because it's ugly, outdated and impractical.'

We're definitely talking about the sabre.

'If you must,' says the gun, 'I could always . . .' It pauses, considers what it's offering. 'Upgrade it slightly? I mean, it'll still be pig ugly, but less likely to get you killed.'

'Hurry it up.'

Wouldn't want the SIG thinking I was grateful.

'Hold it out,' the gun says.

So I unclip the sabre and flick on its blade.

Nothing much happens for a second, and then I realize the cutting edge is getting narrower. The blade is also less thick in cross-section. I think I'm imagining a silvery black sheen.

I'm not.

'Almost there,' the gun says.

A humming inside the handle changes its balance. The sabre now weighs twice what it did and pivots more slowly. In fact, it feels just like one of those pieces of junk I used to carry in the Legion.

Impossible, clearly.

Never ridden a horse in my life. Never even belonged to a cavalry regiment. But I've been carrying a sabre on parade from the age of twelve and it's always felt just like this.

'Stabilizing gyro,' the SIG says. 'Probably faulty for years.'

85

Flicking the sabre from side to side, I can feel its blade counterbalance the weight of the handle behind my wrist. Obviously, that's impossible.

Chapter 11

I CHOOSE POINT AND TELL ANTON TO TAKE REAR. LEONA WILL ride in the middle. Goodbyes from Aptitude and Debro are all that stand between us and our leaving the village. Aptitude throws her arms round my waist and looks upset when I pull away.

'Take care of the SIG.'

'Will do.'

She's decided I don't want to get emotional.

Emotional? It's having her pressed against me that set my reflexes on edge. Debro simply leans her head against my chest and cries.

Not sure how fierce her quarrell with Anton was. Pretty bad, I reckon. He was meant to be helping me, not setting up a bike for himself. Debro barely looks at him as he straddles the Icefeld and flicks it into life.

Leaving Wildeside's borders breaks his parole.

The punishment is death. That's no surprise. Doesn't mean Debro approves of the risk he's taking.

As the gyro fires, his bike's instrument panel glows and his headlight comes up. Sergeant Leona has masked the panels and taped our lights. The beams now show a narrow strip of dirt directly in front of us. The roads between here and Farlight are too poor to ride with no lights at all.

Aptitude doesn't want her father to leave.

But she wants Colonel Vijay saved. She believes Sergeant Leona, her father and I stand a better chance of pulling that off if we go together. Of course, her best chance of getting Vijay back alive involves me going alone.

But I don't say that.

It was obvious her father intended to join us the moment he began removing fairings, replacing optic and stripping pistols from his own armoury. I could almost taste his hunger for excitement.

'Listen,' I say. 'He'll be fine.'

Debro glares at me, before deciding it's not my fault. 'He's being selfish.' She's big on people not being selfish.

'He's protecting the man your daughter wants to marry.'

'Apt said that?' Debro sounds shocked.

'Does she need to?'

Shrugging away my question, Debro says, 'Well, he should be protecting—' We've got to the heart of her anger.

'Trust the gun. Keep Aptitude close. And don't let strangers into the compound. We'll be back inside a week.'

Her gaze asks what it is I'm not saying.

So I lean over and kiss her on both cheeks, the way I've learnt to do. Click my own bike into life and feel the gyro wobble before it steadies.

'Go away,' she says. 'All of you.'

As close as she's getting to telling Anton goodbye. Weird relationship, those two. Live in the same house. Sleep in the same bed. Shared prison, and now share exile. But are divorced because they can't stand being married.

Aptitude's tried to explain it. Told her it wasn't my business.

★

88

People watch us leave. Mostly they watch from behind wooden shutters. A bottle is thrown from an upper window and misses my bike by a finger's breadth to shatter against someone's front step.

I'm tempted to kick down the door of the house responsible and make my feelings known. Only Debro's still watching and I'm trying to be good. So I simply memorize its position and decide to deal with it on my return.

The road spools out ahead.

A strip of crumbling blacktop. It runs through a desert that flickers with shards of light as the moon above us reflects from broken rock and skims the surface of dry lakes that wear their salt like icing.

I remember this landscape as a blur beneath the copter that dropped me at Wildeside. Now it's vast and impressive. A lot more rugged than it looked from up there. Of course, it's also perfect cover for anyone out there with a night sight and a decent rifle.

But the sabre handle is silent. And I trust the SIG when it says I'll get warning of danger.

An hour turns into two and two into three. The road still unravels as straight as ever and I can feel my focus drift. Physically I'm good for another hour, maybe another two or three. But my edge is fading.

I know stopping is the right decision when Anton gets off his bike and falls over as his legs give way beneath him.

'Cramp,' he says.

We've worked that out for ourselves.

Killing the gyro on my bike, I wait for Sergeant Leona to do the same.

'Everything OK, sir?'

'Yeah . . .' I stare out at the blackness.

The moon's position says it's nearly midnight. This means

we've been riding for longer than I thought. The bike's tyre is hot and almost sticky, despite the night wind that has been whipping across the salt lakes towards us.

'*Sven,*' says Anton.

I turn back to him.

'What do you think is out there?'

Furies, smugglers, Horse Hito . . .

It's anyone's guess.

A holster is visible under the open flap of Anton's coat.

He's let his hair grow out after his buzz cut on Paradise. And his face is filling, and he's got one of those small beards the high clans favour. But you can see he's more than a rich woman's husband from the way he holds himself as he stares into the darkness.

It's a combat stance.

And he's fallen into it without noticing.

Sergeant Leona notices it though. She thought he was just another trade lord. Now she's wondering what an ex-soldier is doing married to a senator. I'm the wrong person to ask. Not that she would.

'Well?' Anton demands.

Not sure I like his tone. That's half the problem. Neither of us is sure where we stand. 'Horse Hito? Half a dozen furies?' I shrug, already missing my gun. 'I've just got a sense of . . .'

'Of what?'

'Of being watched.'

At a gesture from Anton, Sergeant Leona steps back. Although she checks with me first. 'You know,' he says quietly, 'if there's anything you want to . . .' He's picking his words carefully. Uncertain where to take them. 'I mean . . .'

'We should get going again.'

'You're certain?'

'About getting going?'

Anton shakes his head crossly. 'About helping Vijay.'

Coming to stand beside me, he joins me in scanning the invisible horizon. For all I know we're being watched from high sat, three little blips of heat on a cold road, and everything we say is being recorded and kept in evidence against us.

Nothing would surprise me.

'Say it,' I tell him.

'If you did nothing and Vijay died,' Anton avoids my gaze, 'his father would be too busy hunting down General Luc to worry about you. In fact, he'd probably want your help.'

'Not going to happen.'

'And then there's Aptitude. I know how you—'

'*Anton*,' I say. '*Enough.*'

Colonel Vijay Jaxx was with us when Hekati died.

Holed up in a scuzzy little mining tug lashed to an asteroid. He didn't belong there. All right, we didn't belong there either. But Vijay really didn't belong there. The boy was scared but he came through.

You go into battle beside someone and it binds you. You don't have to like them or want to spend time with them. But you'll go drinking and stand shoulder to shoulder in a bar fight. If it comes down to it, you'll save their life.

It's come down to it.

Anton must know that.

I've been a loner for as long as I can remember. Wouldn't have it any other way. But I take my debts seriously, and Colonel Vijay Jaxx was my commanding officer. A pretty shit one, admittedly.

'He's Aux.'

Anton's jaw drops. 'He's a colonel in the Death's Head, for fuck's sake. He's the general's son. He'd sacrifice your entire group without thinking about it.'

'Maybe so. But he's still Aux.'

Anton sighs.

Chapter 12

WE PASS THROUGH A SMALL TOWN HALF AN HOUR LATER. Shuttered windows stare as we slow to a crawl. A glow shows beneath one door. That's it. The main street is deserted. Without even dogs, cats or rats.

We're running three-way encrypted comms.

Anyone who likes can listen in. The theory is they won't understand a word we say. Mind you, this is militia crypt we're using. So a passing child could probably break it. Anton says he's never seen a village without animals.

'Eaten,' I say.

He's genuinely shocked.

'It's the drought, sir,' Sergeant Leona tells him. 'Emergency food deliveries never make it this far out. Last year's riots were the worst ever.'

Riots on Farlight?

That's the first I've heard of it.

'We had food at Wildeside,' Anton says. 'Almost all was stolen while we were in prison.' He shrugs. 'There's enough left to feed us for six months. After that . . .'

Anton faces twenty years' exile. After which he's free to

return to Farlight. That leaves nineteen years of shipping food north. And, obviously enough, he's already broken his parole just leaving Wildeside's boundaries.

If he's discovered, OctoV won't be satisfied with just executing him. Our glorious leader will undoubtedly double Debro's exile. If he doesn't simply return her to Paradise, or decide to execute her and her daughter as well.

It's easy to see what made Debro so cross.

'Anton,' I say. 'About that cargo carrier.'

A second later, he's alongside and flipping up his visor. This isn't a conversation he wants to have using militia crypt.

'Not ours,' he says. 'Well, Debro's.'

'It had *Wildeside* down the side . . .'

Stencilled, and then painted out.

No black box. No recognition beacon. All the crew in uniforms with their patches cut off. I'd ask Carl, the cargo captain I dragged from the wreck. But he's back at Wildeside with half his skull still stove in.

'Debro's being set up,' Anton insists.

'That's one possibility. There are others.'

'What are they?'

'You lost any ships recently?'

His gaze slides off mine and settles on the road. The village is behind us, the moon a little higher in the sky. Anton's supposed to be bringing up the rear, but Sergeant Leona drops back to take that position the moment she's realized he's abandoned it. She's a good man to have around.

'Well?' I say.

'Three,' he admits. 'Wrecked in a meteor storm.'

'All together?'

'No. First one, then two others. Four-month gap.'

'How many have you lost in the last ten years?'

'Three,' says Anton. 'And yes, it was those three . . .'

He seems to be reconsidering. But I know Anton. He'll have

considered it already. If he's rejected the obvious conclusion, I want to know why.

'We got salvage,' he explains. 'Plus eighty-five per cent partial for cargo saved.'

'You got scrap on the wreckage? Plus most of what was raised selling the cargo?'

'Debro's insurance paid the difference.'

'Nice touch.'

Anton glances across.

'Scrap, and partial on the salvage.'

Used to know card sharps like that in Karbonne. Three-cup men and dice-rollers. They'd buy you drinks in some scuzzy back-street bar. Let you examine both sides of their cards and win every game.

They'd even buy you beers to show there were no hard feelings. Introduce you to their favourite whores, with necklines so low you never bothered to notice the hardness in their eyes.

Next morning you wake minus their money, your own pay and anything else you might have had worth stealing. If you wake at all.

The second time someone tried that I broke his arm. There wasn't a third. It helps people to know where they stand.

'You think it's a con?' Anton asks.

'Yeah,' I say. 'A good one.'

The village we hit a couple of hours later used to be something else. A cargo depot? The control buildings for an old mine? Why else would it sit on the side of a hill, miles from water and without any defences?

Even round here people aren't that stupid.

The moon's now behind cloud, our headlights are almost useless and killing my lights and flipping down my visor just produces fuzz. Our night vision is militia standard. If you're still alive when it gets dark too bad.

Old buildings. Mostly broken.

A truck without wheels. An upturned bath riddled with bullet holes. An Icefeld, three models older than this one, with razor vine round its rotted wheel. A sign advertising a tavern that wind, age and vandalism have scrubbed back to a floor plan.

'Fuck,' Anton says. 'What a dump.'

Sergeant Leona agrees.

Kicking his side stand into place, Anton kills his ignition and sets the security on his bike. This activates a capacitor that blasts a high-voltage, low-amp shock through anyone stupid enough to try to hotwire the gyro.

'Right,' I say. 'Let's grab some sleep.'

That's the way we're going to make this trip. Ride by night and sleep by day. A light under a door leads us to the only bar in town.

'Closed,' says a voice, before we have time to knock.

A lenz over the door links to a speaker behind a broken grille. Someone's punched a dent in the mesh and then ripped it open. It's not necessary. We get the picture. This place stinks.

Anton knocks anyway.

When that doesn't produce results, he kicks.

The sergeant is looking at me. She knows there's going to be trouble. Wants to know what she's meant to do about it.

'Sir?' she says.

'Take your lead from me.'

She grins and I decide I like her.

'He's shut,' someone announces. Not, *We're shut* or *I'm shut*. *He's shut*. Tells me he doesn't own the place. Doesn't even work here.

Just likes interfering.

'Stand back.'

It's a cheap door with poor-quality hinges. After I kick it out of the frame, it's a broken door with poor-quality hinges. And the weapons-detection system built into its frame is fucked. Either that, or it has the sense to keep quiet. Not a peep comes from it as I stamp my way into the room, side arm in hand.

My kick sent the man behind reeling. And door and man obviously hit the floor together. Something cracks when I climb over them.

Sounds like ribs to me.

'Don't want any trouble,' says a weasel-faced man serving beer.

'We don't start it,' I say.

Sergeant Leona grins. 'No,' she says. 'We finish it.'

Definitely a girl after my own heart.

Chapter 13

THE TAVERN'S NOT THAT BAD REALLY. MUSIC BLARES FROM A juke box. The air stinks of cigar smoke, beer, unwashed men and cheap brandy. For a second, I feel almost at home. The smoke hugs a yellowed ceiling like low-lying cloud.

A dozen men at the bar check out we're not the law, the bailiffs or the husbands of women they've been screwing and most relax. I take note of the ones who don't. One of them is field-stripping his Colt. The barrel sits in a puddle of beer. The gun is only semi AI, but still has enough smarts to complain.

Still swearing, a man crawls from under the door.

He's clutching his side and swaying slightly. Could be pain, but it looks like drunkenness to me. When he lurches towards me, Leona's boot finds its way in front of his. Probably bad luck she treads on his trigger finger as she walks past.

A dozen men stare.

Most have the eyes of those who've seen combat.

The rest have mirror shades. Whose reflection has seen villages burn, boys gunned down, and women offer themselves and see their daughters taken anyway. It's two hours to dawn. Makes me wonder what they're doing up this early.

Apart from playing cards, obviously.

A man with his back to me holds an emperor, two generals and a sniper. Unless the scar-faced man opposite plans to cheat he's already lost.

A pile of coins sits between them.

It's a large pile. Mostly silver, some bronze. A gold Octo glints in the lamplight. A few of the bigger coins look off-world. One is metalhead. I can see the medusa head of Gareisis, their hundred-braid, bug-eyed in the half light.

Only these two are still in the game.

It's a large pot for the man with his back to me to win.

Makes me wonder if he's going to see dawn at all. Or whether one of his colleagues will find him with his dick out, his throat cut and his pockets empty. And the village whore nowhere to be seen. Of course, she'll turn up in a ditch, with her own throat cut, a few days later. When scar-face has left the area.

Old story. I've seen it happen.

Haven't we all.

'Food,' I demand.

The weasel-faced man behind the bar shakes his head. He's a slow learner.

'And a room, three beds.'

He begins to tell me his inn is full and the kitchens closed and none of the rooms has three beds anyway, even if they weren't all taken. His words trail into silence when it occurs to him I'm not listening.

The scar-faced man gets up from the table.

'This is a private party.'

He's definitely losing. Has to be. The speed he ditches his hand, tossing four cards onto the table so they slide into the discarded pile, makes that final hand impossible to call.

His coat is like mine.

Mesh-lined and double-stitched, with thin armour over the

heart and wrapped round the kidneys. A pulse pistol juts from a belt that is studded with turquoise and fixed with a vast buckle that reads *Let God sort them out.*

The motto suggests he's a mercenary.

His stance says he's regular. And his side arm isn't fancy enough for a mercenary. What with their pearl handles and ruby sights, you can usually see them a thousand yards off. Even on a dark day.

'You hear me?' He's talking to Leona, thinks she's the softest target.

'Sorry,' she says. 'You say something?'

Someone at the bar laughs.

The eyes of the man hassling her tighten. 'This place is closed.'

'Not any longer.'

'I don't think you heard me.' He frees the flap on his holster.

'Oh,' she says, 'we heard you, all right. It's just we don't give a fuck.'

Very ostentatiously, the man puts his hand on his revolver. 'One last time,' he says. 'The door's behind you.'

Leona points. 'No,' she says. 'It's over there.'

That's the second time someone at the bar laughs. As the man's cheek twitches, I realize his position in this group isn't secure. A corporal, a freshly made sergeant? Maybe not that battle-hardened despite his scar. It's hard to gauge his age through cheap lighting and a haze of cigar smoke.

'We're taking a room,' I tell him. 'Get your men to bunk up.'

'You're not—'

A step takes me within reach and the palm of my hand connects with his chin, snapping his jaw shut hard enough to crack bone. As I hook back my elbow to drive it into his throat, Anton steps forward.

'*Sven.*'

I knee the man instead.

Stepping over him, I bundle Anton outside.

Outrage floods his face, but it's mixed with fear. I make myself unclench my fist. 'What,' I say, 'is the fucking point of being in disguise if you're going to shout my name all over the place?'

'You were going to kill him.'

'So?'

Anton looks at me.

'He might have lived,' I say.

In the darkness someone snorts. A flame flares, and a bald-headed man touches a match to the end of a cigarillo. Smoke seeps slowly from between his lips. He's leaning against the wall, staring at the sky.

The collar of his leather coat is turned up against the cold.

'Want one?' he asks, twitching his smoke.

Anton says no.

I accept.

The match he uses to light me is military issue. Well used and rubbed back to base metal where it's been hung from a belt. He sees me look and nods approvingly.

'NCO?' he asks.

'Ex-sergeant.' That much is true.

'What happened?'

'Punched an officer.'

His eyebrows rise in the glow from his cigarillo. No one gets away with hitting an officer. I can see him wondering if I'm taking the piss.

'No witnesses?' he asks.

'None . . . My lieutenant decided not to press charges.'

'All the same,' says the man, 'I'm surprised you mention it.'

'The lieutenant's dead and I'm out of the Legion. So it's just my boast against a dead man and no one gives a fuck anyway.'

Dragging deep, I let smoke trickle into the starlit sky. Maybe it's because I grew up in a desert, but I hate city skies. I need to be able to see the constellations, like now. High above me are the howitzer, the whore and the frying pan.

Of course, on Farlight they look different.

I'm used to them looking sharper.

'Off-planet?' asks the man. Maybe he sees my surprise, because he nods towards the howitzer and smiles. 'Always strange, when the sky's not your own.'

His name is Toro, he's ex-Legion. Invalided out after a battle I've never heard of, on a planet that means even less. He worked his way in-Spiral, before ending in Farlight. These days he's sergeant major for a militia regiment in the capital. I ask him if he's with the men inside and watch him try not to be offended.

That's what I thought.

'You were here before them?'

That's as close as I'm coming to asking him what the fuck he's doing in a dump like this. I mean, there are one-horse towns and there are no-horse towns. And this one's missing its horse and most of the town.

'Hunting's good round here.'

So we have a brief conversation about freshwater crocodiles and that leads on to my arm. Ripped off by a ferox sounds too unlikely. So I tell him it's a battle injury. And I'm still waiting for compensation to get it fixed.

We both know how likely that is to happen.

'Where you heading?'

Anton shoots me a glance. Not sure what it's intended to say.

'Farlight. We're looking for a friend. Well, my boss is.' My nod points out Anton. 'He's been out of the city for a while.'

'Anyone I might know?'

'Not unless you're friends with the new duke.'

The sergeant whistles. 'The old bastard himself? I heard he was off-planet. Leading our glorious troops to certain victory.' Toro says this with a straight face. Since to doubt a single word of it is treason, that's probably wise. He's intending to say more but drops his hand to his side arm instead.

Maybe because the card-player I kneed earlier is in the doorway and clutching a pulse pistol. When I step towards him, he backs away and lifts his side arm a little higher. Seems he's brought it to defend himself from another beating.

'Call me if you need help . . .' Sergeant Toro's gaze sweeps over my combat arm and ends at the weapon in my hand. Its muzzle now rests under the chin of the man who's come looking for me. Leona stands behind him. The only reason her gun isn't at his head is mine got there first.

'Not that it seems likely,' he adds.

Chapter 14

'MYBOSSWANTSTOSEEYOU.'

'What?'

'Sir,' Leona says. 'You might want—'

I lower my pistol enough to let the man talk.

'My boss wants to see you.'

'Who's your boss?' Anton demands.

'He'll tell you himself.' The card-player seems happier now Anton's involved. 'His room's at the top of the stairs. He asked if you'd join him.'

Anton nods, as if to say of course . . .

The man with the cigarillo drags a lungful of smoke and lets it out slowly. 'I'll still be out here,' he tells me. 'When you're done. If you fancy a drink . . .' He smiles sourly. 'For old times' sake?'

Once in the Legion, always in the Legion.

I nod, noticing the coldness between him and the man holding the gun. Anton's already heading indoors. You would think being in prison would have sharpened his edge. Instead the relief of being free has blunted it altogether.

'Me first,' I say. 'May as well try to keep you alive.'

Outside, the man with the cigar laughs.

A small man, simply dressed, looks up from a table and then glances back at a map unrolled in front of him. A tumbler and a bottle hold it flat at the edges. Both are filled with water. A quick pass of his hand hides whatever it is he doesn't want us to see.

'You're travelling alone?'

'Yes,' Anton says.

'The roads are dangerous. The whole world is dangerous these days.'

Sounds scripted to me. As if it is phrase and counter phrase. If it is, he's disappointed because Anton stays silent.

The small man gives Anton a steady stare and then nods to himself. His jacket is black and looks expensive to me. He's high clan. Maybe even a trade lord, to judge from the quality of the ring on his finger.

Not long ago I'd have missed that clue.

He wears a shoulder holster, and has a coat hung over the back of his chair. Standing, he leans across the table and offers his hand to Anton.

The two men shake.

'Your bodyguard?' he asks.

Anton nods and I take my position by the wall.

The stranger watches me check the door and the windows to confirm I have enough space to act if necessary and smiles approvingly. Makes me wonder exactly what's going on around here.

'I'm Senator Cos.'

'Anton Tezuka. Travelling to the city.'

'Tezuka. Isn't that . . .' Senator Cos hesitates, on the edge of saying something careless. Like, *Aren't you meant to be in exile?* Unless he's simply worried about being rude.

Reaching for the water bottle, he fills a second tumbler. The senator is careful to take a sip from his own first. 'To a safe journey.'

'And safe roads,' Anton answers. 'For everyone.'

'You're . . . ?'

'My wife,' says Anton, 'is Lady Debro Wildeside.'

He finishes the water in a single gulp and replaces the tumbler on the table. Then he bows slightly, looking surprised when I step forward to open the door.

'You could travel with us,' the senator says. 'In fact, you would be welcome.'

Anton considers this. 'I have business in Farlight,' he says finally, 'that makes it better for me to travel alone.'

'Then travel safely,' Senator Cos says.

'And you,' says Anton, shutting the door behind him.

We make it halfway down the darkened stairs before I round on Anton. 'You want to tell me what the fuck that was about? All the safe journey crap?'

Glancing behind him, Anton checks the door is shut, and I let him steer me to a window. A flare of flame lights the face of the sergeant we met earlier. He's lighting another cigarillo and staring at our window. It's as dark in here as it is out there. So I doubt if he sees anything.

The noise from the bar is muted. As if the senator's men are aware we've halted on the stairs and are worried we might be listening.

'Senator Cos is a doubter . . .'

I get that bit. The water, the simple black jacket. They're clues.

Anton scowls when I say this. 'He's rich,' he says. 'And he's close to the Jaxx. He's been their banker. It doesn't hurt to be careful.'

'About what?'

'Later,' he says. 'Let's talk about it later.'

'Don't leave it too long.'

All this sloping around in disguise is getting to me.

A dozen faces stare at us and then slide away. I'm not sure what the senator told his men before we went up, but a room is ours. Anton asks me which watch I want to take. Way I'm feeling, the answer's easy . . .

'I'll take them all.'

Sleep is fine, but I need less than others and I want to clear my head. Grabbing a bottle of beer from the bar to help that process, I button my coat against the wind and head for the door.

'Sir,' says the owner.

He lets go my arm the moment he sees my face.

'You don't need to keep watch. I lock the courtyard every night and your bikes will be safe . . .'

'Bring me food,' I say. 'In about two hours.'

My order means he'll have to stay awake or risk my anger. And he's seen what I did to the man who didn't open his door.

'On second thoughts, send her.'

He follows my gaze to a girl collecting plates by the far wall. Large hips and full breasts, with dirty blonde hair tied back into a sloppy ponytail. She's doing a good job of avoiding sly hands and slyer comments.

'Your daughter?'

'My wife's niece.'

Thought he was taking it better than expected.

'Stew,' he says. 'I'm afraid that's what we've got.'

'Of course it is.' It's all anywhere like this ever has.

I've eaten stew on three different planets, and in five different cities and half a dozen scuzzy little garrison towns, and it's always that week's leftovers, diced small and boiled to a tasteless pulp that even chillies do little to improve.

'And send out more beer at the same time.'

He nods, glances at me and goes to tell his niece the bad news.

Leona heads inside with my warning in her ears. She's ex-militia if anyone asks. Invalided out. I'm her boss and Anton's my boss. That's all she's allowed to say. No one in that bar is really going to believe her.

But then we don't believe they're mercenaries either.

Senator Cos's own little private army, is my guess. This prompts several questions. Like why does he think he needs an army firstly? And what is it Anton's not telling me?

The Icefelds are where we left them.

Sergeant Leona's armed all their security systems. So I stand these down and go over each bike. No new bugs that I can see. No little transponders telling anyone where we are. The clips are full. Our batteries are charged. The gyros work perfectly. We've even got the right pressure in the tyres.

'Haven't seen one of those for a while,' says a voice. 'Didn't know that model was still in service.' Sergeant Toro drops to a crouch beside me, and runs his hands over a fusion unit.

'They're not.'

'Where did you get them?'

'Stole them.'

He looks at me. 'You serious?'

'Yeah. Completely.'

'And their owners didn't object?'

'Hard to object with your neck broken.'

Leaning close, I watch him trace Anton's optic to the S&Ps, and smile. When I sit back on my heels, it's to discover he's offering me another cigarillo.

'Thanks.'

'No problem. You happy in your job?'

'Why . . . You offering me another?'

Maybe he hears something in my voice because his face stills. 'It's possible . . . I have friends looking for . . . experienced operators.'

'You mean assassins?'

'I mean anyone who's seen real combat.' He sees me grin and

nods. 'Yeah,' he says. 'I know. We've both seen that. So, what do you think?'

'Already got a job,' I tell him.

He jerks his thumb over his shoulder towards the bar. 'Baby-sitting some trade lord in disguise?'

'There are worse ways to earn a living.'

'True enough,' he says. 'And there are better ones.'

Not sure what he's got me pegged as. But it's got to be more than Legion. You can pick ex-Legion up cheap, pretty much anywhere.

'Why isn't your boss flying anyway?'

Most high clans own copters. And you could make Wildeside to Farlight in five hours using a high-speed hover. Of course, you'd need decent roads to do that. As for a ramjet . . . Probably take you longer to buckle in than it would to make the trip.

'He's being . . . discreet.'

The sergeant smiles at my choice of words. 'Thought it was something like that.'

Chapter 15

IT IS SO COLD THAT THE INNKEEPER'S NIECE NODS WHEN I offer her my coat. She's carrying a plate, plus a fresh bottle of beer. The plate has a lump of goat's cheese, a slice of bread and a dollop of chilli jam.

'What happened to the stew?'

Her scowl says this is better; then she realizes I'm teasing her and blushes in the light of the lamp she's carrying.

'Put that out.'

She kills the light.

'No point making yourself a target.'

The girl glances round the courtyard and resists the urge to tell me it's locked and all of its windows are shuttered. In turn, I resist telling her that once you've learnt combat skills you keep practising them, even when they're not necessary.

'This should do,' I say, settling myself against a wall.

It takes me a few seconds to struggle out of my coat. And the girl's eyes widen when she spots my metal arm. 'Lost it to a monster. Bigger than me, with slit eyes and armour across its chest.'

She thinks I'm joking.

'I'm serious.'

'Must have hurt.'

I hide my grin behind the bottle of beer.

Truth is, shock carried me back to the fort, and the lieu-tenant poured so much brandy down my throat that the entire week after I lost my arm is still a blur. He could have used battlefield morphine.

But we didn't have any.

'Come on,' I say. 'Sit down.'

She begins to settle herself next to me. Pouting when I pick her up bodily and put her on my lap. Now we can't see each other and it's hard to wrap my coat round her shoulders. So I swivel her towards me, by which time I'm definitely interested and she's grinning.

'That's better,' I say.

Her name's Mary. She's nineteen.

Maybe twenty. She's not sure.

Mary's father died and then her real uncle died and her aunt married the innkeeper, who isn't really her uncle. She calls him that because it keeps her aunt happy. She stops to check I'm following.

I am, I've known families like that too.

'So life's OK?'

She's not sure she'd go that far. But it could be worse, she agrees.

The bread is stale and the cheese so hard it cracks rather than crumbles. The chilli jam is so hot that sweat breaks out across my scalp.

Just the way I like it.

When I've eaten enough I offer her what's left, and watch as she chews her way through the bread and wolfs down the remains of the cheese. She giggles when I wipe chilli jam from her chin with my thumb. And she doesn't protest when I take the plate and put it on the ground beside us.

Guess we both know what's going to happen.

Not surprisingly, her kisses taste of chilli and goat's cheese and what was left of my beer. She raises her chin and opens her mouth and locks one hand round the back of my head. I like a woman who knows what she's doing. As the kisses get harder, my hand drifts and she opens my coat to make access easier.

She shivers.

Unfortunately, her shivering is from cold, and not excitement.

There's undoubtedly a point at which fucking becomes impossible because your brain simply can't deal with your body being that cold. This isn't it, and I suspect for me that it's not even close. Mary, on the other hand, shivers so hard her teeth begin to chatter.

'Here,' I say. 'Let me.'

Fastening her blouse, I wrap my coat tight around her and button it all the way up, ending with the storm fastening at the collar. Then I lift her slightly, until she gets the idea and kneels over me while I undo my combats and snap free her panties. One yank at the hip is all it takes.

Stuffing them into her pocket, I spit on the fingers of my good hand and find one place where she's definitely still warm.

This time there's a grin to match her shiver.

Positioning myself, I grip her broad hips through the coat, and then I position her in turn, lowering her onto me.

'Fuck,' she says.

The grin on her face is looking less certain. So I hold her frozen in place until she nods, and then lower her more slowly. She takes her weight on her knees. Very slowly, she comes to rest and then lifts away.

I can see the shock in her eyes.

A second later she slides down again and winces.

It takes another three goes before she can drop onto me without gasping. And then she's away, and her hand comes up to grip my skull and her kisses become fierce and she buries her head against me to muffle her cries.

'Oh shit,' she says finally.

I like women who enjoy themselves.

There was a time when I bought my sex in brothels. In the Legion you get the women no one else wants and the ones everyone else has already had. The whores hate us because fucking us tells them how far they've fallen.

Mary doesn't want the coin I offer.

'It's not like you asked for it,' I say, returning the silver to my pocket. Her eyes watch it disappear, but she doesn't change her mind. Asking for money is my definition of payment. Anything else is a present.

Struggling to her feet, she slides off my coat.

So I stand and turn her to face me. Wide cheeks, full lips and pale blue eyes almost lost in the darkness. The fullness of her body hidden under a shapeless skirt, washed-out blouse and thin jacket.

'What do you want?' I ask.

'Told you,' she says crossly. 'Nothing.'

'I mean from life.'

Mary looks at me strangely. 'You're not what I expected.'

Begs a sub-menu of other questions. That's something my old lieutenant used to say. Although it seems right. 'What did you expect?'

She gets embarrassed.

'You know,' she says. 'You're weird.'

Well, she's got that right. My skull is broad, my eyes wide set. I'm a foot taller than most of the men in the inn behind me. My shoulders sometimes scrape both sides of a door. I heal faster and have a higher pain threshold than anyone I've met.

And that's before we deal with my metal arm, my collection of scars, the symbiont slug that's taken up home in my throat or the fact I get strange turns when the slug wakes, and information flows through me like water.

But I don't think that's what Mary means.

'Yeah,' I say. 'Weirder than you imagine.'

Mary shakes her head and wraps her arms around me. 'Sven,' she says.

I'm surprised she knows my name.

'Take me with you.'

'Can't,' I say, watching hurt flood her eyes.

Turning her face to the moon, I wonder idly what I'm seeing.

A girl who sees me as a ticket out of here? Someone so unhappy that anywhere else is better than this? If so, I've been there myself. So I can understand how she might want to get out.

'Now's not a good time.'

She turns to go and swings back when I grab her wrist. Her other hand is already raised to slap me. She lets it drop when she sees my grin.

'Listen,' I say. 'Weird shit's going down.'

Mary looks around her.

'Not just here. Everywhere. Farlight's a bad place to go right now.'

'How do you know?'

The answer is, I don't know *how*. I just know that I do. It's a feeling more than anything. Like static raising the hairs on the back of my neck.

'Just do.'

She nods. 'You'll be back?'

'Should be. If all goes well. In a week or so.'

'Maybe I'll see you then.'

She turns for the broken door of the inn, holding my empty plate and her unlit lamp, and this time I let her go. She's on my fingers and I can taste her on my tongue. Some of the questions she's asked are wriggling in my head like worms.

But I'll deal with them later.

Chapter 16

WHEN I GO IN TO BREAKFAST, ANTON'S AT A TABLE WITH
Sergeant Toro. Leona is sitting opposite Anton, concentrating
on her plate. It doesn't look that interesting to me. Mary comes
out from the kitchens, and puts a plate of cold chicken in front
of me before I have time to sit.

'You want coffee with that?'

'If it's not too much trouble . . .'

She scowls, then ruins it by grinning when I slap her arse in
passing.

The next person to try it gets hot coffee in his lap. Since he,
his boss and his oppos are on the point of moving out, and
I'm looking over, he decides there's not much he can do about
it.

'Sven,' says Anton. 'Our friend has a plan.'

I'm on the point of saying I'm not interested in plans. I want
to get to Farlight, warn Colonel Vijay about General Luc and
get Anton back to Wildeside before anyone discovers he's
missing.

Added to which, the idea of Debro having to defend her
compound against stray furies doesn't make me happy.

'Toro,' I say. 'What do you know about furies?'

He looks up with a start.

'Theoretically speaking.' That's something Aptitude says.

'Theoretically?' Sergeant Toro says it like he knows what it means. 'Ugly bastards . . .' He stops to consider his words. 'I've met them in battle. Only once, Legba be praised. Don't want to meet them again.'

'Where was that?'

He names a planet even Anton doesn't know.

'They guard the Uplift temples at night.' Swallowing most of his coffee, Sergeant Toro wipes his mouth with the back of his hand. As an afterthought, he wipes sweat from his bald scalp with his fingers.

I get the feeling this isn't a good memory.

'That's what we were told. The metalheads wake them up when it gets dark and put them back to sleep come daylight. Use some kind of magic.'

He sees my doubt.

'Just saying what we were told.'

I tell him about the Uplifted temple at Ilseville. I scalped a metalhead and used its braids as a disguise. He likes the story but doesn't know the planet. When I figure I've made enough conversation, I get back to the questions that matter.

'Can furies die of hunger?'

The sergeant's gaze sharpens.

'Just something that occurred to me. You know, maybe they could . . .'

'Sven,' says Anton. 'Did you hear what I said?'

'Yeah,' I say. 'I heard.'

Sergeant Toro glances between us.

And I see his point. This doesn't sound like a conversation between a high clan member and his hired bodyguard to me either. 'Maybe this is a bad idea,' he says, scraping back his chair.

'Wait,' Anton says.

It's only when I nod that the sergeant sits down again.

'You're right about the furies,' he says. 'Well, almost. They hibernate after three days without food.'

'What wakes them up again?'

'The smell of blood.' He says it like it should be obvious.

'Sven,' Anton says. 'If we could get back to the plan.'

'In a minute . . .' I'm trying to work out if giving the SIG to Aptitude was a wasted move or not. Aptitude uses *wasted move*, it's to do with chess. If the furies are going to go to sleep then she doesn't need my gun.

That pisses me off.

On the other hand, the furies might smell blood or attack before three days are up. That means she will need the gun. So then it was a good move. That's why I need the SIG: it does this kind of thinking for me.

And I know what Sergeant Toro's going to suggest anyway.

His version of Mary's plan. Although his reasons worry me more.

Largely because he reminds me of myself. This isn't someone who needs to travel in a pack. In all probability, this isn't someone who even likes travelling in a pack. So why saddle himself with an ex-Legion sergeant, a thinly disguised trade lord, and a militia sergeant, no matter how good?

The sergeant claims to know where Vijay Jaxx lives. This is more than we do. He used to work for the general, seemingly. I guess that means he did things too dirty even for the Death's Head.

'What do you reckon?' Anton says.

He's making it my decision.

Wise choice.

'You know we're on gyros. Single-seaters.'

'So am I.' Nodding to the door, he shows me a canvas heap in one corner of the courtyard. A new-model Icefeld lies underneath. A ground-to-ground missile system is bolted either side of the light. A stripped-down gearbox sits in the dirt. The flywheel of a gyro rests beside it. With a rat's nest of optic.

'Take me ten minutes. Fifteen at the most.'

A man after my own heart.

'You've got until tonight,' I tell him. 'We travel in darkness and you'll need to mask your headlights. 'OK?'

He nods.

Sergeant Toro is as good as his word. His bike is back together, parked next to ours when I get downstairs, and its headlight is masked, and so is its instrument panel. Darkness has fallen, I'm buttoning my fly and Mary is waving from an upstairs window.

'Sven,' Anton says.

'What?'

His gaze slides from mine.

Flicking my bike to life, I feel its gyro settle.

Anton rides behind me, Leona slots into place behind that and our newest recruit rides tail. As we move out, I see his gaze skim the windows to see if anyone other than Mary watches us go. He double-checks for snipers on the roof.

This man's good.

Too good to need our company.

Makes me wonder again what he's getting out of this.

We're all used to the cold, which is interesting. Leona and Toro have done time in sub-zero combat zones. So they say when we stop to sit out the next day in the shade of a sandstone butte. In an hour, the road surface goes from ice-flecked and frozen to hot enough to fry an egg.

Even in the shadows it's so hot it hurts to breathe.

'Never thought I'd miss the cold,' says Anton, and ends up telling Sergeant Toro that he's just back from an ice planet. He leaves out the bit about it being a prison planet. And so I tell them about the siege of Ilseville, which I sat out in a ruined house, with snow banked against our ruined walls.

All that was left of most of the city.

Of course, I was drunk.

But that doesn't change how cold it was.

Ilseville was where I met Neen, who became my sergeant. His sister Shil. A girl called Franc, who slept with her knives, loved cooking and could make rat taste like chicken. The other was a boy called Haze, who turned out to be a baby metalhead, complete with braids growing straight from his skull.

Always wonder whether I should have let him live.

They formed the core of the Aux. Short for Death's Head auxiliaries. A name I gave them to keep the Aux alive when some of the regular Death's Head were showing too great an interest in them.

Even the Death's Head think twice before killing their own.

There was another, but he died quickly and I can't remember his name. We picked up Rachel, our redheaded sniper, after Ilseville fell.

Franc died on Hekati.

That was later, half a spiral arm away. We won. OK, Hekati was destroyed, along with almost everyone we met. But it was a victory. Almost as glorious as Ilseville.

And we left that in rubble.

'Sir,' Sergeant Leona says, 'you're grinding your teeth.'

She takes one look at my face and apologizes. Excusing herself, she heads out of sight to take a piss or something. It takes her longer than it should. So I guess she's sitting out my anger.

Firing up my laser sabre, I strip a thorn bush to twigs and a twisted trunk, then cut the trunk into equal lengths. The dry twigs catch quickly and within minutes I'm feeding the fire bits of trunk.

'What's that for?' Anton asks.

'Breakfast.'

Pulling a dagger from my belt, I check its point.

Not sure why I'm bothering. It's as sharp as it was when I put it away. And I've honed the edge so sharp that flesh cuts like paper. I know that from the trickle of blood on my wrist when I draw the blade across my thumb.

'Keep the fire burning,' I tell Leona.

She nods, still buckling her belt. 'Sir . . . ?'

I turn back.

'You want company?'

'Work best alone.'

She grins. 'Right you are, sir.'

'Leona. You know how to cook?'

'Yes, sir . . . I think so.'

'How about using a knife? Any good at that?'

When she nods, I throw her my blade which she catches cleanly, and tell her to kill something edible and cook it. Then I go take a piss of my own.

That night sees us descend to the low plains, beginning a run that will take us to the slopes of Farlight. We pass villages and small towns, goats eating rubbish on dumps beside the road, and small children who wave.

The older ones spit.

Sergeant Toro asks if I've seen the city before and seems surprised when I say yes. He'd be even more surprised if he knew the story behind my arrival.

Farlight is a sprawl of a city trapped in the bowl of a long-dead volcano. To enter by road you take a track that snakes up the volcano and drops into its crater. Slums cling to the highest slopes of the inside edge. The air there is fresh, but water's rare and so are jobs. The rich bits of Farlight huddle on the floor. The really expensive bits circle Zabo Square and the cathedral.

A virus hit that area years back.

Imagine blowtorching a toy city until the biggest buildings start to melt, then letting them set again. That's what the boulevards around Zabo Square look like. Debro has a mansion there. Aptitude's ex-husband had one also.

Until I burnt it down.

'Ready?' I ask.

Everyone nods.

We fire up our bikes.

The blacktop gets better the closer we get to the city. But the road still twists and turns viciously. And we waste hours running parallel to our old path, only heading in the opposite direction and fifty paces higher. With the next stage of our route switched round again and fifty paces above that. Our pegs grinding sparks as we navigate hairpin bends.

Any army that tried to take Farlight using this road would be hacked to pieces before they reached a third of the way up. In all of this, our lights only show the narrowest sliver of blacktop.

As one hairpin leads into another, it occurs to me we're going to hit a bigger problem and hit it soon.

'What?' Anton demands when I pull us over.

'We're going off-road.'

He wants to protest that on-road is dangerous enough.

Sergeant Toro is watching. As we wait, his eyes flick to the corner ahead, the strip of road beyond that and the road above. He keeps his opinions to himself and his engine running.

A man after my own heart.

'Want to tell him why?'

'Roadblocks,' the sergeant says.

'We can talk our way through,' Anton insists.

'And if it goes wrong? You happy for me to cut their throats? We might as well send a message saying we've arrived.'

Sergeant Leona goes still.

Maybe she's not used to people openly discussing the slaughter of Farlight's finest.

'So,' I say. 'Since we can't kill them . . .'

Anton nods reluctantly.

Chapter 17

THE CITY SPREADS OUT BELOW US. SO VAST IT FROTHS UP FROM the volcano floor right to the crater's edge. A tiny speck in the middle is the cathedral. The gap in front is Zabo Square. You can parade an army there. OctoV has done it.

Just not in my lifetime.

Beyond the square lies an area of big houses, then the river. This is not a river at all. It's a closed-system ribbon lake that cuts the city in two. Although the two pieces are not equal in size and it's years since the river has flowed.

We stand on the eastern rim.

Around here, the caldera rises too steeply for anything but shacks on stilts to be built and scabs of bare rock show where some of those have toppled onto shacks below, sending them crashing onto the buildings below that.

Leona is looking around with a smile on her face.

'Never knew it was so beautiful.'

That's one way of putting it.

In a small square below, barrio dwellers are putting up stalls and unloading three-wheel tuktuks. A woman I know has a stall there.

Supplier of used weapons.

Cheapest price on the planet, guaranteed.

Beyond the little market is a row of rotting houses, built from stonefoam and fibreboard. I own one of the largest. Golden Memories. My bar and brothel . . .

Paper Osamu, U/Free ambassador to this edge of the Spiral, told me they were designed to last less than fifty years. Seven hundred years later they're still going. She knows stuff like that. The U/Free like to study primitive peoples.

In my case, their ambassador liked to fuck them also.

That flat patch of dirt beyond is the Emsworth landing fields. A rotting square of concrete and scrub, edged with crumbling warehouses.

It was here OctoV first landed.

A bronze statue near the gate shows him in a bulky space suit carrying a helmet. He's wearing primitive gravity boots and has an air scrubber on his back.

It is unlike any other statue of our glorious leader. These show him as he now is. Aged fourteen, in cavalry uniform, with elegant ringlets falling to his shoulders, and a sabre belted to his narrow waist.

SVEN?

'*Fuck* . . .'

'Sir. Are you all right?'

I'm on my knees, fighting the urge to vomit. Around me the hard edges of the city fade to leave static in my mouth.

Sergeant Leona's speaking.

Hers isn't the voice I hear in my head.

IS THAT YOU?

Waves of nausea rock me.

We've been here before. In my head is the voice of the only man General Jaxx will bow his knee to . . . Mind you, it's been a while since you could describe OctoV as anything approaching human.

THAT'S NOT KIND.

The words fade and with it the nausea.

Leaving me on my knees, being watched by Anton, Sergeant Leona and Sergeant Toro. Anton looks worried. Toro looks shocked. Leona's expression is harder to read.

Wiping my mouth with the back of my hand, I push myself to my feet and spit.

'What happened?' Anton asks.

Makes me realize he's never seen me do that before. 'You don't want to know,' I tell him. Only he does, and so does Sergeant Toro.

Can see it in his face.

'Wetware.' That's the most I'm going to say.

Toro's stare hardens.

Wetware is illegal. It's also favoured by the metalheads. Since the Enlightened want us dead as badly as we want them wiped from the face of this galaxy, and it's only fear of the U/Free that keeps us from slaughtering each other, owning a symbiont is close to proof of treason.

'The general knows.'

Shouldn't have said that. I'm supposed to be ex-Legion.

'Did some work for him,' I say. 'Like you. Nothing special . . .'

The sergeant smiles sourly. He thinks he knows what *nothing special* means. It means I only just came out of it alive. And I have more sense than to talk about it to him or anyone else, ever.

Five minutes from here is a brothel, with wide beds and fresh food, alcohol and girls who'll be only too happy to help us relax, or not . . .

As I said, I own the place.

Keeping it safe, and collecting their cut for keeping the neighbourhood safe from outsiders, are the Aux, my team.

It takes effort to keep walking. The turn-off to Golden Memories is deserted at this time of the morning. In the distance, a girl with blonde hair splashes water from a pail across a pavement outside.

Looks like Lisa to me. She could be settling the dust or washing away last night's vomit. Depends on the evening everyone had.

Anton's staring around him.

'God,' he says. 'This is grim.'

Sergeant Leona catches my eye. Doesn't look bad to us.

The houses have doors, roofs and windows. Most of their glass is unbroken. All right, the cats are thin, and the only dog we see has three legs, but it's alive, and the cockcrow from a yard behind says chicken is still on the menu. There are cities where cat is what you get served. And the only reason you get cat is that all the dogs have gone.

'What?' Anton demands.

'Just thinking . . .'

He opens his mouth and shuts it again.

All right, I know. Thinking makes me bad-tempered.

I lead them away from Golden Memories and down a narrow lane that skirts the landing field. Somewhere along here is a hole in the mesh. Unless someone's mended it. They haven't. Not sure who would anyway.

Maybe someone owns this field.

Hard to tell, looking at the derelict warehouses around its edge and the fleet of rusting cargo carriers awaiting a wrecking crew.

'Through here,' I say.

We push our bikes to keep the noise down.

Sergeant Leona needs help getting her bike through the mesh. Anton assists her, being the gentleman he is. Between them they manage to get the bars well and truly trapped.

'Out of my way.'

Moving them aside, I rip the wire with one hand and pick up the bike with my other and drag it after me.

'Wait here,' I say. 'Anybody asks, you're looking for work. If they want to know what you did before this, ignore the question. That's answer enough.'

I leave them looking worried.

Probably wondering if I intend to come back.

Guess the landing field looks odd unless you've seen one before. A mountain of engine parts, endless scuttling bots chewing steel down to dust, more broken tugs and cargo carriers than you can imagine.

The man I'm looking for lives in a warehouse. Since he's fucking one of the girls from Golden Memories and he knows that I know he's been drinking on a free tab for the last six months he'll probably help.

That's help, without threats being needed.

It's his kid I spot first.

'Sven . . .' he says.

'You didn't see me.'

'Didn't I?'

'Absolutely not. You understand?'

Blue eyes look from under a fringe. I was ugly as sin as a kid. This boy lacks the ugliness but his intensity keeps friends away. He's ripping legs from a bucket of combat bots he drops in the dirt. After a few seconds, the bots uncurl and begin eating their own weight in shaved metal.

It's the only way to get the bastards to repair.

I taught the kid how to do that.

From the look of things, he's repaired thousands, because I can see them eating their way through huge sheets of space plating. And a rust-stained circle now surrounds his dad's warehouse where other cargo carriers used to be.

'OK,' he says. 'I didn't see you. Didn't see your friends either.' He points into the distance where Anton and the others stand.

'Your dad in?'

The boy nods.

'Is he alone?'

A grin greets my question.

'Angelique's gone home for the weekend.'

He makes it sound like a trip to the country.

Since I know the furthest she's been from Golden Memories is eight streets, Angelique's obviously staying with her aunt, who lives in one of the shacks above the market.

'Here,' I say, emptying coins into his hand. 'Buy me a tortilla and get one for yourself.'

'What about them?'

I nod, and he scurries away.

The stairs to Per's office are rusty. They also creak. So I'm not surprised to open his door and find myself staring at the muzzle of a Colt automatic. It's large calibre, with old-fashioned sights.

His finger is on the trigger.

'Fuck,' he says, lowering the gun. 'Thought you were—' He hesitates, thinks about whether he wants to finish that sentence.

I leave him to it as I look round his room.

A double mattress, a screen fixed to the wall, an old leather chair with a gash across its back, a stack of something that looks like memory boxes, a bucket full of broken combat bots, half of them waving their legs like upturned crabs.

He's tidied up since I was last here.

A bottle lies on its side.

'Angelique doesn't like me drinking.'

'So you drink when she's away?'

He grins, an unshaven grin that doesn't reach his eyes. He's been on a bender for longer than a single weekend. Which might explain why his son is already up and Angelique's staying with her aunt.

'You can feel it?' he asks me.

I look at him, wondering . . .

'Static,' I say. 'That's what I can feel. A flat taste like blood in the back of my throat.'

'Sven,' says Per, 'I didn't mean literally.'

'Oh.' Shrugging, I look at him.

'All the same,' he says, 'that's a pretty good description.'

'For what?'

'Whatever's happening.' He stares at me through bloodshot eyes. 'Van Zill's refusing to pay his taxes. Neen's not happy.'

Federico Van Zill is a scumbag, would-be crime boss we let live in return for one fifth of everything he earns. Neen you know, he's my sergeant. 'Why hasn't Neen handled it?'

'Two days ago Van Zill vanished.'

'Dead?'

'Doubt you'll get that lucky.'

We're silent, and Per looks down at his gun.

It's recently oiled, and I'm willing to bet good money he's field-stripped it and loaded up a few spare clips. Other changes occur to me. The bars over the window for a start.

And those creaking stairs . . .

'Loosened some bolts,' he says. 'To warn me if someone's coming.'

Nodding at the bottle, I say, 'Is that because you haven't killed before, and you're trying to find the courage? Or you have, and didn't like it?'

'The boy doesn't know that.'

Must be the second, then. When I hold out my hand, he hands me the gun.

The weight's good, its clips clean and full. The pin dry-fires with a sharp click and the barrel has been pulled through so thoroughly it's a twist of silvery steel. The broken grip on one side of the handle is recently mended.

All the same.

Pulling a side arm from my belt, I offer it to Per, who looks uncertain. So I put it on the deck beside his empty bottle and add three clips. 'Explosive,' I tell him, tapping the first. 'Take out a truck, no problem.'

He nods.

So I tap the second. 'Hollow-point. Maximum spread and minimum weight loss. No use against ceramic. But take someone off at the knee and it doesn't matter what they're wearing above.'

He looks sick.

Probably because he knows it's true.

'Armour-piercing,' I tell him, pointing at the third clip. 'A thermite core hot enough to melt steel.'

Per's looking at a fortune.

This lot would sell to Angelique's aunt for more than he makes in a month. But he won't be parting with them. I can see that in his eyes.

'Take a shower, have a shave, eat something.'

He nods.

'And teach your boy how to use that.'

Misery twists Per's face as he realizes I mean his original gun.

'Alternatively, let him get killed.'

There's a price to my kindness. I want our bikes serviced and stored safely, I want tyres that don't look as if they've been blasted by a shotgun. And I want Per and his boy to keep quiet about my being here. That means he doesn't tell his squeeze.

Angelique has tits like a goddess, cascades of blonde hair and no inhibitions. Believe me, I know . . . The night we spent together we shared the mattress with Lisa, her cousin.

The one slopping off the steps in front of Golden Memories.

But tell her something when she's flat on her back and half the neighbourhood knows by lunchtime. She's a girl who really can't keep anything shut.

'Understand?'

Per nods. 'I owe you my life already.'

Takes me a moment to work out what he means. A while

back, I came through here, having just landed, and stumbled over a small boy trying to mend a spider bot. Helping the boy brought his father. Had to fight myself for six streets before deciding not to go back and kill them both.

Because that's what I should have done.

'Tell me you didn't,' Per says.

'Do what?'

'Ride those up the face.'

'They're Icefelds. It's what they're for.'

'Sven,' he says, 'gyros exist to stop dispatch riders falling off their bikes.' Per very carefully doesn't ask the others their names or introduce himself. He simply drops to a crouch beside my bike and sucks his teeth at the state of its tyre, the cracked dampers and the broken fairing. His eyes widen at the sight of the spray and prays.

'Expecting trouble?'

'Always.'

'Ain't that the truth,' he says.

If anyone notices Leona rip a piece from her tortilla and toss it down as an offering, they have the manners to keep that to themselves.

Chapter 18

LEONA WHISPERS THAT SOMEONE IS FOLLOWING. I KNOW THAT already. One man, who picked up our tail when we hit Farlight's centre but is still five or six people back. A few minutes ago, he was ahead of us. Before that he was in a parallel street, watching us through shop windows and sightings down side alleys.

He's good. Although that turned-up collar and pulled-down cap must be a bastard in this heat.

'You're grinning, sir.'

'Fuck of a way to spend my leave.'

She smiles. 'You want me to do something about our friend?'

I shake my head. Anton and Sergeant Toro are ahead. My suggestion to break into two groups and make our tracker's job a little less easy. I've got good reasons for not wanting anyone to know I'm here.

And Anton's life depends on it.

For all I know, Toro and Leona have equally good reasons of their own. Which means one of us would have killed the follower if we thought him professional. But if he was professional we wouldn't have seen him.

Unless, of course . . .

I'm tempted to tell Leona to drop back and kill him. Just so I can simplify my thoughts and get back to saving Colonel Vijay and getting Anton out of here.

'How much longer?' Anton demands.

Sergeant Toro tells him ten minutes.

We're walking the boulevard feeding into Zabo Square.

The roof of the cathedral gleams in the distance. Gold domes reflecting the last of the evening light. Leona's counting off the chimes from the tower clock. 'Seven, eight, nine . . .' Not sure why, since she's wearing a standard-issue watch and knows the time already.

Smartly dressed women fill the colonnades.

Expensive hovers skim the road beyond the square.

People like me don't belong. I'm thinking this, when I spot a naked woman, scrawled in red chalk on a nearby wall. A trampled rose lies underneath it. Seems people like me use this area after all.

Flicking the sign of Legba Uploaded, Leona blushes because I notice. So I pull Legba's medallion from my shirt. Soldiers have their own saint.

Not everyone approves.

A truck goes by filled with Death's Head troopers. Cropped hair, hard faces, thousand-yard stares . . . A small boy points and is slapped for his pains. The child's father bustles him away. No one else stares or catches the troopers' eyes. Not that they could; the Death's Head troopers glare straight ahead.

'Almost there, sir,' Sergeant Toro tells Anton.

'You've been saying that for the last ten minutes.'

The sergeant scowls. 'Never approached the colonel's house from this direction before . . .' He's still using the same excuse twenty minutes later, when the clock tower rings the half hour, and I decide it's time to catch up.

'You're lost?'

The sergeant scowls some more.

Cutting under an arch, we find ourselves in a wide street, high walls on either side inset with double doors. The houses rise five storeys above us. Most have lenz over their entrances and weapons systems that track us as we move.

The weapons systems are obvious.

Makes me think they're bluff. And the real systems are hidden. I waste time trying to identify them as Sergeant Toro tries to remember which door.

'You're certain, this time?' Anton demands.

'Yes, sir.'

There's a tightness to the sergeant's voice. Anton has that effect on me sometimes too. Stepping up to a door, Toro knocks three times in quick succession. A double knock answers from inside. I'd do one knock in reply, but the sergeant does three and a small door swings open.

Bombproof, I notice. For all that it's painted faded green. The double doors it lets us enter have electronic locks and deadbolts fat as my wrist.

The soldier who lets us in is out of uniform.

'You're expected.'

We're what?

Colonel Vijay's courtyard is lit by hidden lights. A run of steps leads to its black and shiny front door. Exactly the place I'd expect him to live.

'Fuck,' says Sergeant Toro. 'Look at that.'

A sleek hover sits near the steps. It's got obsidian black windows, a knitted carbon skirt and a grille like a shark's open jaw, with chrome teeth and recessed eyes. A tiny flagstaff juts from its long hood.

The flag itself is rolled and tied.

'How the other half live,' he mutters.

Leona nods.

'Announce yourself,' the soldier says. Seeing my glare, he adds, 'If you would, sir.'

Wise man.

'Lieutenant Sven Tveskoeg for Colonel Jaxx.'

'And the others?' The voice from the speaker grille isn't Vijay. Wouldn't expect it to be.

'Anton Tezuka. Sergeants Toro and—'

The door clicks open before I finish my list. Either the AI is stupid, or we're being covered by so much artillery that chopped meat is today's option if we make a bad move.

At my hip, Vijay's sabre shivers.

Unclipping it, I catch Anton's gaze.

'Sven,' he whispers. 'You're not . . .'

He's right. I'm not.

I'm assuming a software glitch between Vijay's AI and the sabre he gave me. Since the AI outguns the sabre, it makes sense not to make the house nervous.

Putting the sabre to sleep, I reclip it and straighten my coat. We're not in uniform, any of us. But Vijay Jaxx is still a Death's Head colonel.

After knocking at a door, the housekeeper steps back and nods for us to enter. So we do, and that is when our day begins to unravel.

'Good job,' says a voice.

It's talking to Sergeant Toro, who nods his head, accepting the praise.

'And you two . . . What took you so long?'

Clearly, Sergeant Leona isn't important enough to be in this conversation. General Luc sits at a desk. Behind him stand two Wolf Brigade troopers. At the Wolf's signal, our travelling companion peels away to join them.

'*You bastard . . .*'

'Shut it,' I tell Leona.

'Sorry, sir.'

Toro's a sergeant, all right. In the Wolf Brigade.

'Like puppets,' General Luc says. 'Pull the strings and watch them walk. Knew you wouldn't be able to resist it.' He's talking to me. Grinning at Anton, his gaze slides to a halt when it reaches Sergeant Leona.

'Where did you find her?'

'Picked her up on the way,' Anton says. 'Shortly before we met—' He jerks his chin towards the wall. 'Whatever he's called.'

'Toro,' says the Wolf. 'My staff sergeant.'

'If I might, sir,' Toro says.

'Feel free.'

Pulling down his eyelids in turn, our travelling companion pops first one and then another coloured lens from his grey eyes.

'Bastard things, sir . . .'

'All in a good cause, Toro.'

Leaning forward, the Wolf takes a closer look at his map of the city. It's a paper map, so old that it curls at the corners. However it's not Sergeant Toro's deceit, General Luc's smugness, or the map that raises my blood pressure. It's the girl sitting on the edge of his desk, swinging her legs like a teenage hooker.

'Hi Sven,' she says, trumping my scowl with a grin. 'Wondered when you'd get round to me. Long time no see.'

'Not long enough.'

Ms Osamu pouts. 'That's not kind.'

Paper Osamu is the daughter of the U/Free president, and a one-time lover of mine. She's also their ambassador. Today her eyes are blue and her skin pale. Her dress is thin enough to leave nothing to the imagination.

'Yes,' she says, 'I'm still wearing the same body as last time.' Bitch.

'*Tveskoeg*,' General Luc says.

My hand is on my gun.

'How many darts,' he says, 'do you think are trained on you?'

Now is when I need the SIG-37. My real gun could shut down the AI, or fool it into thinking we're friends. At the very least it could tell me how much of the general's confidence is bluff.

'Madame,' he says. 'If you could stop swinging your legs.'

Paper pouts again.

Sliding her gaze round the room, she looks for weapons. There are none visible, obviously enough. House defence systems use needle guns. Steel darts blown from hidden tubes in the walls and ceiling and floor. A good AI can kill one man in a group of fifty and leave the rest untouched.

'I heal fast. And she'll be dead whatever happens.'

'And your friends?' he asks. 'Do they heal fast too?'

Chapter 19

WE'RE DELIVERED TO A PRISON FOUR FLOORS UP, LOOKING down on an empty street. It's at the back of General Luc's house. Because it was to his house that Sergeant Toro led us. Those were the Wolf's poisonous ancestors smirking from the paintings on the stairs we just climbed.

Paper comes along for the fun.

'I'm sure you'll be comfortable,' she says.

The room is stripped bare and has one window. A single light panel glows sullenly overhead. The floor is tiled. There is no piece of furniture in sight.

'Fuck off,' I tell her.

'Sven,' she says, 'I'm only trying to be friendly.'

Across the empty street is a smaller house. It has less grand carving around its windows. The other difference is those windows don't have bars.

'I know we have history,' the Wolf tells Anton. 'But use tonight wisely. Think about where your loyalties really lie.'

'And me, sir?' Leona says.

General Luc looks amused. 'Oh,' he says, 'I'm sure my men can find a use for you somewhere.'

Sergeant Leona reddens.

'As for you,' he says, staring at me. 'Your choice is simple . . .'

'Not interested.'

'You haven't heard what it is.'

'Don't care. Not going to happen.' Betray Colonel Vijay or be killed. I don't need the Wolf putting my options into words to know what tomorrow will bring.

The door that slams on us is good-quality steel. I know this, because, having tried to put my fist through it, I try to kick it off its hinges and that doesn't work either.

I'm missing my combat arm, obviously.

Also my gun, my boot knife, and the sabre handle.

Although Sergeant Toro misses the blade I'm wearing between my shoulders, in memory of Franc, who used to carry her own knife there.

When the time comes I'm going to kill the sergeant. Also General Luc, Ms Osamu and the smirking guards. But I'll kill Toro fast because he's a professional and he'd pay me the same respect.

'Sven,' says Anton, 'we need to talk.'

'When we're out of here.'

Anton scowls.

I ignore him.

The cathedral clock strikes for ten in the evening. It strikes again for the half-hour. We're still no closer to getting out.

I run through the list in my head.

Twelve paces by twelve paces. One door, locked. One window, barred. One lighting panel, sunk into the ceiling. One tiled floor, now chipped. There's mesh beneath. A grille leads to an air vent, for a cooling system that no longer works. My hand is large enough to cover the grille, and the duct behind is narrower than my wrist.

Sergeant Leona jumps when I toss the grille down.

'Sven,' says Anton.

He shuts up when I glare at him.

My head hurts. General Luc and Paper Osamu. Paper Osamu and General Luc. As U/Free ambassador, Paper obviously attends local dinners and functions. So they could have met anywhere.

But something stinks.

A *tension*, that's what lay between them.

The Wolf's scowl. Paper kicking her heels like a spoilt brat, using his desk as her chair because she can. She's the U/Free ambassador, who's going to stop her? And that map on the table.

Why a paper map, and not a screen? The answer hits me the moment I stop thinking about it. The Wolf uses a paper map for the same reason Colonel Vijay uses a machine that punches letters into paper when writing to Aptitude.

He's hiding something.

Who from? I wonder.

'Sir,' says Leona.

She steps back when I glare at her.

'You're grinding your teeth again, sir.'

If Leona had my headache she'd be grinding her teeth too.

When the lights in the panel die I think someone's turned them out. I'm wrong, because stars begin to appear in the Farlight sky. That's strange enough to take us all to the window. As we watch, the sodium glare fades a little at a time. Blackouts are common in the barrios.

But not here in the centre.

The high clans would never stand for it. And yet it's happening. One after another the lights lining the street below go out.

'Try the door.'

It's locked. The bolt's electronic, but we're not that lucky. We're still locked in. Although there's obviously a

139

lever that will open it. Equally obviously, it's on the other side.

'Face it,' Anton says. 'We're trapped.'

I make another circuit of our prison in silence. I'm not interested in being trapped. I'm interested in getting out of here.

'Yell "Fire",' I tell Leona.

She looks at me.

'Do it.'

When she hesitates, I take three steps towards her and raise my fist. Her yell has real emotion in it.

'See? That wasn't difficult . . .'

Her voice echoes off the walls until she's deafened us.

'Well,' Anton says, 'that doesn't work.'

He's wrong. It works perfectly. If no one comes, that's because 1) there's nothing in this room to burn. And 2) they obviously don't have time to shut us up. Which means 3) we're being left alone.

Not because they want to soften us up. They'd have to be stupid to think that's possible. The answer is they're busy with something more important than us. The next question is, *What?*

It has to do with that map.

And what is Paper doing here? That thought won't go away either.

It nags like a hangover. She's the U/Free ambassador and General Luc commands the Wolf Brigade. His job is to protect OctoV. Her job is to make our glorious leader do what the U/Free want. She'd put it differently. But that's what it comes down to . . .

If General Luc and Ms Osamu are not allies, and they're not enemies, what the fuck does it make them?

That was Paper's hover.

Not sure why I didn't grasp it earlier.

She always did like her toys. I was one of them. Sven, the barbarian. So crude in bed. So exciting to bring to parties.

Anton chooses exactly the wrong moment to demand we talk about Colonel Vijay and Aptitude. He thinks we should accept that the colonel's probably beyond saving. What the Wolf wants the Wolf gets . . .

I'm so used to hearing that said about General Jaxx that it's a shock to hear it said about someone else. And I don't agree about Colonel Vijay. Giving up now would be like handing his heart to the Wolf on a plate ourselves.

Not going to happen.

Anton scowls when I say this. So I decide to explain a few home truths. Being me, I try to keep them simple. Three sentences into explaining how Apt's husband died, and Anton is accusing me of cold-blooded murder. So I start again, from the top . . .

'On Paradise, Debro said look after Apt, right?'

Anton looks at me.

'Isn't that what she said? Look after her . . .'

He nods abruptly.

'That's what I did.'

Holding up my hand silences him.

'You know what my orders were . . .? Begin with Senator Thomassi, finish with Aptitude, kill the lot, burn down their house too. You know who issued that order?'

Anton shakes his head.

Of course he fucking doesn't.

'Vijay's father. *That's* why he wants to kill me. Not because I brought you back from Paradise. Because he discovered I disobeyed his order to kill Apt. You know why I killed Senator Thomassi and saved your daughter?'

'Sir,' Leona says.

Might be because I've got Anton against the wall.

'Not your quarrel. Be grateful.'

Anton's eyes are wide and his face purple. Guess it's time to step back. Taking my elbow from his throat, I listen to him drag air into his bursting lungs. His eyes take a second or two to focus.

Something's changed behind them.

There's watchfulness. He knows less about me than he thinks. And there's something else. A realization of how little he knows about what happened during those months he was in prison. But we've still got one question outstanding and I want it answered.

'Tell me why I saved Aptitude.'

'Because you promised.'

He's got it. I promised Debro, who reminds me of my sister. This is the dumbest fucking reason I've ever heard for putting my life on the line. But the only one I've got and it's the only one I can offer. Not that I bother to say that.

Sergeant Leona stands by the window.

She's wondering how dangerous I am. It shows in her eyes. You'd think I was good at reading faces. Only, that's not it. The expressions round here are pretty obvious.

'Anton,' I say, 'what kind of hover has flags?'

He blinks at the change of subject.

'Official ones, right?'

'Yes . . . Empire ministers. Full generals. Senior senators. Ambassadors.' Anton shrugs, tries to think of some more important people and lets his voice trail away into silence.

'What does it mean when they're tied up?'

'They're not on official business.'

Rubbing his throat, Anton looks at the street below and glances away. 'We're talking about that girl?'

'Paper Osamu. U/Free ambassador to the Octovian Empire.'

It hasn't occurred to me he doesn't know who she is. But why should he? After being released from Paradise, Anton was flown straight to Wildeside. This is the first time he's been in Farlight since his original arrest.

'I met Paper at Ilseville,' I tell him. 'When she was the U/Free observer. She witnessed our surrender of the city. And confirmed our later victory. It was Paper who asked General Jaxx if she could borrow my team.'

'You've met her socially since?'

That's the high clans for you.

'Yeah,' I say. 'Several times.'

'What's she like?'

'A scorpion.'

Anton looks at me. 'Sven, tell me you didn't—'

Obviously enough, I did.

Every which way. Enjoyed it too.

Chapter 20

THE BARS ON OUR WINDOW ARE AS THICK AS A CHILD'S WRIST.

Beyond them, the jumble of roofs fades into darkness. A narrow street, more of a back alley really, lies empty below us. The air stinks, because the air in Farlight always stinks.

The house opposite is lower than this one. A light shows from one window. A lamp, presumably. We can't see into the room because its shutters are closed for the night. That's to be expected, since the cathedral clock just struck eleven.

A quick scrape with my nail reveals rust under the paint of the bars. Another scrape reveals dull steel beneath.

'Sven.' Anton's voice is hoarse. 'What are you doing?'

Plainly he's talking to me again.

Apart from being hacked off I didn't collect the Aux on my way down . . . ? I'm thinking. I know it's a novelty. I'm sure the SIG would have something to say about that. But I'm trying to get us out of here. I don't say that to Anton, obviously. But why not think? Nothing else is working.

'Grab one of these,' I order.

Anton wraps his hands round the central bar and tugs.

Gripping the bar next to it, I pull in the opposite direction. We were right first time, the bars are beyond bending.

'And again.'

Grit drops onto my fingers.

'Help me off with my shirt,' I tell Sergeant Leona.

The blade in its neoprene sheath between my shoulders is narrow. This is a knife for stabbing or throwing, rather than slashing. That's good, because I need the point to be fine.

Positioning the blade parallel to a bar, I jab at the ring of mortar around its upper end and smile when more grit drops onto my fingers. Too much pressure and the blade's end will blunt. Wrong angle and it'll snap.

The others have the sense to let me work in silence.

If you've ever built a jail, you'll know the deepest hole for the bars always goes at the top. The bar slots into that and drops into a shallower hole in the lintel below. Otherwise the weight of the bars sinks them into the setting mortar.

That's how these are fixed.

About an inch in, the mortar becomes softer. Between scraping mortar free, I sharpen the point of my knife on the wall beyond the window. I could use the lintel, but the street below is empty and I'm hoping to get out of here without leaving too many clues how we did it.

'Right,' I say. 'Grab this and twist.'

They do, until the bar turns slightly.

So I tell them to twist it back and repeat until I tell them to stop . . .

The room's hot, the night is muggy in a way only central Farlight can manage, and they've been worrying the bar so long sweat runs down their faces and sticks their clothes to their bodies. I can smell Leona from where I stand.

When she thinks I'm not looking, she examines her hands. Their palms are blistered and raw.

'Piss on your fingers,' I say.

She thinks I'm joking.

'Leona,' I say, 'you've been squirming half an hour . . .'

Now I've embarrassed her as well. Can't think why. You need to piss, you need to piss. She might as well do something useful with it like harden the sores on her fingers. Although, come to think of it . . .

'Cross your legs for another minute.'

Anton looks appalled.

Sergeant Leona simply nods.

Gripping the central bar, I twist until the muscles lock in my back and ligaments pop in my shoulder. I can almost hear flesh tear.

'*Sir* . . .'

'Almost there.'

With a squeal, the bar turns one complete rotation. And then another and another until I can turn it freely. After that, all Anton has to do is push upwards as he turns it. So the end of the bar buried in the lintel grinds against its mortar.

Eventually the bar works free.

'All right,' I tell Leona. 'Now you can piss. Bring a handful over here when you're done.' I'm going to mix it with the grit to make new mortar.

'We'll turn our backs,' Anton reassures her.

I do what Anton suggests. But only because I want a proper look at the wall outside now the bar is gone. I need to know how hard it is going to be for us to reach the roof above.

The answer is, impossible.

Chapter 21

THE WALL ABOVE OUR WINDOW RISES TWENTY FEET TO A LOW parapet that probably runs around the entire building. The wall's flat, no ledge, no drainpipes and no handholds. The plaster I stab flakes to reveal stone beneath. No way can we cut holes in this.

Even the hiss of Leona pissing isn't enough to raise my spirits.

'What about that?' Anton says.

Yes, I've seen it.

Fifteen feet below, a rusting girder straddles the street.

It stops the back wall of the building opposite from collaps-ing into this house. As cheap fixes go it's effective. And for all I know it's been there since the original virus bowed the walls round here into their current state. Has to have historic value. Or someone would have replaced it with something less ugly.

If I'm wrong about the house opposite not having bars, we're fucked. But we're fucked if we stay and fucked if we fall. So we might as well try using the girder as a bridge. Not least because the other house is lower than this one, and the girder ends five feet below an attic window.

Anton winces at my reasoning.

'Sir . . .'

A slick of liquid stains the tiles. And Leona's cupping a hand-ful of piss so rank it would poison rats. I'm not surprised: it's hot and we've been sweating and no one's bothered to bring us water.

'Here,' I say.

She dribbles liquid into the little mound of grit I've made on the windowsill and I have my mortar.

'Right. You go first.'

'Yes, sir.'

That's when it occurs to me she doesn't know about our girder. Leona thinks I'm telling her to drop four floors. The fact she's willing to obey impresses me. Anton is looking at her as if she's insane.

'There's a metal strut,' he says. 'About ten feet below us.'

'Fifteen.'

'If you say so.'

'Yeah,' I say. 'I do.'

Climbing onto the ledge, Leona wriggles between the bars, grips my hand and winces. Her palms are sticky with blood.

'Ready when you are, sir.'

She finds herself dangling four floors above the street, with her boots a few feet above the girder. Looking up, she gives me a twisted smile, and nods.

So I let go.

Landing on the girder, Leona tries to balance, loses her nerve and panics, throwing herself forward to wrap her arms round the rusting bar. Her yelp of pain when she hits is louder than I'd like.

I think she's going to fall to the street below, but she locks her hands and holds tight. It's not enough to stop her slipping sideways.

'Fuck,' Anton says.

As we watch, Leona tips off the edge and finds herself hanging. Should have locked her knees round the girder first.

'You can do it,' Anton says.

'Swing your legs up. Lock your knees. Work your way round.'

She nods at my order. It takes her longer than it should to scrabble upright. When she does, her face is white with pain.

'Ribs,' she says. 'Sorry, sir.'

'Broken?'

'Yes, sir. Sorry, sir.'

'They'll mend.'

She rewards me with a sour smile.

Anton drops next. He's taller than Leona, so once we've locked wrists and he's dropped over the ledge, his boot almost touches the girder. All the same, he decides against Leona's plan. No balancing for Anton. Opening his legs, he lands on the girder as if riding a gyrobike.

'Shit . . .'

Not sure it's a method I'd choose.

The girder is old and rusting and fixed in place with only three bolts at each end. No point Anton and Sergeant Leona having their brains dashed out if my weight is too much and the bolts decide to give.

'Crawl towards the attic window. Make yourselves secure.'

My first problem comes when I try to get through the bars. Even with one bar missing, the gap is tight. Gripping the window frame, I drag myself through, one-handed, and hear ribs crack. Feels like Leona got her revenge.

My next problem is staying put while I repair the bars. Sliding the missing bar into its upper slot and bedding it down is easy. Replacing the mortar is harder. Scraping what I don't use off the ledge with my knife, I flick it to the street below. Should have crumbled it. Still, it looks like dog shit from this distance. So maybe we'll get lucky.

'Sir,' Leona hisses.

Three soldiers are turning into the street.

Give me three bricks and I could kill them all. But we're out of bricks and don't want to attract attention. So I wait until they're gone, before dropping from my position to hang by my one hand from the window ledge.

SVEN, IS THIS WISE?

For a second, with metal creaking and dry mortar trickling from the three bolts at each end of the girder as I hit rusting steel and cling fast, I feel icy smoke swirl through my thoughts. Then it fades.

The air is hot and Farlight breathless.

Night hangs heavy, and sweat slides down my ribs. It drips from my eyebrows and runs through my cropped hair. As the kyp roils with excitement in my throat, a fever tries to shake me free from my perch.

'You OK?' Anton whispers.

'*Of course I'm fucking*—'

What's the point of saying OctoV is watching me?

Even if it is true, which isn't definite . . . But a wave of static makes the kyp sour my throat, and I suspect it is. The kyp's faulty. Can't remember if I mentioned that. It's been faulty since it was fitted.

Gaining a kyp is a one-time action. Well, mostly. You could replace it. But then you'd need to rip out my throat and give me another.

I've never been worth that kind of money.

'Catch,' I tell Leona.

A second later, she's balanced at the far end of the girder, gripping a shutter with one hand. We all hear the click as she uses my knife to lift its lock. What happens now depends on what we find.

Legba is kind.

Our attic has no bars. And its window is partly open.

Lifting it, Leona tumbles through the gap. Anton follows.

Takes me longer. Reaching back, I close the shutters and click their latch in place. Then I shut the window and lock that.

'*Sir*,' Leona says.

Something strange about her voice.

A young woman struggles in my sergeant's grip. Leona has one hand over the girl's mouth and my dagger to her neck. She's young, with blonde curls falling across her naked shoulders. Her dress is low-cut. So low, her breasts threaten to spill free as she struggles.

Anton's spellbound.

'Deal with it,' I tell Leona crossly.

Dropping my blade, she digs her thumb into the girl's elbow and grips. When Leona lets go, the girl's too shocked by the pain to resume struggling.

Works for me.

'Scream,' I say, 'and we'll kill you.'

'*Sven!*'

I ignore Anton. 'Understand me?'

Blue eyes grow huge with tears.

This girl is pretty, in a useless sort of way. Some men like that. From the look on Anton's face he's one of them.

'*Do you understand?*'

She nods.

'OK,' I say. 'Release her.'

As the girl fills her lungs to shout, Leona muffles her. The look Leona gives me says it all.

'You're not listening,' I say, picking up my blade.

Now the girl's watching the knife.

Very carefully.

And she's still watching when Leona removes her hand to leave the four of us alone in the attic with silence.

'Anton,' I whisper. 'Try the door.'

It's locked. Now how did I know that?

The attic is clean. Someone recently scrubbed its floor, but badly. There's a bed, with a mattress, both old. There are no clothes on hangers, no hangers come to that. This isn't a room for living in. It's a place families dump junk they can't be bothered to throw away.

'You being punished?'

That's the usual reason to be locked up in places like this.

'No,' she whispers. 'At least, I don't think so . . .'

'My dear.' Anton comes forward.

His face is grave. Something about her worries him. I should have known it would be her accent. 'What's your name?'

'Sef Kam— Lady Serafina Kama.'

Leona slides me a glance. My face is neutral.

'That's high clan?' I say.

'Obviously,' Serafina says. Then mutters an apology. Can't work out why she's bothering, until I remember she's seen me tell Anton what to do. And he's obviously from her world. So . . .

So simple these people.

'Have you come to rescue me?'

'Do you need rescuing?' Anton asks.

Since she asked, the answer is obviously yes. But Anton and Sef are too busy being polite to follow the logic of that. The captive has a lamp by her bed. An old-fashioned lamp with a wick.

Power cut. Lamp.

What are the chances of that?

The attic has a small alcove containing a lavatory. So this was a bedroom once, before it was a storeroom. I do what my old lieutenant told me to do when entering any new situation. Take an inventory.

One door in, locked. One window, now bolted.

Shutters safely closed and locked.

One skylight in the alcove, too small to let me or Anton through. Although Sergeant Leona might manage it.

'I could climb out, drop down, unlock the door from the other side,' the sergeant says. She's obviously been watching me read the attic. Bar, brothel, bedroom or battlefield, doesn't matter which, there are times you need to lock them down or get out fast. First rule of anything: Know where you are. Second rule: Know how to get somewhere else.

I glance at Sef Kama.

'What?' she asks, seeing me look.

'Nothing.' The fact she hasn't tried escaping through the skylight tells me all I need about how much use she's going to be. 'How often do you get fed?'

Her mouth is open, but it's not saying anything.

'You got fed this afternoon?'

'Pancakes.'

'Last night?'

She shakes her head. 'I wasn't . . . I only . . .'

OK, she's only been here for a day, and hasn't yet got her head round the fact she might be here some time. Except, she won't be. Because Anton is telling her she'll be all right now he's here.

He shuts up when I glare at him.

'I can't believe it,' Sef says.

Anton wastes a couple of minutes coaxing out what she can't believe. Apparently she's been locked in by Paulo. She breaks off telling him this to ask why Paulo would do such a thing. Since Anton doesn't know who Paulo is, it's a pointless question.

When asked, she says Paulo designs dresses.

Doesn't sound that dangerous to me.

Lady Serafina is only here because her aunt insisted more lace was needed for the dress.

'What dress?' Sergeant Leona demands.

Sef's glance is cold. 'I'm getting married.' You can see she

153

thinks talking to Leona is beneath her. 'In the cathedral.'

'Who's the lucky man?'

'Vijay Jaxx. You wouldn't know him.'

Anton grabs me before I can finish wrapping my fingers round her throat. And then he's on the floor, clutching his gut, and Sef is wailing and Leona is trying very hard not to show any expression at all.

'How long have you known him?' I demand.

'All my life. We've been engaged since childhood.'

'We're talking about Vijay? Been away recently? Only just come back?'

'Landed this morning,' she says. 'Why?'

Because, I'm going to kill the little shit. And a Jaxx or not, I'm going to cut off his tackle and fuck him with his own bits first. Don't realize I've said it aloud, until Leona grins and Sef starts wailing.

'What's he ever done to you?'

It's what he's done to Aptitude that pisses me off.

Anton's dragging himself to his feet. He looks sick, but not upset enough for someone who's just discovered his daughter's fiancé is cheating. I'm getting ready to call him on it, when Leona grabs Sef and chokes off her wails.

'Sir . . .'

We hear footsteps on the stairs.

'We'll be in there,' she tells Sef, pointing at the bathroom. 'With the door slightly open. Betray us and it won't just be Paulo's throat we cut . . .'

She really is a girl after my own heart.

154

Chapter 22

A KEY TURNS AND THE DOOR OPENS. THE MAN WHO ENTERS IS balding, middle-aged, and slightly thick about the waist. He wears small spectacles, a flowery shirt and carries a bottle of water and a glass.

Not my idea of a kidnapper.

'My lady,' he says. 'I heard you moving around.'

Not sure what Paulo sees in Sef's face, but his voice falters. Putting down his offering, he begins to back towards the door. He's not doing this because he thinks Sef might attack. It's embarrassment that keeps him bent double.

'Try to get some sleep,' he suggests.

'*What?*'

'It's for the best.'

'Paulo,' Sef says. 'You locked me in.'

'Lady Isadora said—'

Shouts from General Luc's house stop anyone finding out what Sef's Aunt Isadora said. Scurrying to the window, Paulo slides it up and throws back its shutters. A street door opposite opens hard enough to hit the wall. The Wolf has returned to find us gone.

At a sound of feet on his stairs, Paulo freezes.

No chance it's General Luc. He's still busy issuing orders on the street below, his voice tight and angry. He sounds a bad man to have as a CO.

Had a few like that in my time.

'*Serafina . . . my dear.*'

Treacle sliding down razor blades. Maybe Sef feels the same, because her face tightens. Although she forces a smile, and turns from watching the street to face her visitor.

'You have no idea how hard it was to track you down.' Both Serafina and the newcomer are young, both blonde, both blue-eyed. There the likeness ends. Although they're obviously twins, the newcomer got the brains.

Behind Sef and her reflection stands a man, looking concerned.

'You've come to take me home?'

'Of course,' she says. 'We've been looking all day. Vijay must be worried sick. As for you . . .' Her gaze hits Paulo. 'You'll be dealt with later.'

The man behind the newcomer interests me.

He's U/Free, dressed in elegant robes.

Some kind of smart silk that swirls through carefully chosen colours. His hand on the newcomer's hip says he's already had her. And his smile as he examines Sef says he'll be happy to have her as well.

'So,' he says. 'This is your sister?'

The reflection nods.

'Ladies Simone and Serafina Rivabella y Kama.' Although he sweeps them a low bow, there is something predatory in his gesture. And his grin is mocking as he strips Sef with his eyes.

'Sir,' Leona whispers.

I'm gripping the door frame tight enough to crush wood.

★

156

Morgan Trefoil is married to Paper Osamu. We have history. He cost me a corporal who could skewer an abseiling spider across a crowded bar with a single throw. We were lovers, Franc and I. She still throws that knife some nights in my dreams.

I've killed Morgan once already.

Unfortunately, he's U/Free. So he had a back-up.

You can tell he's U/Free from his smug little face. The puffy cheeks, the arrogant sneer. His type might preach equality, but only because they can afford to. They control the richest civilization the galaxy has ever seen. We're the ones still scrabbling our way out of ditches.

You've probably worked it out.

I want him dead.

Again.

'Time to go home,' he tells Lady Serafina.

As Sef nods, something strange happens. Although Paulo's obviously terrified of Morgan, he thrusts himself between the U/Free and the open doorway. Men like Paulo don't do well in Farlight. It's probably only his ability to dress the high clans that keeps him safe. Now, he's risking it all. And for what?

'Please,' he begs. 'Lady Isadora said—'

Morgan's face tightens. 'Stay out of this,' he snaps. 'You're meddling in matters far above you.'

That's Morgan all over. Patronizing bastard.

'My lord,' Paulo says.

A scowl floods Morgan's face.

'The U/Free don't recognize titles,' he says. 'We certainly don't use them ourselves. All people are equal in our eyes.'

Self-righteous, as well as patronizing.

'But Lady Isadora insists—'

'I don't give a fuck what *Lady* Isadora insists.'

'My lord . . .'

One second the dressmaker is standing there, the next he's against a wall and his feet dangle six inches above the floor. Morgan has him by the throat. The U/Free's muscles are augmented. Nothing else explains the speed at which he reacts.

Never seen Morgan lose it before.

Pretty impressive, if you take it at face value. I don't . . . Taking things at face value gets you killed, according to my old lieutenant. Mind you, he read meanings into the number of vultures at the water hole, how many flies swam in his brandy and what time of day he first farted. Took bets on it too.

U/Free aren't supposed to lose it. That's for barbarians like us. So if Morgan is going apeshit he's pretending or he's scared. And why would a man like Morgan be scared?

Paulo's eyes are popping.

The way they do when pressure builds behind them. Much more of this, and it'll be a dead tailor Morgan holds.

'You're nothing. Understand me? You'll do as you're told. All of you . . .'

'*All of us?* Really?'

General Luc stands in the doorway.

Light glitters from a lamp in his hand, and the flash of purple behind his rank badges shows almost black in the shadows. He has a smile on his lips at odds with the barely restrained fury in his eyes.

'We'll do what we're told?' General Luc repeats the words softly. As if he can taste them.

'You know the agreement.'

'Do I? Really?'

The Wolf steps into the room. A captain and Sergeant Toro step into the room behind him. His immediate staff from the look of things.

'You know,' General Luc says, 'I don't remember agreeing anything at all.' He nods stiffly to the women. 'My ladies.

158

It's late to find you out. And in such strange company.'

General Luc glances at Paulo.

The little dressmaker is on his knees, holding his throat.

It's obvious the Wolf knows Serafina and Simone Rivabella y Kama. Equally obvious that Sef's sister is unhappy to be recognized.

'This has nothing to do with you,' Morgan says.

'It has everything to do with me.'

'Paulo locked me in,' Sef complains. 'I don't know why. He said he had some special lace he'd been saving for a dress as beautiful as mine.'

Yes, that sounds stupid enough for her to believe.

'It didn't occur to me he'd . . .'

The Wolf shows his teeth. 'No,' he says. 'Obviously not. So, he asked you to travel all the way across the city just to look at lace?'

'No.' Sef looks more puzzled than ever. 'That was my aunt.'

'Lady Isadora?'

Sef nods. 'She said Paulo had mentioned the lace to her and . . .'

As Sef's words trail away, I wonder if she's ever finished a sentence in her life. And decide I don't care and it doesn't matter. What matters is the friction between General Luc and the U/Free.

'We're taking Sef home,' Simone says.

The general ignores her. 'Tell me,' he says to Paulo. 'Why did you lock her in?'

'Lady Isadora said it would keep her safe.'

'From what?'

'I don't know, sir.'

'Maybe not. But that's the question. Isn't it?'

Morgan draws himself up, and I know the man's an idiot. If you have to *draw yourself up* when facing someone like the Wolf, you're in the wrong fight.

159

'You should stay out of this.'

'Should I?'

'Yes,' says Morgan, nodding. 'You should.'

When General Luc grins, yellowing canines gleam in the half dark of the room. And it's obvious how he got his nickname. 'My dear,' he says to Sef. 'What do you think your little dressmaker is keeping you safe from?'

She doesn't answer. She just looks wide-eyed and beautiful and stupid. When she realizes General Luc is waiting for an answer, she shrugs to show she's waiting for him to tell her.

Instead he asks if her aunt is kind to her.

'Always,' Sef says, tears in her eyes. 'Very kind.' She says this as if the rest of the world has been nothing but cruel.

'So you trust her?'

Sef nods.

'Then perhaps you should stay here?' Walking over to the open shutters, General Luc looks at the windows opposite and glances at the rusting girder, judging the drop from the window where we were trapped.

'You opened this window yourself?'

'Yes,' Sef says.

'When?'

'When I heard the noise outside.'

The Wolf nods to himself. 'What's through there,' he demands, pointing at the door we hide behind.

'A bathroom,' Sef says.

'You don't object if I take a look?'

'*Don't* . . .' Her voice is a squeak.

'Why not?'

'Because . . .' She's now bright red. 'I didn't . . .'

'Flush it,' the Wolf tells her.

'The power's gone.'

'I can wait while you close the lid.'

That's the high clans for you. Perfect manners and strict propriety, mixed with vast sums of money, extended lifelines, and a certainty everyone else exists to keep them amused. Much like the U/Free really.

Chapter 23

SIX MONTHS AGO THE U/FREE WERE MYTHICAL BEASTS TO ME.

And I'd only ever met one member of the high clans, my lieutenant, Bonafont de Bonafont, and I didn't even know that's what he was. He was just a drunk who insisted his plates be piping hot, even in the middle of the day in the middle of summer in the middle of the desert.

'Sir,' Leona whispers.

Sef is walking towards our door.

I move aside to let her enter, and she shows me an anguished face as she walks to the pan and shuts its lid with a clatter. It's not necessary, but she does it anyway.

'I'd know,' Morgan snaps, 'if anyone was in there.'

The Wolf ignores him. The U/Free hate that more than anything.

'My lord,' Paulo is saying, 'I only had orders to detain Lady Serafina. There's no one else here. I swear it.' His voice is honest, his embarrassment plain.

'All the same.'

It's Morgan's anger that saves us from discovery.

I intend to thank him someday. Before killing him, obviously.

Drawing himself up again, he says, 'It would be best for everybody, General, if you simply did your job. I'm sure you and your men have places to go, duties to perform. Perhaps you should go perform them?'

Self-righteous fuck.

Leona grins beside me.

Even the Wolf, seen through the door's crack, looks as if he can't believe what he just heard.

Stepping close, he halts a hand's breadth from Morgan's face. 'Talk to me like that,' he hisses, 'and I'll cut out your heart.'

'I'm U/Free.'

'Believe me,' he says, 'that's the only thing keeping you alive.'

The Wolf has one hand on his dagger. Maybe he's hoping to make good that promise. Morgan, however, refuses to back down.

'Serafina,' Simone calls.

Leona pushes her towards the door.

Anton puts his finger to his lips and smiles. Leona's approach is more basic. She mimes cutting Sef's throat.

'I've shut the lid,' Sef says, sounding close to tears.

'We're taking you home,' Morgan says.

General Luc shakes his head.

It's become a point of principle for both of them. As far as I'm concerned there's nothing more stupid and nothing more dangerous. 'She has rights,' Morgan says.

The Wolf grins. 'Such concern for those less fortunate.'

'We make dangerous enemies.'

'You speak for the whole U/Free?'

Morgan nods.

'Good,' says General Luc. 'Because I speak for Clan Luc and the entire Wolf Brigade. And we don't give a fuck if you think you're dangerous or not.'

It's the first time I've heard him swear.

'But if you're that concerned, why not ask? I'm sure Serafina can tell us her wishes.'

Everyone looks at Sef.

'She's coming with us,' Simone says. 'Aren't you? We're going to take her to find Vijay.'

'I'm staying here,' Sef says.

'*Serafina.*'

'I mean it. It's only one night, right?'

She looks at Paulo, but it's the general who nods. 'Wise choice,' he says. General Luc is so busy steering Morgan and Sef's sister towards the attic door that he forgets to search our little alcove before he goes. Instead, we get the click of a lock, the grate of a bolt and then steps on the stairs outside.

When the Wolf hits the street, I'm at the window, stepped back so I can't be seen. He growls something to Sergeant Toro and the waiting troop break into three groups. One group follows General Luc, one follows Sergeant Toro, and the last follows the captain we saw earlier.

All wear battle rattle.

Not dress uniform. The full kit. Eighty pounds of Kevlar flak jacket, combat boots, 1.5 litre camelback, carbon helmet, with flip-down visor. They're carrying short-barrel 18s, adapted for urban combat.

'Fuck,' Leona says.

'Yeah.' Anton opens the door. 'That was close.'

Don't think she's talking about our near miss with General Luc. This is Sergeant Leona's city. You'd have to be blind and stupid not to know something very nasty is going down.

After a few minutes, the noise dies. Half an hour later, you wouldn't know there had been a troop of Wolf Brigade on the street at all. And it is exactly half an hour, because the cathedral clock strikes.

I'm still in the attic, considering choices.

Sergeant Leona's just finished washing herself in the bathroom.

And Anton's telling Sef how brave she is for the fifth time, when a step squeaks at the top of the stairs and someone halts outside our door. When Sef grabs Anton, Leona rolls her eyes. Not good discipline. But Anton's not a soldier and Sef's an idiot.

So I guess it's allowed.

'Hide,' I tell my two.

Running to the bed, Sef pretends to sleep.

At least, she curls up on the rancid mattress like a cat, rests her head on one arm and shuts her eyes. A second later her breathing steadies.

'So brave,' Anton says.

I think of pointing out she's a brain-dead little idiot and he's married to Debro. Then I remember he's not. They're divorced. For all they share exile.

Not my business anyway.

Although, what he sees in a vapid blonde with pneumatic breasts who clings like ivy . . . I kill that thought, knowing I've answered my own question. I expect Paulo to be our visitor, maybe with food. But it's too silent out there.

Very slowly, a bolt slides back.

The figure in the doorway hesitates and then appears to nod.

Sliding into the room, it moves towards the bed. When it steps through a sliver of moonlight, I see blonde hair spilling from under a raised hood. Lady Simone Kama hesitates as her eyes adjust to the unexpected light.

She freezes when Anton shifts slightly, her head flicking towards where we hide. Stepping towards us, she changes her mind. Maybe the darkness unnerves her. Maybe she simply wants to get Sef out of there.

Turning back, she steps towards the bed . . .

And Leona hurtles past me.

Body-slamming Simone into a wall, she draws back her elbow and cracks it into the side of Simone's skull, dropping her to the floor.

'*Sergeant . . .*' Anton sounds outraged.

Leona's not listening. Crouching above her victim, she has one arm back to drive a straight-fingered blow into Simone's throat.

'*Easy.*'

For a second, it looks as if she'll ignore my order. Instead, she drags air into her lungs and makes herself sit back.

'*Why did you do that?*'

Sef's wailing again. At least she's got a reason this time. Anton kneels by Simone's body, his fingers to her throat.

'Well?' I demand.

'Still breathing.'

'Put her on the bed. Let me know when she wakes.'

Nodding to the sergeant, I walk her to the window and open its shutters. The street is silent, the stars clear against a deep black sky. There's a heat tonight and a humidity that clings. The whole city feels oppressive.

'Sir,' says Leona. 'You all right?'

Not the kind of question she should be asking. 'Leona,' I say, 'you want to tell me what that was about?'

She looks uncertain.

'That's an order.'

'The woman had a knife.'

The sergeant looks sane. That's good enough for me. Anton wants to know why we're searching the floor. So does Sef. At least, she stops fussing over Simone long enough to ask why we're on our knees.

I don't answer either of them.

I don't find a knife either.

What I do find is a puddle. At least, the remains of one.

Most of the liquid has disappeared down a gap in the boards.

Dropping to a crouch, Leona wipes her fingers across the floor and tastes it.

'Water,' she says.

Leona's right. I'm thinking about this when it occurs to me she's still staring at me. 'What?' I demand.

'Sir,' she whispers. 'I saw a blade.'

On the bed, Simone is groaning. She sits up, falls back and struggles up again. It's a bravura performance. 'What happened?'

'You slipped,' I tell her. 'On a puddle of water.'

Something says she doesn't believe me. Anton's staring, and Sef has her mouth open to protest. Although she shuts it again when Leona glares.

'Get your cloak,' I say. 'We're taking you home.'

'But I want to see Vijay.'

My sigh has Leona smiling.

All five of us make our way down the stairs. I've told Sef and Simone what will happen if either one makes a noise. It involves letting Sergeant Leona loose on them. This probably explains why we almost reach ground level before Paulo appears.

The sight of my knife freezes his protest.

'Lock the front door after us,' I tell him. 'Raise an alarm and I'll come back and burn your house to the ground. With you inside . . .'

He believes me. It shows in his eyes.

'Paulo,' says Sef. 'It's going to be all right.'

Although he keeps his mouth firmly shut, he shakes his head and slides his gaze between my face and my knife, his mouth twisting in anguish.

'Please . . .' he blurts.

Courage impresses me, whatever form it takes. When Paulo realizes he's not going to get punched or stabbed, he relaxes slightly. 'Let her stay here,' he begs. 'I promise to keep her safe.'

'She'll be safe with me,' Simone says.

Paulo dares to disagree.

This makes me wonder what he knows.

And that makes me wonder why Simone is so keen her sister sleeps somewhere other than this. I might be slow. But I get there. Too many things about this that make no sense.

'You know where Vijay lives?'

Sef nods. She doesn't say where, of course. Or give me directions. She simply nods.

'Sir,' Paulo says.

'Sef and her sister go with us. End of story. You want to protect her, find me a piece . . .'

The little man looks puzzled.

'A gun,' Sergeant Leona says, translating it into language he can understand. 'Do you have anything resembling a gun?'

Paulo grins.

'You take point,' I tell Leona.

She nods.

'I'll bring up the rear.'

'Yes, sir.'

'Anton, you and the Kamas travel together. Anyone asks, you're on your way back from a party. Didn't realize it was curfew.'

We have one piece and a collection of kitchen knives. Paulo's contribution to keeping Sef safe until she finds her fiancé. He's also tacked my empty sleeve neatly across my jacket to stop it flapping.

Anton thinks this hysterically funny.

Not sure why I let Paulo do it. Except he wants to make the jacket look neater and obviously has Sef's interests at heart. And he did give me his revolver.

It's huge, uses a calibre I've never seen, and pivots open

168

beyond the trigger, rather than having a cylinder that flips out to one side. The cylinder only takes five rounds, despite its size. But each one is fatter than my thumb.

Seems Paulo had a friend who worked in an abattoir.

This was what he used to kill oxen. All right, it's rusting and we've only got twelve rounds in all. But even empty it's going to make a good club. Pity it's not AI, it would probably spit like a campesino and demand to be cleaned only with cooking alcohol.

'Sven,' Anton says. 'You're grinning.'

He's in a better mood than he was a moment ago. Mind you, I was hammering crosses into the top of each round using a kitchen knife and a pestle borrowed from Paulo's kitchen. Think he thought ammunition this old might explode.

'Right,' I say. 'Let's go.'

Between them, I'm hoping Anton, Sef and Simone can muster enough high clan outrage to cow the militia we're likely to meet. If we meet Death's Head, or anyone from General Luc's own troop, then we're fucked.

Anton knows that even if the others don't.

Chapter 24

HALF A MILE DOWN THE ROAD, I SLIP FORWARD AND TELL ANTON our change of plan. His group's on its own from now on. At least, that's how it will look to those watching. Anything happens, we're there. Otherwise, Leona and I don't exist.

Anton is in Sef's hands for directions.

As Simone and Sef argue which route to take, we slip away. Simone has the brains, and Sef the sickly sweetness Anton finds so attractive. They both have that high clan smugness that makes me want to slap them.

Voices come from an upper window as we cut under an arch.

A dozen men talking, maybe two dozen. The voices mute as Anton, Sef and Simone pass without seeing us. I can't shake the feeling they're being watched, as they turn down streets that change their names halfway and bicker about which side of a square to walk.

As if it matters.

Blank colonnades stare at them as they tramp across flagstones.

Sef and Simone's constant arguing, all done too loudly, and

with an obvious high clan accent, acts as their passport. I hear men in a garden behind one of the walls. They fall silent. Just as the men in that upstairs room fell silent. Although two guards peer through a small gate.

Leona and I freeze.

The men stare at Anton and the twins. Anton nods, Serafina wishes them a good evening and Sef waves.

Still muttering, the men disappear.

In a courtyard beyond, troops wait. Fifty soldiers, maybe more. Sergeant Leona's seen them too. Anton doesn't notice. He's too busy listening to Sef complain that her route is better. Although, as Simone points out, as they're almost there it doesn't really matter.

'Fuckwits,' Leona says.

Don't think I'm meant to hear that.

Slipping after them, we find Anton, Sef and Simone standing by the river. They're admiring its blackness. At least Sef is. Anton's merely agreeing how very black it is. While Simone's look is unreadable.

Should have known Vijay would have a mansion round here. For all that the river is stale and stinks, these are still the most expensive houses in the city.

'I'll go ahead,' we hear Simone say. 'Make sure it's safe.'

We follow her.

She's good, Leona. Moves swiftly, efficiently and silently.

Makes me wonder if she's really militia. I'd have her pegged as elite, if I didn't know the elites only take men.

'Sir,' she whispers.

'What?'

'Back at Paulo's . . .'

'You did see a blade?'

She scowls, then smiles when she realizes I believe her.

The sergeant and I are close enough to smell each other. And I notice the way her fringe slicks to the side of her head.

Another thing I notice is that the badges are cut from her uniform. I've only her word she's a dispatch rider. Although why would anybody bother to lie about a thing like that?

'On Paradise,' I tell her, 'people used ice daggers all the time.'

'You were a guard?'

'A prisoner.'

I watch her reassess me.

'Sir,' she whispers, 'what do you think is going on?'

Her question takes me back to an evening a month earlier. Another soldier, although one of my own this time. The same hot wind and smell of stale sweat. I'm in the slums on the upper slope of the crater, staring down at the centre of a city that celebrates Indigo Jaxx's promotion to Duke of Farlight.

Behind me, my bar is crowded.

A goat turns on a spit over a fire pit. The girl rubbing black pepper into its crisping sides is Aptitude. She doesn't know I've asked OctoV for her parents' freedom. She thinks this is her life now.

Maybe things should have been left like that.

As I sit, and watch the fireworks explode above me, the soldier next to me drains the last of our shared bottle and rests her head on my shoulder. She wants to know what I smell on the hot night wind.

Her, obviously. Although I don't mention that.

People stink in the barrio. People stink on campaign. They stink in the desert. Face it, people stink anywhere they're expected to exist without water. So I tell her the night smells of dog shit. Also, leaves, flowers and weeds. Plus a bush sour enough to be thorn. My childhood was ringed with razor thorn. This is less vicious, but no less pungent.

Shil nods, says she's identified them as well.

It occurs to me now she was just making conversation. The

way women sometimes do. So they can listen to you talk. At the time I thought she really wanted to know.

'There's something else,' I tell her.

She looks interested.

Something ranker than all the other smells put together. It tugs at the back of my throat and wakes the kyp, making it spasm so violently I want to vomit.

'What is it?' Shil asks.

I've never seen the point of lying.

'Trouble.'

And here, as soldiers hide in the shadows, and conversations still in upstairs rooms or behind the high walls of high clan houses, and Anton and Sef flirt, and Simone hurries towards the gates of a darkened mansion, I know I was right.

Trouble was what I smelt on the wind that night.

I smelt tonight waiting for me.

Don't know how. Only know it's true. The stink of unborn violence thickens the streets like cheap scent. Without thinking about it, I say the prayer for soldiers going into battle. Sergeant Leona looks across.

'You think we're going to die?'

My shrug asks if it matters.

From the look on her face it obviously does. So I toss her a fresh grin and add, 'Not if I have anything to do with it.'

Farlight's volcano was extinct before machines landed to make earth from rubble and begin the process to create atmosphere. Drunks joke about it blowing again. No one expects it to. And yet, if ever a city felt on the edge of exploding, it's this one. As Aptitude says, Farlight is proof ignorance isn't bliss.

If it was, we'd all be happier.

Simone can't see us. Because we're in shadow, and she's not looking. Nor is the man who opens the gateway to greet her.

'Took you long enough.'

'Little bitch is with me.' This is her sister Simone is talking about. Like I said, most families are more trouble than they're worth.

Morgan looks at her.

'Don't ask,' Simone says. 'She had back-up.'

'Supplied by Luc?'

'Imagine so. Where's her fiancé?'

The U/Free shrugs. 'Not here, anyway.'

'He must be.'

'I've searched.'

She grabs his arm. 'But—'

'Don't you understand?' Morgan hisses. 'He crossed the river before curfew. Looking for Serafina.'

'So he's still trapped?'

'The bridges are shut. The boats are all on this side. Paper's locked down airspace until tomorrow. What do you think?'

Sounds like more than a lovers' quarrel to me.

A couple of soldiers appear at Morgan's side. City militia. Armed with Kemzin 19s, body armour and night helmets, visors flipped up.

One of them asks a question. Morgan nods. They disappear.

I'm thinking this is getting interesting, and Morgan is opening his mouth to say more, when Sef comes hurrying up. With Anton following. They don't see us either, and they don't see Morgan swap his scowl for a sympathetic smile.

'I'm sorry,' he says. 'Vijay isn't here.'

Sef's lips tremble.

At the last moment, Anton resists wrapping his arm round her shoulders. Just as well. The U/Free is watching closely. Stepping forward, Morgan holds out his hand and his smile widens.

Anton shakes.

'Don't think we've met.' Morgan's voice is casual, friendly. The impatience and anger we heard earlier is gone. Reminds me how dangerous he is.

174

'No,' says Anton, smiling. 'I don't think we have.'

Morgan can demand a name or let it go.

'Anton is a friend of Vijay's.' Sef's voice is bright.

She's got over her disappointment at not finding her fiancé at home. Grasshoppers have better attention spans. This is what happens if you inbreed for generations, with an emphasis on looks. You get beautiful little idiots.

'Really?' says Morgan, his voice thoughtful.

Simone and Morgan exchange looks. 'You should go,' Simone says. 'It's going to be a busy night.'

The U/Free scowls at her.

Sef is oblivious, of course.

As for Anton, he's so busy looking at Sef's magnificent chest he barely notices Morgan leave. It's possible he's running a clever bluff. But I wouldn't stake my life on it.

Wars have good and bad sides.

The good guys fight for freedom, justice and most words that don't put food on the table. The bad fight to scrub those words from our speech. Only problem is, both sides claim to be good.

Stay with me, there's a point to this.

Now, I've seen cities after the Uplift finished with them. I've walked down alleys the Silver Fist have filled with ripped-open bodies and stepped over the dead children who've had their brains cored. I've seen braids sprout from the skulls of sobbing captives as the Enlightened virus corrupts flesh to metal.

And if I haven't raped children myself, or tortured dogs for fun, when all the humans are gone and animals are the only thing left, then I've looked the other way while people on my side did so.

I'm not saying we're better. I'm saying we're not worse.

The United Free are *meant* to be better.

They have no emperor or hundred-braid to issue orders. Death is not their automatic punishment for disobedience.

They are a commonwealth, united in their love for art, culture and freedom. Concepts that never trouble our glorious leader, or his triple-damned enemy Gareisis.

Kite-flying is a career for the U/Free. So is breeding gold-fish, or collecting ancient silicon chips, ferox furs or every kind of jade in the galaxy. Most of which they own anyway. Their ships rip holes in space to arrive before they leave. No one carries a bigger stick or speaks more softly.

We believe we're the good guys.

The Uplifted believe the same.

Only the U/Free *know* they're on the side of right and justice. And they don't need fancy words to make up for lack of food on their tables, because the Commonwealth of the United Free is the richest civilization ever to exist. Their tables put food on themselves, and their clouds rain to order.

You think I'm joking?

I went to Letogratz once, their capital.

It's vast and crowded and full of buildings that turn into what you want them to be. Most of the women spend their time dis-cussing poetry, parties or politics. The men waste their lives building elaborate kites.

Almost everyone is bored out of their skulls.

Until I met Paper Osamu, I *believed* the U/Free were better than us.

It was as simple and non-negotiable as the fact that the sun rises and the sun sets. Now I know the only reason the sun never sets on the U/Free is that Legba doesn't trust them in the dark.

They're just richer and better armed than us.

Although it helps that they talk nicely. Morgan has the morals of a rattlesnake. That is, no morals at all. He feeds, he lies in the sun. If threatened he bites. He's just not used to lowlifes like me.

Who hit back.

Chapter 25

AS THE MILITIA PASS UNDER AN ARCH, THEIR VOICES ECHO OFF cut stone above. Something changed when the cathedral clock struck one. The soldiers no longer bother about hiding in the shadows. Their voices get louder. Almost as if they want to be heard.

'Sir,' says Leona. 'Permission to speak freely?'

Can't believe people still use that phrase.

'Go ahead.'

'Any idea what's going on?'

My laughter draws Simone to my side.

Anton's still fussing over her sister. After a moment, he nods at something Sef says and heads for Vijay's house. Stopping at the top of the steps to listen, he holds Paulo's abattoir pistol combat-style as he goes through the door.

I send Leona to stand guard. As for Sef, she adjusts her gauze-like shawl. It's probably coincidence her fingers lightly brush the top of her own breast. Actually, I'm sure it's not.

'Not your taste?'

Simone grins at my expression.

'Thought not. You like the dyke.'

Takes me a moment to realize she means Leona.

'Just needs a good fuck, eh?' Her voice is mocking. 'Think you would be up to it?'

I tell Simone the thought never entered my head.

Stepping close, she says, 'It's really true? My sister's fiancé is a friend of yours?'

There's a smartness in her eyes missing from her sister. A deadly, snake-like smartness, which watches me watching her and calculates something.

My price, probably.

'Well?' she says.

I nod.

'Can't imagine where he'd have met you.'

Obviously, it doesn't matter, because she steps closer still. Her breasts brush the front of my jacket. She knows it well enough. Her nipples stand hard, despite the warmness of the night.

'That man,' I say. 'The one who walked away. He's U/Free?'

Simone's gaze narrows.

'He looks U/Free,' I tell her.

My hands are on her shoulders. And then they're not, because one rests on her hip, and the other has dropped to the upper slope of her breasts.

My taste in women always was appalling.

Back in the day, women wanted to kill me for the silver in my pocket. Or because I couldn't pay their price and they'd been too trusting to take the coins in advance. Now, it seems, they simply want to kill me.

Simone reminds me of Paper Osamu.

Both know that lust blinds men to their flaws and makes us stupid enough to do what is asked. And Simone intends to ask something. Her lips keep moving. It's not passion or some strange sadness. She's working out the words inside her head.

'So,' I say. 'He's U/Free?'

Simone nods.

'Met a U/Free once,' I tell her. 'On a battlefield. She was there as an observer. To make sure we slaughtered each other according to the rules.'

Simone glances at me to see if I'm joking.

I'm not.

Still, she's relieved. She thinks that's how I know what U/Free look like. As if it's hard. They look like us, just richer and smugger and better-looking.

'Where did you meet him?'

'At a party,' she says, deciding the truth can't hurt. 'The Senate gave a party for the new U/Free ambassador and her husband. I was invited.'

Simone says this with real pride. So I guess most people weren't.

Weird place, Farlight.

Somehow my hand slips to caress her buttock. From the way her mouth opens, the tip of her tongue appears and her pupils get larger, she's acutely aware of what's happening. 'Look. Your friend's in danger. People are hunting him.'

How does she know that?

She must see the query in my eyes. 'Doesn't matter how. Rescue him. Get him out of this insane— What?' she asks.

'Just wondering. Are you a guard or an inmate?'

Simone forces her face into a smile. 'He's trapped south of the river,' she tells me. 'You need to bring him back. Only the bridges are locked down and the boats this side. So you'll have to talk your way past roadblocks or find a ferry. Understand?'

Yeah, I understand all right.

I understand she's telling me the truth. But it's still a lie. I heard her talking to Morgan about Vijay, remember?

'Be discreet,' she stresses.

Maybe I shouldn't laugh. 'I'm ex-Legion. We don't do

179

discreet. We do bloody and vicious and insanely violent.'

And because we do, we don't need to do it nearly as often as other people believe. Death's Head. Wolf Brigade. Légion Etrangère. Our reputation is worth its weight in gold and extra guns.

Simone sighs. 'Come with me.'

Five doors down is a less grand house, with a front door that exits onto the street. Fumbling in her pocket for a key, Simone clicks the lock and we're facing an empty hall and a long flight of stairs leading into darkness.

At the top is a study, with an oil lamp already lit on the desk.

It's a man's study, because a hunting rifle hangs above the fireplace and a ferox skull stares from a vast shield on a wall behind me. The heavy brow ridge and skull crest show it to be a fully grown male.

Never knew a woman who collected trophies.

Not that kind.

'This could be dangerous . . .'

Simone abandons her pep-talk. Probably because I grin. People like her don't know how addictive danger is. Except I'm wrong and she does. It's in her eyes and the swiftness of her pulse and the way her mouth opens slightly when I steer her towards the desk. She keeps glancing at the door as if she expects someone to enter.

I can't tell if she hopes someone will.

Or fears they might.

She says nothing when I lift her onto the desk. And nothing when I hook that expensive silk round her hips. It takes me a second to free her breasts.

'Don't tear my top,' she says.

Too late.

Having got her breath back, Lady Simone Kama reaches into a drawer of the desk and produces a small box, flipping it open.

Inside is a silver ring, showing a ferox skull in an enamel circle. The circle contains a motto.

Senatus Populusque Farlightus.

I've no idea what it means. But I've seen a hundred like it. Every Senate officer and NCO wears one. As do a thousand others, who cadge drinks in scuzzy bars, based on having been something they never were.

I take it to the lamp.

That's the second time she's proved me wrong.

The ring is platinum. Its enamel a mosaic of rubies. And the skull is not yellow and black, as I expect, but two shades of purple used only by OctoV and the members of his Senate.

Not here, not now . . .

That's something a fully grown ferox said to me once. I've been waiting for Death to catch me up ever since. So far he hasn't dared.

'Use it wisely,' she says. 'And take this . . .'

Simone scrawls three lines on a piece of paper from a different drawer, and signs it with a flourish. Safe conduct through the city. Signed by Augustus, Archbishop of Farlight.

At least that's what the signature says.

She grins, eyes glittering. 'He won't mind.'

Finally, she rips her scarf in two, pulls a jewelled bottle from her pocket and splashes several drops on one half. She ties that half round my arm. 'Once you find Vijay,' she says, 'remove the ring and lose the band. Your lives depend on it.'

'What—?'

'Don't ask questions.'

She kisses me on the lips and steps back, adjusting her top.

'Go,' she says.

So I turn for the stairs.

'One last thing. I don't know your name.'

'I'm Sven.' Habit almost makes me add the rest. *Sven Tveskoeg, lieutenant, Death's Head, Obsidian Cross, second class.*

181

'Just Sven?'

'Yes,' I say. 'Just that.'

'Take my sister with you then, Sven. Keep her safe.'

Chapter 26

THERE IS AN ORNATE BRIDGE HALF A MILE TO OUR LEFT. Another, much simpler, roughly the same distance to our right. The first is gilded, made from cast iron, and decorated with underage nymphs and naked boys holding tridents.

The second is built from slabs of basalt, and has OctoV's crest carved into its sides. Different eras. Different tastes. Although not that different. Each nymph and boy stares out with wide eyes, a sweet smile and perfect cheeks. Our glorious leader's face is the model for every one.

'Well?' says Anton. 'Which bridge?'

'Neither.'

Anton, Sef and Leona follow me down a flight of steps to a jetty that has three boats tied to its end. Only one boat is big enough for all of us. The problem is that five militia stand between us and its rope. All are armed, and their sergeant is already raising his rifle. It's a Kemzin, obviously enough.

'Recognize the regiment?' I ask Leona.

She mutters the name of a high clan that means nothing to me. Five of them, three of us. Plus Sef, of course. Although there's little point relying on her for anything. Unless . . .

'Tell them we're taking the boat.'

'We're taking your boat,' Sef says. 'If you don't mind.'

The sergeant with the gun looks worried. It's Sef's voice. So obviously high clan. The rest of us look like rabble. But she's trouble.

'Madame,' he says, 'my orders—'

'Are of no interest to us,' I tell him.

The NCO thinks dealing with me is going to be less grief than dealing with Sef. Shows what he knows. Particularly as he's let us get too close.

'Listen—' he says.

And then says nothing. Instead we get muted gurgling. Must be my hand gripping his throat.

'*Sven . . .*'

For fuck sake.

How many times do I have to tell Anton not to use my name?

'Sorry,' he says, 'but I think . . .'

A corporal next to the sergeant has the muzzle of his rifle under Leona's chin. 'Let go,' he says. 'Or I'll shoot him.'

'It's a her, fuckwit. And you think I care?'

Leona's face goes blank.

Guess the corporal doesn't see her fingers edge towards a kitchen knife in her belt. She's going down fighting. The other militia stand there, undecided. We've got their sergeant and corporal on our case. So they're going to sit tight, and see what happens. That's militia for you. Being cannon fodder doesn't mean you have to like it.

'I said . . .'

'Yeah,' says Anton. 'He heard you.'

My fingers close a little, and the sergeant starts struggling. 'Drop your weapon,' I tell the corporal. 'Or he dies.'

The idiot obeys.

And I know they're amateurs.

Getting your sergeant killed should be every junior NCO's dream. Instant promotion, plus you haven't broken a basic rule: never surrender your weapon. It's a good rule, since the pain OctoV is likely to inflict if you do is infinitely worse than anything an enemy can threaten . . .

I let their sergeant drop. He hits the deck of the jetty and we rock a little. Stepping over his body, I begin untying the boat. When Leona dips to grab the sergeant's rifle and I hear a snap as she clicks its slide, I know it's going to be one of those nights.

'Boss,' she says. 'We've got company.'

There's a tightness to her voice. Now, Leona is not a trooper to get jumpy without good reason.

Very slowly, I turn.

Although I retie the boat first.

Don't want the bloody thing floating off while I sort out our latest shitstorm. A dozen rifles point at me. Make that two dozen. A handful of seconds later the number is up to three dozen and militia are jostling each other in their eagerness to take aim.

'Sven . . .' says Anton.

He looks at me.

'It's OK? I mean, if I call you Sven?' Anton nods at the soldiers. 'You don't think it's going to make matters worse?'

Not sure what's got into him lately.

A captain stands at the top of the stairs.

Two militia NCOs grab me before I can reach him. One goes down in silence. Don't imagine he'll get up for a while. The other sits on his arse whining that I've broken his arm. If it was smashed he'd have shards of bone sticking through his skin.

'Dislocated, moron.'

Yanking him to his feet, I fix his shoulder. OK, I do it by bouncing him off a stone wall, but the joint pops back into place and he's able to move his arm again.

'*Enough*,' the captain says. He's got his Colt to my head.

I can take him, and the corporal with the light machine gun behind that. It's the sergeant beyond who worries me. When I glance back, I see Anton and the others on the jetty. Leona, at least, holds the Kemzin she took.

'Your ID,' demands the captain.

'Not carrying them.'

Since this is a crime he's surprised I'd volunteer that information.

Most people in my situation would be patting themselves down and protesting that they'd had their papers a moment ago. I'm not most people.

'What's your name?'

'What's yours?'

The captain scowls. 'I have a weapon to your head,' he reminds me.

As if I'm going to forget.

'Might be more use if you took it off safety.'

Glancing at his piece, he realizes the safety is already off. But he's just made himself look a fool. It's been a while since I enjoyed myself like this.

The captain is tall, thin and elegant.

He probably thinks it's original to sound that bored with life. Maybe he should see more of it before deciding it's something he's willing to toss away. This strikes me as dangerously close to intelligent thought on my part.

So I decide to sneer at him instead and watch his eyes tighten.

'Take him to HQ.'

'What about the others, sir?'

'Take them as well, obviously.'

One of the NCOs glances at another. The captain isn't popular. I file that information for use later. As one of the soldiers starts down the stairs, Leona readies her rifle.

A dozen rifles point in turn.

'Lower it,' I tell her. 'I want to see this idiot's CO anyway.'

The militia captain slicks me a glance. I'm not behaving how freshly taken prisoners are supposed to behave. No one grabs Leona when she reaches the top, with Anton and Sef behind.

'Sven,' Sef says, sounding anxious, 'we have to find—' She stops, smiles brightly. 'I know,' she says. 'We can ask them.' Turning to the nearest trooper, she says, 'Do you know Vijay?'

A hard-faced sergeant starts, then stares straight ahead. A callus of hard skin is visible beneath his jaw. I'm right, this man is ex-Legion.

'Sven,' I say, sticking out my hand.

He ignores it.

The man hasn't got me pegged as an officer yet. Thinks I'm hired muscle for whoever Anton is. But he's beginning to wonder if Anton is someone. And you'd have to be an idiot not to know that Sef is trouble, however you cut it.

'Brandon,' he says, after a while.

'What regiment?'

'Fifteenth.' Sergeant Brandon's eyes flick to my jawline. It's hidden in shadow. 'How about you?'

'Third.'

'Ah, right . . . Posted at Zami.'

The third haven't been near Zami. Not in my lifetime. 'Karbonne,' I tell him. 'One of the forts south of the capital. If you can call a dogshit market and three brothels capital of anything.'

He grins, nods in recognition.

'So,' I say. 'Does Vijay Jaxx ring any bells?'

Sergeant Brandon's eyes flick to his captain.

'Man's a fuckwit and I'm over here.'

The sergeant has trouble not grinning again. 'Arrested someone of that name an hour ago.'

'What for?'

He shrugs. 'Not my business.'

'I really do need to see Vijay,' Sef insists.

'Madame,' says the captain, voice tight, 'I'm sorry, but . . .'

'Call me Sef,' she says, putting out her hand. 'Lady Serafina Rivabella y Kama.'

'Rivabella y Kama?'

'Yes,' Sef says brightly. 'That's right.'

Picking the captain up, one-handed, I move him out of my way.

No one stops us when we turn for the final twist of stone steps that take us from the embankment to the street above. Although Sergeant Brandon follows without being ordered. So does everyone else eventually, like an untidy shadow.

The HQ is someone's house.

Not sure if it belongs to an officer. Or has simply been commandeered for the night. Either way, it's heavy on gilt, marble tiles and oil paintings, and the occupants have made themselves at home. A lieutenant stands by a candlelit table, scowling at a paper map of Farlight's river.

An aide de camp is offering him a drink.

The boy looks about twelve.

Their CO sits at a coffee table, peeling a pear with a tiny knife. The way he has his boots on the chair opposite makes me think the house stolen. I've got two questions for him.

'The Wolf,' I say. 'Has he been here?'

The major stares at me.

He's facing a one-armed intruder. And it's his HQ. But I'm also taller than him, broader and holding a rusting pistol in the hand I do have. So he does what I'd expect of a man like him. Orders someone else to arrest me.

A lieutenant hits the wall.

'Let's try that again.'

'No, sir . . . He hasn't.' The ADC shakes his head, then blushes.

Walking to the drinks table, I pour myself a triple brandy and feel it warm my throat and heat my gut on its way down. A roast chicken sits on a silver salver on the sideboard. I'm wrong; it's bigger than a chicken.

'Anton,' I say. 'What's bigger than a chicken?'

'A turkey.'

See, he knows things like that.

Ripping off one leg, I toss it to Leona who tears off half the meat with her first bite and looks up, muscle fibres sticking from her mouth.

'What, sir?' she demands.

'Didn't say a thing.'

It feels hours since we ate and my gut's empty. Also, the brandy is strong enough to go to my head. So I bite a chunk out of the other leg and offer the rest to Sef, who's looking round the room. Probably seeing if she knows these people socially.

'Want some?'

'I'm fine,' she says. 'Thank you.'

Anton gets fed instead.

'Sir,' says a voice behind me. 'I'm sorry. I couldn't . . .'

Yes, he could, he just didn't, there's a difference. And the fact the captain let us go into his HQ first and trailed after tells me everything I need to know about him.

'You know this man, Captain Vard?'

'Yes, sir. He said he wants to talk to you, sir. And the woman with him is Serafina Kama, sir.' The captain no longer drawls, and he's uncertain where to look. Glancing at me, he looks at the major and then looks away from him as well.

He ends up staring at Sef. She has that effect on people.

'I'm here for a prisoner.'

The major raises his eyebrows.

'Vijay Jaxx.'

'We're getting married,' Sef adds.

The major's still thinking about that as I head for the door. 'Stay here,' I tell Sef. 'You two, stay with her.'

Sergeant Brandon is waiting in the corridor outside. Since he's alone, issues no orders to stop and makes no attempt to raise his Kemzin, he's obviously been waiting for me.

'You don't like what's happening, do you?'

He shakes his head.

'Nor me.'

It seems enough.

I'm turning away, when he says, 'The Wolf was here, sir. About two hours ago. He also asked about a Vijay Jaxx. And about a one-armed lieutenant. Dangerous, and a traitor, seemingly . . .'

'That's what you wanted to say?'

'Didn't say anything, sir.'

A flight of stairs leads to the cellars. As I open the upper door, the major, the captain, the lieutenant who hit the wall and the little ADC come bundling out of their room and head towards me.

'You can't—' the major says.

He freezes when I reach into my jacket. Man's an idiot. If I wanted him dead he'd be dead already.

The major takes the paper I offer.

Blood drains from his face. It really does. He goes pale faster than someone with a severed artery. Over his shoulder, Captain Vard reads the first two lines and steps back. It's a reflex action.

'I'll have to check,' the major says. 'Really, I really should check.'

He's having trouble meeting my eyes. The major tries to say he must see if my safe conduct is real. Only he doesn't dare. And he doesn't need to check, either. He's just trying to save face in front of his staff.

I could help him out, of course. But why would I bother?

Instead I thrust Simone's ring in his face. It takes the major's eyes a second to refocus.

'Shit,' someone says. Think it's the little ADC. 'That's . . .'

The ADC's looking at Captain Vard, who is staring at the major. The major's open-mouthed. Probably wondering what someone like me is doing with a ring like that. Anton might get away with pretending to be high clan.

I never will.

He reaches the only conclusion possible. The Senate is rumoured to employ killers. Highly paid, never mentioned and beyond the reach of the law. I must be one of those.

'Sir,' says the major. 'If we could . . .'

But I'm not interested in talking. I'm only interested in rescuing Vijay Jaxx before someone decides to find General Luc and tell him the men he's hunting for are here.

Chapter 27

SHIT AND FEAR, THE SMELL OF SWEATBOXES EVERYWHERE. THE cellar beyond the door has no ventilation. It's high summer in Farlight, fifty or more people are down here in pitch darkness, with more being brought in while we wait.

Half will suffocate before the night is out.

'Jaxx,' Sergeant Brandon shouts.

A thin man stumbles towards the door. He's blinking against the sudden brightness of the sergeant's torch and wiping rivers of sweat from his face. Dark patches blossom under the arms of his once-white shirt. It could be piss staining his trousers, equally well it could be sweat.

'Where is Vijay Jaxx?' I demand.

Pale blue eyes blink at me. 'I'm Vijay Jaxx,' he whispers.

Never seen him before in my life.

'You know the general?'

He wants to tell me everyone knows the Duke of Farlight. Only, he has no idea who I am and he's being dragged out of a stinking cellar in the middle of the night. Traditionally, that means execution or torture. For someone not sure which, he does a good job of raising his chin and meeting my eyes.

'Jaxx is my great-uncle,' he says. 'And you won't—'

Captain Vard smirks. 'Oh,' he says. 'Believe me. We will.'

Dragging this Vijay through the crowd around me, I bundle him up the stairs and park him next to the front door. He stays put without being told while I fetch the others.

'We're out of here.'

Anton takes one look at our captive, and opens his mouth. So I jab him in the ribs with my elbow. He's still trying to draw breath when I push past.

'Sir?' Sergeant Brandon asks.

'Get that boat prepared. I want it fuelled, and ready to cast off. I want Kemzins if you've got nothing better, helmets, and ammo and flak jackets.'

He salutes.

The major is approaching.

'Sir,' he says, then regrets it. His gaze stiffens. 'I need to know where you're taking my prisoner.'

Reaching across, I remove his pistol from its holster.

'Believe me,' I say, jacking its slide. 'You don't.'

Two shots crack the night. From habit, I slip the discarded shells into my pocket.

Vijay and Sef are looking aghast.

Think that is the right word. Anyone else, I'd say they were scared shitless. Must be because I had Sergeant Leona march them round the corner into a narrow side street. Where I put two bullets into the wall beside their heads.

Throwing both arms round the boy's neck, Sef twists one foot behind his leg like she's a piece of ivy and bursts into tears. We don't have time for this.

Wrapping my hand into her hair, I pull.

She unpeels easily.

The boy glares.

'Don't,' Leona tells him. 'He'll kill you.'

'Right,' I tell him. 'Let's start with who you really are.'

Turns out this Vijay Jaxx is the first cousin once removed of my Vijay Jaxx, and they're both variously removed to another two Vijays in the Jaxx clan. I wonder if I knew about the eldest born of each clan branch sharing the same name and decide I did.

A captain in the Death's Head told me. At the time I was trying to blow up an enemy mother ship. So I probably didn't pay enough attention.

'We must save the others,' the boy says.

'What others?'

'The other prisoners.'

'They're dead.'

'No,' he says, and then stops. Understanding what I mean.

'Maybe it's a mistake,' Sef says. 'And they'll be released later . . .' No one bothers to correct her.

'Spend tonight somewhere safe. Then get the fuck out of this city.'

The boy's eyes are wide. His glance at a dark doorway tells me he thinks we need a private conversation. Ordering Anton and Leona to cover the street, I walk the boy somewhere private.

'Is that true?' he demands. 'General Jaxx has been arrested?'

'*What?*'

'They said.' He takes a deep breath. 'That captain said Jaxx was arrested earlier this evening. But one of the prisoners said the general was ordered to surrender but is refusing and no one dares arrest him.'

'Who's meant to take his surrender? The Wolf?'

'Apparently he refuses to be part of this . . .' The boy hesitates. 'And Sef says . . . She says Simone offered to help you find me?'

'Why? What of it?'

'Simone had me arrested.'

'Shit. Sure it was her?'

He nods. 'I was in a café, with a friend. Simone turns up wanting Sef. I say she's with Lady Isadora. As she leaves, Simone points me out to a girl.'

'Describe her.'

He does. Young, pretty, strangely dressed.

It's Paper Osamu.

The boy can't work out how Paper can order militia around. That's because it hasn't occurred to him she's U/Free. And Simone's a snake. All that fretting as Morgan tells her Vijay is trapped south of the river, and she knows he's here all along.

I have one last question. Although I know the answer already. 'The other prisoners. Who are they?'

They all have one thing in common.

Obvious, really . . . They're supporters of General Jaxx, hangers-on to his family, senators who have taken the new duke's side against the Thomassi. This hasn't occurred to the boy before, probably because he inhabits a world where the idea of not supporting the general is absurd.

'That ring,' he asks. 'Can I see it?'

His face falls and something bleak enters his eyes as he turns the ring over in his hand and squints at its jewelled ferox skull.

'So it's true,' he says. 'The Senate plan to ruin us, because of the murder of that Thomassi . . .' He stares at me. 'You know the one. He married Senator Wildeside's daughter. But we weren't behind his killing. The general swore an oath to that.'

Did he now?

'Listen,' I say. 'Leave, and don't come back until it's safe.'

'What if it's never safe?'

'Then you never come back.'

He wonders if I understand what I'm saying. Then he nods and walks to where Serafina stands, and puts one arm round her shoulders. Whatever he says, it's enough to make her follow without complaint.

Chapter 28

OCTOV WAS THE FIRST PERSON TO SET FOOT ON THIS PLANET. Every child in the empire knows this. He crashed onto its surface in a tiny one-man plane named *Polygon* and lived in a cave while the seeds he planted turned to cities and trees and oxygen and rivers.

It was a bad seed that created the oil rain in the rift. And a good seed that grew Farlight, although a bad seed almost melted it before our glorious leader blew on the stone to make it cool again.

Everything exists because OctoV grew it.

As other planets were seeded so his garden grew. Until it spanned a quarter of the galaxy. But a snake-headed thief stole some of his stars. OctoV has been fighting since then to get them back.

This is the story I was told as a child.

Until I met Debro, I thought it true. When she realized how upset I was, she told me it wasn't that it *wasn't* true. It simply wasn't true in the sense of happening. That's Debro for you. It's a creation myth. A post-singularity attempt to simplify something or other. I give up listening after the myth bit.

★

'You're not serious?' Anton demands.

I nod. We need to get out of Farlight, but first we have to save the real Vijay. Saving a pretend one doesn't count. I reckon Simone was right without knowing it – he's on the south side of the river.

Anton is unhappy with my plan. Mind you, he's unhappy with everything. He's been sulking since Serafina walked away without looking back, and that makes me think of something else.

'Why didn't you say there were other Vijays?'

'Thought they were all off-planet.'

Something feels wrong about that. Maybe Anton doesn't want Vijay found, that's what his behaviour says to me. But Aptitude dotes on General Jaxx's son, and Debro seems to approve. So why would . . . ?

'We're crossing that river.'

'Sven . . .'

'It's not up for argument.'

Catching my scowl, Leona glances away. Anton trails after us in silence as we head for the stone steps down to the jetty. Sergeant Brandon's loaded everything on my list into the largest of the boats.

Except a radio.

'No radios, sir,' he says. 'Orders from above.'

'*What?*'

'No point anyway. System's down.'

Taking a step back when I glare, he catches himself and adopts a combat stance instead. When I grin, the tension goes out of his eyes.

OK, no radio it is.

He has found us three standard-issue Kemzins, some ragged-looking flak jackets and a jumble of ready-loaded clips. We've even got a square of cheese, some dry tacos and a big bottle of beer.

'Sir,' he says, stepping closer. 'You think it's true, sir? About . . .' He hesitates. I don't blame him. My brain won't process the idea either.

'Listen,' I say. 'General Jaxx is my general.'

'Yes, sir.' Stepping back, he salutes. Then he unties our line and tosses it into the belly of our boat.

'Take point . . .'

Leona does, a rifle ported across her chest. Anton sits in the middle, still sulking. And I take the small tiller. The boat's lights are taped. Not sure if Sergeant Brandon did that or if it was done anyway.

We're running the fusion unit from a truck, bolted crudely into place and too big for the cavity allowed. It's a replacement for whatever was there before. A diesel motor from the look of the piping left over.

The river is sluggish around us and smells stale.

We have the whole stretch of dark water to ourselves. There are no other craft on its surface at all. Not even one of the police launches that usually plough the river at night.

'Sir . . .'

Troop trucks are gathering at the northern end of one bridge. As we watch, a light tank rolls along the embankment behind us to join them.

Tracks clattering in the night.

Looks like an AX 31.

'Fuck,' says Leona. 'That's . . .'

'Yeah,' I say. 'It is.'

Other trucks begin blocking off the northern end of the next bridge along. A rumble of tracks says other tanks are on the move. As we watch, a scout car flicks on its searchlight and a beam stabs the sky.

'Sven,' says Anton. 'This is a shit idea.'

'Got a better one?'

'Almost anything is better than this one.'

'Sir,' Leona says. She's pointing at the sky. Locked in the beam of the searchlight is a vast cigar-shape, blocking off a hundred stars. It's black, slung with a cargo pod, and running without lights. Largest zep I've ever seen.

'Oh shit,' Leona says.

One side drops from the pod, and spins briefly, before crashing into a house on the side of the river we're approaching. The figures who follow it spreadeagle to slow their fall.

They jump without parachutes, wings or power packs.

As a siren breaks the night and the bells of Farlight cathedral start ringing behind us, I expect the tanks to open fire, but they're silent.

'Sergeant,' I say. 'Concentrate on the South bank.'

'Yes, sir. Sorry, sir.' Leona unports her rifle as the embankment approaches and I steer for a flight of steps. There's too much noise for anyone to hear our engine, and far too much going on in the sky for anyone to bother with the river. Leaping ashore, Leona drags us in and ties our rope.

'Take these,' I tell her.

She catches an extra three clips, one after another. Ceramic hollow-point. The standard issue for militia everywhere. She thrusts them into her belt, then drops out her clip and checks it's fully loaded.

Should have done that already.

Anton catches the weapon I toss him.

Jacketing up, Leona velcros the tags at the side and pulls down the ceramic skirt to protect her thighs. Anton joins her. There is no way I'm going to fit into the flak jacket that Sergeant Brandon found me, so I leave mine behind.

I'm glad the real Vijay Jaxx doesn't plan to marry Sef. Apart from the fact she's a brain-dead idiot, it would be a waste to rescue him, only to have to rip his heart out myself.

Anton's staring at the zep again.

'Silver Fist?' he asks.

That was my first thought. But even assuming an elite force of the Enlightened are suicidal enough to attack OctoV in his capital, how could they get this far in-system, and why has no intelligence reached Farlight of their coming?

Chapter 29

ANTON'S NEXT GUESS IS MERCENARIES. HE'S WRONG. THERE are a dozen reasons but I don't have time to list them all. Although top of the list is that mercenaries are mercenary. If you're in it for the money, you don't throw yourself out of zeps without a parachute, even low-flying zeps.

Mercenaries don't want to face death. They want other people to face death. They like living. That's the only way you get to bank the gold.

'Up here . . .'

We climb steps from the water's edge. Knives in our belts and Kemzins in our hands. Soldiers are meant to like K19s. But they're cheap cookie-cutter shit. If those were mercenaries, we could kill a couple and arm ourselves with something better.

Bells are still ringing in the cathedral across the river.

Don't know yet if it's a warning or a signal.

Sergeant Brandon told me most of the Death's Head are off-planet. And everyone knows the Legion aren't allowed near Farlight anyway. Plus, half the militia are on a training exercise outside the city boundaries. The rest are here.

So, some are on an exercise. Others aren't.

Anyone can see that's bad.

A square waits up ahead. With a church on its northern edge, and a decaying colonnade around the other three sides. Uplights usually pick out the clock tower but the whole square is in darkness.

The little statue of OctoV looks weird unlit.

No light either on a statue under the colonnade, of a young girl with a cryptic smile and perfect breasts. She's nude. Most statues in this city are. This one looks like Aptitude. That's no surprise, the model was her great-grandmother.

Didn't know more than one had been made.

I touch its arse for luck. Me, and a thousand men before. Most of her is a greasy green. But her right buttock is shiny enough to have been cast yesterday.

'Friend of yours, sir?' Leona asks.

'Something like that.'

Our glorious leader never told me to betray General Jaxx. He did, however, order me not to tell the general – or anyone else – that I was working for him. That he, our glorious leader, was my boss. Of course OctoV is everybody's boss. He just doesn't talk to everybody.

He talks to me.

'Sir?' Leona says.

'Thinking,' I tell her.

'About what the fuck we're doing here?' Anton asks.

'No. Why the fuck this is happening.'

Nothing political occurs on Farlight without OctoV's approval. The laws that underwrite this city don't come more basic than that.

'Not mercenaries?' Anton checks.

Sergeant Leona and I shake our heads together. Not mercenaries. Not Silver Fist, or any of the Uplifted and

Enlightened's shock troops. Every time the list gets shorter, it gets nastier. And when we run into the only choice left, it gets very nasty indeed.

'Sir,' says Leona. 'Three o'clock.'

When a figure slinks under the arch on the far side of the square I'm beyond surprise. Leona's not. Flicking down her visor, she stares in disbelief.

Silver skin, hollow chest, a face like someone slit its nostrils and hacked off its ears. The one we faced at Wildeside was obviously half grown. This one really stinks. Even from here we can smell its vinegary stench.

'Fuck,' she says. 'What's that?'

'I don't know,' I say. 'Let me go and ask.'

Anton scowls. 'It's a fury. Go for the guts. Don't let it get close.'

She glances at him.

'Feeds through its fingers.'

Leona shivers.

The fury is focused on a man a hundred paces away. The poor bastard hasn't seen it yet. When he does, he tries to run.

You can't outrun furies. Well, maybe I could, given a head start. He doesn't stand a chance. Closing the gap in easy strides, the creature slams its fist into the man's back, breaking his ribs and dropping him to his knees. The second strike uses straight fingers that split flesh and displace bone as they reach for his heart.

We hear him scream from where we stand.

Leona's first shot kills the man and the fury steps back, puzzled.

Her second, third and fourth shots release what blood it has swallowed from the fury's gut. Although it's hard to tell if the creature even notices. All Leona does is attract its attention.

'Don't waste your ammunition.'

'*Sven*,' Anton says.

'I mean it.' Nodding towards the creature, which now waits like a coiled spring, while it decides whether to attack us or a group of civilians pretending to be invisible against a far wall, I say, 'Does it look injured to you?'

To me it just looks irritated.

We win the contest of who it wants to kill next.

'Behind me,' I order. Anton decides the order applies to him as well.

The creature racing towards me is used to its prey running, so it doesn't expect me to step forward, and stops when it should attack.

Bizarrely, that's bad, because now I'm off its list of targets.

It wants Leona instead. Trying to move round me, it side-steps, as Leona takes bigger ones to stay behind me. Fighting one-armed is hard. Doing so against a fury should qualify as suicide.

Well, for anyone but me.

But, like I said, the fury doesn't want to fight me. All it wants is for me to get the fuck out of its way so it can kill Leona. As it tries to push past, I side-stamp its knee. Anything without steel joints would be down, but it keeps standing. So I slam the Kemzin into its throat and hear the rifle's plastic stock break.

The damn thing barely rocks on its heels.

Been a while since I fought anything my size. And the lack of my combat arm leaves me feeling . . . *lopsided*. That thought just has time to flick through my head before the fury decides it's facing an enemy after all.

Bemusement turns to . . .

Anger is the wrong word. It's colder than that.

I watch it happen and – a split second ahead of it happening – watch the fury's red eyes flick to the rag round my upper arm. That is what's holding it off. Not my stepping forward, not my size.

'Sven . . .'

'It's sir,' I say.

Sergeant Leona's holding out the rusting abattoir pistol. Damn thing's so large she can barely lift it with both hands.

'Let me get back to you.'

Don't know what it means. Something Debro says.

As the fury punches for my ribs, I grab its wrist, and slam my knee into its elbow as hard as I can . . . Hurts like fuck. When the joint doesn't break first time I try again and something snaps. So I twist, grinding broken steel against itself.

Vile breath hisses from the fury's lips.

'*Sergeant . . .*'

'Here, sir,' she says.

Catching the revolver, I thumb its oversized hammer, jam the muzzle into the creature's neck and pull the trigger. Fuck knows what the calibre is, but that recoil would break most people's wrists. Bits of spine exit the fury in a spray of metal, wiring and wizened flesh, as the explosion echoes around the square.

'How many more?' Anton asks.

'What?'

'In total . . . How many furies?'

A memory of the drop flicks through my mind. One pod, a line of maybe ten furies. Five waves of figures falling.

'No more than fifty . . .' Yeah, reckon I'm right. Looking at the fury at my feet, I knock the figure down to no more than fifty, minus one.

Taking the abattoir revolver from me, Leona breaks it open to extract the case, pulls a new round from her pocket and slots it into the cylinder, flicking the revolver shut with a satisfying snap. She's good like that.

Anton is looking appalled.

That's because another two furies have entered the square. Large bastards too, even bigger than the one we've just killed. If that's possible. And both are heading our way. Ripping

Simone's scarf from my arm, I tear it in three and thrust one strip at Leona. 'Here,' I say. 'Tie it on, now.'

Anton ties one on too.

The fury nearest us hesitates. The one behind bumps into it. Both snarl their irritation. A guttural hissing. Before returning their attention to us.

'What's happening?' Leona asks.

'They're deciding whether to attack.'

'The rags, sir?'

'Yeah.' She catches on fast.

'Sir?'

'Sergeant?'

'Looks like they've got proper bands. Maybe we could . . .'

She jerks her head towards the colonnade. Killing the fury has brought us to the attention of three militia officers. All wear white bands stencilled with a ferox skull wrapped round their arms.

We're obviously the topic of their conversation.

'Good idea,' I say.

Edging towards them, we bring the furies with us. Never quite attacking, unwilling to let us escape. Our audience wants to back away, but there's a wall behind, and they're in the corner of the colonnade.

As we get closer the furies lose interest.

Our makeshift armbands, combined with their official ones, stand the furies down. Instead, the creatures turn for the group of civilians we saw earlier. Three men, one woman and a child, all neatly dressed.

'Doubters,' Anton says.

Surprised he can see that from here.

Realizing they're the new target, the family run for a church door. The battle is brief, brutal and one-sided. 'Watch,' I order, when Leona begins to turn away. We need to work out their methods.

See if there's anything we can learn.

'But sir,' she signals our audience, 'shouldn't we . . . ?'

Join them? Why not?

Sergeant Leona has other plans.

Ripping free her knife, she stabs it into the base of their captain's skull, jerks her wrist to cut his brain stem, and combines extracting her blade with a rapid sweep that opens the throat of the lieutenant next to him.

Their junior lieutenant goes for his gun.

He exits this life with a broken knee, a crushed larynx and his head twisted far enough to sever his spinal cord. It's good to find something that dies as it should.

'Sergeant,' I say. 'Who gave you that order?'

Leona looks at me. 'Sir. You said it was a good idea, sir . . .'

I take the ferox-skulled armband she offers, nodding as she ties the next one to her own arm. Interesting. She kills the officers in order of seniority. Now she's handing out their bands according to our rank. I get the first. She gets the next. Anton's rich, but Leona's decided he's a civilian and disposable.

Wonder if he realizes that.

Stuffing my original band inside my shirt, I rifle the nearest man's pockets for what I can find. Five gold coins and a handful of silver from off-system. Plus a bundle of high-denomination notes.

The paper's worthless, obviously.

Anton says nothing when I pocket the gold.

Doesn't need to, his scowl says it all. The man's had money so long he's forgotten what it's worth. Leona takes the silver I offer with a smile.

'Take this,' I say, thrusting the safe conduct and ferox-skulled ring at Anton.

He shakes his head.

Anton's not keen to re-cross the river.

Why would he be? All the same, the safe conduct and ring are going to make it easier. 'Send her,' he says. His comment is contemptuous enough to make Leona bridle. Worries me that he doesn't notice.

'I need you to go.'

'Why?'

'Because the Aux know you.'

Anton can't deny that. He's Aptitude's father. The Aux met him when he and Debro came to collect her from Golden Memories, the day after his audience with OctoV. Neither Debro nor Anton told me what our glorious leader said.

Doesn't surprise me. He saw them separately.

I doubt they've told each other. Our glorious leader can be very persuasive when he wants you to keep things to yourself.

'Find Neen,' I say. 'Tell him to hurry. I want full battle rattle, but no Death's Head patches and I want them fully armed. If you can steal armbands on your way up, that's good. If not, tell Neen to collect some on his way down.'

'Sven—'

'We need to find Colonel Vijay. Then we need to get both of you out of here and back to Debro's. We have to make sure Wildeside is safe.'

'Wildeside's not in danger,' Anton says.

It's not in danger?

He's said too much. But a pack of furies are loping from under an arch, as the stink of blood on the hot wind draws them our way, and Anton decides I didn't notice his slip; or I'm too stupid to put things together if I did.

'I'd better go,' he says.

'Yeah,' I say. 'You had.'

Chapter 30

ON THE CORNER OF A STREET SOUTH OF THE RIVER, LOCAL militia smash a jeweller's door from its frame with a sledge-hammer. They're drunk to the last man. Cheering the corporal with the hammer to keep their courage up.

'*Fucking heretics,*' one says.

Two of the others spit. Doubt they even know they've done it.

The door goes down and the jeweller dies in his own door-way. I see it happen as we walk past, protected by our ferox-skulled armbands from the militia and the furies. Fuck knows what's on the bands to make the furies docile around us.

'Pheromones,' Leona says.

She has to tell me what these are. They're animal stinks that trigger fucking or fighting. Leona says humans don't produce pheromones. I ask her if she's sure.

A woman drops a baby from an upper window. The child is still alive after hitting the sidewalk. It survives as long as it takes an NCO to stamp on its head.

The woman doesn't know it's dead, because she's trying to lower herself by her hands, but she slips and lands badly.

Slamming her face into the sidewalk, the NCO holds it there as he pulls her nightie to her hips and spits on his fingers.

She keeps trying to look round.

Wants to see the kid on the sidewalk behind her.

The NCO cuts her throat a second before he pulls out. An accidental kindness, since she dies with the dead baby unseen.

Leona has never seen a city sacked before.

At least, that's what I assume. She looks outraged at my suggestion. Seems she's seen cities sacked, just never seen one sack itself. Have to admit, that's new to me too. And the crowd around me is getting bigger by the minute and more out of control. According to my old lieutenant there's a sliding scale for these things.

You get people, crowds, mobs and riots.

I'm wondering where we are on that scale . . .

A grinding of gears announces the arrival of a scout car, complete with machine gun, searchlights, a dozen militia hanging from the back, and a freshly painted and still wet stencil of a ferox skull. It's obviously been allowed over the bridge.

'Over there. Doubters.'

Three men freeze in the glare of the searchlight.

A fury flicks its gaze towards them. In its grip is an old woman, whose head flails from side to side as she screams. As the fury hesitates between the meal it has, and the larger one it could have, a group of youths swagger from the shadows into the brightness of the scout car's light.

They're not militia. But they are organized.

One holds the torch, now redundant. The rest have knives stolen from a food stall. Crudely painted skeletons drip from their clothes. A single white line for the lower leg, a blob for the kneecap, and a thicker line above. The hips, ribs and arms are equally crude. Whitened faces and darkened eyes make them look as though they're celebrating the Day of the Damned.

Blood splatters their ankles and boots so thoroughly it looks as if they've been wading through puddles of the stuff. Fanning out, the gang keep half their attention on the fury and the rest on their new targets.

One of the doubters tries to flee and falls to his knees with a cleaver in his back. The boy who throws it stops to take a bow. Amateurs. My least favourite kind of killer.

'Out of here,' I tell Leona. 'This way.'

'What about them?'

She means the gang in their festival clothes.

'Who knows?' I say. 'If we get lucky the fury will kill them.' Having finished with the old woman, the creature now flicks its attention between the gang and the doubters. Personally, I know which I'd kill.

A doubter family lie in the courtyard of their own home. Rich merchants from the look of it. A hunting rifle rests near the dead man. His wife has a bullet through her head. So does he. His son died fighting. Aged thirteen, maybe younger.

All the boy's wounds are at the front, apart from the one that killed him. A bloodied brick shows how he died. His sister lies behind him. A year younger still, her gown ripped open.

'Fuck,' Leona says.

Yeah, I agree. No one who kills for a living likes killing children.

Eyes watch me kneel to take the rifle and I realize the girl is still alive. Her throat's been cut. The problem with amateurs is they're amateur. Furies leave nothing but dried husks behind. And troopers, even militia ones, don't leave jobs like this half done.

'It's going to be OK.'

Hard to tell what colour her eyes are. She tries to speak but the words are lost in bubbles from her throat. The cut ends just before her artery. All it needed was half a second's more professionalism and she'd be dead.

I place my hand over the gash.

'Help me,' she whispers.

'Of course,' I say, bending closer.

'We have a regeneration tank,' the girl tells me. 'In the cellar.' She tries to look to where her mother sprawls behind me. 'Is she . . . ?'

'Unconscious.'

'Really?'

'A bad fall.'

Takes Leona a while to work out what my back-stretched arm means. And then she kneels beside me and I feel the warmth of a wooden handle and the comfort of a blade that takes the girl under the ghost of her breasts.

A single flicker of shock signals her end.

Don't have a prayer to say over dead children. So I recite the only prayer I do have. The one which wishes dead comrades deep sleep and a better life next time. My voice is distant. Cold as ice. Has to be me speaking because I can taste the bitterness of the words and feel the anger behind them.

'Sir?'

'I'm going to hunt down whoever ordered this. And I'm going to kill him, slowly . . .'

'Do we find Colonel Jaxx first, sir?'

Good question.

Taking the rifle, I drop out its clip and find it empty. Spent cases tell me why. The militia have removed their own dead, and left their victims. Come morning, this whole area will be an abattoir.

The gun room is at the back of their house. A steel cupboard lies open, with its safety chain left hanging slack in the owner's hurry to fetch his rifle. A box of .762 is tipped on its side. He

212

should have taken those too. His son and daughter might be alive if he had.

'Doubt it, sir,' Leona says.

She's right, of course. But he could have extracted a higher price. That would be worth something. Fastening the suppressor into place with a single twist, I thumb ten rounds into the clip and find I have enough .762 left over to make my pockets heavy.

It's a game rifle, complete with scope.

A very expensive game rifle.

And I stuff my jacket with round after round until I run out of pockets to take more. Jacking the first shell into place, I hook the webbing sling round my elbow and wrap it once round my wrist.

We swapped our Kemzins for weapons carried by the militia officers we killed, and now I've swapped my pick of those for this. Leona gets my previous choice, a light machine gun with curving clip.

Times like this I could do with having both hands.

Mind you, I could also do with my SIG-37, not to mention the sabre General Luc's sergeant took from me when he removed my combat arm.

'Right,' I say. 'Let's do this.'

Sergeant Leona wants to ask, *Do what?*

If I knew, I'd tell her. In fact, when I do know, I will tell her. Until then she's going to have to wait.

Out on the street, four militia NCOs break down another door. They die silently; one after another in the time it takes me to sight. The last one goes down desperately trying to work out where my shots are coming from.

My next round blows half a fury's head away.

The creature barely notices. Next time I see it, the fury is in an upstairs window, feeding from a girl who tries to throw herself into the street below.

Dropping to one knee, I centre the scope's cross hairs.

The hollow-point takes the fury under its chin, spreads on impact and blows fragments of spine through the smashed mess I made of its skull earlier. My second shot kills the screaming girl. Like most people in this city she's beyond saving.

Chapter 31

'SIR?' SAYS LEONA.

'What?'

'You think Anton will get through?'

How the fuck would I know? He's wearing an armband, and he's carrying a ring and a half-decent rifle, and he's got enough rounds to start a small war . . .

But the city's rioting.

At least, the bit south of the river is. No idea what's happening across the river. Maybe nothing at all for all we know. But on this side, we have a mob on the streets, unprotected by armbands, but loaded for bear with kitchen knives, iron bars, broken bottles and anything else that looks like a weapon.

They freeze when the furies appear.

Sometimes that is enough.

Other times they die. The furies kill anything that runs. Unfortunately, the instinct to run when faced with something more dangerous than you overwrites common sense. Doesn't matter how many times their friends scream, *Stay still*.

People don't.

A few of the doubters being slaughtered are high clan.

Slightly more are merchants or bankers, the kind of people who own houses along the river or around that square we left behind us. But most are poor, little different to those killing them. And the shout in the streets around us is changing.

At first it was *Death to the doubters*. Now it's *Death to the general*.

The mob works to a pattern. Having watched the militia break down doors, they wait for the furies to go in, and then loot the place when the furies are done. Jewellers, bakers, chemists, computer stores. Doesn't matter, the pattern is the same.

1) Steal anything valuable.

2) Destroy everything too heavy to move.

3) Burn the shop back to a shell when that is done.

Ash falls like rain around us. Already warm, the wind from the river grows hot as it takes heat from the fires and is sucked into new fires to heighten the flames.

We see a woman carrying an oil painting.

A man pushes a wheelbarrow full of painted china plates. One girl wears a priest's hat. Another, a senator's cloak joined at her neck by a silver chain. Both grinning and both blind drunk.

'This way,' someone shouts.

Excitement hisses through the crowd around us.

I follow, with Leona behind me, drawn by the word *Jaxx*. Our group streams into a bigger one, which joins a bigger one still. When the movement stops we're standing in front of a huge house overlooking a small square. The coat of arms above the door is one I recognize. It's carved on the general's pinkie ring.

Two Death's Head NCOs guard the steps.

Black uniform, silver braid, three stripes on each arm.

Their faces are impassive. They know they're going to die. All the same, their pulse rifles are ported across their chests as regulations demand.

When they smell vinegar, they know how it's going to happen.

The crowd freezes as a fury enters the square, herded by militia who wear armbands, and carry rags on sticks to stop the beast from attacking. The creature's leathery skin reflects searchlights and torches as it approaches the door.

Another follows.

Both are puzzled by the stillness of their prey.

Away to the side, a looter claws a stone from the cobbles, and weighs it in his hand as his friends split their faces into grins. Opening her mouth to shout a warning, Leona shuts it again when I shake my head.

What will happen will happen. Legba's rule.

Plus, I've no plan to get killed before I find Colonel Vijay. Actually, I've no plan to get killed after that either. Although that doesn't mean it won't happen. Drawing back his arm, the man hurls his stone.

He's dead, bullet through his skull before the cobble even lands at his killer's feet. But the guard's movement gives the fury its next target. As the creature lurches forward, the other guard sights his pulse rifle. The blast burns through the fury, fries a hole in the guts of a militia corporal behind and sets on fire the hip of a woman beyond.

Makes no difference.

Closing on the Death's Head NCO, the fury reaches for his heart.

Blood pumps up the creature's arm and pisses from the hole burnt in its gut. Staring death in the eyes, the NCO thrusts his rifle under the fury's chin and pulls the trigger.

They fall together.

Scooping out the first guard's guts, the other fury plunges its fingers into his ribcage and reaches for his heart. The man dies in silence. But he still dies.

Job done, the creature turns and the crowd falls back as it exits the little square. Pot belly protruding from under silver ribs as its minders with their armbands and rags on sticks lead it away.

'Fuck,' Leona says.

A corporal beside her nods.

'Yeah,' he says. 'Wouldn't want their job.'

He's noticed Leona's ferox-skull armband, for all that she is out of uniform.

'Which battalion?' he asks.

Leona looks at me. The wrong thing to do.

'Let it go,' I say. 'You don't have the clearance.'

Those magic words. He nods reluctantly, checks out my coat and weapons. Probably without even knowing it. Not sure what he sees. A blood-splattered, one-armed ex-Legion sergeant clutching a hunting rifle, a dagger at his hip, an over-sized abattoir revolver in his belt, and an official band wrapped round the arm he does have?

Maybe.

Alternatively, he hears the warning in my voice. Who knows how other people make their choices? Well, maybe you do. I don't give it much thought.

At the top of the blood-slicked steps, a militia sergeant catches a crowbar, rams it between the door and its frame and dies nastily. A thousand darts dicing him down to chopped meat. What did he think? That the house of General Indigo Jaxx would be undefended?

'Use explosives,' someone shouts.

The militia corporal who likes Leona grins.

Pulling a grenade from his belt, he yanks the pin and hurls it at an upper window. I'm out of there, dragging Leona behind me, before his grenade has time to bounce from the bombproof glass and roll back to his feet.

A trooper next to him loses everything below her knees.

The corporal loses his balls. And they both lose their lives shortly afterwards, as their blood spreads out in little rivers from the cobbles beneath them. The crowd's night of happy looting has just turned sour.

Can't say I'm upset.

I'm waiting to see if anyone else has a bright idea, when the sound of a battle tank comes from behind us. That obvious rattle of ceramic treads, and the low rumble of an engine designed to grind its way across pretty much anything.

The crowd scatters.

That's just to give the tank space.

'Old-model Tusker,' Leona tells me. 'RR52–MBT. Heavy plating, fully rotating turret, two main guns, five LMG . . .'

I'll take her word for it.

Main battle tanks combine heavy and medium capacity. Their plate is thick enough to survive a direct hit. But the chassis is light enough to allow them reasonable manoeuvrability and distance, supposedly.

Never used them at Ilseville. There were no powered vehicles on Hekati. And something that clumsy wouldn't last many minutes in the sands round Karbonne. Can't see the point of tanks myself.

Slowly, the Tusker halts.

Its turret begins to swivel. Inside, someone turns a dial or taps a touchpad or whatever the RR52 needs to raise its gun. The barrel steadies, quivers and then drops slightly.

The first shot blows off the door.

Actually, it blows the door's frame out of the wall, takes a hundred bricks with it and reveals a spider's web of pipes powering the needle gun. It also demolishes three internal walls and leaves a hole in the back of the house you could drive the tank through.

OK, I'm beginning to get tanks now.

As the crowd cheers and the hatch flips on the Tusker's turret, allowing the gunner to take his bow, dust billows from the doorway and settles to reveal a man standing halfway up a flight of stairs holding a side arm.

His first shot drills the gunner through the head. And the crowd's cheers turn to anger.

'*Jaxx*,' shouts a voice.

'Get him,' someone screams.

They're shocked by their own courage. It's the courage of crowds.

Everyone is shouting and no one wants to make the first move. Even the senior militia officers look stunned as General Jaxx descends broken stairs towards his missing front door.

None of them raises his own side arm.

That's going to prove temporary, of course. All the same, it's impressive to see the whole square still and watch General Jaxx's sheer presence reduce the crowd to silence. This is the general after all.

He's tall and thin.

Wire-framed glasses are his only affectation. And his uniform is immaculate. Even the silver and black dagger at his hip looks recently polished. From his neck hangs an Obsidian Cross, with oak leaves and extra crown. The general has dressed for the occasion.

Right down to a ferox-skulled armband.

'Back,' someone shouts.

As the crowd scatters and then freezes, three furies enter the square, herded by half a dozen militia with their rags on sticks. Red eyes watch us, snub noses wrinkle at the smell of blood. Needle-like teeth grin from narrow jaws.

The vinegar stink is unmissable.

I seem to be the only person to recognize the cylinder strapped to the general's back and the nozzle that juts from his hand. A braided hose stretches from cylinder to nozzle. Although the hose is nearly invisible in the dust, shadows and darkness. The hose is black, obviously. Like the general's boots, his uniform, his cap and the pressure tank on his back.

General Jaxx smiles. A cold, brutal and brilliant smile.

As he steps into the doorway I tell Leona to move. She doesn't obey quickly enough. So I push her in front of me as I force my way towards the edge of the crowd. A militia colonel watches us leave but breaks eye contact when I glare at him.

The general's attack comes without warning.

A flash of ignition that lights sticky liquid pumped from the high-pressure cylinder strapped to his back, and then a dripping hose-length of flame. I've faced it before, dropped from planes and poured down shafts to burn out underground bunkers.

Most of these people don't even know flamefire exists. The furies have obviously never met it. Wrapping their leathery skin, it burns so fiercely that skin peels like tissue paper to reveal burning flesh and melting machinery beneath. Steel bones twist with the heat and joints rupture themselves.

The general achieves this without appearing to move.

When a militia NCO goes for his gun, General Jaxx redirects his nozzle, incinerating the NCO, the men either side of him and half a dozen of those behind. The furies died silently. These die screaming.

'You can surrender,' he tells the crowd. 'Or we can play some more.'

'*We're going to kill you.*'

The voice is rough. Too rough. Like someone pretending to be campesino. The general sneers. 'You think I don't know that? I knew my time was up the moment our glorious leader decided to cancel his meeting.'

He glares at the crowd. And laughs harshly when they cringe as he twitches the flame-thrower nozzle. Ice-blue eyes sweep over us.

'Come on,' he says. 'Surely one of you rabble has the guts.'

I'm not sure he can see our faces, because the searchlight on him must put most of us in darkness. We can see him, however.

And no one can miss the contempt in his face. Until tonight, General Indigo Jaxx, Duke of Farlight, was the most powerful man in this city. What's more, he's held my life in his hand and opened his fingers more than once. I owe him my membership of the Death's Head and my promotions. For all that he now wants me dead.

An order is given.

Five militia rush the door and burn like candles, falling in flames at the general's feet. Having kicked the closest down the steps, he searches for the colonel who gave the order and smiles.

'Guido,' he says. 'You can do better than that.'

A cobblestone is thrown, then another. Neither hits, and the general doesn't react. He is looking over the throwers' heads to what is behind them. Eight furies and a dozen minders, appearing out of a side street and hesitating at the opposite edge of the crowd.

Seeing this, the crowd moves back and freezes.

The general's smile widens.

God, you've got to love this man.

He might be a murderer, commander of a regiment feared on a thousand different planets, as unremitting as thirst in the desert, and implacable as a blizzard or ice closing over a lake, but his bravery is beyond question.

As the furies advance, he steadies himself.

The rest of us are irrelevant. He sees only the silver-skinned creatures moving towards him with their loping gait and sloped faces. Their fingers flex as the hunger takes them and they head for the kill only to hesitate when they sense his armband.

Three turn to writhing pillars with his first blast.

Another two attack and he flames them as well. All die in silence. No one doubts the intensity of their pain or the depth of agony that drops them to their knees, before leaving them blackened and stinking husks on the cobbles.

'Sven,' he says suddenly.

People turn to see who he's addressing.

'Come to see me die?'

I shake my head. That's not my reason for being here.

The general shrugs, and says something too quietly for me to hear. Guess he's talking to himself. As a fury shambles forward, General Jaxx sets his feet, twists his body, and steadies the nozzle again.

Flame streaks from his hand and bathes his attacker in fire, dripping in molten splashes around its feet.

'Fuck,' says Leona.

She's not talking about the fury.

The general must have known this would happen eventually. The flamefire that roars from the nozzle suddenly splutters, splutters again and begins to weaken. In all, he's killed nearly fifteen of the creatures.

'You ready?' I ask Leona.

'Always, sir,' she says.

Reminds me of myself, that girl. 'Right, then cover my back if needed. And be prepared to fall back when I give the word.'

A dozen militia watch me drag the revolver from my belt. Officers, NCOs and men. Only their colonel, the man General Jaxx called Guido, looks as if he might react. He doesn't say anything, however, or issue orders. The light machine gun Sergeant Leona points at his guts sees to that.

Turning to where General Jaxx stands, I hold up the piece. I don't give a fuck that he was intending to have me killed. Hell, I'd have had me killed if I were him.

'Sir,' I shout.

He almost stumbles under the gun's weight.

'Sven,' he says, 'what is this?'

'An abattoir pistol.'

He breaks it open, counts the rounds and flicks it shut again. Then he stares round at the dead bodies, the burnt furies and the waiting crowd. 'An abattoir pistol? How apt. And Sven . . .'

I wait.

'It's an abattoir pistol, sir.'

Who knows how the general thumbs the oversized hammer while ducking an attacking fury's first blow? Maybe his muscles are boosted. Takes General Jaxx two shots to kill the leading fury. A single shot to kill the one behind. Two rounds left and three furies to kill. He lived a bastard and will die a hero.

He'll be happy with that.

I don't stop to watch it happen.

Chapter 32

DEATH TO GENERAL JAXX BECOMES *DOWN WITH OCTOV.*

Beginning raggedly, the chant gathers force. The crowd in the next square finds courage in its anger. All the militia units around them do is nod. Someone rips a picture of the emperor from a bar wall and that's enough. The crowd turns from looting doubter houses to destroying posters and breaking statues.

As the window of a liquor store goes in, a boy clambers over brandy bottles to smash a figurine of OctoV in full uniform. When Leona steps forward, I grab her and swing her into a wall. 'Get yourself killed in your own time. Until then, behave.'

The rumours start a few minutes later.

OctoV has been captured. He has been killed. He has taken refuge with our enemies the Enlightened. No, the Enlightened are our friends. OctoV's on the run in Farlight. Then it is Vijay's turn to drive the rumour.

The general's son hides in a house on the next street. This is untrue, as we discover when we reach the building. He's crossing the river. One of the rusted wrecks on the Emsworth landing fields is really a combat craft in disguise.

I don't bother to follow the splinter group heading north.

The landing fields are a mountain of rust, broken spider bots and shacks. Anything in there that works was stolen years ago. And Per Olsen would have told me if anything strange was happening on his patch.

The crowd's need to find Vijay is interesting.

Not so much what drives it.

As who drives it.

In twenty-nine years of life, most of those with the Legion, and one in the Death's Head, I've seen my share of slaughter and looting. But something other than anger and alcohol is driving this crowd.

It goes one way, houses burn.

The crowd chooses another and a temple goes up in flames.

Bars are looted and shops destroyed, doubters die. Yet whole streets remain untouched. Some suffer only broken windows. And always, the cry *false* or *true* is what decides the crowd. At first Leona and I think there are a dozen voices making the call.

Then we realize there are only three or four.

Word comes that Vijay Jaxx is hiding in a hotel near the river. It has to be true, because sappers take apart roadblocks to allow us passage. The furies left don't follow, being satiated and dazed with overfeeding.

Most are already in mobile cages, herded there by men holding those rags on sticks. Dropped from a zep, picked up on the ground. For all its seeming chaos, this night has had military planning from the beginning.

We're jostling across an embankment. Well, Leona is. The crowd keeps its distance from me. Might be the blood on my coat, my height or the broadness of my shoulders. Might be the fact I punch the first jostler in skeleton clothes into unconsciousness before stamping on his ankle and tossing him into the water.

'*Sir*,' Leona says.

The rest of her sentence goes unsaid.

General Jaxx's death leaves me sick in the gut. You can't expect a general to be like other soldiers. And you can't expect soldiers to be like other men. We're different. Simply killing doesn't make a soldier. We fight for what we believe. And if we forget what that is we fight until we remember.

The people around me will never be soldiers. You think I have contempt for this rabble in their carnival clothes? You're right, I came from far worse. I can't say I made good, but I made different.

'Sir,' Leona tries again. 'Permission to—'

'Get on with it.'

'Where are we going?'

'To save Colonel Vijay's hide.'

She shoots me a glance. 'How will we do that, sir?'

How the fuck would I know? When I've got an answer, I'll share. Then again, maybe I won't. Must be something in the air, but I'm starting to mistrust Anton and Leona both. Don't doubt myself though.

Armoured cars at the embankment end draw back to let us through. Militia officers sneer from open hatches. Makes me wonder what they think we've done that they haven't. We're not the ones who turn back doubters fleeing for safety.

'Grim,' says Leona, looking round.

Her first comment on the events of the night. Although *night* is the wrong word. Darkness is passing and I can see dawn shimmer on the distant slopes.

'This way,' someone shouts.

It's always someone. We never see who.

But a voice shouts, and the crowd surges towards the old wrought-iron gates of a riverside mansion. Grabbing Leona, I drag her out of the crush and towards an alley. If people object, they keep it to themselves. And if they show any emotion, it's to gaze sympathetically at Leona, who lets herself be dragged behind me.

I know this place . . .

A very grand hotel where Paper Osamu stayed when the U/Free were having their embassy redecorated. The thought makes me consider how little I've seen of the United Free tonight. Surprising in itself, since the U/Free pride themselves on their role as unbiased observers to the galaxy's trouble spots.

I spit, and a smartly dressed man glares before turning away.

Can't believe the idiot doesn't recognize me. Mind you, seeing Federico Van Zill does wonders for my anger. He's that ex-gangster Per Olsen mentioned. The one who went missing from the slums below Calinda Gap. For all his current aura of importance he was born a slimebag and will die one.

Preferably soon.

These days, it seems, he's wearing suits and expensive shoes and working for . . . ? Now there is a question.

Mind you, I know why Vijay's here.

You don't run black ops out of your regular base and this has U/Free written all over it. I thought OctoV was behind tonight until the crowd changed its chant. Now I know it's Paper's mob who are driving the slaughter. And since they're not going to run this out of their embassy, and she or Morgan will want to be on site, this is the next best guess for their centre of operations.

Looks like Colonel Jaxx has been playing the guessing game too.

Chapter 33

A NAKED CHAMBERMAID CLUTCHES THE REMAINS OF HER uniform at the top of a flight of stairs. She has blood on her lips and between her thighs. A puddle of piss darkens the red carpet beneath her.

Three ex-guests, a slaughtered floor manager, and someone from security who has been kicked to death. Leona looks sicker by the second, which makes me wonder if I was wrong about her. She's meant to be experienced.

We've gone in the back way and we're ahead of the crowd. What does she expect us to find? This stuff can't come as that much of a shock.

Next floor up a bellboy huddles over a gut wound. The terror in his face says he knows it's going to kill him. He's lost too much blood to lift his stolen gun for more than a second and his shot shatters plaster ten paces away.

Kneeling, I take the piece from his grip.

The knife I slide under his ribs topples him sideways.

'You mean it, don't you?' Leona says, when I recite the soldier's prayer over him. 'You really believe there will be a better life next time.'

'Can't be worse.'

On the stairs to the next level, I catch her watching me. It's not the look a militia sergeant gives an officer. Mind you, it's not the look a woman gives a man. I'm not sure what it is. Other than strange. 'What are we searching for?' she asks.

'I'll tell you when we find it.'

The penthouse of this hotel can only be reached by a one-stop elevator that begins in the lobby way below us. Since the power in this city is out, and the emergency stairs don't rise that high, we need another plan.

It's rusting. But it's waiting where I hoped it would be.

'We're going to use that?' says Leona, then remembers to add *sir*.

'Yeah. And you're going first.'

Leona climbs out of the window, sighing as the grating creaks beneath her boots. The fire escape sways as she yanks a ladder down and paint flakes from its steps as she begins to climb.

She moves slowly.

Her stolen machine gun is ported across her chest and I get a good glimpse of her arse as she goes. The uniform looks standard issue. But since when is standard issue that well cut? Also, the rest of us are filthy but the dirt drops off her.

Cloth like that is expensive.

Filing that thought, I watch her go. It's a day for doubt and darkness. These are not doubts I usually get. Because I don't get doubts. Only, Farlight has changed me. The harsh simplicity of my life in the Legion is too far back for me to recover.

I find that thought shocking.

Not least, because it never occurred to me I'd want it back. Certainly not when I was living it. When Leona reaches the top, I slide myself through the corridor window and stand on the grating below her.

It protests under my weight, as does the ladder.

Leona offers her hand to help me onto the upper level, stepping back when I ignore it. We face a steel door, bolted from the other side. On the plus side, it's old, with hinges that slot together.

All I've got to do is lift it off its hinges.

One-handed.

My arm locks and muscles tear as sinews pass popping point. Finally, it occurs to me that it's not the weight that's the problem. Rusty hinges make the door hard to move.

'Scrape those down.'

She does, as silently as possible. And then I lift it free.

A scullery, complete with bucket and a mop that chirps happily to see us waits on the other side. It's obviously been a while since anyone used the fire escape.

'Wait here,' I tell Leona.

She looks like she wants to protest.

'*Sir*,' she says.

'Later.'

This corridor has marble tiles and expensive rugs. Oil paintings hang from the walls. A portrait of OctoV in cavalry uniform, his hand on the hilt of a sword. Beyond it is a cityscape of Farlight, as it must have been when first built. And beyond that, a seated nude. The nude is particularly tasteful. Little body hair, the slightest tint of nipple. Painted to give the minimum offence.

I've come to the correct place.

A desk by an elevator is where the receptionist sits. She's probably only there when VIPs check in. Marble steps lead to double doors. One of the handles shows a man's face. The other shows a woman.

Try to remember where I saw that before.

One of the double doors is slightly open. Comms noise comes from inside. The sound of AI chatter, the whirr of memory boxes, the beep of incoming calls. Remember, this is

231

a city without power. So now I'm certain I'm in the correct place.

I'm right about one thing and wrong about another.

Paper Osamu's husband Morgan has set up his HQ in the most expensive hotel in Farlight and filled it with enough machinery to run a war. He's even had the door handles replaced with his and her faces to make himself feel at home.

'*Sven . . .*'

Not sure which one is more shocked to see me.

Colonel Vijay Jaxx, who carries a blade of his own. Or Morgan, who is still wearing one of those flowing robes and looking tense. That's because Vijay has his blade to the U/Free's throat. Paper is nowhere in sight. Probably trying to avoid getting her hands dirty.

'Don't let me stop you,' I say.

Morgan scowls. It's instinct. He can't help himself.

'What are you doing here?' Colonel Vijay demands.

'Could ask you the same question, sir.'

He raises his eyebrows. 'Thought that would be obvious, Sven. I'm following the U/Free example in making the world a better place.'

'Sven,' whispers Morgan. 'I know we've had our—'

Differences? Vijay Jaxx draws his blade hard across Morgan's throat. He does it fast, putting all his strength behind the cut. Blood spurts halfway across the chamber and redecorates a wall. Eventually, Morgan's heart loses its battle and the spurt is reduced to a trickle that stains tiles and finally runs down his leg.

Morgan only falls when Colonel Vijay remembers to let go.

'Fuck,' the colonel says.

A handful of steps takes him to the bathroom and I hear him retch. The retching lasts longer than it should. Long after the colonel's stomach has emptied. When Colonel Vijay returns, he's wiping his mouth with the back of his hand.

'You know,' he says, 'they killed Sergeant Hito.'

The old man's pet assassin. He gave me a dagger that saved my life once. If I remember right, he was the man who taught Vijay unarmed combat.

'Worse than that, sir. They got the general.'

He closes his eyes. Swallows. A tear squeezes from under a lid to remind me how young he is. Nineteen last birthday. That's what he told me on Hekati.

'Sir,' I say. 'You planning to destroy Morgan's back-up?'

Colonel Vijay looks at the body.

Then he looks at the room, as if seeing it for the first time, with its blood splatters and stained tiles, and the inevitable puddle of piss, and the stink of shit from where our dead U/Free shat himself.

'Or shall I do it, sir?'

'If you would,' he says.

Rolling Morgan onto his front, I steady my blade.

Morgan's memory unit is at the back of his skull, just below the curve. It's expensive, which I expect. The surgeon cut away bone to let the unit fit flat. This means the symbiont running the unit can access both brain and spine.

It twitches when I prod it.

And when I begin to saw, Morgan's whole body begins to thrash. So I saw harder and listen to Colonel Vijay vomit. Doesn't matter that he doesn't reach the bathroom this time. There's nothing in his gut to throw up.

'If you'll allow me, sir.'

Dropping the symbiont to the tiles, I crush it under my boot heel until the last tendril stops thrashing. There's sourness in my gut, and a taste of vomit in my own mouth. The kyp in my throat feels Morgan's symbiont die. It must do, because it convulses as I flush his next life down the pan where it belongs.

'All done, sir.'

'Sven . . .'

'Yes, sir?'

'I'll need a moment alone.'

Chapter 34

I'M WONDERING HOW BRIEF TO MAKE COLONEL VIJAY'S moment, without wanting to push him into fury or despair. Since I never knew my parents, their death didn't touch me. Can't imagine what it would be like to have the general as a father. Suspect it's one of those things you don't want to think about.

While Colonel Vijay gets over his misery, I go check on Leona.

She's missing.

That is, the fire escape is empty.

A sound of water splashing leads me to a door.

At first I think she's taking a piss but it lasts too long. Twisting the handle, I find myself in another bathroom. The biggest I've seen. More a room with a shower for its ceiling.

Sergeant Leona stands in the middle, stark naked.

Hot rain falls from above onto the coloured pebbles at her feet. A cactus grows from the pebbles in one corner. Damn thing is soaking wet, but it has to be a cactus because it has spikes. A little bridge joins her part of the room to mine.

The stream separating us is fed by water that runs down a

marble slab set into one wall and disappears into a floor-level slit in another. I have no idea how the fish living in the stream survive the hot water raining down on them or stop themselves being swept away.

Unless they're an illusion.

As Leona tosses her hair, shampoo sprays upwards and she raises her face to the ceiling to rinse herself. She's humming something loudly. Sounds classical. A march, or one of those strange pieces Debro likes.

The sergeant's body is perfect.

I mean it. Firm buttocks, soft waist and wide hips. Legs that combine elegance with looking like they could squeeze the life out of you. Her breasts would fill, but not quite overflow my hand. A flash of nipple as she turns slightly takes my breath away.

And when she kneels to wash her feet, I'm speechless.

I'd know that arse anywhere.

There isn't a man in Farlight who wouldn't.

Only the arse I remember is bronze. And its owner kneels beside a different stream. She sits in a park in the oldest part of Farlight, near the cathedral. *Serenity*, says the plaque on her base.

No idea if that's her name, or why she's supposed to be peaceful. Sitting around naked by a stream with a body like that can only attract attention. As Leona stands she sees me watching.

'Shit,' she says.

Having clicked her fingers to stop the shower, she grabs a towel and wraps it tightly around her. She wears it like armour.

'*Sergeant . . .*'

'Yes and no,' she says.

Her feet seem small for the boots she's been wearing. The tattoo on the inside of her wrist has a barcode and number I don't begin to recognize, and the dog tags around her neck are not standard issue. Hanging beside the tags is a weird-looking key.

'Oh well,' she says, seeing me look. 'You were going to work it out eventually.' Her voice is sad as she adds, 'I used to love this place.'

You used to . . . ?

Sergeant Leona holds her ground as I stamp towards her, fists bunched. This is a militia NCO, I tell myself. An NCO who disobeyed an order.

A *direct* order. I could shoot her now; no court martial and no appeal, and still be within my rights. Only, she's not really militia, is she? And that's no way to treat soldiers, militia or not.

The thought stops me dead.

'*Nature*,' she says. '*Nurture*. They're a bastard pair.' Obviously enough, I have no idea what she's talking about. 'I need to get changed,' she tells me.

Then waits for something.

'You plan to watch?' Leona asks after a while.

When I say nothing, she shrugs.

'Guess so.'

Dropping her towel, she reaches for a sodden singlet and wrings it out, before dragging it over her head. Climbing into a thong, she yanks up her combats and slides herself into a shirt and then her flak jacket. Her light machine gun, boots and helmet stand in one corner, away from the water.

'How's Vijay?' she asks.

'You knew he was here?'

Leona shrugs. 'It seemed likely. Although it was hard to be certain with the nodes down. There are only a few left. As I'm sure you realize.'

I'm sure I don't.

She opens the door for me.

At a window, we stop so she can look at Farlight.

I'm not sure what she sees that I don't, but when she turns away there are tears in her eyes. 'It wasn't supposed to be like this,' she tells me fiercely. 'Not now, not then, not even in the beginning.'

She's talking to herself.

She has to be. Nothing she's said so far makes sense. 'You didn't answer. How is Vijay taking the general's death?'

'Badly.'

'Good. Better he gets over it now.'

Leona agrees that cutting Morgan's throat probably helped. The U/Free was behind this. She nods when I say that. Not just him, she tells me. But he was part of what happened. And now the general is dead, killing Morgan, I tell Leona, will help Colonel Vijay negate some of his inevitable guilt.

Inevitable guilt?

Where does this stuff come from?

'Your head,' says Leona. 'Intelligence is a construct. Well, mostly . . . You have yours locked down.'

'Fuck,' I say. 'You're—'

'Run in survival mode long enough, you'll believe that's all there is.'

I'm not sure if she's talking to me or about me. Maybe both. And I notice that, not only did she interrupt me, I allowed it to happen. That tells me we both know she's not a militia sergeant.

'Actually,' she says, 'I'm—'

'One of OctoV's handmaidens.'

Taken me long enough to work it out. They're stuff of rumour and fantasy. Only the most intelligent, most talented, most beautiful and most deadly are ever chosen. The official version says all are virgins. Their relationship with OctoV is chaste and he's interested only in their beauty and weapon skills. Obviously, that's bollocks.

'You don't believe it, do you?'

Of course not.

You don't put a fourteen-year-old in a harem and expect him to be interested in needlework, sword skills and musical talents. I imagine OctoV screws himself stupid most days. If he exists at all.

Leona looks at me. 'Ah yes,' she says. 'I forget.'

She forgets I've talked to our glorious leader. And to his mother. At least that was how he introduced Hekati, the autonomous and self-aware habitat on the edge of Enlightened space. The ex-habitat.

Hekati no longer exists. I still hear her screams in my head.

'Sven,' Leona tells me, 'there are no handmaidens. There haven't been handmaidens for years . . . Centuries,' she corrects herself. 'Not for centuries.'

'Then what are you?' I demand.

'Good question,' she says. 'A monster, I guess.'

She stares through the window at the burning city, and then looks at the black zep still hanging in the sky. 'They lied,' she tells me. 'They said the furies would be programmed to kill only specific, pre-chosen targets.'

'You don't programme furies,' I say. 'You release them.'

'These ones were supposed to be different. The U/Free promised.' She shakes her head, runs one hand through her hair and flicks sweat from her fingers. Her mouth trembles and she looks close to tears again.

'Leona. Who are you?'

'Doesn't matter.'

'Believe me,' I say. 'It does.'

Don't want to kill her. But if she's a traitor, I will.

Chapter 35

'LET US START,' SHE SAYS, 'WITH WHO I WAS . . . LEONA ZABO,
third in command of App 85. An exploratory mission with
terraforming abilities. Five officers, fifteen NCOs, one civilian
physicist, two biologists, a pet geek, and sixty passengers.'

Leona shrugs.

'They were frozen, obviously.'

Obviously?

'Thirty pairs,' she says, adding, 'the passengers,' when I look
blank. 'That was our minimum for long-term DNA mixing.
Sixty disparate sets. All of us had been screened for hereditary
diseases, genetic weaknesses, the usual.'

Leona turns back to the window. She's looking for something. When she finds Calinda Gap, she stops. So I guess she's
found it.

'That's where our lander crashed,' she says. 'Caught in the
bow wave. Its core went critical. All that fallout fucked
the carefully chosen DNA . . .'

'Caught in the what?'

'Bow wave,' she says. 'The singularity bow wave. A hundred
and fifty years out. We'd been left behind and then the future

overtook us.' Her mouth twists and she bites her lip without realizing it. 'Pods fell out of the sky, oxygen scrubbers failed, half the food coming out of the Drexie was poisoned.'

She wipes her eyes.

'I assumed command when Colonel Farlight died. Major B didn't disagree. Of course, she was dying by then. I named our base after the colonel, and our landing fields after Major B . . . Betty Emsworth,' she adds, in case I'm not following.

'And then,' she says, 'I went to sleep. When I woke . . .'

Leona nods at the city beyond the glass.

'Most of that was already there. We had oxygen, water, grass and trees. A main street, a square, a cathedral. All it needed was people. And that wasn't a problem because Calinda down-loaded minds into meat as fast as she could.'

A bit of me is worried I'm not following what Leona is saying.

A bigger bit is fucking terrified that I'm following every word. She's one of the originals. That makes her high clan. High clans live longer. What I don't get is why she'd pretend to be a militia sergeant.

What was she doing delivering messages from Vijay Jaxx?

And what the fuck does she think she's doing out on a night like this? Anyone with her money should have holed them-selves up behind high walls or abandoned the city when the riots went out of control. For most, leaving Farlight means using roads. But the clans have planes and copters. Some are said to have gates. You enter one side, you exit somewhere else.

'Sven.' She takes my face in her hands. 'You still don't get it.'

'What?' I say crossly. 'What the fuck don't I get?'

'Take a good look at me.'

'I did, remember? You're Serenity.'

Leona smiles. 'That's one of my names,' she agrees. 'Major Zabo is another. A few people, like you, know me as Leona. As for the rest.'

She hesitates.

'It gets complicated. I died, you see. So Calinda held me while my new body grew. Only I liked being inside Calinda, and she liked having an interface. This was before Hekati made the AIs unite. And that was long before Gareisis . . .'

Oh fuck. 'You're . . .'

'*No one betrays OctoV while I'm around. Don't care if it's pretend. Don't care if it's a trick. We're not signing.* Wasn't that what you told Colonel Vijay on Hekati?'

She's got it word for word.

'So you'll keep this quiet, right?' Leona says.

That's not really a question. Turns out, she's *M'OctoV.* Mission eighty-five. Made flesh in the person of Captain Leona Zabo . . .

'But OctoV's a boy.'

She sighs. 'This body's older,' she says. 'Usually I'm younger. Think about it. Curly blond hair, soft hips, puppy fat. Everyone says I look androgynous.' She stops to explain what that means. 'It began years ago. The questing prince. Strong but defence-less. Young but timeless. We never bothered to . . .'

Her words dry up.

Colonel Vijay looks less pale than he did. His floppy hair is pushed from his eyes. He's obviously washed out his mouth, because droplets stain his flak jacket. Although now isn't the time to mention it.

'Sven,' he says. 'If I might have a word.'

As Colonel Vijay nods towards the door, Leona shoots me a look that tells me to keep her secret to myself. OpSec, apparently. So I grin and she scowls, which only makes me grin harder.

The body of Paper Osamu's husband lies where we left it, blood glazing the tiles and staining the grouting between them. A greenness tinges his face. Meat rots fast in this heat, unless he was rotten already. Who knows how long he kept that body?

'This savagery is planned,' Colonel Vijay says. 'The light tanks on the bridges, the zep with its furies, half the militia out of the city, the rest corrupted. It suggests an intentional strategy.'

Thought that was obvious.

Furies don't appear by accident. They're illegal, even here. You have to source them, make shipping arrangements, grease palms and fix paperwork.

'The Thomassi,' he tells me, 'are behind this.'

I don't doubt they're involved.

For all I know, they planted stooges in the crowd to say which houses to burn and which shops to loot and which to save. But this is bigger than a bitch fight between the Jaxx and the Thomassi over who gives the best supper parties, or whatever these people really quarrel about.

And even if you throw in Farlight's archbishop, the mistrust believers have of doubters and the city's previous history of rioting, it's still bigger than that. He must realize it. There's a crowd in the street below calling for OctoV's death.

OctoV's *death.*

They want peace with the Uplifted. Trading rights between planets, votes for all, not just male members of the high clans. The death penalty must be abolished for all but the most major crimes.

'Sir,' I say. 'It's—'

Colonel Vijay's not listening.

'The Thomassi insist we killed their senator.' He sounds outraged at the slur. No, he sounds young and scared and furious. 'Everyone knows that's a lie.'

'You did kill their senator.'

The colonel gapes at me.

'Sir,' I say, 'I killed him. That was how I met Aptitude. On her wedding day, as her wedding feast was about to begin. I should have shot her as well. Before the ceremony began—'

'But why?'

'Because those were your father's orders.'

Vijay shuts his eyes.

'Look,' I say. 'I don't do whys. I do whats. So I don't know *why* the general had Senator Thomassi killed. *Why* he chose then to do it. Or *why* I was chosen to carry it out. But he did and I did and the senator died. Your father declared war on the Thomassi and they fought back. Your father knew something would happen.'

'Not this,' Colonel Vijay says.

I wouldn't put anything past the old bastard. His conscience wasn't deleted, so much as overwritten to military standards, and the technicians who oversaw it taken out and shot. All the same, I agree.

'No,' I say. 'I doubt he expected this.'

There is a lot that doesn't make sense. This control room for a start. Just who are the U/Free controlling? The Thomassi? The archbishop? General Luc's Wolf Brigade? The city militia? The crowd of believers looting shops below?

All of them? Or none?

Now is the time to tell Colonel Vijay about Leona. Something stops me. Partly, that he's close to cracking and I'm not sure how much more he can handle. But also I can see an advantage in not telling him. Hell, there can't be that many people in history who've had the emperor on tap.

'Sven,' he says, 'where are your friends?'

He means the Aux. 'Anton's gone to fetch them, sir.'

'Are we expecting them any time soon?' His drawl is returning, the smile on his lips is supposed to suggest it's all so amusing. That's how I know he thinks this is the end. If not here, then near here. If not now, then soon.

He's putting on his armour.

Colonel Vijay Jaxx, teenage son of General Indigo Jaxx and new Duke of Farlight, although I don't think he realizes that yet, is getting ready to die. Being Death's Head, he intends to do it well.

Me, I intend to live, until that stops being an option.

Then I'm going to join him.

Chapter 36

A KNOCK AT THE DOOR MAKES ME TURN. IT OPENS A LITTLE and Leona sticks her head through the gap. 'Think you should take a look out the window, sir.'

The street below is filling with soldiers.

An armoured car locks off one end. A troop of militia guard the other. On the steps of the hotel a man harangues the crowd. We're too high to hear what he says but we can hear their responses. As the man finishes, he throws his arms to heaven and soldiers channel the crowd towards the doors of the hotel.

They can't know about Morgan's control room, that's my first thought. My second concerns us. 'Leona,' I say. 'How do they know we're here?'

'Someone must have told them, sir . . .' She glances apologetically at Colonel Vijay. 'We left some people alive on our way up.'

Little bitch.

'Had to happen,' the colonel says, picking up his rifle. 'Suppose we might as well go meet them.'

Leona shoots me a glance.

'Sir,' I say.

'Sven?'

'Leona and I will go. You need to gut those, sir.'

My gesture takes in a bank of semi AIs, plus some dumb slabs and a couple of stacks I don't recognize. 'We'll need their contents . . .'

'In God's name, why, Sven?'

'Give us something to negotiate with, sir.'

Vijay Jaxx looks at me. Something hardens behind his eyes, and he nods to himself. Putting down his rifle, he reaches for a memory crystal. Then he puts down the crystal and walks over to where Morgan lies on the carpet.

Hooking the toe of his boot under Morgan's side, Vijay Jaxx rolls the man over and kneels beside his body.

MilCrypt keys, three of them.

Ever eaten an octopod? Eight legs, good grilled. To kill it, you turn it inside out and bite out its brains.

. That's what MilCrypt does to raw data. The crystal slivers twist info on the way in; then twist it back on the way out. One can be broken, supposedly. You can buy failsafe milhackers in every market. They don't work, but it doesn't stop idiots buying them. Two keys, everyone knows two keys can't be broken.

As for three . . . Makes me wonder exactly what Morgan wants hidden.

'Buy me time,' Colonel Vijay says. 'Then get out of here.'

'Sir . . .'

'That's an order, Sven.'

'Yes, sir.'

On her way out, Leona turns. 'Sir,' she says to the colonel. 'Permission to speak freely.'

He looks surprised.

'Destroy the cores, sir. When you're done.'

'The cores?'

She walks back, stopping by the frame that supports the semi AIs. Flipping down a keyboard, she signals a sequence of hot keys. 'Starts a Guzzman Swab, sixty-seven overwrites.'

'*Sergeant.*'

'Take you about ten minutes . . . sir.'

Not yet sure how I feel about OctoV being a fourteen-year-old girl.

Except that she's not, of course. Any more than Gareisis is really a multi-braided metalhead with eyes that glow and a pump station's worth of pulsing glass hoses going into his gut. They're manifestations.

Even I get that.

Not even manifestations of the whole. I've talked to OctoV, a mind bigger than anything I can imagine. With a breadth of knowledge wider than the gaps between the stars. Leona is OctoV's manifestation.

An interface.

Won't stop those soldiers below our fire escape from hanging her, though.

The grin she gives me is borderline insane. On the wrong side of that border too. Startling blue eyes catch my gaze and she grins again and shows a mouthful of white teeth. I wonder how I ever mistook her for a militia sergeant.

'Easy mistake to make.'

'Can you be killed?'

'Planning to try?'

'Some of the shit I've been through, you deserve it.'

Leona scowls, climbs in the window after me, and grins again. 'Yeah,' she says. 'I can be killed.'

'I probably owe you that.'

'Owe me what?' she says, sounding puzzled.

'A clean death . . . If we get trapped, and we're going to die or be captured, I'll kill you myself rather than let them do it.'

Leona looks at me. 'Sven,' she says. 'You have no idea how reassuring that sounds.'

Now I know she's mocking me.

Flicking a lever on the hunting rifle I took from the merchant's house, I drop out the clip to check it's full, tighten the suppressor slightly from habit and snap the clip into place. Franc's throwing knife is at my hip, a Colt tucked in the back of my belt.

Checking the list makes me wonder something.

'Banned inside the city limits,' Leona tells me, before I can ask why we've seen so few pulse rifles. The general's two guards carried them, that's all.

'And those were illegal,' she says.

One floor down, and we see no one in the half light that filters through the stairwell windows. Two floors down, and we can hear the crowd inside the hotel, but they're still way below us.

We meet, when we meet, at the top of a wide set of marble stairs five floors below the fire escape we used to reach the penthouse. The ballroom at the foot of the stairs is full of rioters. Not a militia officer, NCO or trooper to be seen.

Leona winces when a shot flicks past her ear. Not sure why. The bullets you hear are the ones that don't kill you. They're already gone.

'Put down that rifle,' someone shouts.

Most people hit the floor when I shoot over their heads. A few roll out of sight. They're the ones I need to deal with.

'You missed,' says Leona, sounding shocked.

'That was strategy.'

Leona snorts.

One of the rollers raises her head. A second later she fires. She's not Death's Head but her K19 is, right down to its black barrel and the silvered D-ring on its sling. Looted from Jaxx's house, most likely. Centring her in the cross-hairs, I put a round through her skull and watch slivers of bone blind the man behind.

Two for one.

'You're grinning.'

I don't deny it.

Another couple of rollers die just as fast.

Showing myself briefly gives the wall behind us battle acne. Someone down there owns an anti-tank rifle, because it punches a round into the wall hard enough to drill marble, destroy both skins of brick, puncture a steel plate and reveal air behind.

Now that's the kind of gun I like.

'Eight o'clock,' Leona says.

Tell her I know that.

For his first shot our target stands, resting his rifle on the carved fluting of a marble pillar. For his second, which blasts a bigger hole through the wall behind us, he kneels. The next time he looks round the pillar, he's at ground level and I slick his brains all over the floor behind him.

'Shouldn't be that predictable,' Leona says.

After that we get silence. So Leona stays down on my orders and I stay silent and it takes longer than it should to occur to the crowd that we've stopped firing back.

Ten minutes since we left Colonel Vijay, and Leona reckons he'll need twenty to extract the information, run the Guzzman Swab and destroy the data cores. The information bit I get. But running sixty-something overwrites? A couple of rounds a core sounds quicker to me.

Leona smiles when I say this.

A voice we haven't heard before asks questions. Someone answers and the crowd mutter their agreement. Seems the military have arrived.

'They won't like that,' Leona says.

'Like what?'

'Having to involve the militia. Vijay Jaxx should have been

250

killed by the mob before the authorities had time to prevent it.'

'And now the authorities are here?'

'You've got it.'

After more muttering and quiet orders, we hear steps on the ballroom stairs. Gesturing Leona back, I position myself flat to the corridor wall.

A corporal turns into the corridor and I grab his throat, thumb one side and forefinger the other, closing them on his windpipe. It's a bad way to die. So I jab my blade under his ribs and lower him to the floor.

A finger to my lips tells Leona to keep silent.

She nods, looks from me to the corporal. Occurs to me that for all the planets taken and planets lost, maybe OctoV hasn't seen death this close for a while. And yes, I know she's not OctoV. She's a manifestation.

She's real to me.

When their corporal doesn't answer a shouted question, his commanding officer shouts again. I expect him to send a sergeant next. Because I'm imagining he'll work his way up the food chain until we reach someone I'll enjoy killing . . . Like some spoilt little militia major with a chest full of medals he hasn't earned.

But their CO has more sense than that.

'What's your price?' he shouts.

Has to be talking to us.

'Sir?' Leona says.

Make him wait or answer now? A quick check of my watch says Colonel Vijay needs another five minutes, which means we need a diversion.

It comes from somewhere unexpected.

A stamp of boots says others are joining the fun. Voices rise in the ballroom, then die abruptly as someone fires a side arm. Into the ceiling, from the sound of falling plaster and screams from the crowd.

'Wow,' says a voice. 'Vulgar paintings, cheap marble, mirrors to disgrace a brothel. No wonder Sven feels at home.'

'That's enough.'

'Enough nothing. You should have used incendiary.'

'And destroy this place before we reach the boss?'

'Serve him right.' That gun's got all the personality of a hung-over bouncer who's been dumped by his girl, had the bailiffs repossess his apartment and is having a really bad attack of piles, but I'm still delighted it's here. If only because I know the voice of the sergeant holding it.

Although I still want to know what took him so long.

'Neen,' I say. 'Get your arse up here.'

'Right you are, sir.'

'And hurry it up.'

'What about this lot, sir? Kill them?'

Voices rise and weapons cock. Seems we're going to have to go to them after all. When Leona and I make the turn in the stairs, our hunting rifle and light machine gun turn a two-way stand-off into something more interesting.

The first thing I notice about my team, apart from the fact they're in Death's Head black, minus their shoulder patches, is that they wear ferox-skull armbands. The second thing is they're splattered with blood.

Other people's . . .

Guess that answers the question about what took them so long. Been fighting their way through Farlight and stealing armbands from the look of it. The final thing is that Rachel and Emil are missing.

So is Anton, but I'll get to that later.

The militia have clocked their uniforms and armbands. Although it doesn't impress their CO enough to have him make his troopers lower their weapons. They do, however, part to let Leona and me through.

'Sir,' says Neen. 'Reporting for duty, sir.'

He snaps the words out and the Aux stiffen. They'd stand to attention but then they wouldn't be able to cover the militia with their rifles.

'Good to see you, Sergeant.'

Neen looks at me, trying to work out if I'm mocking him.

He's clutching my SIG-37, and has a Kemzin 19 slung over his back. His sister stands beside him, with a scowl on her face. That's fine. The day Shil turns up not looking sour is the day I start worrying. Obviously, I don't need to start yet. Shil takes one look at Leona and scowls harder.

Standing behind her is a blond boy with broad shoulders and a wide smile. When he sees Leona, his smile gets wider. Ajac is the newest official member of the Aux. A survivor from the death of Hekati. Beside him stands Carl, with staples holding shut a gash in his skull.

'You stole my coat,' he says. 'Want it back.'

It's the girl on Neen's other side who really raises my eyebrows. Curves overflowing in all the right places, sweet smile, puzzled eyes. Iona isn't a member of the Aux at all, which explains why she's not in uniform.

She is, however, Ajac's cousin and Neen's lover, much to Shil's disgust. That's nothing new, because pretty much everything is to Shil's disgust. So we've got Iona who I don't expect, but we're still missing—

Neen nods upwards.

A strange little balcony overlooks us, fed from different stairs. It has a low balustrade with fat pillars. Between two of these I see a flash of red hair. And peeking from behind a pillar's base is the muzzle of an 8.59 calibre Z93z long-range sniper rifle. The new model, the one with the adjustable cheek piece, $\times 3$–$\times 12$–$\times 50$ spotting scope, laser sights and floating barrel.

No idea how Rachel managed to get up there.

But I'm impressed she did. Not going to tell her that,

obviously. Rachel's our sniper. As the saying goes, a good sniper is worth ten troopers. In Rachel's case you can make that a hundred. Snipers are high-maintenance and so are redheads. Put them together . . .

Rachel's as high-rent as all fuck.

The militia are watching us. Uncertain which side we're really on. After all, we're wearing official armbands. The crowd is watching the militia. Mobs need simplicity. Kill these people, sack that house, burn this building. Too much complexity muddles them.

'Sven,' Leona mutters. 'You're being cynical.'

'No. It's the truth.'

At the rear, someone mutters Colonel Vijay's name and we're back in business. Voices take up the mutter. And the voices get louder until they become a shout. The crowd has re-found its focus.

'Give us Jaxx,' someone shouts. 'We know he's up there.'

'Death to Jaxx.'

They're back in a place they understand.

'Boss?' says Neen.

It's my call. Obviously it's my call. We're outnumbered, which means nothing. In battle experience this lot don't come close. And we're better armed. Although Neen still holds the SIG-37. He must realize that, because he holds it out.

'About fucking time,' the gun says loudly.

The militia and the crowd go suddenly quiet.

'Aptitude OK?' I ask.

'You think I'd be here if she wasn't?' It scans the ballroom, doing a little dance with its diodes. 'Fifteen Kemzins, three side arms, a shotgun (unloaded), assorted kitchenware, pry bars and bits of scaffolding . . .'

My gun sounds disappointed.

'Hell,' it says. 'Hardly worth getting out of bed.'

'Behave.'

'Aptitude didn't even let me kill rabbits.'

Carl's grinning. 'Debro sent it back. Think she thought it was a bad influence. Lent me her copter.'

Wondered how he got here so fast.

'Jaxx,' a voice says clearly.

A small man at the back, dressed in a filthy shirt and wearing a campesino hat. Doubt he's ever lived in a favela, or would recognize a barrio if he got knifed in one. His skin is too fresh and he looks well fed.

He scowls when he sees I've spotted him.

I consider shooting the man with the campesino hat. But then we'd have a battle on our hands. So I weigh my other options. The thought stops me dead. This must be *strategy*. My old lieutenant used to talk about that.

Strategy is working out how high to bet on each hand.

'You,' I say. 'Come here.'

The man looks behind him. Realizes I mean him and considers losing himself in the crowd. Only it's not big enough. And Rachel's already targeting him. I see it in the way the suppressor of her Z93z shifts. Those around him see it too. In the little red dot that blossoms right in the middle of his forehead.

'Shit,' someone says. 'Sniper.'

'What's your name?'

'Juan . . .'

'Bullshit,' my gun says. 'Try again.'

The man looks at the SIG. He wants to say that's illegal technology and he's right. Only how would a man in a campesino hat, who comes from the favelas, know what's on the banned weapons list?

Unless he's not from the favelas.

'Well?' I say.

He gives me a name.

Since the gun remains silent I guess it's real.

'So,' I say. 'You're leading this group, right?'

The man's not happy to be the centre of attention like this. And some of those around us, mostly militia, are scowling at him. They're the ones who didn't realize they were being led.

'We're all together,' he says. 'We want the same thing.'

'And what would that be?'

'Vijay Jaxx . . .'

'Why?'

He looks at me, eyes opening wider. Wondering whether to appeal to the militia CO, he glances from the officer's face to us, and decides it's a bad idea. So he answers my question instead.

'He's the general's son.'

Indigo Jaxx is dead, his house burnt and his city in ruins. But his enemies still call him the general and stand a little bit straighter as they say it. Weird fucking place, Farlight.

Think I've said that before.

Leona tries to catch my gaze. Who knows what those insane blue eyes are meant to be saying? Not me.

'Sir,' she says.

Neen's wondering if he's got a rival. Those chevrons on her flak jacket have him worried. And I don't imagine he's missed the casually competent way she holds her light machine gun.

'Sergeant?'

'Perhaps we should . . .'

'Perhaps we should what?'

'Negotiate, sir.' She flicks her gaze towards the stairs. A smile crosses her face and she nods. Something's going on inside that head. It would be good if she let me know what.

'Neen,' I say. 'Anyone moves, kill them.'

He snaps me a salute.

Grabbing Leona by the arm, I march her out of the others' hearing.

'You're hurting me.'

'I'll hurt you a fuck of a lot more if you don't tell me what's going on.'

She really shouldn't grin at a threat like that. 'I believe you would,' she says, sounding impressed.

'Count on it,' the gun tells her.

She files that for later. 'Colonel Vijay's done. I felt the cores die. He's making for a different fire ladder. I imagine he's trying to reach the roof next door.'

'You can sense that stuff?'

'Jacked a couple of lenz.'

I'll take her word for it.

We reach a simple deal with the militia CO. His troopers and the crowd will part to let us leave. And we let them live and make their way upstairs unhindered. It's going to take them a while to reach the penthouse.

When they do, Colonel Jaxx will be gone.

The little man with the campesino hat grins. He thinks we're cutting our losses rather than fight. From the look on Neen's face, he thinks the same. Although he's not grinning about it.

Chapter 37

'THIS IS SERGEANT LEONA,' I TELL THEM. 'SHE'S AUX UNTIL WE find someone better.'

When Leona scowls, Shil shoots her a sympathetic glance, and I have one less problem on my hands.

'Guess that makes you senior sergeant.'

Neen finds his grin.

'Shil, you're the new corporal.'

My old one died, twice . . . It's a messy story.

Rachel has removed the suppressor from her rifle, now she's breaking the barrel from the stock. She slides the barrel into a long pocket in her jacket and slings the stock under one arm.

The Aux are booted, suited and wearing helmets.

But I've still got two problems.

'Where's Anton?'

Neen looks at Shil, who glances at the dirt. Rachel decides to check her stock hangs correctly. And Ajac simply looks worried I might ask him. Only Iona's dumb enough to speak. 'He had things to do,' she says. 'Said he'd catch us later.'

'Did he say how he'd find us?'

Must hear something in my voice. Because her smile fades

when she realizes the others are carefully not looking at her. 'No, sir,' she says. 'Sorry, sir. Not that I heard . . .'

'And where's Emil?'

Otherwise known as Emil Bonafont de Max Bonafont, Death's Head captain and a traitor whose life we saved on Hekati. Although *spared* may be a better way of putting it. He was our newest recruit. Newer even than Iona and Ajac.

'Missing, sir.'

'Neen,' I say. 'Care to explain?'

'My fault, sir. Should have been paying better attention.'

He means Emil slipped into the crowd. The Ninth Death's Head, Emil's regiment, will be heroes now. Supporters of a glorious revolution that has finally arrived. Instead of the traitors they were yesterday.

If I were Emil I might do the same. But I'm not and he must know I'll kill him if we meet again.

We're outside the hotel now. The street is crowded, but less than it was. The air is hot and stinks of blood and shit and river. A faint wash of sunlight outlines the roofline behind us. As we look, a street light comes on, and a murmur breaks like a wave over the crowd as more and more lights come on around us.

'Not good,' Leona mutters.

I can work that out for myself. You don't withdraw troops or bring power back to a city until you're certain you have it locked down. My helmet's earpiece starts crackling as the semi AI built into its neck pad returns to life and begins scanning the emergency frequencies.

Although it doesn't matter which one it scans.

They all say the same. *An important announcement will be made shortly.* From the way my team have their heads tipped to one side, their helmets are picking up the same promise.

'You're fucking dead.'

That gets their attention.

'All of you,' I say. 'A sniper could have shot the lot.'

Neen wants to tell me it's not true. Politely, obviously. But he knows it is and surprises me by apologizing. It's been a long night for everyone, we're not through this yet, and from the armbands they wear it's obvious they did their share of killing on the way down.

In our ears a voice is telling us that a new dawn has broken for the peoples of the so-called Octovian Empire. No longer will we be oppressed by evil members of the high clans and their leeches among the merchants. Prince Sebastian Thomassi promises this in person.

'Prince,' Leona says, sounding outraged.

The others look at her.

No longer will we be denied our potential. Uplifted technology will be made available to Farlight, and to all the other worlds newly freed from the evil grip of OctoV, self-styled emperor and stealer of hope. Those who wish to become Uplifted will be granted that priceless opportunity.

'*Uplifted*,' Neen says.

Prince Sebastian Thomassi promises this in person too.

I bet he does. There are no prizes for guessing where the furies came from and who financed this revolution. Our newest recruit looks stunned, all the colour draining from her face as she stumbles, then rocks backwards and forwards.

Shil shoots me a glare when I wrap my arm round Leona. And an even filthier one when our new sergeant throws her arms round my neck and buries her face in my chest. 'Wasn't supposed to be like this,' Leona sobs.

'Wasn't it?'

Shaking her head, she whispers, 'This isn't what I agreed at all.'

Chapter 38

'SVEN . . . THOUGHT YOU MIGHT BE HERE.'

Carl goes missing between the hotel and where we are now. Maybe he figures he's paid his debt. Maybe he simply disappears for a piss, loses track of us and can't find his way back. I get to keep his coat; he gets to keep the ferox-skull armband, the side arm Neen gave him and the Kemzin he picked up on his way into the centre.

Having lost Carl, we find Anton.

It's one of those nights.

Or rather he finds us, standing in the early dawn, staring at what remains of the general's house. Flames have gutted Jaxx's mansion and reduced it to a smouldering shell. An impressive, five-storeyed shell, with half its roof in place, and a twist of marble stairs, seen through the hole that tank made below in the wall.

But a shell all the same.

We're here because I'm worried Colonel Vijay will want one last look at where he grew up and his father died. Don't know if the colonel knows about Sebastian Thomassi declaring himself a prince. Or the traitorous deal Clan Thomassi has agreed with the Uplifted. If he does, then the colonel knows he's a dead man for sure. If he doesn't, he must still suspect it.

General Shadow Luc is no longer his worst enemy.

When the U/Free want you dead there's nowhere in the galaxy to hide. I'm beginning to realize that. We need a plan. When you're up against the U/Free or the Uplifted and Enlightened it has to be a big plan. When you're up against both together . . .

Sweat sticks my shirt to my back, and the morning air is hot and static around me. Iona's already vomited once. She now looks as if she's about to do it again. Shil's scowl has closed down to an empty blankness. Even Neen looks shocked by the carnage around us.

'Fuck, sir . . .'

He doesn't bother to finish.

The whole area south of the river stinks of death. Each new street is a makeshift abattoir. We stand, watching Jaxx's house, with our backs to other houses that smell like open-doored butchers, and the stench is impossible to ignore. Walking up to Iona, I punch her lightly in the stomach.

She vomits up the rest of last night's food.

'Find her some water,' I tell Neen. It's bad enough he brought Iona along without her having hysterics on us.

Between drinking and squabbling, the civilians in the square wait for the mansion's roof to fall in. As they do so, a scout car pushes through them, as if they were as much a part of the stench as the air itself.

Obviously, it's been a long wait. Most of the crowd are falling-down drunk. One man sits in the gutter, beating out a march on his naked belly. When he sees Leona look, he laughs, and laughs louder when she looks away.

'Fuckwit,' Rachel says.

When the roof falls, the crowd cheers.

Sweeping his field-glasses over the crowd, the man in the

scout car ignores their noise. Seems the Wolf has the same idea as us.

'Looking for Vijay,' Anton mutters.

Think that is what he says.

Hard to tell, given the mess he's in.

Helmet missing, side arm minus its clip. Bottom lip split. Blood from a broken nose splashing his flak jacket's urban camouflage. One of his eyes so badly bruised its lid is inside out.

He's sliced the bruising to release blood.

Either that, or it burst.

'Iona . . .'

Neen's squeeze hurries forward. Large breasts, generous hips. I must have been mad. Having someone this attractive in the unit is a shit idea.

'Boss,' she says.

'It's *sir*.'

Iona looks from under her lashes. She's checking if I'm still cross.

'Boss when we're off duty. Sir when we're on duty. Got it?'

She nods enthusiastically.

'Right,' I say. 'Sew up Anton's cut eye.'

Pulling thread from her pocket, she hesitates. Turns out, she's deciding where to start. Her choice is good. Tacking the middle, she ties it off. You stand a better chance of getting a clean scar that way.

A couple of loops close the cut.

She sews the bridge of his nose without being told.

When she's done, Iona returns her thread to her pocket, puts the needle back in its case and risks a glance at Neen. He smiles and she smiles back. Shil sees me watch her watching her brother's first serious lover and scowls. My sour grin only makes her own scowl fiercer.

Leona looks on with interest.

'He's going,' Anton says.

Seen it already. That tells me three facts. One, General Luc hasn't seen us. Unless we're not that important in his scheme of things. And two and three . . . Either the Wolf thinks he's waited long enough, or he knows something we don't. And the Wolf strikes me as a man who waits as long as it takes.

'We're moving out.'

'Yes, sir,' Neen says.

'Want to tell me where you've been?'

I wait till we're moving before asking Anton my question. Leona and Rachel are far enough ahead to be out of hearing. Shil's buried in her own thoughts five paces behind and Iona's five paces behind that. She's going to be our medic.

The crowd lets us through without really knowing why. Neen takes point, with Ajac at the rear, because it's time he started earning his place.

'Went to get this.'

Reaching into his pocket, Anton produces a small black disk. It lights when his thumb brushes the middle and he checks no one has seen.

'Five million credits,' he tells me.

Must see the shock in my eyes, because he shrugs. 'Debro's escape fund. Figured I should collect it.' Anton smiles sourly. 'Only Debro,' he says, 'could glue it under the leg of a cousin's chair for safety.'

'It's tied to her DNA?'

'Unformatted,' he tells me. 'Totally open.'

Fuck . . . I could kill him, lose myself in this crowd, talk my way off-planet and drink myself stupid, surrounded by the most beautiful whores five million credits can buy. A house the size of a city, a hot tub that can take ten, plus me.

'Put it away,' I say. 'Before someone mugs you.'

'Not likely,' he says. 'With you around.'

Stupid bastard means it. Leaving Anton to his fortune, I push forward until I reach Neen's side.

'Copters,' he says.

The first we've seen since this began.

Three black wasps hang over the river bank, door gunners hanging from open hatches, their long-magazine Kemzins tied with bungee cords to the sills above. One of the copters has an underslung thermal scanner sweeping the roofs. When three wasps become five, I know it's serious.

'Jaxx,' says Neen, flicking frequencies. 'They've got him cornered.'

'Vijay?' I say.

Neen looks surprised at my question.

I know it's Vijay. What interests me is Neen calling him *Jaxx*.

The beginning of an idea is stirring. It's an insane idea. All my best ones are, but this is a long-term idea, a big idea . . .

Never had one of those before.

I'll tell the others later. If there is a later, because my idea depends on us getting out of this alive. And it's not even a starter unless we can get Colonel Vijay out of this alive as well . . .

A hand signal stops my team where they stand. Civilians push around us, irritated we're in their way. The first man to voice his opinion gets punched to the ground by Rachel. The man goes down and stays down. They're better behaved after that.

My second signal says close up.

When I'm certain we're gathered, armed and ready for anything likely to happen, I pass control to Neen, tell them to stay close and begin pushing my way towards a side street leading to the river's edge.

Shil wants to know why I've given her brother operational control. It shows in her face. I surprise myself by telling her.

'Going to let the kyp feed.'

Her eyes widen. Shil knows how I feel about that.

Static, fever, a sourness in my throat. The side effects of feeding the kyp follow the same pattern every time. Going to do it all the same.

'Almost there,' Leona says.

The others think she's talking about the river.

Hidden pipes and buried pumping stations form a ghostly overlay in front of me as Farlight's AI comes on line. Looking deeper reveals electric substations and underground walkways.

A maze of tunnels ends at a filter house so old its filters are clogged with a century's worth of waste. No way into the houses in front of us, though.

'Earth to Sven,' the gun says. 'Anyone home?'

'The system is up. But OctoV has gone.'

'Sven,' it says, 'that's impossible.'

It isn't. I have no sense of our glorious leader's presence. The information is waiting, overlaid and organized, but there are no thoughts behind it. No one watches while the last of the data unravels itself for me. And the kyp in my throat is almost well behaved, which is proof enough – barely a roil of its exoskeleton or an aftertaste of static.

Won't last, of course.

The Uplifted will take over. For all the U/Free guarantee our freedoms, and our new leader Prince Thomassi promises life will get better . . . The Enlightened will want our lands, our trade routes, our data havens.

Well, not *my* lands, routes and data, obviously. Because I own fuck all of fuck all. Unless you include Golden Memories, and we own that between us, and something says we won't be seeing it again for a while anyway.

'Your choice,' Leona says.

She's talking to me, has to be. Since I'm the one she's looking at.

'*Sergeant*,' Neen warns.

When the SIG suggests we let her speak Leona nods, a little too gratefully. My glare warns her to behave. 'I don't imagine,' I say, 'Prince Thomassi will be kind to his prisoners.'

She scowls. Maybe at my use of *prince*. Mostly likely at the threat. Neen's scowling for a different reason. He doesn't know what is going on.

'Leona's precog.'

'Like Iona?'

'Different skill set.'

Neen doesn't like that idea.

That is fine, because I don't like it either. In fact, if Leona turns out to be a problem I'll kill her. She's only a temporary manifestation of our glorious leader, after all. An *avatar*. The word finds its way into my mind.

It's not like she's the real thing.

'Actually,' she says, 'it's exactly like.'

'In your dreams.'

I've talked with OctoV, felt the power of his mind as it turned from a million problems on a thousand different battle fronts, to concentrate on the tiny irritation I represented the first time we met.

'Sven,' says Leona. 'Think bigger.'

'You call him *sir*,' Neen snaps, stepping forward.

Leona looks at him, then nods. This time she means it. After a long scowl to make sure she knows he's the senior sergeant round here, he steps back.

'We'll talk later,' I tell Leona.

That sounds enough of a threat to satisfy Neen.

Chapter 39

A COPTER HANGS DIRECTLY OVER THE HOUSES WE'RE approaching. Most of the crowd are busy pointing at the roof of the one in the middle, where a single figure edges along a balustrade, before dropping from sight.

A second later, he reappears.

There's no balustrade on this house to protect him from falling. Just a drop to the road and his audience below. Half of Farlight has turned out for Colonel Vijay's last performance. Including the Wolf, who stands scowling in his scout car, surrounded by his men who keep the crowd back.

'Shit,' Rachel says.

A low moan, somewhere between upset and excitement, sweeps the crowd as Colonel Vijay begins climbing the tiles towards a roof light and slips slightly. His fingers grab at the tiles, but he can't get a grip.

'Oh fuck,' Neen says.

Doubt he knows he's said it.

Tiles come loose as Vijay's slide gets faster.

My plan's fucked. The thought comes as one of his feet clips guttering, which breaks away and begins to fall. He's going over the edge, when his other foot hits the bracket that held the guttering in place and his slide stops.

The crowd sighs.

Very slowly, Colonel Vijay reaches for a handhold and restarts his climb.

'Well,' says the SIG, 'that was exciting . . .' Telling me to watch the Wolf, it blips a laser dot on his helmet and removes it just as quickly. 'Ninety-nine yards, one foot, eight inches,' it says. 'Barely worth aiming.'

General Luc is now smiling. So I imagine his earlier scowl was at the thought of not being able to slaughter Vijay Jaxx himself.

'One shot,' the SIG says. 'How hard can it be?'

'That's not why we're here.'

'Kill Luc. Save Vijay.'

'Enough . . .'

'Just saying.'

'Well don't, all right?'

'You know,' it snarls, 'I think I preferred Aptitude.'

As we watch, Colonel Vijay claws his way to the roof light, and punches out the glass. Even at this distance we hear it shatter, before we see him roll over the window's lip and disappear into an attic below.

The colonel must know he is trapped. I'm not sure what he found downloading those data cores of Morgan's . . . May the bastard sleep badly and have a hideous life next time. But it's got the plotters riled. Unless this really is just about killing Indigo Jaxx's son.

One of the copters watches the front.

Another watches the river behind, while a third locks off the far end of the embankment and a fourth locks off the nearer end. A fifth wasp hangs right overhead. That one flies the pennant of Sebastian Thomassi from its tail.

Now is when we need the anti-tank rifle I wanted earlier.

The crowd knows Vijay Jaxx is cornered. Pushing and shoving, they jostle for a better position, hoping to get close to the steps leading to the house where he's taken refuge. It's like watching water come to the boil. Everyone is waiting for a sign. It comes when a man climbs the steps and turns to bless us.

The Archbishop of Farlight.

As one, the crowd bow their heads.

Every single word that man says is a lie.

I refuse to believe this dawn is glorious, that the collection of whores, looters, pickpockets and rapists around me is anyone's army for freedom, or that those who follow Sebastian Thomassi are doing God's will.

Bullshit, the lot of it.

The person behind Augustus, Archbishop of Farlight, convinces me of that. And if he wasn't proof enough, the U/Free next to him is.

The last time I saw her, Emerald Schott was wearing a dress made from slashed red silk. More slashes than silk. Certainly enough to show her breasts, all four of them . . . It was at a party in Letogratz. Tonight she's wearing something simpler.

Black, low-cut, but almost decent.

Next to Paper Osamu's mother-in-law stands Federico fucking Van fucking Zill, wearing a suit, dark glasses and a smirk.

'Sir,' Neen says.

He's waiting for orders.

'Nothing we can do,' Anton says. 'Vijay knows that. He wouldn't want you to sacrifice the Aux. We've still got time to get away.'

Anton is right. If we walk now, we can make it out of the crowd while the Wolf's attention is still on Colonel Vijay. But then, if I mug him, the rest of us can change our faces and names and live out our lives in luxury.

I'd no more do that than desert.

Besides, I gave Aptitude my word.

'We're probably going to die here.' Don't imagine I'm telling them anything they haven't worked out for themselves. 'Anyone who wants out, step back now.'

No one moves.

Not even Iona, who's sobbing.

If at first you don't succeed, destroy the evidence that you tried.

When the crowd get bored trying to pry-bar their way into the house where Colonel Vijay is trapped, someone drops the bar down a drain and sends for explosives. That's what a woman in front of us says. She's heard it from a man in front of her.

'Must be true then.'

There's a sourness to Neen's voice that makes her look away. *'Explosives coming through.'*

My gun begins its chant and those nearest us suddenly decide we must be the ones bringing the means to blow down that door. They part willingly.

'SIG . . .'

'Just trying to do my bit.'

As the four-breasted U/Free mutters anxiously to Van Zill, the Archbishop of Farlight stares at the disturbance we're causing, obviously wondering what's going on. Pretty soon, General Luc is going to stop looking hungrily at that door and start wondering what's going on as well.

Happens sooner than I'd like.

A shout goes up that the explosives are coming. And it's enough to attract the Wolf's attention.

'Fuck,' Anton says.

The SIG shivers in my grip.

Yeah, I know. We've been seen.

On the far side of the crowd, General Luc snaps out an order and his men start to move. They head for the steps. Same as we do. The Wolf follows, seemingly oblivious of those who scatter to avoid being crushed by his wheels.

Fifty paces from the steps, Luc realizes we're going to get there first.

He mutters an order to the man jogging beside his vehicle, and Sergeant Toro snaps out an order of his own. A second later, the sergeant and a splinter group cut free from the Wolf Brigade and start pushing towards us.

'Two o'clock.'

'Seen them,' I tell the SIG. 'Keep scanning.'

And then something happens that changes it all.

The crowd don't realize at first. Because half are watching us, and the rest are watching General Luc or his splinter group. But inside the house someone slams back heavy bolts and the door begins to open.

'Fuck,' says the SIG.

Hard to disagree.

Stamping onto the top step, Colonel Vijay clips down his boots as if he's on parade. Only then does he lift the hand hanging at his side. His opening shot drills Emerald Schott through the head.

So fast and clean is it she remains standing for a second, with a neat hole in one side of her skull and a bigger hole in the other. The Archbishop of Farlight is wiping his face frantically. He's wearing most of her brains.

Colonel Vijay's second shot kills Van Zill.

Personally, I'd have taken the archbishop before that scumbag, but it's the colonel's call. I think he's forgotten about Emerald's implant.

Not a bit of it.

Rolling her over, he drops to one knee and puts his gun to the back of her skull. His next shot blows the implant apart. Killing a U/Free and destroying her memories. Vijay Jaxx just made himself a galactic outcast.

'Interesting move.'

Even the SIG sounds impressed.

'Sven,' Colonel Vijay says. 'Thought I told you to get out of here?'

Now the crowd know we're not bringing explosives. I'm about to say, *Did you, sir?* when three things happen at once.

The first militia officer to raise his rifle goes down with a broken knee and a blade in his shoulder. Ajac's looking shocked, but then it's his blade and he forgot to keep hold of it. So now it juts from the screaming officer.

Ajac catches the spare Iona throws.

The archbishop begins to back away. That's the second. The third is that General Luc arrives just as Colonel Vijay points his gun at the archbishop.

'Don't,' the Wolf says.

This is a man used to being obeyed.

And Colonel Vijay does obey. Nodding, he lowers his weapon and the crowd surge forward. Actually, four things happen.

If not five.

'No one will touch Jaxx,' the Wolf announces. To back it up, his corporal turns his machine gun to cover the crowd.

'My son—' the archbishop says.

A second later he's reeling down the steps into the increasingly puzzled crowd. General Luc having just slammed his elbow into the archbishop's head. The final thing is that my gun shivers to let me know Luc's splinter group are behind us.

Not that I'm bothered.

We're Aux. We don't retreat anyway.

'Flechette,' I say, then change my mind. 'Make that incendiary.'

The SIG–37 whirs as it does what it's told. A diode lights to say it's loaded and a little red dot appears between General Luc's eyes. When he twitches, I know the SIG's made the dot hot this time.

It likes doing that.

'Earth to Sven,' my gun says.

'Sir,' I say. 'Stand away.' I mean Colonel Vijay, obviously. 'And you,' I tell the Wolf. 'Stand your men down.'

Grey eyes watch me.

His lip curls beneath his heavy beard.

And then his gaze flicks behind me and I feel the cold kiss of an automatic to the side of my head. A second later, it jags slightly. So I'm obviously supposed to have done more than simply notice it.

'Drop your piece.'

Sergeant Toro holds a Colt, with underslung sight, and a clip that juts indecently beneath its handle. But it's a single clip, with hollow-point at the most.

There's no way I'm backing down.

'Covered, sir.'

Neen has his rifle to Sergeant Toro's head. Although a Wolf Brigade corporal is pointing a rifle at him. I try to see who's targeting the corporal. Only, I don't want to turn my head that much.

'Got him covered,' Anton says.

I do the maths. Luc dies, I die, their sergeant dies, Neen dies, their corporal dies, Anton dies . . . Would help if I knew how many Wolf Brigade are behind me. Iona and Rachel, definitely dead.

Maybe Ajac.

The question is whether Vijay can be saved.

Back when I joined the Legion my old lieutenant tried to teach me chess. Good players take and lose as few pieces as possible. Until they're ready to roll up the opposition. Drunk or sober, but usually drunk, he'd win, no matter how many pieces he gave me first.

He played the long game.

I killed the first pawn to offer itself.

Looking round, it occurs to me I've improved. Maybe not by enough, though. Since my instinct is to pull the trigger. Don't want to get this wrong.

'Sir,' says Neen. 'How are we going to play this?'

Ignoring the weapons completely, someone slides through the crowd and stops at my side. 'The long game's waiting,' Leona whispers. 'If you want it.'

Chapter 40

WE NEED GENERAL LUC FOR THE LONG GAME. LEONA WILL explain why later. Although I'm supposed to know already. The fact he's commander of the Wolf Brigade, the private guard of Farlight's emperor, should tell me. It doesn't.

'But OctoV's dead.'

She pouts.

'You said you felt him die.'

'Yes and no,' she whispers, before telling me it's unimportant. I should concentrate, in the short term, on not getting killed.

The Wolf is watching me.

Still wearing that red dot between his eyes.

Sergeant Toro has his side arm to the side of my head. Even Colonel Vijay looks bemused not to be the centre of attention. But I'm not sure I'm going to let this go, so I hiss another question at her instead.

'If our glorious leader is dead then General Luc is out of a job, right? You can't command the emperor's guard if there isn't an emperor.'

'You're all out of a job.'

That thought shocks me. Colonel Vijay as commander of a

reborn Third Regiment is the heart of my plan. Only, the Wolf wants the colonel as well. He wants to wrap his heart in a bow and give it to Aptitude on a plate.

So there is no long game.

Killing General Luc is the right move.

'About fucking time,' says the SIG-37, when my finger tightens on the trigger. 'Hate to think you'd lost your nerve.'

'Sven,' Colonel Vijay sounds clipped. 'You will lower that damn gun.'

'Sir . . .'

There's a sudden flare of interest in the Wolf's grey eyes as he watches me wonder whether to obey.

'I mean it,' the colonel says. 'That is a direct order.'

'But, sir—'

'Stand your team down, lieutenant.'

'Fucking great,' the SIG says. Diodes fade along its chassis as I flick it into sleep mode.

'You heard the colonel,' I tell the Aux.

Very slowly, Neen lowers the muzzle of his rifle so it no longer points at Sergeant Toro, and Anton takes his blade from their corporal's throat. Sergeant Toro's first punch takes Neen from his feet.

Anton is raising his blade when the Wolf's snarl demands silence.

'Enough . . .' He nods to me. 'Your men will put their weapons on the ground. And you,' he scowls at his sergeant. 'Don't let that happen again.'

'Let the Aux keep their weapons.'

That's not me talking, obviously.

'If you will accept my parole,' Colonel Vijay says, 'I guarantee no one under my command will use their weapons against you or your men.'

Fucking idiot.

'Your word as a Jaxx?'

'No,' Leona says. 'His word as the new Duke of Farlight.'

Both men stare at her and the Wolf sneers. 'Have an heir, do you?' he asks Colonel Vijay.

The colonel shakes his head.

'Then it's going to be a short dukedom, isn't it?' The Wolf grins, showing yellow teeth. When he tells Colonel Vijay his parole is accepted, the colonel bows slightly. Nodding at me, the Wolf says, 'Get your rabble in formation.'

I pass this command to Neen.

'My son,' the archbishop says. He's keeping his distance from General Luc, which seems wise given the blood dripping from a cut over the prelate's eye. 'You must give him up for trial . . .'

He gestures. As if pointing the way to the promised land.

'Here comes the truck.'

Two police officers hang from its doors, riding shotgun. They look young and excited to be part of history. Their chief should have chosen two who knew what they were doing.

'Close ranks,' General Luc says.

The Wolf Brigade tighten their formation.

We could use their new focus to fight free. Colonel Vijay must know what I'm thinking, because he catches my gaze and shakes his head.

'Boss,' Neen says. 'Can't we ignore him?'

I've been wondering that myself. It's not like we're high clan ourselves, so why should we be bound by Vijay's stupidity? Except the colonel was our CO on Hekati, and for all I know he's the highest ranking Third Regiment officer alive on Farlight.

'No,' I say. 'We can't.'

But we can stop Sebastian Thomassi getting his hands on the man. I have the Aux fall in beside the Wolf Brigade. Colonel Vijay gave his word we wouldn't fight General Luc's men. He said nothing about not fighting anybody else.

Halting, the truck opens its doors and ten prison guards

jump out. They're everything you'd expect, from the guts hanging over their gun belts to the coffee stains on their flak jackets. They've even got cattle prods and extendable batons in little leather pouches at their sides.

I don't like prison guards.

Given the number of prisons I've been in that's understandable.

Stumbling to a halt, they only take formation when their NCO barks an order. The police officers look less happy than they did a few seconds before.

'Sir,' the older one says.

He is addressing Colonel Vijay.

Instead of being offended, General Luc laughs. And it occurs to me the officer only talks to Vijay because he's afraid to talk direct to the Wolf.

'I need your surrender for trial, sir.'

'On what charges?'

'Being a member of an illegal organization.'

'*A what?*'

'You're a colonel in the Third Regiment. That regiment of the Death's Head is now proscribed. All officers, NCOs and soldiers are to surrender immediately. Failure to surrender is punishable by death.'

He's reciting from memory. Obviously enough.

'Death?' The Wolf looks interested.

'Refusal to surrender constitutes treason to our newly elected leader Prince Thomassi.'

'Who elected him?' Leona demands.

The police officer ignores her.

'And he's not a prince,' I add. 'And he's only a senator because his brother died.'

'Sven,' says Anton, 'you're not helping.'

That's fine. I'm not interested in helping. I want the Wolf Brigade to attack the police and guards while we spectate. A little friendly fire, and the Wolf's down and Colonel Vijay's conscience is clear.

Unfortunately, the colonel is regretting he can't oblige. He has surrendered already and it's impossible to do so twice. He says this politely. Of course, should the Wolf decide he doesn't want the colonel's surrender . . .

General Luc's lip curls.

The police officers go pale.

Nodding to his driver, the Wolf climbs into his scout car and we hear its engine start. He nods again. To Colonel Vijay, this time. I have no doubt that General Luc intends to cut out his captive's heart. But he still offers him a ride.

High clans. Fucking insane, the lot of them.

Chapter 41

'SVEN . . .'

Yeah, I know. The road's this way. Grabbing my bars, I blip the throttle and jump a ditch, missing a man who opens his mouth to swear. Only to shut it again at the sight of my face. Wise move. Although I'm too drunk to go back and kill him. So maybe he's not in that much danger after all.

Given I've finished a bottle of cane spirit, it's a miracle I can steer this thing. Mind you, it has three wheels and that probably helps. An Icefeld couldn't cope with the state I'm in.

Someone got splashed the last time I vomited.

Shil probably, knowing my luck. Something else for her to get sour-faced and tight-lipped about. Luckily, I've got a second bottle in the pocket of my coat. So I don't care that much.

We're getting out of Farlight.

So is half the city from the look of it.

But we're having a better time of it than they are.

A broken-down truck with an armchair tied to its flat-bed sits up ahead, guarded by an old doubter woman, who slumps on the chair, with a crying child on her lap. The child clutches a doll.

A hover taxi lies burnt-out in a ditch. Given its age and rust, and the patches of rot pocking its neoprene skirt, I'm surprised it made it this far. Gyrobikes wobble under the weight of two adults and more children than their riders can afford to feed.

The city obviously started emptying hours ago.

But we plough our way through the lot. General Luc doesn't bother with sirens. Vehicles and people move out of our way or get driven off the road as the Wolf Brigade convoy roars by.

Three personnel carriers, five scout cars, sporting light machine guns. A pair of anti-tank missile launchers, with pintel mounts. Three transporters, loaded with food, water and ammunition . . .

The SIG gives me the list.

I tell it to shut up.

It tells me Aptitude was more fun than this.

Everyone in the Aux avoids me. Don't blame them. Not their fault if I'm drunk. Apparently, Shil thought I was over behaving like this. Fuck knows where she got that idea. Don't appreciate the SIG telling me either.

I blame Sergeant Leona. She landed me with the shit about thinking ahead, long games and people changing. Undoing my second bottle, I swear when the SIG says that's a bad idea, and swap them around. The SIG-37 goes in my pocket and the bottle goes in my holster, an altogether better arrangement.

My combat trike is really just a fat-wheel with added light machine gun. I'm riding one. We're all riding one. The bastards have even left the LMG's belt in place. A clanking strip of 7.62 knitted with twists of ceramic. The LMG is automatic, gas-operated, belt-fed, air-cooled . . .

Our glorious leader's usual shit. I wonder the Wolf is stupid enough to leave us loaded guns given the way I feel. The SIG tells me he's not.

The pin has been shaved.

General Luc is up ahead. His vehicle identical to the one at

Wildeside. Long snout, short back, weird turret. Painted grey, flying his flag. Still looks like a wolf's skull on wheels.

'Same one, fuckwit . . .'

Being in my pocket makes the SIG sound muffled.

The road we travel steams with early rain. The clouds have burnt away, and with them our protection from the early-afternoon sun. It will be worse later, when we hit the wastelands. Everyone rides in silence, staring ahead. No one knows what to say. And I'm not ready to say anything. Not yet.

So we wrestle with our fat-wheels, set our faces to the hot wind, wipe dust from our visors and head down Farlight's slopes towards a gash through the wastes beyond.

Our route to the high plains.

There are seven of us and there should be nine.

Like I said, General Luc rides ahead. The personnel carriers ride behind. Four of the fat-wheels are used by Luc's men. They act as our guards and as the Wolf's outriders. Five hundred Wolf Brigade in all.

Drones fly overhead, all stubby wings and afterburners. They're worked by a pale-faced girl who sits up front in a scout car, with a pad on her knee that she scratches with one nail as she flicks them round the sky. Not sure what she's—

Oh, fuck it.

Upending the bottle, I swallow half in one go.

'Sven,' the gun says. 'This isn't helping.' Shows what it knows.

The trucks are being loaded with supplies. The officers will travel separately from the men, and the NCOs separately from both. There's even less mixing of ranks in the Wolf Brigade than in the Death's Head, and there was little enough there.

Imagine it reflects General Luc's tastes.

This is a memory, in case you didn't realize. Not even the second bottle of cane spirit is enough to wash it away. So I guess I'll be living with it for a while.

In my memory, we line up and the Wolf walks himself down our line.

As if we're on parade, and he's inspecting us. Colonel Jaxx is two paces behind. Still in his uniform and wearing his side arm. His loaded side arm, because General Luc lets him keep his rounds. The colonel looks younger than he is. And, God knows, he's young enough.

The Wolf stops twice.

Once in front of me. Staring me up and down, he asks if I'm glad to have my arm back.

'Yes . . .'

'You call him sir,' Colonel Jaxx snaps.

'Yes, sir.'

General Luc nods. 'That's better.'

'I was talking to my colonel.'

The Wolf's eyes tighten. Leaning close, he takes a long look at my skull. I know it's wide. I'm just not used to people making their interest so obvious.

'So,' he says. 'The last human.'

I salute so fast it's like a spring uncoiling. General Luc isn't sure how he feels about that. 'Checked your record,' he says. 'Did you really destroy an Enlightened mother ship?'

'Not by myself, sir.'

He smiles. 'Now we get to the truth. What help did you have?'

'That lot.' I jerk my head towards the Aux.

The Wolf's wondering if I'm mocking him. Takes a moment for him to decide I'm not and he likes that even less. 'Near original,' he says. 'Isn't that what the Uplifted said?'

'Yes, sir.'

How the fuck does he know about that?

I'd always assumed I'm human, plus. Not that it matters since our glorious— our late, no longer glorious leader declared all forms of human equal. But it seems I'm not. Everyone else is human, minus.

They probably believe they have the bad bits cut out.

The second time he stops is at the end of the line where Anton should be. Anton, who is with us right up to the point General Luc announces he's abandoning Farlight for the Wolf Brigade's mountain HQ; and then vanishes, along with five million credits on an open chip, although that's not something the rest know.

'Ah yes,' he says. 'Our missing hero.'

'Sir,' I say.

Grey eyes flick towards me.

'Anton wasn't Aux.'

The Wolf smiles. 'No,' he says. 'You're right. He wasn't. Was he?' There's something dangerously silky in his voice. 'You're saying your colonel's parole didn't apply to him?'

I shrug. The Wolf is not amused. I'm not sure I care.

'Well?' he growls.

'How the fuck would I know? My childhood was spent stealing food on a planet you've never heard of, sir. It took the man who shot my sister to teach me not to eat with my fingers, shit in public and kill animals for fun.'

'Is there a point to this?'

'Yeah . . . If it wasn't for Colonel Vijay I'd have killed you by now, set fire to your corpse and pissed on the ashes.'

He stares at me. 'Are you really a Death's Head lieutenant?'

'General Jaxx's choice.'

'That true?' the Wolf asks Colonel Vijay.

'My father was an astute judge of men.'

'Anton Tezuka and I have history,' General Luc tells him. 'Did Anton mention that? Such an ambitious young man.' The general bares his teeth. 'You know,' he says, 'I always wondered what Anton saw in my well-connected, beautiful, absurdly rich fiancée.'

'Senator Wildeside?' The colonel looks shocked.

'Yep,' I say. 'Debro.'

The general's eyebrows rise at my use of her first name. 'Of course,' he says. 'I forget. The dashing young lieutenant saves the disgraced senator from the insane and ravening inmates of an ice planet. Demands her freedom as his reward for destroying an Uplifted mother ship. Are you in love with her?'

My expression makes him bark with laughter.

'I'll take that as a no.'

It wasn't the five million in credits that made Anton desert us. At least, not entirely; although no doubt that helped his decision. As General Luc walks up and down our line, I replay his words in my head. *You're right. He wasn't. Was he?*

Anton didn't trust the Wolf not to take his revenge.

Right now, General Luc is pretending to talk to himself and we're listening carefully, because our lives depend on it.

'I could keep some of you and kill the rest,' he says. 'Or simply kill all of you. Only I can't kill your colonel, can I? Because he's given parole and, anyway, his heart needs to be fresh.'

Vijay Jaxx says nothing.

So I guess they've had that conversation already.

'And tempting as it is I can hardly kill you, can I?' he says, looking at me. 'Last human and all. What with you having freed Debro. Given I intend to marry her daughter . . .'

Colonel Vijay's head does twitch at that.

'But,' he says. 'Someone has to pay for Anton's desertion.'

Stopping by Rachel, he raises her head. 'Hard enough to find snipers as it is.'

Neen he passes without comment. Good sergeants are as valuable as snipers. Noting the corporal's stripes on Shil's uniform, and the sour way she scowls at him, the Wolf grunts his approval. Ajac stares straight ahead. Iona is in tears . . .

'You,' General Luc tells her. 'Step out of line.'

'Take me instead,' Ajac says, stepping forward.

'You're lovers?' The Wolf sounds amused.

'Cousins,' Ajac says. 'And she's precog. That has to be worth something.'

The Wolf looks between them, eyes hard as flint, noting their family likenesses. 'Your accent,' he demands. 'What is it?'

'Hekati,' says Iona. She manages to hiccup in the middle.

'You're from Hekati?'

Iona nods, not realizing she's saved. No way will the Wolf kill the last two survivors from the oldest of habitats. The first one to become sentient and aware. Keep Iona as his mistress, and make Ajac his servant, quite possibly.

But not kill them.

'That leaves you,' he tells Leona.

She smiles. 'Yes,' she says. 'It does.'

'You think that's amusing?'

Leona runs her gaze up his uniform, stopping at his face. Grey eyes, swept-back hair, a scar that whitens his cheek. 'General Luc, commander of the Wolf Brigade, bound to protect the emperor by blood and oath.' Her smile grows wider. 'You have no idea how funny it is.'

Chapter 42

IN A CORNER OF THE WOLF'S PARADE GROUND IN FARLIGHT, under an oak tree that looks as if it's been there as long as the barracks, which must have been there since the beginning, Leona says goodbye to me. She wraps both arms around my neck and holds tight, resting her head on my chest. I shouldn't let my hand slip, but I do.

Her bottom is as perfect in the flesh as it is in bronze.

I can feel her grin.

'Sven,' she says. 'They're about to shoot me.'

'For real?'

She prises herself away. Lets me see her face. She's still smiling, but looks slightly puzzled. 'How do you mean *for real*?'

'You'll die like everyone else?'

Snuggling close, she rests her head again, and I feel her nod. 'We've been through this. When the bullets hit, flesh will tear and muscles will rip. My lungs will fail, my vision cloud. I'll be fighting for life long after any chance of it has gone.'

Leona grips me tighter when I try to pull away.

'Sit for a second,' she says. 'Luc's given me time to say goodbye.'

Dropping to a crouch, she points to a patch of dirt next to her. So I sit cross-legged beside her.

'Sven,' she says. 'Can I look at the gun?'

She field-strips the SIG so fast my eyes barely follow her fingers. And she lays it out in front of her according to the official manual for a Colt-37, which is what it used to be before it was upgraded to full SIG AI and cinder maker capacity.

Having done that, she slides free its chip.

Breaks the chip into five smaller pieces and reassembles it just as swiftly. Less than thirty seconds later the SIG-37 is swearing blue murder and Leona's nodding to herself with a pleased smile on her face.

'You've done that before.'

'At my age, it's hard to find something I haven't.'

I'm not sure who's talking. But I don't think it's the girl in front of me.

So we sit in the early morning light, under the shadow of a huge tree, with a sticky wind rustling oak leaves and stirring dust. Her hair is damp at the neck and her skin smells of soap and sweat. I promise to kill General Luc the first chance I get. I promise it will be a slow and painful death and he will die in absolute—

Leona tells me this isn't what she wants.

She wants me to pay attention. So I try not to notice her scent or how the skin of her neck feels under my touch. Although it doesn't help my concentration when she shifts back and starts to unzip her jacket, revealing a vee of sweat beneath.

Her breasts shift either side of three dog tags that hide behind her vest's green cotton. One tag to be buried with her body, one to be returned to her regiment, and one for central records so everything is up to date.

Don't imagine that will happen.

Removing the chain, Leona ignores her dog tags, and holds

up the key next to them. This would be simple, if not for its handle, which looks like the bastard son of a circle and a square.

Then she leans forward and unbuttons my shirt.

Next to my tags is a planet buster.

I took it on Hekati from a man who tried to kill me. He'd been given it by members of the Silver Fist. All he had to do, they told him, was twist its top and all his enemies would disappear.

He should wait until the next full moon.

By then, the shock troops intended to be somewhere else.

Somewhere that turning time inside out and destroying a sentient ring world wasn't going to cause them problems. Because the U/Free can be very strict about things like that.

Only I screwed their plan and their ship too. Screwed the lot of them. But the ring world still died and I heard it happen.

'Remembering Hekati?' Leona says.

I nod abruptly.

'It will get better.'

She smiles when I growl that I'll take her word for it. Reaching out, she opens my hand and drops her chain into the middle, folding my fingers around it.

'Fuck,' the SIG says. 'That's—'

'None of your business,' Leona replies.

A tingle like static burns the centre of my palm.

'Profiling,' the SIG says. 'Genotype human equivalent. Status DH class 2, override complete . . .' It sounds like someone else.

My planet buster has a flip-up top, a purple ring that needs turning to set the core and a locking mechanism to stop the top opening accidentally. The key Leona gives me is simply a key.

'What do I do with it?'

'What do keys usually do?' Taking her chain from my hand, she hangs it round my neck and buttons my shirt, before resting her forehead on mine. 'The empire is not a thing,' she says. 'It's an idea. You understand?'

'No. I don't understand at all.'

'The long game.'

'Leona, I can't play chess.'

'Then learn fast,' she says firmly. 'Or find people to play it for you.'

My face is to the sun and hers in shadow. Over her shoulders, half life-size in the distance, are the Aux, a dozen officers from the Wolf Brigade and the Wolf himself.

I'm impressed he's left us alone this long.

'Yes,' Leona says. 'I know. It's time.'

Reaching out, she touches my face and her eyes glisten.

As we climb to our feet, she takes my hand and walks me back to where the others wait. And she keeps her face turned to mine and her smile in place, as if I am the one about to die.

Leona refuses General Luc's offer of a blindfold.

She does, however, beg a cigarette from Neen, whose fingers shake badly when he lifts his hand to shield the flame. Trickling smoke between her lips, Leona glances round and nods towards a wall.

'That'll do, I guess.'

Soldiers from the Wolf Brigade continue loading trucks.

Food and ammunition and crates of weaponry. Kemzin 19s, half a dozen Z93z long-range rifles, a couple of mortars, a heavy machine gun, on a tripod so unwieldy it takes three men to carry.

They turn to watch us as they pass.

We're a minor part of a play parallel to their own. Nodding to Colonel Vijay, the Wolf says, 'I'll leave the arrangements to you.'

Colonel Vijay says nothing.

'Sir?' I say.

Both men look in my direction.

It's easy to read the colonel's eyes. The last twenty-four hours have filled them with horror, sadness and a sense of hope-lessness. The Wolf's stare is harder to translate.

'Permission to carry on, sir?'

It is the Wolf who nods.

Pulling my SIG–37 from its holster, I switch to hollow-point while the gun is still at my side and walk towards Leona. She's still smiling when I raise the SIG and blow out her brains. No one said she had to be against a wall. No one said there had to be a firing party.

'Find shovels,' I tell the Aux. 'Get yourselves over to that oak and dig a grave. I want her buried and prayers said before we move out.'

Sergeant Toro sends for entrenching tools, those flip-down spades with spikes one side and shovel blades the other. I could crack the Wolf's skull with one blow. Only my idiot colonel gave his word and we're stuck with that.

Ajac breaks the first of the dirt, hacking through a root that gets in his way. He's broad and blond and strong as an ox. But he grew up on a deserted ring world in a goat-infested village that called itself a city. He digs until the sweat running down his face hides the tears he's ashamed to show.

Then Neen volunteers.

He didn't know Leona. None of them did, not really. But, by the end, she was one of us and that is enough. When Neen is exhausted, I take my turn.

Shucking off my coat, I strip off my shirt, wrap both hands round the handle of the entrenching tool and cut through roots in short, brutal strokes. Each one is General Luc's skull being smashed beneath my blade.

A crowd begins to gather.

At first I think they're drawn by the ferocity of my digging. But it's the scars on my back that have them muttering to each other. They've never seen an officer who's been whipped before, and my scars are clear enough to be counted.

Most men would be dead.

'Lieutenant,' says a voice. It's the Wolf. So I don't bother to look up.

'Sir?' I say, slamming my entrenching tool into a root.

'Your back . . .'

'Whipped for hitting an NCO.'

'You were a trooper?'

'Yes, sir.'

'But you made sergeant?'

'Made sergeant, sir. Lost it for hitting an officer.' Another crack of the entrenching tool and its blade skids off a root to split a block of black stone. Obsidian, I've seen it before.

'You were whipped for hitting an NCO. But not for hitting an officer?'

'The penalty for hitting an officer is death, sir.'

General Luc knows that.

There is probably an army somewhere with different rules. I imagine they'll lose to the first serious enemy they meet. Militia exist to die. Conscripts hold the enemy's attention while the professionals get on with the real job.

As for the rest of us . . .

Legion, Death's Head or Wolf Brigade, it doesn't matter. Our officers can be trusted to behave in public. The rest, and I include myself in that, are in for life. We're a fuck of a lot less dangerous to other people that way.

Scrambling from the grave, I discover it's as deep as I'm tall.

So I carry Leona to the edge and have Neen pass her down to me.

From the front, as she lies face up, staring at the blue sky above, you'd never know that most of the back of her skull is missing.

'Fill it in,' I tell the Aux.

One of Luc's officers checks his watch.

The Wolf shakes his head, and the major goes back to staring straight ahead. The men who finish loading their trucks drift over in twos and threes and find themselves staying. When Leona's grave is full, and its overspill heaped into a mound, as overspill always is, we seem to have most of the Wolf Brigade around us.

Several hundred people bow their heads when I say the soldier's prayer.

Chapter 43

THE EARTH IS RED ROUND HERE. SCRUB CLINGS TO THE EDGES of a road, which is broken and scabbed and full of badly mended holes. Stunted trees dot the distance. Twisted pines and cork and something that sheds its bark in leprous strips.

For all that it is hot and dry, the air is cleaner than in Farlight. Much cleaner and much clearer. In the distance a low line of hills stands between us and snow-covered mountains.

Birds circle a clump of distant thorn, wide-winged and lazy.

On the bike ahead, Rachel shifts her gaze. *One, two, three, four . . .* She's just judged their speed and distance, allowed for deflection, wind and the diffraction that heat induces, and mentally shot each buzzard through its head.

Colonel Vijay rides at the front.

He won't look at me.

Actually, he won't look at anyone.

He just stares ahead and keeps his eyes on the red earth.

Still, if I'd delivered myself into the hands of a man who wants to cut out my heart and fuck my girlfriend, I'd probably be concentrating on the road too. Mind you, I wouldn't give my parole. So the problem wouldn't arise.

'No,' says the SIG. 'You'd invent a whole new category of fuck-ups. You know the value of teamwork?' It waits for my answer, then sighs. 'You get to blame someone else.' When I don't reply to that either, it puts itself to sleep.

We pull into a hill village that afternoon.

There are a thousand like it dotted across the wastes.

An old church, now peeling whitewash. A small square, surrounded by broken buildings. The handful of children who watch us arrive get slapped into silence and dragged inside. Not sure if their mothers expect the Wolf Brigade to eat them, rape them or use them as target practice.

General Luc obviously feels happier to be out of the city, because he commandeers the village bar, its owner, the serving girls and its cook and settles himself at a table out front where he can keep an eye on what is going on.

As he waits, he sends for our colonel.

We're too far away to hear their conversation. But it ends with Colonel Vijay's clumsy salute. Never met a senior officer who could salute properly yet.

Turning on his heel, Colonel Vijay heads for where we sit in the shadow of the church's faded bell tower. When he tells us to stay as we are, we stop climbing to our feet. 'Sven,' he says, 'how are you feeling now?'

'Better, sir. Thank you. Vomiting helps.'

He sighs. 'Where are Ajac and Iona?'

'Inside, sir.'

I imagine they're lighting candles for Hekati.

'I eat with General Luc's officers.' The colonel's words are addressed to us all, but he's staring at me when he says this.

'Understood, sir.'

He looks relieved.

What does he think? I'm going to tell him he's an idiot in front of the others? I'm not even going to tell him he's an idiot when we're alone. For all that giving his parole is one of the stupidest things I've heard.

The next time I see Colonel Vijay he's next to the Wolf, slicing ewe's cheese with a blunt knife to eat on fat slabs of dark bread, which he washes down with a local wine. The general is asking his opinion on how many hours it will take a courier to ride from the Wolf's Lair to Wildeside.

The man's torturing Colonel Vijay with politeness.

Imagine we're handcuffed or held in a cage, stripped of our weapons and uniforms and badges of rank. Both sides know where they stand. We're the naked, shit-covered ones and they're our captors.

We get to hate them.

They get to regard us with contempt. Everybody is happy.

This way is crueller. The Wolf's officers reply politely to the colonel's conversation and let him take his food before them, but there isn't a single one who doubts their general's intention to cut out Vijay's heart.

And he will do it. This is Shadow Luc we're talking about. Who slit the throats of a Silver Fist's five children.

God knows, we've all cut throats.

An Enlightened eleven-braid, a three-braid and several Silver Fist in my case. But the Wolf did it in cold blood to make a point, because their father refused to surrender.

'Sir, you OK?' Shil sits beside me without being invited. Since these are the first words she's said to me all day, I assume she's been sent by the others.

'Why wouldn't I be?'

My corporal slicks a sideways glance.

She's scowling, which might be the light in her eyes, because the sun is eating the edges of the shadow where we sit. I can smell the sweat on her. As surely as I can smell the smoke and stink that clings after any battle.

If that's what last night was.

'Colonel Vijay mentioned Leona took his message to Aptitude . . .'

Shil's choosing her words carefully. There's a reason for this. Actually, there are a couple of reasons. I'm her lieutenant, and I've been known to lose my temper with her. And we've talked a couple of times; alcohol was involved and nothing happened, at least not that I remember.

She's come to see how I feel about executing Leona. How does she think I feel? It occurs to me she doesn't know.

'I'm sorry,' she says. 'Really, sir. We all are.'

The idea the Aux are discussing this behind my back doesn't improve my hangover any. They're cannon fodder, wasn't that what I told them at the start? I'm about to remind Shil of this, when a thought closes my mouth.

Leona delivered Vijay's letter to Aptitude.

'Later,' I say.

Stamping to where Colonel Vijay sits, I come to salute.

The Wolf watches me, his ADC watches me. My own troop watch me from where they sit near the church tower. Apart from Shil, who watches from where I was a few seconds ago. Her scowl has nothing to do with the sun this time.

'Join us,' Colonel Vijay tells me. He gestures to a bench opposite. So that's where I sit. 'Sven,' he says, sounding formal. 'I'm so—'

I nod away his sympathy.

The colonel clicks his fingers and a girl appears. Huge eyes and a tight smile. She hides her fear behind a fringe that half-covers her face.

'More wine,' he says. 'And some food.'

Her smile falters. Might be my metal arm. Might be the fact my uniform is so stained with blood I can't remember whose most of it is. Alternatively, the fact I stink of vomit and alcohol could have something to do with it. Vijay Jaxx is far too polite to mention that fact. But then Colonel Jaxx is high clan.

'What he had,' I say.

The cheese is so hard I use my own knife, wiping its blade before hacking myself a chunk. The loaf that arrives with it is oily and tough as old leather. Polite people tear their bread. My old lieutenant taught me that. Luckily I'm not polite.

'You seem to have found your appetite.'

Looking down, I discover the colonel is right. All the cheese is gone and most of the bread. 'The kyp's quieter these days, sir,' I say.

Colonel Vijay flicks a glance towards General Luc.

The Wolf is concentrating on the glass in front of him. He tastes his wine with the restrained ferocity that underlies everything he does.

There is a tightness to Colonel Vijay's face . . .

He doesn't like me talking about the symbiont in public. Actually, it's not that. His father is dead, he's going to his own death and the house where he was born is a burnt-out ruin, all of this inside the last twenty-four hours. Having to pretend it hasn't happened is killing him.

'Sir,' I say. 'Perhaps we could take a walk?'

General Luc watches us leave.

For all I know, he watches us the entire way round the village square, because that is where we walk, our heads together and my questions low. As we return to where we started, Colonel Vijay retakes his place and dismisses me with a nod.

He demanded a messenger.

Leona appeared.

There is no mystery. No significance. Senior officers often use militia for non-essential messages. He's sorry for Leona's death, and understands my action was a kindness, although he doubts if the Aux understand that. When I mention his father our conversation is over. That's a subject he's unwilling to discuss.

'Sir—'

'Leave it,' he orders. So I do.

After my dismissal, I don't expect us to talk again until the evening. I'm wrong about that as well.

Iona sits on a broken wall watched by two Wolf Brigade troopers at a table. As she leans back and raises the hem of her dress to sun her knees, I think she's pretending not to notice their interest.

But no, they're invisible.

Only the sun, the wind and the sound of cicadas hold her interest. The insect noise probably reminds her of life on Hekati.

The way she leans back tightens the cloth across her breasts, which are full anyway, and seem fuller because she wears a belt beneath. Her eyes close and she opens her mouth to taste the wind; has to be that, can't think what else she's doing as she flicks her tongue like a lizard, a dozen of which hug the wall where she suns.

When one of the two troopers attracts her attention by putting his hand on her knee, Iona jumps.

'Heart rate up, pupil dilation, rapid breathing . . .' The SIG counts off the shock signs. 'Yep, she really is that stupid.'

'Unworldly,' Colonel Vijay says.

'Sir . . . Sorry, sir. Didn't hear you come up behind me.'

His attention is on Iona, who is finding it hard to move now the Wolf Brigade trooper grips her knee. Every time she struggles, he tightens his fingers and she stops struggling again. Iona needs to crack that pain barrier.

'Damn it,' the colonel says.

Must be at the way Neen's now scrambling to his feet, one hand reaching for a knife in the back of his belt. Seeing he has competition, the Wolf Brigade trooper grins.

'Sven . . .' Colonel Vijay nods to where General Luc gestures.

'What rank is your man?' the Wolf asks.

'Sergeant, sir.'

Pretty obvious I'd have thought from the stripes on the jacket Neen's now wrapping round his left arm as protection against the trooper's blade.

'And my man?' he demands, pointing to his own trooper.

'A private, sir.'

'Exactly, Lieutenant.' He waits impatiently for my response, then hisses with irritation. 'A sergeant fighting a trooper. Hardly fitting, is it?'

'That's his girlfriend,' I say.

General Luc looks at me as if I'm mad. 'What has that to do with it?' he demands. Emptying a wine glass in a single gulp, he pulls a face.

'You want me to stop the fight, sir?'

'I want you to use your discretion.'

'Never had any, sir.'

'Is that a joke, Lieutenant?' He stares at me. 'I'm not a general who appreciates jokes from junior officers.'

'I imagine not, sir. And it's not a joke.'

Ignoring my reply, he holds his glass to one side. An orderly comes running so fast he almost falls as his boots skid on the grit beneath him. 'Find me something drinkable,' the Wolf demands.

The orderly wants to say it's not possible. We're in the middle of nowhere, for fuck's sake, but he simply nods.

'Well, Sven . . . ?' Colonel Vijay demands.

Neen and the trooper circle with sideways steps, like angry crabs, as they jab and feint. They're testing each other's defences. Can't be long before one of them draws first blood, maybe even gets in the killing blow.

'General Luc doesn't approve of sergeants fighting privates.'

'Then you'd better stop it, hadn't you?'

This is more of an order than a question. But I'm not happy with anything that makes the Aux look as if we're backing down.

'*Sven . . .*'

'I'm going, sir.'

Both men stop circling as I step between them. Six or seven men jeer. They're all Wolf Brigade, which is just as well. I'd have the hide off any of mine who behaved like that.

'Fight's over,' I say.

Neen steps back, and returns his knife to his belt. The Wolf Brigade trooper stares at me.

'Your man not up to it . . . sir?'

'My man was killing Silver Fist while you lot collected medals for guarding empty corridors in unused palaces.'

There, I've just managed to insult his whole brigade.

'*Lieutenant . . .*'

General Luc is so angry, the glare he shoots at the trooper who started this is enough to have the man staring at his boots. Meanwhile, Neen still waits, stripped to the waist, with his jacket wrapped round his arm. You'd have to be blind to miss the scar on his ribs or the puckered mess of an old bullet wound over his hip.

'You,' the Wolf says firmly. 'Stand down.'

He's talking to Neen, but my sergeant isn't the one holding a blade.

All the same, Neen unwraps the jacket from his arm, then salutes the general and returns to his original spot by the wall, where Iona now sits between Rachel and Shil.

'Of course,' General Luc says, 'sergeants not fighting privates doesn't mean privates can't fight privates . . .'

He leaves his comment hanging.

'Mine,' Ajac says, scrambling to his feet.

★

302

Ajac's big, but he has little real muscle and no scars. He's also young enough for his chest to be almost hairless. Taking one look at him, the trooper laughs and Ajac's face tightens.

If the Wolf Brigade trooper lives, I'll buy him a beer for that.

Wrapping his arm the way he saw Neen do, Ajac pulls his knife and scowls at the man. He was angry on Iona's behalf. Now he's furious on his own. All he has to do is turn that into something useful.

'Neen,' I say. 'How good is Ajac?'

My sergeant looks worried.

'Five gold coins we win.' My voice is loud enough to carry. Those simply wondering what is going on decide they might as well come over and find out.

The trooper looks unhappy at my confidence.

Ajac simply looks shocked. Probably the thought of my temper if he loses me the money I won in Farlight. A moment later, Sergeant Toro appears at my side. His general has taken my bet.

'Have you got five in gold?' Colonel Vijay asks.

'Yes, sir.'

He looks surprised.

'Go brief Ajac,' I tell Neen.

'Sir,' he says. 'I'm not sure that's in the rules.'

'What rules?'

Given his general is watching, it's understandable the trooper goes for a five-second knockdown. Instead of starting to circle as he did facing Neen, he launches a strike.

One second he's opposite, the next his blade slashes towards Ajac's guts and his friends start cheering. Their cheer dies as Ajac jumps sideways and jabs wildly, his blade aimed at the trooper's face.

Although he misses, their man still flinches. Ajac doesn't notice, because he's trying to find his balance, but Neen certainly does.

'What orders did you give?'

'Watch his eyes. Fight dirty. Get it over fast.'

Neen's right about all three. Unfortunately, Ajac refuses to obey. At least, he refuses to obey the last two. He circles instead, blocking a couple of clumsy attacks, and just dodging a slash at his throat that looks slicker than the previous two blows, unless it's simply lucky.

Iona watches slack-mouthed.

I'll be having words with her about blind stupidity later. I imagine the others know that, even if she doesn't.

'Get it over with,' Neen growls.

The Wolf Brigade trooper glances over and something tightens behind his eyes. He thinks Ajac is toying with him, that the blond boy plays a waiting game.

'Another five gold coins on Ajac.'

I'm lucky. No one takes my bet.

But it does the job and the trooper's next attack is so panicked that half his friends believe it's a feint, until he follows through and leaves himself wide open.

'*Now*,' Neen orders.

Ajac steps back.

His blade should be in that man's kidneys. And the man should be down, pissing the dregs of his life into the dirt. There is no excuse for the anguish on Ajac's face, he's not even injured.

That changes when Ajac's opponent decides to go on the attack. Feinting in one direction, he juggles his blade from one hand to the other, and jabs. We all hear Ajac's gasp of pain as blood starts running from his hip.

'Sir . . .' Shil stands beside me.

'Not now, Shil.'

'It's about Ajac, sir.'

'What about him?' I ask quietly.

When the trooper swings his blade at Ajac's throat, Ajac

blocks, using his jacket-wrapped arm. From his whimper, he didn't wrap it well enough.

'Ajac hasn't killed, sir.'

'*What?*'

She nods towards the fight. 'Iona doubts he's done more than slaughter a goat. She says he'll keep circling until he dies of blood loss or that man kills him.'

'Get me Iona.'

'Sir . . .' Iona looks terrified.

Given how I feel about her that's a sensible reaction. Ajac might make a good soldier five years down the line, if he lasts that long, which looks unlikely. Iona, I can count on one finger of one hand what she's good for.

'Do you and Ajac share a dialect?'

She looks at me blankly.

'*Do you share . . .*' A dozen Wolf Brigade stare as I raise my voice and Iona nods quickly. Telling me that yes, her tribe has its own dialect.

'Good,' I say. 'Tell him if he loses I'm giving you to the trooper.'

Iona looks appalled.

Almost as appalled as Shil, who stands beside her.

'Tell him it's tradition. He wins, you go free. He loses, you belong to the Wolf Brigade. They don't have female soldiers or medics. So I guess they'll just have to find some other use for you.'

'*Sir . . .*'

Shil shuts up when I glare at her.

Their trooper is looking more confident, his friends are looking happier and Ajac is obviously exhausted. His collection of wounds now includes a slash that reveals a glistening rack of ribs.

'Tell him,' I say.

Pushing her way to the front, Iona almost gets Ajac killed by reaching out to touch his shoulder. As he turns, the Wolf Brigade trooper slashes, and only Iona's scream shocks her cousin into ducking.

The Wolf Brigade jeer.

But it's at their own man for screwing up his attack. There are some sizeable bets being carried here, and the few who went heavy on Ajac at the beginning are starting to look worried.

In reply, Ajac asks only one question.

I know it's a question from the way Iona nods when she answers.

Looking at her, Ajac looks at me, then looks at his opponent and something changes in the boy's face. The question is, has that change come too late to save him? Now's when I discover whether I get a soldier or a corpse out of this fight.

Their man is stronger, uninjured and experienced.

But he's also a braggart. A small step up from a coward. I guess every regiment has at least one.

'Finish it,' a friend of his shouts.

Unless it's someone who simply has money riding on the fight.

'Yeah,' says Neen. 'Finish it.'

As the trooper steps in, Ajac jabs hard for the man's gut and almost lands his blow. Twisting aside, the trooper slashes at Ajac's face, and stumbles as his anxiety and the fury of Ajac's attack tip him off balance.

'*Do it*,' I order.

Ajac nods, draws back his arm.

He's on the point of striking when one of the friends objects. Sidekicking the back of Ajac's knee, he waits for our man to drop and then drives his boot into Ajac's face.

'Fuck this,' Neen says.

'*Sergeant.*'

Neen's hand freezes at my tone. And I watch him make

himself release his own knife. The Wolf watches also, from across the circle.

'Sir . . . ?'

'Ajac's fight.'

Spitting teeth, Ajac gets to his knees.

His face is pulped, and he's having trouble breathing through the blood that must run down the back of his throat. His original opponent decides the result is a foregone conclusion. Wrapping his fingers into Ajac's hair, he drags back his head and slashes.

Iona screams and the crowd gasp.

When the trooper steps back to take a bow, he thinks it's over. It's not, because Ajac caught the blow across his palm. As we watch, he jacks his knife sideways into the man's leg.

'Twist,' Neen yells.

Ajac does, viciously.

And with the man frozen in agony, he rips free his blade and rams it into the trooper's groin, twisting hard. The man screams like a castrated pig, falling as Ajac rips his knife free one final time and crawls up the man's shuddering body to drive it into his throat.

A knife's point beats edge every time.

The trooper dies within seconds and is buried by his oppos, who dig through rocky dirt to their own depth, then stand to attention in the blazing sun to say the soldier's prayer for a man who lost them money and standing.

I make the Aux join in, Ajac included.

No one in the burial detail blames him for what happened. There isn't a Wolf Brigade trooper who wouldn't have done the same.

The real surprise is that Ajac can stand, function and say the prayer. He can do this because Sergeant Toro turned up with

307

five gold coins from General Luc, and a wizened major who turned out to be the Wolf's own doctor.

A very good one too.

Having sewn Ajac's ribs, hand and hip, and bent the boy's nose into shape, he staples it at the bridge, before washing the teeth we collect in milk, coating them with protein coagulant and pushing them back into Ajac's gums.

Then he gives the boy three jabs of battlefield morphine and tells him not to pick any more fights for a few days.

As we ride out, the Wolf tells the innkeeper not to cut down the trooper who tripped Ajac until he is dead. General Luc is very clear about what will happen if this order is disobeyed.

He leaves the trooper crucified to the tavern door.

Chapter 44

WE MAKE CAMP THAT NIGHT IN THE PLACE WHERE LEONA, Anton and I first met Senator Cos, and I smoked a cigarillo with the Wolf's sergeant.

Sergeant Toro is still around.

Who do you think just gave me another bottle of cane spirit?

Mary, the girl from the inn, takes one look at the convoy that rides into her village and decides she doesn't know me.

'Wise decision,' the SIG says.

'How do you—?'

'Fight, flight or fuck.' The gun sighs. 'You're pretty basic. I could run you through the body chemistry, biological triggers and neural responses. But I'd only end up explaining every other word.'

'Biological what?'

'Your brain went, *pretty*. Your dick went, *again* . . .' The SIG stops, thinks. 'Actually, it was the other way round.' My gun hasn't forgiven me using its holster to store alcohol, but can't resist being snotty.

If Mary has any sense, and she has, she'll keep her head down and her opinions to herself and wait for us to roll out of here tomorrow. Then she can come up with a better plan for escaping. One that doesn't involve me.

'You'll be all right, Sven?'

'Yes, sir.'

'Good.' Colonel Vijay tries to smile. 'Earlier, when you asked . . . I appreciate your concern, Sven. And I know we'll all be happier when this is over.'

That's his own death he's talking about.

'Sir . . .'

He turns back, finds his smile. 'Have a good evening, Sven. I'll see you in the morning.'

As is the way in the wastes, the temperature plummets the moment the sun sinks behind the horizon. Iona asks why it's so cold here when night in Farlight is hot and humid.

Taking this as an excuse to wrap his arm round her, my sergeant invents a theory to do with the city's volcano trapping clouds. He does this between taking his turn at the cane spirit and cupping the underside of Iona's breast when he thinks we won't notice.

His sister opens her mouth to object.

And I interrupt her to talk the Aux through how things stand between the Wolf and Colonel Vijay. Although they hear about General Luc's visit to Wildeside for the first time, it's only when I mention Aptitude that Shil and Rachel start looking at each other.

The colonel dines with General Luc at the inn, while we sit round our fire, draining the bottle and watching sparks fly into a moonlit sky. The sparks should remind us of what happened last night, all those burning houses and looted shops, but they don't. They simply look like sparks disappearing into the darkness.

Neen's twenty, Iona's eighteen.

They've been together less than six months.

Their lust is understandable, although Shil doesn't look at it that way. She's ten years older than her brother. Old enough to remember the dirt poor, Uplifted planet on which she was born, and the punishments the Enlightened inflicted on girls who let men get too close.

'Neen,' I say. 'Check the perimeter.'

Scrambling to his feet, he disappears into the night.

I don't mind members of the Aux fucking. Battle can take you like that. Actually, anything can take you like that. Battle, loneliness, alcohol, just the sheer bloody number of miles from home. But I'm not having it cause problems.

'All quiet, sir.'

Neen has the sense to sit opposite Iona this time.

It should be all quiet. At least, quiet in the sense no one's likely to attack. We've got five hundred Wolf Brigade camped around us. I'm more concerned with General Luc's people listening in.

'So the Wolf says he's going to kill Colonel Vijay?'

Iona sounds puzzled.

'He'll do it too,' Rachel says.

'Then why doesn't the colonel run away?'

A chorus tells Iona that the Death's Head don't run.

'Escape then,' she says. 'Withdraw.'

You can tell she doesn't know the difference.

'Because,' I say, 'he's given his surrender to General Luc. He would have to take it back. And then the general would know he was planning to escape.'

'That's stupid,' Iona says.

Neen's torn between agreeing and telling her why it isn't true. He sees me watching and bites his lip. He still looks like a farm boy half a spiral from home. Pushing hair out of his eyes, he says, 'The colonel's high clan. They have their own rules.'

'And those rules bind us?'

It's the first sensible question I've heard Iona ask, ever.

The fact she's Neen's lover isn't enough to earn her a place here. She travels with us because her safety was the price put on me by a tribal woman who nursed me back to life after I'd taken more damage than my body could handle.

Iona will never make a soldier.

She's built for bars and bedrooms, children and gardens full of flowers. Some women are. So are some men. Iona never makes any secret of what she wants from life. What she hopes Neen will eventually give her.

All the same . . .

'They bind the colonel,' I say.

Something in my tone makes Shil glance my way.

Without a word, she clambers up and removes the cane-spirit bottle that has found its way into my hands again. What's more, I let her. A few minutes later she reappears with a mug of coffee. It's hot, bitter and black.

Chapter 45

EACH MILE TAKES COLONEL VIJAY CLOSER TO HIS DEATH.
Although he knows this, he's far too polite to make a fuss about
the fact. Instead, he shrivels inside himself, becoming paler and
more upright with every rut and pothole that vanishes under
our wheels.

Makes me want to slap him.

We've been climbing all day, in serious heat, towards distant
mountains. These aren't the high plains that spread around us
in a grey mess of gravel, broken walls and half-fossilized tree
stumps, these are the wastes.

The high plains are beyond the pass.

Bocage, not wastes. These were orchards once.

When did I start thinking shit like that? Meeting Leona fucked
with my head. Fucked with it far worse than killing her did. Even
the SIG-37 knows it. My gun's keeping quiet around me.

'Why?'

'To give you time.'

'To do what?'

'If you knew that,' it says, 'you wouldn't need more time,
would you?'

Even threatening to toss it under the wheels of my combat trike and keep going doesn't produce a better answer.

This looks like a retreat. Only General Luc didn't lose a battle, so it has to be a power play. But surely his position would be stronger if he remained in Farlight, or brought his troops from their barracks into the city centre, rather than moving them out altogether?

We're back to the long game.

Tapping the brakes on my fat-wheel, I wait for Shil to slide alongside. She's surprised I'm out of formation. Not least because I told her anyone fucking up formation would be shot.

'Sir?' she says.

I open my visor.

Takes her a moment to do the same.

'Do you play chess?'

She looks at me. Wondering if it's a trick question.

'Well, Corporal?'

'Yes, sir,' she admits.

'Good,' I tell her. 'I need you to teach me.' She's about to flip down her lid when I shake my head. Haven't finished yet.

'Sir?'

'I should warn you. My old lieutenant tried and failed.'

The Aux, and for all I know, the entire Wolf Brigade, hear her swear over the comms channel. Luckily none of them knows what about.

That night Ajac carves me a chess set. He does it swiftly, from chunks of cork hacked from a dead tree on the edge of a village where we stop. When he's done I don't recognize any of the pieces.

That doesn't surprise me.

But Shil doesn't either. So she gets Ajac to cut her a new set, and tells him how she wants each piece to look. Ajac does it without complaint. His cousin and my sergeant use the diversion to disappear into the darkness. Iona and Neen think Shil won't notice. They're wrong. She does.

'Let it go,' I tell her.

'That's easy for you to say.' Seeing my scowl, she adds, 'Sir . . .'

'No. It's not. He's my sergeant. Until she proves herself, she's just a camp follower who almost got one of my men killed. I don't carry dead wood on campaign.'

'Is that what this is, sir?'

Good question.

'Can't see what else it is,' I say finally.

When Neen and Iona return, Shil goes to talk to them. I'm not sure what she says but Iona scurries off. When she comes back it's with a basin so I can shave. And she offers to mend the rips in my uniform.

God knows where she stole the water.

Shil watches impassively as Iona wastes half our thread tacking a piece of cloth under a hole in my shirt the size of my fist.

'That's better,' Shil says.

Later, Iona brings me food. It's chilli stew (meat undefined). Biscuits, dry (two). Cheese, processed (not yet mouldy) and chocolate pudding in a tin that heats itself when I rip the lid. For all I know the stew heats the same way, but she prepared that for me.

The pudding tastes like glue.

That's fine. I like army rations. And I know Colonel Vijay gave us a little talk about eating with the Wolf Brigade. But one thing at a time. We're still finding his bit about not killing them hard enough.

'Sir,' Rachel says.

I look up. So do the others. Rachel's not given to starting conversations on her own.

'What does General Luc gain from cutting out the colonel's heart?'

She has a part-stripped Z93z long-range rifle in front of her.

She's already cleaned its scope and laser sights. And the 8.59-calibre floating barrel lies on an oiled sheet, momentarily forgotten.

As said, snipers are high maintenance.

If a target's out there Rachel can kill it, moving or not, distance no object. In everything else she's a mare. A sullen, slightly podgy one who hides behind a curtain of red hair. Lash marks for abandoning her position scar her shoulders. And an Obsidian Cross second class hangs on her dog-tag chain for saving our lives.

Being her, both incidents took place at the same time.

'Rachel?'

'You say he plans to marry Aptitude. So why would he kill Colonel Vijay?'

Why would he . . . ?

What kind of question is that? This is the man who . . .

It's a long and bloody list. Dead babies, crucified women, impaled officers, and spies hung with their own guts or returned to their own side with their noses slit, ears cropped and balls stuffed into their mouths and their lips sewn tight.

The general, our general, used cruelty as an art.

The Wolf is cruel by nature. The difference between Generals Jaxx and Luc couldn't be greater. If the Wolf says he'll serve Colonel Vijay's heart on a plate to Aptitude why should I doubt it?

I wouldn't put it past him to cook it first.

'Sir,' Rachel says. 'Don't think you're right.'

The Aux go silent. Neen glances at Shil, then looks away. I could have Rachel whipped for insubordination and that would make twice in a year. As it is, I'm seriously considering having Neen flog Iona for what happened earlier today.

'Want to tell me why?'

Rachel bites her lip. She's not good at judging what she's allowed to say. All she knows is she's said too much already, and she only knows that because the others have gone silent.

'Aptitude would hate him if he did.'

I open my mouth to call her a fool and shut it again.

Maybe she's right? Perhaps General Luc doesn't want Aptitude the way men usually want women? If he did, he'd simply marry her, rape her and burn Wildeside down around her head if she dared whine.

Have to say, that's what I thought he had in mind.

'Shil. What do you think?'

She hesitates. Makes me wonder if Rachel's mentioned this before.

'Well?'

'It's a good threat, sir. But I'm not sure he'll go through with it. Not unless the colonel refuses to give Aptitude up. The Wolf might *want* to. But he'll need things to be right with Aptitude and her parents.'

Shil's showing a touching faith in the Wolf's nature.

'Vijay gives up Aptitude in return for his life?'

She nods.

'What if Colonel Vijay would rather die?'

From the look on her face, Shil wants to say he won't be that stupid. Only he will. Vijay Jaxx is dumb enough to die for love.

'Sir,' Iona says.

'*What?*'

Maybe I say it too roughly, because she bites her lip.

'It's just, General Luc reminds me of Milo. You remember . . .'

Yeah, I remember. Although it's a stretch to compare the head man of a village on a ring world with the commander of one of the most feared regiments ever to exist.

'They called him the Fox.'

And we call Luc the Wolf. OK, she's got an animal thing going. All the same . . . I glance round, seeing faces edged by firelight. It should soften our features but all it does is harden them. We're good, I remind myself. Anybody who survives what we've survived has to be good.

'Where's this going?' I ask Iona.

Looking up, she meets my gaze. Her eyes are huge and seem different in the dark. As if an owl watches me through her eye sockets. Static travels my spine and I shiver, despite myself.

'He won't offer Colonel Vijay his life, sir. Not for giving up Aptitude. He's too cunning. He'll offer her his life for rejecting him.'

I want to check I understood that.

'He'll spare Colonel Vijay? But only if Aptitude renounces him? And agrees to marry General Luc instead?'

All three women nod.

Chapter 46

AS THE STARS GET CLEARER AND THE SKY DARKER, THE NIGHT gets colder and colder, until everyone huddles inside their combat jackets or sleeps under the engines of trucks and scout cars that are too cool to make any difference.

The sappers have built slit latrines at the village's edge. But I've told Shil, Rachel and Iona to make their own arrangements and not stray beyond the glow of our fire. No point taking chances after what happened earlier.

General Luc and his staff occupy an inn.

Its main door is bolted against the wind. All of its shutters are closed and locked, but they still bang endlessly, like boys hammering on fences. Noisy, smoky and crowded; I know where I'd rather be.

'Yeah,' my gun says. 'We know. You'd rather be cold.'

I'm sat by myself, watching stars.

The brushwood Neen stole, and the dried dung he had the others collect, has burnt to a white ash that dusts sullen embers like sugar on one of those sticky pastries you can buy in Zabo Square.

'Behind you,' the SIG says.

If it was anyone dangerous, it would have warned me before this.

'What are you thinking?' asks a voice.

You'd think women would get bored with that question. They never do. At least not the ones I meet. Shil sits herself down uninvited, and puts her back to the wall that's protecting me from the worst of the wind. Takes me a while to realize she hopes for an answer. I thought she was just making conversation.

'About the stalls in Zabo Square. The ones that sell pastries.'

She smiles. Not sure why.

'Can I ask you a question, sir?'

'You can ask . . .'

Shil hesitates. That's how I know I'm not going to like it.

'Were you and Sergeant Leona lovers?'

'*Shil.*'

'Were you, sir?'

She's waiting for my answer.

First Rachel's insolence. Now Shil's question. I'm not sure what's got into everyone tonight. I could tell her to fuck off, which wouldn't be the first time. Or I could give her sentry duty for the rest of the night, which would send the same message, but something stops me . . .

'No,' I say. 'We weren't.'

She closes her eyes. 'I'm not sure if that makes it better or worse,' she mutters. I'm not supposed to hear that bit. When I shift to stop her hip pressing against mine, she looks hurt.

'You cold?' I ask.

'Sven—' Shil catches herself. 'I mean, sir. What do you think?'

'Me? I think you probably shouldn't squat to piss in case your bits stick to the ground.'

Her laugh is rough. 'Guess you're never going to change.'

I wasn't aware I needed to.

320

'Shil,' I say. 'Listen . . .'

My idea that your first kill is harder than the second, and your second is harder than the third sounds strange when I say it aloud. Particularly when I get to the bit about how it starts getting hard again.

'What's that for?' I ask. She definitely shouldn't be holding my face in her hands. Her mouth tastes of salt, stew, chocolate pudding and alcohol. When I sit back, she smiles and then sighs.

'I miss the desert . . .' Not sure what makes me say it.

The alcohol, probably.

Shil shakes her head. 'What you miss,' she says, 'is the simplicity.'

I stare at her.

'*Sir*,' she adds.

That's not why I'm staring.

I'm staring because she's right. And, then again, she's wrong.

I *do* miss the silence and the simplicity. Doesn't mean I want to go back to who I was then or how I was living. I'm just not sure I want to replace it with where I am now. My shock is not that I realize this.

It is understanding I have a choice.

'Sir,' Shil says. 'We're going to die, aren't we?'

'Yeah,' I say.

Her eyes widen. Maybe she expects me to say no.

'Shil,' I say, 'everyone dies. Unless you're U/Free. And even those bastards must die eventually. That's why we hope for a better life next time.'

'You believe that?'

I look at her. 'You mean some people don't?'

Her eyes are wet. Usually, where Shil's concerned, that's anger. Not this time. 'Sven,' she says, 'I don't mean in fifteen years, or ten, or five. I don't even mean next year. I mean, do we die tomorrow? If not tomorrow, next week?'

'Would it matter?'

'Yes,' she says. 'It would.'

So I wait for her to tell me why.

'I don't believe we come back,' she says. 'We're born naked, wet and hungry. Then things get worse. Then it stops.' She touches the medallion at her neck. I see her fingers make the shape for Legba Uploaded. Her lips move to the familiar words.

'I try to believe,' she tells me. 'God knows.'

That's the saddest thing I've heard. Taking her face between my hands, I turn her so I can see her eyes in the moonlight. They're huge, and tracks cut the dirt on her cheek. The air is so cold her tears steam as they fall.

'Believe me,' I say. 'This isn't everything.'

'How do you know?'

'Because . . .' How do I explain touching the mind of an AI?

'They're machines,' Shil says.

'Maybe once. But if Hekati thinks there's more than this . . .'

'Machine heaven,' says Shil sourly, but she's smiling as she turns her face towards me. Her kiss is clumsy, but enthusiastic. So I drop my fingers from her face and cup the breast barely discernible beneath her uniform. When she shifts, I start to say sorry, but she simply pops open a storm flap at her neck and tugs a zip behind. When my hand still won't fit, she tugs again.

'Fuck,' she says. 'That's cold.'

Her singlet is warm under my fingers.

Closing her jacket as best she can, she wraps both arms tight round my neck. Our next kiss is deep. As my fingers grip a breast, she winces. So I stroke my fingers across a nipple instead.

'Thought you were going to die,' she says. 'That night in Ilseville.'

'So did I.'

The cracked bones mended within a week, and the pain went within a month. All that remains now is scarring to remind me that my heart was once visible through a hole in my chest.

Knife wounds you stitch.

But bullet wounds are different, because stitching those can kill. Some need air and others maggots. So medics pack broken flesh with sterile bandages, if they have any, and hope unpacking them doesn't finish what the enemy started.

But that wound in Ilseville . . .

Shil tied me to a chair to hold me still while she cut away ruined flesh. Washed the wound with water and vinegar and kept me sedated with brandy. She smiles sourly when I remind her of this.

In the cold of the high plains, with a freezing wind at our backs, and only a broken wall to protect us, our fire burnt down to embers, and the stars clear above us, with the Aux talking in the darkness or sleeping, and five hundred Wolf Brigade camped around us, we unfasten zips, undo buckles and free Velcro straps.

Fuck knows, it's taken us long enough.

Her body is whipcord thin, her breasts as slight as I remember from seeing her strip once. Give me two twigs and I could beat out a march on her ribs. We're not naked, because the cold would kill us before we could dress again. Colonel Vijay might consider being found frozen in his lover's arms romantic, but I'm not the colonel, and Shil is not my lover; although she opens her thighs readily enough as I slide my hand into her combats.

'You don't mind?' she asks.

Body hair crinkles beneath my fingers. 'About what?'

'Oh,' Shil says. 'Franc didn't—'

My other hand stills her lips.

Yes, I know, Franc shaved her whole body with the edge of a knife, every day, and wore her scars like badges of honour. When the U/Free removed her scars, they took away her reason to live. So she died for us. Because dying was the only thing she could do to make sense of being alive.

Shil listens in silence as I say this. Then she reaches up and hooks her fingers around the back of my neck.

We kiss again, because that's polite.

Kiss first, take the weight on your elbows, make conversation afterwards, and leave the money discreetly on the table before you go. That last bit of my old lieutenant's rules doesn't apply, obviously.

At least I hope not.

Rolling Shil to face the wall, I curl myself behind her and reach round to cup my fingers over her breast.

'Ready?'

She gasps when I enter.

So I pull back. A part of me wants to grip her hips and bury myself. A bigger part knows I should behave.

'Fuck,' Shil says at last. 'I thought she was joking.'

It hadn't occurred to me Franc talked about us. Not that there was much *us* where Franc was concerned. The only person she loved was Haze, my intelligence officer. And that was sexless.

We lie still for a few seconds as Shil's body adjusts, and we feed on each other's warmth. And then she reaches for my fingers and takes my hand from her breast and pushes it between her legs, locking her thighs tightly.

'Slowly,' she whispers.

Sliding myself out, I roll Shil over and kiss her forehead. Reaching up, she grips my neck and kisses my mouth. If I didn't know better, I'd think she was saying goodbye.

'Whatever happens,' she says.

'Whatever happens?'

'I've had you . . .' She grins. Has to be my expression, because I can't think what else would make her grin like that. 'You realize,' she says, 'you're a bastard?'

She asks if I'm in love with Aptitude.

This is an improvement. The last time she asked about Aptitude she wanted to know if I'd fucked the kid. It's the same answer this time.

No, I'm not . . . No, I haven't . . . I don't intend to now or ever.

Around dawn, when it's light enough to see each other's eyes clearly, we fuck one final time. It's brief and awkward, as if she needs the darkness to be comfortable. 'Sven,' she says, when we're done.

'What?'

'If we live, I want out of the Aux.'

'That's what this was about?' My question is rough enough to make her scramble away from me, holding her jacket closed, while she fumbles at the zip of her combats with her other hand.

'Of course that's not—'

'Not going to happen,' I say, adding, 'What about Neen? He want out too?'

'Neen makes his own decisions.' This is the Shil I recognize, although it turns out her anger isn't with me. At least, not entirely.

'I thought Iona was your problem?'

'She doesn't help,' Shil replies, still waiting for my answer.

'Shil. Conscripts don't resign.'

Her mouth sets in misery.

'You could fix it.'

'But I'm not going to. Only you and Neen remain of the originals.'

'And Rachel,' she says.

'No,' I shake my head. 'Rachel joined after Ilseville fell.'

Shil thinks about that. Eighteen out of twenty-five died within minutes of hitting the ground. Six out of seven made it through the first skirmish. Haze is off-planet, the others died later. Only two of her troop remain.

I know exactly how she feels.

Me, I'm one out of five hundred. Because that's how many we were before the ferox attacked Fort Libidad. Everyone has a story and most of them are grim. That's why we get drunk to remember, and drunker still to forget.

I grip Shil's shoulders and she's not expecting that. She fights briefly and then folds herself into me. I don't have to look to know she's crying.

'You're still a bastard,' says a voice at my side.

Chapter 47

THE SCOUT CAR AHEAD CHANGES GEAR AS THE ROAD STARTS to rise towards its distant pass through the mountains. Slopes stretch both sides as far as we can see. Well, as far as Rachel can see and that's further than most. Even using field-glasses, I can't make out where the heat haze ends and the sky begins.

Buzzards circle us.

They've been following for three days. They can't believe a convoy this big doesn't leave them a trail of dead. Rachel says they'll come through the pass. Ajac says not, he's seen birds like this before. They'll turn back. Ajac and Rachel ride side by side, their visors flipped up and their words whipped away by the hot wind.

Neen and Iona's communication is strictly non-verbal.

They clutch hands occasionally, making their combat trikes wobble until tiny gyros kick in to stabilize them. You shouldn't need gyros on a fat-wheel, my gun tells me crossly.

It's in a foul mood.

Not the only one. Neen and Shil aren't talking. And Iona spends most of the morning giving Neen sympathetic glances.

Occasionally she stops to glare at Shil, when she thinks we're not looking.

Colonel Vijay is oblivious to it all.

I'd be so lucky.

As the scout cars pull ahead, and the incline increases, and the transporters fall back behind us, we're left on our own in a little huddle. Six Aux and the colonel, on combat trikes, each of us in a uniform so dusty it needs no camouflage.

Even our outriders have scattered.

Sergeant Toro is hunting goat for General Luc's supper. His corporal is thirty minutes back helping a trooper who shredded his tyre. Not sure where the final one is. Out of our sight somewhere.

We'll never get another chance this good.

Neen sees me loosen the flap on my holster. We haven't discussed this, because you don't discuss mutiny. You act and live or die with the consequences. Tapping the SIG-37 awake, I tell it to keep quiet.

'Fucking great,' it says. 'You're about to do something stupid.'

'I'm saving Colonel Vijay's life.'

'What I said.'

For once I wish the SIG was less lethal. 'Neen,' I say, 'what rounds are you carrying?'

A Kemzin is strapped to his back. At the hip, he has a simple Colt automatic. Almost no brains and zero attitude. 'Seven six two, sir. Full metal.'

'Cut a cross in the top?'

That's illegal but everyone does it.

'No, sir,' he says. 'Uncircumcised.'

Seeing my surprise, Neen says he took the side arm from a militia officer in Farlight. An amateur, obviously.

'Right,' I say. 'We'll swap.'

Neen looks at the SIG, and nearly runs himself off the road. Only instinct and gyros save him. 'Sir?' he says.

'He'll want me back,' the SIG says.

'Don't count on it.'

Taking my weapon, Neen slides it into his jacket for safety, while he flips up his own holster flap and hands me his automatic. Only then does he put the SIG-37 in his own holster. He checks three times it's fastened safely.

'Scan for comms traffic,' I tell the SIG.

It takes so long to answer I think it didn't hear, but it's sulking. 'No traffic,' it says, which surprises me.

'Check again.'

The SIG does. It was right first time.

'Cover me,' I tell Neen.

He wants to ask, *from what?*

Seeing us, the colonel nods, then forces a polite smile.

Shil appears on his other side. A fact that darkens Neen's face, as swiftly as it wipes the smile from Colonel Vijay's own. She positions herself well. A little back from the colonel, but close enough to stop him making a run for it.

'Sir,' I say, 'I'm taking over.'

'Mutiny is a capital offence, Sven.'

'Not mutiny, sir. A temporary redesignation of command.'

His mouth twists, and he looks almost impressed. 'And you're going to shoot me if I refuse to accept this redesignation?'

'Yes, sir.' I have Neen's gun aimed at his heart.

'No, you're not,' he says. 'I've read your file. You're clinically incapable of killing your CO.'

Dropping my hand, I re-sight on his upper leg.

A leg wound can kill, but only if you're unlucky. As I switch my aim, the colonel realizes I'm holding an ordinary weapon. It's this, more than anything else, which convinces him I mean it.

'Sven,' he says. 'Wait.'

'Colonel, I'm taking control.'

'On what grounds?' His voice is calm.

'Grief makes you unable to command, sir.'

'Temporarily unfit,' Shil says, supplying the term I want. Neen glares at his sister and then glances at me. He decides we've discussed this already, without him knowing. He's wrong. She just learns fast.

'Grief at what?' Colonel Vijay demands.

'The death of your father, sir. The massacre of doubters. The arson that destroyed your family home. The Thomassi's coup. The call on officers of the Third Death's Head to surrender. Our capture by General Luc . . .'

It is quite a list.

'I see,' he says. 'And this grief manifests how?'

Takes me a moment to work out what he's asking. Ahead of us the scout cars increase their lead, while a drone overhead drifts to one side. I can barely see the transporters that should bring up our rear.

'Refusal to escape, sir.'

He nods, as if expecting no less.

'Every officer's duty,' I remind him. 'Kill your captors and escape. In certain circumstances, to be judged by a later court martial, simply escaping may be enough to wipe out the disgrace of being captured in the first place.'

'Sven, General Luc is not the enemy.'

'Well, he's not a friend, sir. We should be fighting the Thomassi. The rules state—'

'I know the rules.'

'Yes, sir. I don't doubt it.'

'My father wrote most of them.'

Looking from me to Neen and across at Shil, Colonel Vijay checks how far back the rest of us are in his mirrors. Then he nods to the gun in my hand. 'You're going through with this,' he says. 'Aren't you?'

'Yes, sir.'

'And you'll give me back my command. Knowing I'll have you court martialled and shot for mutiny?'

'Yes, sir.'

Colonel Vijay buries his face in one hand.

We ride in silence, the colonel's trike bracketed by mine on one side and Shil's on the other. Neen rides to the left of me, keeping a slight distance. The others keep their positions, still wondering what's going on.

'Your NCOs didn't know about this, did they?'

'No, sir. They didn't.'

'Of course not. Otherwise they'd be liable for mutiny.' Colonel Vijay's lips twist. 'Sven,' he says, 'take a look around you.'

In that moment, he sounds exactly like his father.

'I have, sir.'

'Take another.'

Scout cars up ahead, transporters and trucks way behind. An incline of rock, grit and gravel on both sides, rising to that mountain pass ahead. We're in the middle of goddam nowhere. Even the buzzards are beginning to turn back in disgust.

'What do you see?' the colonel demands.

'Nothing, sir.'

'Exactly,' he says. 'You see nothing.'

Neen and Shil scan the slopes, wondering what they're missing.

'It's a trap, Sven,' Colonel Vijay says. 'The moment we make a break, those outriders will reappear. The Wolf's probably got snipers on that mound.'

He jerks his chin to a low hill ahead of us.

'And those scout cars? They'll birth extra trikes the moment they're needed.' Colonel Vijay sounds apologetic for stating the obvious. 'Sven,' he says, 'they want us to run.'

'Sir,' says Neen, 'It's not—'

He doesn't get to finish, although Colonel Vijay's glance is almost kind. 'Sergeant,' he says, 'I'm not going to get myself shot while escaping. Certainly not so General Luc can keep a clear conscience.'

He raises his eyebrows.

'Assuming it is clear, of course.'

Personally, I doubt the Wolf has a conscience at all, clear or otherwise.

'Since he's going to kill me,' Colonel Vijay adds, 'I might as well make him go through the pretence of due process.'

Nodding politely, he edges his bike forwards and, after a second, I fall back to return Neen's side arm.

'You know,' the SIG says, 'I'm not sure chess is your thing.'

That night, after we've made camp on the far side of the pass, Colonel Vijay excuses himself from the Wolf's company and joins us round our fire.

He smokes a cheap cigar with Neen, takes a swig from Shil's brandy and tries not to choke on either. He even shares our rations. And if he pays a little too much attention to Iona's breasts and gets slightly drunker on three swigs from a bottle than is decent, that's fine. We've all been there at his age.

Although Ajac still is.

And Neen's only a year or two more.

You'd think, given the death of his father and the fate await-ing him, that Vijay Jaxx would look older. Not a bit of it. He still looks what he is: a well-brought-up late teen, with floppy hair and a tiny beard so blond it's almost invisible.

After supper, he excuses himself politely.

He sounds apologetic when he says he needs to return to General Luc. As if he regrets being forced to leave our cheap cigars and cheaper brandy and outdated rations for real food and a requisitioned hunting lodge.

Maybe he does.

Even the best meals taste sour when you're prisoner.

'Who takes first watch, sir?'

Neen looks surprised when I say no one. No watches and no pickets, Colonel Vijay's orders. We're under the protection of the Wolf Brigade. I hope he finds the words as hard to say as I do to hear.

'I'm not tired, sir,' Neen says.

'You want to walk our perimeter, that's fine. Wake me if you get bored.'

He salutes, collects his Kemzin and takes himself out to the edge of our fire, while I settle myself in the shelter of a rock that rises like broken bone from the slope we're descending, with the others round me in a sprawl. Our fire burns to ashes faster than we'd like and, come morning, our uniforms are frozen so hard they creak when we move.

I sleep in my boots. We all do.

Our rations might taste vile, but they're still better than any I ate in the Legion. These merely taste bad, those were some-times poisonous. I've known fifteen-year-old pressed meat slaughter more than a full-on tribal attack.

Telling the Aux to quit whining, I flick my trike to life and wait for my team to saddle up. We edge through a sprawl of Wolf Brigade troopers folding their camp and pulling faces at their own rations.

We're the first to the road. So we wait, as we did yesterday.

It's worth being early to see General Luc's scowl when he finds us drawn up in order, waiting for his men to sort them-selves out. Unless he knows how close we came to falling into his trap and scowls because we pulled back before it snapped shut.

We are half a day from his lair. A small castle perched on the top of a basalt mountain a hundred miles from the rift. The walls are cut from the mountain's rock, making them almost invisible.

Or so I've been told. Few visit it willingly.

'Mount up,' Sergeant Toro tells his outriders.

From the tightness of his voice, the Wolf's had words about being late on parade. The glare Sergeant Toro shoots me is blasphemous. So I grin back and that upsets him even worse.

His men ride us tight for the rest of the morning. So maybe he's also upset we didn't fall into yesterday's trap. We respond by pretending they don't exist. And the sergeant doesn't like that much either.

We stop once, an hour before noon.

There are usually two stops a day. One before the sun reaches its highest. Another an hour before sunset begins. That means we ride through the heat of the day. General Luc probably has his reasons. Not sure what they are, mind you.

'Sorry,' the sergeant says. 'Not enough to go round.'

We're not allowed to join the others filling their camelbacks and bottles from the water truck. So I tell Sergeant Toro he's a dumb fuck, and I can't believe General Luc is stupid enough to think we'd fall for a trap. Just how fucking dumb do they think we are?

He doesn't know. How fucking dumb are we?

Not as dumb as a bunch of bastards who've never fought a real battle in their lives and run at the first sign of danger. Thought that would hit a nerve. Sergeant Toro doesn't know why we're retreating either.

If I wasn't an officer, he tells me.

So I say not to let that worry him, because I never have. 'Behind that,' I suggest, nodding at the truck. 'Who's going to know?'

He looks tempted. 'And the injuries?'

'You can tell them you fell over.'

His laugh is harsh. 'And what will you say?'

'I saw you trip.'

Chapter 48

'KEEP YOUR WITS ABOUT YOU,' I TELL THE AUX. 'ONLY ATTACK IF I give the order.'

'That was a joke, all right?' Colonel Vijay's voice sounds tired. 'For anyone listening over the comms system: that was a joke.'

He brings his trike alongside for a quiet word.

The Wolf's Lair hugs the top of a peak that has been flattened to take it. There's one road, which crawls round the mountain in a slowly rising spiral, cut into the living rock. This forms the only way in.

High walls, looking down on the spiral, mean every step of the approach can be targeted from the ramparts. The black rock into which the spiral is cut is studded with steel doors for its final twist, which must be vast to be visible from here.

'It's hollow,' I tell Neen.

He nods. 'Yes, sir.'

Maybe Colonel Vijay told him that, as well.

My guess is one of the earlier COs decided he needed more space, so had the rock beneath his base quarried to provide it.

The quarrying will be deep and the rock strong. This is not an easy place to capture.

As General Luc approaches the castle, a steel door slowly opens and his vehicle disappears, presumably inside. We're two spirals below, with twenty scout cars ahead, each one leaving a safe distance, in case of mines . . .

Although I'd like to see someone dig this road.

As we finish our second loop around the mountain, the faces around me tighten. Neen looks determined, Shil resigned. Rachel is reciting a table of distances, wind speeds and deflection settings, her default position in times of stress. Ajac is doing his best to look like Neen.

Iona simply looks scared.

'Being scanned,' the SIG says. It shivers as it handshakes the castle's security settings. No idea what it tells it. That it's General Luc's new housekeeper, probably. 'Sven,' it says, a moment later, 'I think you should . . .'

Yeah, I know I should.

This is the bit I always hate.

The kyp in my throat leaps as I swallow the information the SIG is feeding me. There's a taste of static, and my combat trike lurches as a spasm locks my muscles. But it's fleeting and the gyros kick in anyway.

'You OK?' Shil asks. 'Sir?'

'Yeah. Just busy.'

Floor plans blossom inside my head. The hidden part of the castle is vast. There are dormitories for a thousand Wolf Brigade, and enough weapons for twice that number. Real weapons: pulse rifles and missile launchers, grenades and smart bombs. The armoury, fifteen floors below, is lined with mesh behind ceramic plate. It holds more ammunition than I've ever seen in one place.

The Wolf is ready for war.

That's interesting. General Jaxx had an intelligence service

336

second to none. So how come he didn't know? Unless the Wolf's naturally suspicious, and his suspicions are accidentally right.

'Paranoid,' says a voice.

'*What?*'

Neen looks across, sees my expression and glances away. Most of this conversation is inside my head anyway. So, as far as he's concerned, I'm just talking to myself.

All the same, I'm not sure I knew I'd said that aloud.

'That's the word you're looking for. Paranoid. *Displaying an extreme or unnatural distrust of others.* A character trait often found in senior officers. Well, in mine . . .'

'OctoV?'

'He's dead. She's dead. Doesn't make much difference.'

'So who are you?'

'A ghost.'

'Oh Sven. Can I stroke your gun, please?' The SIG-37's impression of Leona's voice is good enough to startle me.

'Little bitch.'

'My feelings exactly.'

We're approaching the last of the spiral, which means an open door blocks our way. Its hinges are larger than me, and now it's open, its outer edge extends over the drop, making it impossible to ride round. A steel iris in the rock reveals a tunnel, with luminescent strip lights and gun encampments every hundred paces.

Close the iris to lock off that tunnel, and open the steel door, and you halt your enemy in his tracks. General Luc may be paranoid but he has good defences.

The cavern into which we're led could hold Farlight cathedral. Maybe not its clock tower, but the main bit. And it has the same churchlike lighting and high ceilings. Even the grey walls rise in the same way.

'You OK, sir?' Shil asks.

I'm touching stone for luck without even realizing.

'Yeah,' I say. 'Never better.'

She scowls.

So obviously I grin.

And that's how General Luc finds me a few seconds later, as he filters between scout cars, ignoring the salutes of those around him. 'You,' he says. 'What happened to your lip?'

'Fell over, sir.'

He scowls. 'So did Sergeant Toro.'

'Really, sir?'

The Wolf's scowl deepens. 'Be glad I need you . . . This is your chance,' he adds. 'Don't waste it.'

'To do what?'

'Impress me.' His tone says that should be obvious.

'Why the fuck would I bother, sir?' My gaze takes in his convoy of trucks and scurrying troops. 'You've got enough . . .' I look at Shil. 'What's the word?'

'Acolytes, sir?'

No idea what it means, but she's probably right.

Shades of grey camouflage my Icefeld. A fat tyre bites dirt to leave a trail of dust that must be visible miles away. A Wolf Brigade stencil decorates a fuel tank that's really an ammo box stuffed with cartridges for an 8-gauge pump-action shotgun slotted into the holster on my tank's right side.

Insects commit suicide so often I stop at the first village to scrape the screen clean. The village is broken and has only one bar. A man in the shoulder patch of a Wolf Brigade veteran looks up, sees my Icefeld through the closing door and decides to leave by a side exit. I guess his patch isn't real.

'Beer,' I demand.

The cane shot comes free.

I eat most of their spiced nuts, drink a second beer and piss against a rusting car out back, because that's what everyone else uses. The barkeep takes one look at the 5000 Octo note I slap down on the counter and his face goes white.

'Sir,' he says, 'I can't possibly . . .'

'Give me a rag and a bowl of water to wash my screen. Keep the change.'

He's grinning madly as the door swings behind me, so I guess the events in Farlight haven't reached this far from the city. A boy wanders over looking for a lift to the next ville. When I shake my head he shrugs.

Children stare as I leave.

Since ruins outnumber people and this place is on a road so obscure it appears only as dots on my nav pad, I'm not surprised. From the Wolf's Lair to Wildeside is not a ride people often make.

The general probably has some NCO logging every last piss and beer break. And I could make the trip faster, but I've been given a day to travel there, and another back and I'm not looking forward to arriving.

'One-fifty miles,' says the SIG.

A couple of hours at this rate. Maybe slightly less. Depends how many more stops I make. In my pocket is Vijay's memory crystal. The one containing the download from Morgan's data cores. Vijay is one step ahead of me. He knew where I was being sent, and wants the crystal delivered along with the Wolf's message, discreetly of course. You probably know what discreet means. I have to be reminded.

The next village is so small it has no bar at all.

It has a rusty bike, however, so old it's double-wheeled, one at the front and one at the back. The naked child who rides it forms his fingers into a pistol and shoots me as I pass. Maybe General Luc comes this way after all.

'Sven,' my gun says.

'Yeah, I know . . . Concentrate.'

The wheel spins in grit as my road disappears.

Since I can see it up ahead this has to be flood damage washing out the blacktop. We skid and slide, until I get bored with that. A long patch of grey scabs a slope to my right, so I gun the Icefeld. Traction when we hit rock powers the bike forward and I'm at a crazy angle, dodging a boulder, when my hip shivers.

'Sven,' my gun shouts. 'You want to kill yourself, just pull over and do it properly.'

Twelve-pot brakes squeal, and only the gyro keeps us level as my bike skids to a halt, leaving a strip of smoking rubber behind it. Clambering from the Icefeld, I undo my holster.

'Look,' the SIG says. 'Let's talk about this.'

A boulder explodes a hundred paces away. Splinters of rock buzz past my head like wasps. None hit, though. A second boulder explodes, then a third. When I run out of boulders I burn a thorn tree back to ash and then a bush.

'*Fuck, fuck, fuck.*'

Wisely, the SIG-37 keeps silent.

When I'm twelve and only just in the Legion I watch my lieutenant have a screaming fit. His CO, a boy half his age, has issued an order that gets twelve troopers killed. And though the CO would be within his rights to have Lieutenant Bonafont court martialled he does nothing.

Later, Lieutenant Bonafont tells me there's a knack to losing your temper. You do it at the right time and in the right company.

For me, the right time is now, and alone.

We make the rest of the trip in silence. Although the SIG relents on the way into Wildeside village. 'Roadblock,' it says. 'Danger seventy-eight per cent probable . . .'

That's high to me.

'Militia. Plus I've added a thirty per cent Sven fuck-up weighting.'

It hasn't relented that much.

One of the soldiers waves me down as the other raises a rifle to cover me. It's the old-model Kemzin with the short clip. He'd be more convincing if he remembered to jack the slide first.

'Get off your bike.'

I shake my head, although I flip up my visor.

'Debro around?'

Strangers on Wolf Brigade bikes don't call Senator Wildeside *Debro*.

At least, not in the world they occupy, which is about to change beyond all recognition. In the way of these things, it will probably look and sound and feel and taste the same to anybody not bothered by the difference.

Unfortunately, Debro and Aptitude aren't on that list.

'Farlight was sacked,' I tell them.

Mouths drop open. They stare at each other, wondering if I'm telling the truth. Wish I wasn't. There are few things I'd wish away in my life, but I'd wish away the last week, and pay ten years of what's left for the pleasure.

'The Uplifted?'

Silver-skulled and ruthless, riddled with tubes and the virus. Our traditional enemies. You know where you are with the Uplifted and Enlightened. They want to kill us and we want to kill them. Even the militia can get their heads round that.

'If only.'

Must be something in my voice.

'General Jaxx was killed on Senator Thomassi's orders. Half the city has been massacred. Men, women and children. Their houses burnt, their shops smashed, their warehouses ransacked. You will tell no one else.'

'But OctoV wouldn't—'

'The emperor is dead.'

Shock slackens their faces. Both know what I say is true. No man would dare say that if OctoV were still alive. It has never occurred to them, just as it never occurred to me, that he would not still be there after we are all dead.

The ghost in my gun is no more OctoV than Leona was.

They are avatars. Subsets. Encased memories. I wonder where those definitions come from and realize it's the kyp. Somewhere between the gun, the ghost and the kyp I'm floating in information.

'*Enough,*' I say.

Both NCOs think I'm talking to them.

Saluting, they step back and offer to escort me to meet Senator Wildeside.

The village is quiet, locked down with shutters tight and barred doors where bead curtains should be. An old woman sits on an upper balcony, resting a double-barrelled shotgun that is older than she is on her lap.

Her eyes follow me as I head for the square, riding no faster than the two militia corporals can walk. Up ahead is the arch to Debro's compound. Another two NCOs occupy an encampment in front of it, made from sandbags.

A belt-fed sits on a tripod behind its defensive wall. The machine gun is old but clean, with the breech locked down and the belt in position and correctly folded. The gunner has chained himself to the belt-fed by his ankle.

Been a while since I saw that.

The corporal on my right tells me why. 'Those creatures,' he says. 'We had an attack.'

'I thought they were dead?'

'So did we. This lot were alive.'

'How many?'

'Three.'

That's enough. Three furies can do damage.

'We were lucky,' he says. 'A man saw them coming. All the

same, they killed ten troopers, plus two families. All of them,' he adds. 'Even the children.'

'You did well to fight them off.'

My praise makes him braver. 'The Wolf Brigade,' he says finally. 'What do you guys want with us?'

'I'm not Wolf Brigade.'

He looks from my combat jacket to the bike I ride.

'I'm delivering a message from General Luc to Lady Aptitude Wildeside. The name's Sven Tveskoeg, I'm a Death's Head lieutenant.'

Chapter 49

'SVEN . . .' DEBRO COMES BOWLING DOWN A PASSAGEWAY AND flings her arms around me. 'How are you?' she demands. 'Where's Anton? Why are you carrying a shotgun?'

Guess I took the pump action from the bike without thinking.

'Anton is—' Maybe she notices me hesitate. 'He's still in Farlight. We got separated.'

'Separated?'

'I'll tell you about it later.'

'Let me get you some water,' Debro says. 'You look parched.'

'A beer would be better.'

'Water first,' she says firmly.

The corporal is standing to attention. So I salute briefly and dismiss him. He walks away, wondering how someone like me knows someone like her. I might be a Death's Head lieutenant, but I'm a lieutenant in a regiment where most other junior officers are in their late teens or early twenties.

I'm almost thirty.

And with my arm, plus the scars, I look older. So I'm up from the ranks or bad at my job.

'You OK?' Debro asks.

'Just thinking.'

She's going to tell me that's a novelty. But she changes her mind and leads me down a set of stairs to the kitchens. A glass of water is followed by a cold beer. Then she suggests a tortilla or a breast of chicken. But for all that it's welcome, the beer tastes sour in my throat and I'm not in the mood to eat.

'Debro,' I say, 'I need to see Aptitude.'

'A message from Vijay?' She thinks about that. 'How is—'

My scowl cuts her question dead. 'A message from General Luc. I need to be back at the Wolf's Lair by daylight tomorrow. And Aptitude is going to need time to think. So I'd better see her now.'

The woman in front of me doesn't block my way.

But she doesn't get out of it either. She simply stands between me and the door. I could walk round her, but Debro commands respect. She also reminds me of my sister. You have to have met my sister to know how scary that is.

'I'm not going to like this, am I?' she says.

'No,' I say. 'You're going to hate it.'

I don't mention that it's all I can do to deliver the message. We talk about the furies on the way. I'm almost at the gardens before it occurs to me that Debro hasn't asked about what's been happening in Farlight. Makes me wonder why not.

'Our screens are down,' she says in reply. 'They'll be back up later.'

'Who says?'

'The house AI.'

'And how long has it been saying this?'

'Since yesterday . . . Sven,' she says. 'Tell me what the Wolf wants with Aptitude.'

'Can't. Gave my word.'

'To Luc?'

'Colonel Vijay.'

We climb the steps to the garden in silence, and walk out under an arch that leads to an ornate array of hedges. I only know they're *box* because Debro told me last time I was here. A small fountain plays in the middle of raked gravel. Water is a luxury in a landscape this hot.

Red flowers sit in clay pots. A cascade of bell-like blooms tumbles down a red brick wall. Since Wildeside is grown and its natural colour is grey, the wall has to be built so that flowers can cover it.

'Clematis,' Debro says.

Even now, her manners are perfect.

Aptitude sprawls in a hammock, one bare leg draped over the edge. She's not lying along it, and she's not sitting in it; somewhere between the two. In her hand is a slab and she's playing some question and answer game.

Debro watches me hesitate. More than anything this tells her how bad it's going to be. I killed Aptitude's husband with a single shot to the head. I ruined her wedding feast, slaughtered half her guests and burnt down the villa in which she was due to live. I've never felt a second's guilt for any of that.

Guilt and I don't mix.

Anything else drives you insane.

But I'm about to ruin Aptitude's life. She never wanted to marry Senator Thomassi, but her parents were in jail and she was a minor. She did what her uncle ordered. This is different, she loves Colonel Vijay. He is the first person she's really loved. She's young enough to believe he's the last.

'Sven!' she says, clicking off her book.

Aptitude rolls out of her hammock and flings her arms around me.

'You smell,' she adds, stepping back and wrinkling her nose. Then she catches Debro's expression and begins to say sorry. 'Shouldn't have said that,' Aptitude says, leaning forward to kiss me on the cheek. 'But you do.'

Of course I do.

Ride a gyrobike for several hours across baking wastes and you'll smell too. I can feel the sweat under my arms and down my spine. The only reason it's not dripping into my eyes is because I keep wiping it away.

'What's wrong?' Aptitude demands.

Where to begin?

The young woman in front of me is not the girl who served behind the bar at Golden Memories; nor is she the spoilt little rich kid from that wedding party in Farlight; she's an older version, somewhere between the two.

'Aptitude. We need to talk.'

She glances at her mother, who nods.

'I'll leave you to it,' Debro says. She goes without looking back.

Aptitude suggests we use the hammock, but we settle on sitting with our backs against the only bare patch on a flower-covered wall. I know I need to start talking. I just don't know where to begin . . .

'Sven,' she says. 'You're scaring me.'

The horizon stretches to dark clouds over the rift. Dying olive groves give way to scrub and then gravel where only salt grass can live. I recognize the colour, the flat green that looks grey in direct sunlight. The same grass that edged the strip between scrub and sand north of Fort Libidad when I was a teenager.

'The Wolf has Vijay prisoner.'

Aptitude looks at me, her mouth open.

Without knowing it, she folds her hands across her chest and draws up her knees, hugging herself tight. 'I thought General Luc was just being cruel,' she says. 'When he said—' She can't bring herself to finish the sentence. 'He couldn't,' she says. 'He wouldn't.'

This is General Luc we're talking about. Of course he would.

'Why are you here?' Aptitude asks.

'General Luc offers you Vijay's life. In return—'

'He'll let Vijay live?'

'In return—'

'We've got money,' Aptitude says. 'He's always wanted our land bordering his estate. We could give him that. And there are trade routes and concessions, we've got the fission monopoly on—'

'Aptitude. Listen to me.'

My tone is harder than I intend. Hard enough to shock her into silence. She waits for me to continue. 'You have to give up Vijay. That's his price.'

'I renounce Vijay?'

'Yes,' I say. 'You renounce Vijay.'

'What else?' She glares at me. 'I know you,' she says. 'I know when you're not telling me everything. Tell me what else he wants.' She's half turned towards me and her fingers are fists. This is the girl I faced on the steps at Villa Thomassi. 'Tell me,' she demands. 'Tell me.'

'He wants you.'

Her face changes as if someone has flicked a switch. All the life goes out of it, leaving only a mask. A very beautiful mask, with blue eyes and long blonde hair that tumbles around her shoulders.

Seeing it is looking at Aptitude's future.

'As his mistress?'

'Aptitude,' I say, 'he wants you as his wife.'

'Lady Aptitude Luc.' She tries the words for size. Tears magnify her eyes, not yet falling. She bites her lip hard enough to cut flesh. The fingers that were fists now dig nails into her hands. They dig so hard her knuckles turn white.

'You don't have to say yes.'

'Of course I do.'

Her anger is enough to make the tears fall.

'You know I do. If I don't Luc will . . .' She looks at me, some of the fierceness leaving her face. 'He'll cut out Vijay's heart. I can't let that happen.'

'Aptitude.'

'I love him,' she says fiercely. 'In a way I can never love anyone else.' Not sure what she sees in my eyes, but she looks away. 'Tell the Wolf my answer is yes. But Vijay must be free first. And I want his word he won't hurt Vijay once we're married.'

She glares at me.

'I was going to wed Senator Thomassi,' she says. 'How can this be worse?'

Chapter 50

DEBRO WALKS ME TO MY BIKE. SHE GIVES ME BREAD AND dried beef and a flask of water and an ice-cold bottle of beer that will be warm by the time I drink it. Then she kisses me on both cheeks and steps back.

I have no idea what Aptitude said.

All I know is I haven't seen Aptitude since she stood up from the wall in the garden, smoothed down her skirt and said good-bye as politely as if I was a stranger.

'Don't blame yourself,' Debro says.

Her words increase my rage.

'Sven,' she says, 'I mean it. You're just the messenger.'

My link with this family will go, I think as I fire up the gyro. General Luc will marry Aptitude and Vijay Jaxx will go into exile. I'll be someone Debro met, from a time she no longer wants to remember.

Rage is a habit.

One I learnt young and traded, turning it into something I could use. But this is a cold fury. In part with Debro, that she can let go this easily. But mostly with General Luc, although it's not that simple.

My fury feeds on memories of OctoV's deviousness. It feeds on my hatred for the U/Free, which now burns fiercer than my hatred for the Uplifted and Enlightened, which burns fierce enough . . .

'*Listen*,' I say.

Debro steps back.

'Farlight is burnt, most of the area south of the river anyway. The furies that attacked you? Many more ripped through that area, killing doubters. That's why your comms system is down. Vijay's father is dead. The head of the Thomassi has declared himself Prince of Farlight. The U/Free have accepted his claim.'

'But OctoV . . .'

Funny how everyone comes back to that.

'He's dead.' Seems fussy to point out he was actually a she. And there are more important points to consider. 'OctoV betrayed General Jaxx and the U/Free betrayed OctoV, Senator Thomassi is their choice. You know what that means?'

'We're in danger?' That's only half a question, but she has a real one. 'Sven, how could this happen?'

What I ask myself.

I run Debro through events on Hekati, some of which she knows and more of which she doesn't. I'm putting it in words to give myself thinking time. For someone who doesn't like thinking I'm doing too much of it lately.

'General Tournier offered Jaxx a dukedom and a planet to change sides. OctoV made him send Vijay to kill Tournier. And then made Jaxx a duke anyway and gave him Farlight City, which isn't a planet, but it's still capital of the empire.'

Debro nods.

'Suppose OctoV decides Jaxx is too powerful? So he cuts a deal with the U/Free, who blame General Jaxx for the empire's failure to sign that treaty with the Uplifted.'

'Though you said Paper didn't want the treaty signed?'

'Who knows what she wants?'

We're back to bloody board games again.

Before she left Golden Memories, Aptitude bought me a T-shirt that read *My computer beat me at chess. It was crap at kick boxing.* It was a joke, but not much of one.

The problem with the U/Free is that while you're congratulating yourself on planning three moves ahead, they're winning the game after next.

I give her the memory crystal Vijay filled with data from Morgan's AIs before trashing them.

'There might be something on them you can use to negotiate.'

Debro looks doubtful.

Although she doesn't doubt the U/Free are involved, she's more worried by what a Thomassi victory means for Wildeside. Nothing good. If she's been left alone for the last three days it's because Sebastian Thomassi is still locking down Farlight.

The favelas will riot.

They always do after something like this.

Sebastian Thomassi's first job will be to strip power from the crowds who gave him his victory. After that, he'll cut deals with some high clans and kill others. Only then will he begin to tidy up outside. As for the other planets, in the short-term the war against the Uplifted and Enlightened will go on, because it will take months, if not years, for the news of a truce to reach them, and longer still to be believed.

'Targeted,' the SIG tells me.

It sulks when I say that is obvious.

The Wolf has me targeted from the moment I reach the road to his castle. For all I know, he has me targeted my entire trip from Wildeside to here.

A comm sat could do it.

Something hanging in geostationary orbit. Say a simple targeting laser, particularly if it ties to a signalling—

'*Earth to Sven*,' the SIG says.

A long shot of our planet, with bright dotted rings showing communication satellite orbits, fades inside my head. The world's edges vanish, and for a split second I'm near vomiting as a mountain range rushes towards me.

'*Sven.*'

The spiral flicks into focus.

'Don't,' the SIG–37 says. 'All right? Just don't.'

'Do what?' Can't remember the gun talking to me like this. Mostly it's just snotty, now it sounds somewhere between angry and worried.

'Choose now to format. OK?'

I'm still thinking about that when a steel door opens ahead to lock off my route. A door behind also opens and I'm trapped, with rock one side, steel barriers front and back, and a long drop on my outside edge.

A dozen Wolf Brigade exit the doors carrying pulse rifles. The visors on their helmets are down and all wear grey flak jackets. I'm flattered.

Just how dangerous do they think I am?

'Unbuckle your holster,' shouts a major. 'Put it on the ground.'

'Fucking great,' the SIG says. 'See what you've done?'

No, I don't.

'*Now*,' the officer insists.

I reckon I can kill him before they get me. If I can reach the edge and use a boulder as cover, I can probably kill a lot more . . .

'Sven,' the gun says. 'Just fucking unbuckle me.'

I step back from the SIG.

There's a knife in my boot. Actually, there's a knife in each boot, and the webbing between my shoulders holds another, its blade honed to a sliver of steel, carbon and molybdenum. Never did get that laser sabre back.

The first trooper to pick up the SIG collapses. Must be an electric pulse that has him wetting himself, as if someone poked his arse with a shock stick.

'Deactivate it,' the major orders.

'Nothing to do with me.'

He stares, not sure what to do next.

'Do I get to see Luc?' I ask. 'Or do we stand here?'

'You call him General Luc,' he tells me. 'Or the Wolf.'

'Yeah,' I say. 'Him.'

A second trooper drops twitching.

I can't work out if the SIG is simply enjoying itself, or doing something more useful, and now seems the wrong time to ask.

'Let's leave them to it,' I say.

Chapter 51

'APTITUDE REFUSES?' GENERAL LUC GLARES FROM THE FAR SIDE of his desk. 'That's her answer? *She refuses?*' Nodding, I keep my eyes on his.

I don't want there to be any doubt about this.

'You offered her Colonel Vijay's life?'

'Yes, sir.'

'And she turned it down?'

'She turned *you* down, sir. Some prices are too high.'

He bites his lip and glares some more. Yellow teeth glisten like old bone. Then he turns his fury to the window, although I doubt he sees anything much through the glass. General Luc is shaking with rage, and his fingers clench into fists as the heel of his boot grinds against the tiles. He's squashing something imaginary underfoot.

Me, probably.

'*What?*' he demands, when a buzz from his desk makes him jump.

An officer apologizes for disturbing him.

I don't hear this. But it's obvious from the way the Wolf jerks his head in irritation. Indigo Jaxx would never show anger like this. The general could be furious, he could be cold, ruthless and unforgiving. But he would regard shaking with rage as beneath him.

'No,' General Luc snarls. 'I don't care how you do it. Just pick up that fucking gun and get it inside.'

The Wolf's ADC passes me to a captain, who hands me to a lieutenant, who summons a sergeant I've never seen. None of which improves my temper. By the time I reach my destination I'm looking for an excuse to hurt someone.

Usually, I wouldn't need one.

But there's that stupid oath our colonel gave.

'In there,' the sergeant says.

'It's *sir.*'

He looks at me.

'Enjoy your stay, sir,' he says.

When Colonel Vijay looks up from his mattress I'm shocked at the change. His face, always thin, has hollows. Dark rings circle his eyes. His skin is so pale it matches the blond wisps of his beard.

'*Sir,*' Neen says.

The colonel is forcing himself to his feet. 'What did she say?'

Grabbing my jacket, he tries to stop shaking. But he's as useless as a cheap gun spring and only his grip keeps him upright.

'She turned him down, sir.'

'That's the truth?'

'Yes, sir.'

Colonel Vijay gives a huge sigh of relief.

His fingers let go my lapels, and Neen catches him before he cracks his skull on the floor. Taking the flak jacket Shil offers, Iona makes a pillow for the colonel's head and crouches at his side, wiping his forehead.

Catching my gaze, Rachel returns her stare to a tiny slit

window, and resumes her sniper's exercises, muttering angles and distances to herself.

'Tell me they didn't torture him . . .'

'We're on bread and water,' Neen says. 'The colonel's been sharing his with us.'

'Sharing?'

'Giving,' he says.

'And you ate it?'

'Orders, Sven,' says Colonel Vijay. 'Orders.'

He's right, of course. If he says eat his food and the Aux refuse they're disobeying a direct order and that's a capital offence. We both know that.

'No point wasting it,' he says.

'Sir,' Rachel says. 'You might want to see this.'

A second after she says it, I hear the clang as something metal drops in the courtyard.

'Sergeant . . .'

Walking Neen to Rachel's window, I move her aside.

Sappers drag lengths of scaffolding to pile in one corner. A second squad unload planks from a forklift. Sergeant Toro oversees both. As we watch, he nods to a man with a chainsaw, who starts cutting wood to length.

'I'm gone two days. Want to tell me what happened?'

Glancing over his shoulder, Neen says, 'Wouldn't sleep, wouldn't eat, wouldn't even drink his share of our water. All he did was wait for your return.'

Little idiot.

The bars separating us from the landing are old, but sound. The hinges are hidden, and the lock looks new. Nothing shakes free when I slam my steel arm against the lock. A second blow brings dust, and a captain, a sergeant and a corporal.

They've been talking something over between them.

'Stop that,' the captain says.

He's curly-haired, smug and good-looking enough to make

me want to rearrange his features. A wolf pelt drapes from his shoulder and a row of medal ribbons decorate his chest. Three of them are probably for being able to wear the wolf skin elegantly.

'Or what?' I demand.

A third slam of my arm rattles the door in its frame.

'Lieutenant,' he says, 'I'm warning you . . .'

'I want food,' I tell him. 'Proper food. Meat, bread, beer.' Glancing over my shoulder I meet Shil's gaze. 'And fruit . . .'

She's always eating fruit.

'And I want it now.'

'That's not going to happen.'

'Yes it is.'

The captain makes the mistake of stepping closer.

Think he's planning to do something stupid like jab his finger at me, while telling me to behave. He doesn't get beyond the first word. My hand slicks through the bars, and I grasp him by the throat. After that, he can't say anything anyway.

'Release him.'

'Not a chance.'

When the sergeant reaches for his side arm, I introduce the captain to the bars as a warning, hard and fast. I do it twice for luck and the NCO decides to leave his gun where it is. The blood on his CO's face probably helps. Or maybe it's the metal sheen of my fingers gripping his throat.

'*Sven* . . .' That's Vijay, obviously.

'What, sir?'

'I gave my parole.'

'Which means what, sir?'

He's going to say I know what it means. Then it occurs to him that I don't. We didn't have things like parole in the Legion, and I haven't been Death's Head long enough to understand the ins and outs of it.

'We don't try to escape.'

'In return, sir?'

'They treat us with respect.'

'See?' I say, bouncing the captain off the bars. 'Respect. That means you feed us properly . . .'

'Lieutenant Sven Tveskoeg?'

The officer who asks introduces himself as Major Whipple. He's followed by an ADC and a handful of staff from the castle canteen. He knocks on our door, which has me grinning.

'Please . . .' Colonel Vijay invites him in and our food is delivered. It seems Captain Fowler took his smashed jaw to General Luc, and the Wolf decided to feed us after all. The captain is on a charge for being generally useless.

Major Whipple salutes Colonel Vijay.

On his way out, he stops. 'Hekati,' he says. 'Is it true you talked to her?'

The man's face is impassive but there is something in those eyes. Something turns on my answer. But it turns for him and not for me.

'Yes,' I say. 'Right at the end.'

'She killed herself?'

'And took an Uplifted mother ship with her. It was like watching one of the gods clap her hands.'

The major fingers a medallion around his neck.

'And they say . . .' he hesitates, 'you once ate human flesh. A woman . . .'

I'm grateful for the food, but this isn't a conversation I'm interested in having. 'Oh you know what they say. I like women as much as the next man, but I couldn't eat a whole one . . .'

He raises his eyebrows.

'But if I was going to, I know where I'd start.'

The major snorts, despite himself.

'An orderly will come by to collect your trays,' he tells me. Then he's gone, in an abrupt turn and a clatter of boot heels on stone stairs. His ADC has left our door unlocked. I wonder if that is intentional and decide it is.

'A trap?' I ask Colonel Vijay.

'Maybe a sign of trust.'

Fucked up, the lot of them.

Only I'm coming to realize something else.

That major in the Wolf Brigade has more in common with Colonel Vijay than either one has with a civilian. Doesn't matter we hate them, or our troopers beat the shit out of theirs in every available bar, and the other way round. Makes me wonder if a Silver Fist has more in common with us than our own civilians.

I decide that's a thought too far.

Ripping a chicken apart, Neen gives half to Iona. She finishes her half in a couple of bites, watched by Shil who can be odd about food. As for Rachel, she fills her fist with salted almonds and returns to her window.

I think she's working on distances. Turns out, she's watching a man bolt lengths of scaffolding together. 'You know what he's doing, sir?'

'No,' I lie.

She goes back to watching.

'Certainly,' Colonel Vijay says, when I ask if we can have a word. That's one of his phrases, but it's beginning to stick. He makes space for me to sit and offers me a plate of chicken breast.

'I've eaten, sir.'

'It's about Shil?'

I stare at him. 'Why would it be about her, sir?'

'Thought it might.' He nods to where she sits in her corner. There's a darkness round her eyes, and a hauntedness to her face that I haven't seen since the siege of Ilseville. There's an air of barely restrained fury as she watches us watch her.

'You realize,' the colonel says, 'she loves you?'

'*What?*'

It was a fuck against a wall, and a couple of conversations since.

As far as I'm concerned we called a truce to her low-level grousing. If she sees it differently that's her problem. Not mine, because I don't need more problems. I have enough of those with the fallout from what happened in Farlight.

'You serious, sir?'

'Yes, Sven.'

My sigh sounds like bellows emptying. *Fuck it, twice . . .*

Is she that smart? The answer is yes, she's smart. Probably the smartest person we've got in the group now Haze is off being important somewhere. But I don't think it's a plan. Maybe I just don't want to think it's a plan.

'OK,' I say. 'She wins. I'll have to throw her out after all.'

He stares at me. 'You mean that, don't you?'

'Afraid so, sir.'

An orderly comes to collect our trays.

He says nothing as Neen piles what's left of the fruit onto one plate and puts it near the wall. We get a fresh bucket as a latrine and a sheet for Vijay's mattress, although a blanket would be more use.

Something occurs to me.

'Why aren't you in a better room?'

Colonel Vijay shrugs.

'Sir,' I say. 'When we were on the move, you messed with the Wolf Brigade. Suitable accommodation and proper food.'

'I asked to be with the Aux.'

'Why?'

'The company.' Looking round the cell, Colonel Vijay smiles slightly. 'You'll look after them?' he says. 'If you can?'

'Sir . . .'

'We both know what they're building, Sven.'

'A scaffold,' I say. 'They're going to hang you.'

'Behead me,' he says. 'I have that right.'

'To be beheaded?' My voice is louder than I'd like. Don't know what the others heard, but my scowl is enough to make them look down again.

'General Luc intended to shoot me.'

The colonel's voice is calm.

'Through the head, obviously. He doesn't want a bullet ruining my heart. But I've insisted on the sword.' He nods, his blue eyes meeting mine. 'And I've demanded he wield the blade himself.'

'You have that right?'

Colonel Vijay smiles, almost angelically.

Chapter 52

THE NIGHT RETREATS IN A CRUNCH OF BOOTS AND THE CLANK of ratchets, as sappers work through to build the scaffold on which Colonel Vijay will die come morning.

We hear chainsaws, and the flat slap of a nail gun, which sounds enough like small-arms fire to comfort me and keep everyone else awake.

Apart from Colonel Vijay, who sleeps curled in a ball. One arm folded under his head, the other wrapped round his knees. He looks too young to take the weight of General Luc's hatred for Indigo Jaxx, and whatever warped need for revenge makes the Wolf want Aptitude because he couldn't have Debro.

Shil's shocked when I mutter this.

Sitting up, she peers into my face. There's enough light coming through the slit window for us to see each other's eyes, and I don't know what she sees, but she leans forward and kisses me carefully on the cheek, while the others pretend not to notice.

'Say it, sir,' she whispers.

'You get your wish.'

'I what . . . ?'

'You're out of the Aux. Soon as this is over.'

She's meant to be happy about that. Not spend the rest of the night slumped in the opposite corner, with her legs pulled up and her arms holding them in place and her head buried in her knees, crying.

Outside our window the nail gun falls silent. Colonel Vijay's scaffold is bolted together, the boards now form its floor. A strip of railing secures the back and runs along both edges, but the front is open.

Makes the execution easier to see.

A second platform sits in front of the first. It's longer and lower, with newly built wooden benches to either side of two ornate chairs. I was wondering what kept the nail gunner so busy.

Do I have a plan?

I have several. Unfortunately, I don't know which is right. Although Leona's comment about the long game won't leave my head. And her strange silver key feels heavy next to the dog tags and planet buster around my neck.

The long game.

What does a key usually open?

I think I've left it too late to learn to play chess. Coming to stand at my shoulder, Rachel sees the scaffolding outside and her face tightens.

'Yeah,' I say. 'He's getting an audience.'

'Bastards.'

We both look at Colonel Vijay at the same time. He's still curled in the dawn light like a baby, head on his arm. Makes me wonder if he's really sleeping, or just being kind to the rest of us. Wouldn't put that past him either. A few minutes later, the colonel stretches and yawns.

'Breakfast, sir?' Iona asks.

He takes the fig she offers, and peels it carefully, lifting first one sliver of skin and then another with his fingernail. Don't think I knew people peeled figs. Only when he has eaten and wiped his fingers does he climb to his feet and walk to the window.

'Interesting,' he says.

'Sir?'

'Those seats . . .'

Before the colonel can explain his interest, an ADC knocks at our door.

The boy is barely wide enough at the shoulder for the wolf skin General Luc's officers wear. His boots have thick heels as if the extra height will make a difference. 'If I could trouble you, sir?'

Colonel Vijay turns from the window.

'I meant your lieutenant, sir.'

Wolf Brigade troopers watch as I stalk through their base.

Some meet my eye, and others glance away. A few stare. An old lieutenant in a uniform jacket frayed at the cuffs nods, as if he recognizes me. Or maybe he simply recognizes the type. He's me, twenty years down the line. If I'm lucky enough to live that long.

I return his nod.

A sergeant, I decide. Up through the ranks.

Not rich and not well-born, but good in a scrap and forgiven his filthy jacket, poorly cut hair and greying moustache for battles fought and victories won. He would know the answer to the question occupying my mind.

'*Parole?*' I say.

He stops, stares at me.

The ADC keeps walking, only to stop in his turn. Looking back, he sees something in the lieutenant's face that makes him stay where he is.

'You spoke?'

The lieutenant's voice is rough. His accent as raw as mine.

We speak traveller, because that's what people on Farlight use. Something says it's not his natural tongue either.

'How does it work? Parole?'

'The generality?'

'What does it *mean*?'

'You don't know?' The lieutenant considers this. His slow nod says he approves of my ignorance. 'One officer gives another his word not to fight or try to escape. In return, the officer is treated as a guest and not as a prisoner.'

'Invited to dine? Doors left unlocked?'

The man nods.

'That's it?'

Another nod. The ADC is getting worried. Which means whoever sent him outranks this officer. He's worried enough to start shuffling his feet.

'When does it run out?' The only question to matter.

The lieutenant grins. 'When you take it back.'

'What if I didn't give it myself?'

'Your colonel?' He obviously knows about us. I guess everyone in the Wolf's Lair does. Even those who didn't make the retreat when we did.

'Sir,' the ADC sounds anxious.

'Wait,' the man demands.

The ADC does.

'Interesting question.' I have his attention back. 'Until his death, certainly. After that? Keeping parole would show respect.'

'But personally . . . ?'

He shrugs, turns to go. Then looks back. 'Personally, we both know it's a crock of horseshit. It ends when you decide so.'

'Yeah,' I say. 'That's what I thought.'

He returns my salute with a smile.

Our boots ring on the stairs as we go up a level. Officers that outrank me move aside. Must be the glare on my face and the urgency with which the ADC leads me across a lobby and towards a new flight of stairs. He's on the general's staff, that much is obvious.

Those who don't watch me, watch him pass, and mutter.

We're in a long corridor.

Huge portraits of Wolf Brigade COs line both walls, with gilded frames and brass plaques giving each a name and his dates. These are counted in the years then ruled by OctoV, the glorious, victorious and undisputed.

Doesn't say undisputed what.

The wolf skin begins five commanders ago, the grey jacket lined with leather three COs before that. The brigade's first two commanders wear no uniform. The ADC stops when I stop, and hesitates, too nervous to tell me to hurry.

He opens his mouth to protest when I tap the final picture.

It's life-size, with a flat and shiny surface, like a news screen that has frozen or a holo cube that has lost its ability to rotate.

The man in the picture wears a bulky suit, like OctoV's in that statue at the Emsworth landing fields. He even has the same bubble helmet. What he doesn't have is OctoV's ship.

'What's that?'

'Wolf's landing.'

'No,' I say. 'That weird shape behind him . . .'

'A hexagram, sir.'

That's the shape of the handle of Leona's key. See, I knew he was the kind of ADC who would know stuff like that.

'Actually, sir, it's probably a hexatope.'

'A what?'

'Reroutes reality through six dimensions.' He blushes. 'Well, that's what we're taught at the Academy.'

'And the man next to it?'

'Major Wolf,' the ADC says softly. He could be talking about a saint.

'Major?'

'Before he became a general.'

'He went from major to general? That's some promotion.'

The ADC stares at me, to see if I'm mocking him. He's afraid to tell me to hurry up, but not so afraid that he won't defend Major Wolf's reputation. A man dead seven hundred years, or six or five, or however long it is.

'I mean it,' I tell the boy. 'I'm impressed.'

His nod says that's natural and we pass a door I remember leading to General Luc's study and head for another flight of steps. There's daylight at the top, and a huge H painted on the deck to say I was right, the round tower doubles as a copter pad.

'Sir,' the ADC says. 'I've got Lieutenant Tveskoeg.'

When Colonel Nswor is sure I've registered his glare, he returns to scanning the horizon. The H-pad has an inbuilt ground-to-air defence system, but a trooper still sets up a belt-fed on the parapet to face the courtyard. Beyond him, a corporal manoeuvres a rocket launcher into place, using hand-held controls.

Hydraulics are meant to damp the recoil and prevent the launcher from skidding, but the way he double-checks wires used to shackle the unit suggests they're less than successful.

The launcher has four barrels, like goat tits, fed from a single magazine holding eight rockets. A dozen magazines sit on a trolley. The launcher faces outwards, which is interesting, but not as interesting as the fact other launchers are appearing.

'Sir . . .' Major Whipple hands the colonel his field-glasses.

Scanning the horizon, Colonel Nswor nods when he finds what he's looking for. Everyone else has to wait until the copter comes into sight. It's sleek and grey and flying so low it raises dust as it skims the dirt.

It is bigger than it first looks.

There's a lazy thud to its rotor that speaks of untapped power. Twin cannon hang both sides of its nose, and the flight window is a narrow wrap tinted the same grey as the sides.

'The general's own,' the ADC whispers.

I could have guessed that for myself.

Only General Luc's not aboard, because he's down below inspecting his engineers' handiwork. Having climbed onto the viewing platform, he seats himself in one of the two chairs. Then he stands and nods to Sergeant Toro. It seems the view is everything he wanted.

'Prepare to receive our guests,' the colonel snaps.

An NCO shouts orders and the honour guard comes to attention.

Banking as it reaches the mountain, the copter starts a twisting approach that tracks the spiral road towards the gates, hugging the rock as it goes. Impossible to tell if the pilots are AI or human, but they've obviously done this before.

Maybe the flight path is tradition.

Most of the pointless things you find are.

As the copter skims the road, a rocket launcher starts tracking its movement. So maybe there is a logic to that approach pattern after all. Like a dung-fly dance, get it wrong and you get eaten.

'*Present arms . . .*'

The cockpit membrane slides back and slabs of chitin shift as the craft settles and its wheels touch the deck. The first person out is Debro, the second is her daughter. The guard behind them holds a pulse rifle, sloping down.

'Sven,' Debro says.

We air-kiss. Then Debro grabs me and hugs me tight.

'Why isn't General Luc here?' she hisses. 'Surely he has the manners to meet his bride?'

'He's busy inspecting the scaffold.'

It takes her a second to understand my words.

Now, I've seen Debro angry and I've seen her outraged. I've

369

seen her stark naked, standing in steely silence, while a guard cavity-searches her. The only emotion she showed then was to shiver at the icy wind that blew through our underground corridor. Didn't think Debro did shock.

'*Who for?*'

'One for Vijay. Another to seat the audience.'

'How could he?' she hisses. 'After Aptitude agreed.'

Debro glances back at her daughter, who wears a simple white dress, and complicated braids. Apt's losing her battle with tears.

Behind me, Colonel Nswor and his men remain at attention. Only the trooper manning the belt-fed has the honesty to stare.

'Vijay refused Aptitude's offer.'

Debro's mouth drops open. '*What?*'

'He denies her right to sacrifice herself.'

She doesn't challenge my statement. In fact, Debro accepts it without question, turning away to wrap one arm round Aptitude's shoulders. Mother and daughter stand side by side, then face to face, their foreheads touching.

Seeing them like that makes me want to kill someone. Their escort must read that in my face, because he grips his rifle tighter. We stare for the second it takes me to remember him for later. And then he steps around me to present himself to Colonel Nswor.

'Reporting with your prisoners, sir.'

'*Prisoners?*' Stepping forward, the Wolf Brigade officer back-hands him so hard the man goes down. 'They're *guests*,' he says furiously.

Seven hundred pairs of boots stamp courtyard dirt as the entire brigade comes to attention. Their chief warrant officer salutes a captain, who turns on his heels and marches to where Colonel Nswor stands.

The WO salutes the colonel, who about turns and presents

himself to General Luc, who accepts his salute with hurried elegance.

If they weren't my enemies I'd be impressed.

Not a word passes between the Wolf and his guests. His bow, which is slight, is met with the briefest of nods.

'If you will, Lady Aptitude,' says the little ADC, offering his arm to help her up the steps, but she ignores him entirely, still fighting back tears. Everyone waits for Aptitude to move, even Debro, who steps forward.

I'm already there.

Apt takes my hand.

Helping Debro up next, I step back for Colonel Nswor, and then let Major Whipple follow, but the Major is watching the sky. Dark grey eyes and a hard face and something close to regret. He's impressed by Aptitude, which doesn't surprise me because I've never met anyone yet who wasn't. And he's impressed by Debro, because she's Senator Debro Tezuka Wildeside, and Debro impresses everyone.

He's even impressed by us, the Aux.

But he wants this over.

And when General Luc follows his major's gaze, the answer hits me. They're expecting an attack. That's what those mortars and rockets and belt-feds are about. Dragging his attention from the sky, General Luc nods to Sergeant Toro. 'Housekeeping first,' he says. 'We can deal with the Thomassi afterwards.'

Chapter 53

COLONEL VIJAY ENTERS THE COURTYARD ALONE.

If he's seen Aptitude he doesn't let on. He must have seen her, you can hardly miss a sobbing girl in a white dress. Debro sits beside her, one hand lightly on her daughter's wrist to steady her.

'Any last words?' General Luc demands.

Colonel Vijay shakes his head.

'None at all? No pleas for mercy, requests to be remembered, fond words for your ex-beloved?' The Wolf looks at Aptitude, who sits as if cut from stone. Except no statue ever cried, whatever wise women and fools say.

Colonel Vijay opens his mouth to answer.

Then shuts it again.

His eyes, which watch General Luc, flick to the sky. And we hear what he hears, a low buzz in the distance, like mechanical wasps.

'Too late to save you,' the Wolf says. 'Not that they'd bother.' He shrugs. 'You should thank me for saving you from a Thomassi show trial.'

On cue, Sergeant Toro steps from under an arch carrying a

sword as long as he is tall over his shoulder. It is double-handed, with a heavy hilt, and weighs enough to make him stoop on one side.

Aptitude whimpers.

But Debro is looking at the sky, which is now dotted with a hundred tiny black specks getting closer, with more specks behind.

'Last chance,' says the Wolf.

'For what?' Colonel Vijay demands.

These are the first words he's spoken since he walked from under that arch. And they're calm, almost reasonable. He knows Aptitude is here, all right.

'To plead,' Luc says. 'Surely you want your life?'

'Not at any price.'

At a touch from Debro's hand, Aptitude stifles her sobs, and her swallowed gasps sound worse still, like a child drowning in misery. Only Aptitude is not a child, she's a major piece in a game so messy the only person to understand it is dead.

Take ground, keep ground.

Keep taking ground until you can take no more.

Die rather than let the ground you've taken be taken back.

There is nothing in those rules you'll find hard to understand. At twelve I understood them perfectly. Every one of the Aux understands them perfectly now. I'm just having trouble making them fit what's happening around me.

'Steiner 3 Combat copters,' Major Whipple mutters.

Not sure if he's talking to me, his colonel or himself.

Mixed in with the copters are gliders. And worse than that, the gliders are spilling white globs like drops of milk. Each dot a parachute.

Up on the battlements, a rocket launcher opens fire and shuts down just as fast. The Wolf refuses to let what is happening beyond his walls interfere with what is happening inside.

'If you will go first, sir . . .'

Nodding to the sergeant, Colonel Vijay climbs the steps. He stands aside to let General Luc climb after him. Sergeant Toro follows, and Colonel Vijay steadies him when he stumbles under the weight of that sword. Next to me, Major Whipple grunts approvingly.

In my pocket I have the planet buster.

Its lid is raised and its priming ring already turned. All I have to do is push the button and this is over. Everyone dies. But that is not a long game, so there has to be a better answer.

A warm wind blows into Colonel Vijay's face and tugs at the edge of his white shirt. The shirt is clean, the colonel's hair still wet and he's been allowed to shave. Only the hollowness around his eyes suggests last night's sleep was fake.

'Ready when you are,' he says.

The Wolf scowls. As we watch, he tests the sword's balance.

And then, standing firm, his shoulders twisted and his boots glued to the boards, General Luc draws back the blade to take Colonel Vijay's head from his shoulders.

'Ready for death?'

Colonel Vijay smiles. 'I'm a Jaxx,' he says. 'An officer in the Death's Head. What do you think?'

General Luc sighs.

'I think you're a fucking little idiot. And every bit as insane as your father. What do I think . . .?' He grounds the sword. 'I think this world's gone to hell in a handcart and you two deserve each other.'

We have the long game.

Things change swiftly after that.

'I release you from your parole,' the Wolf tells Colonel Vijay. 'You can take your chances here or try to break through those.' He nods towards the falling chutes, then turns to where Aptitude sits, and says, 'I renounce my claim on his life. You too may stay here, or go . . .'

'*She's staying. They're both staying.*'

All three turn to look at me.

Of course they are. There's a war going on out there and I'm not about to lose my major players at this point. General Luc's halfway down the steps when I block his way.

'*Sven*,' Colonel Vijay says. 'No.'

'I want my gun back.'

The Wolf shows yellow teeth. It's a grin, of sorts.

He tells me it's an illegal piece of shit, ideally suited for scum like me. Then he orders Sergeant Toro to make sure the Aux are freed and our weapons returned to us.

'Anything else?' he asks me.

'Yes, sir,' I say. 'We need to talk.'

His nod takes in the men scattering to their positions. 'It can wait.'

Chapter 54

AS APTITUDE SCRABBLES PAST, I GRAB HER. SHE FIGHTS UNTIL she realizes who it is and stops, puzzled.

'Listen,' I say, pulling her close. 'I told Vijay you refused General Luc's offer. It's what he expected,' I add, hearing her gasp. 'He was proud of you.'

'So he didn't refuse to let me . . .'

Shit, I hadn't thought that through at all.

When her gaze flicks over my shoulder, I know who stands there.

Orders might stream from General Luc: belt-feds to be manned, pulse rifles to be broken out and mortars positioned, more anti-aircraft missiles brought from the armoury, but he still watches as Aptitude flings her arms around Colonel Vijay, and buries her face in his shoulder.

Say you rejected Luc's offer.

I have to mouth it twice before he understands.

The colonel's nod is slight, and then he's stroking Aptitude's hair and whispering things men should only say to women in the darkness of a locked room at night. Except it doesn't matter and, strangely, I need the Wolf Brigade to see this.

Vijay Jaxx and Aptitude Wildeside.

It's going to be a long hard fight and a good myth is worth a dozen battalions. A good prophecy is worth ten times that. Get us to believe luck's your whore and the next battle is half won. Alternatively, this is where we die.

The choice is General Luc's. He just doesn't know that yet.

'Sir,' says Neen. 'They've got tanks.'

'How the fuck—'

'Slung under triple-rotor copters, ready manned.'

Shil stands behind him, her eyes on Aptitude. Rachel, however, has eyes only for her rifle. She's running her fingers down its stock, like she just remembered she wanted to take it to bed. Ajac is keen but unfocused and Iona simply scared.

'Go sew people up,' I tell her.

She disappears.

To Rachel, I say, 'Up on the battlements. Kill the officers first.' She doesn't need telling, but saying it gives me a warm feeling inside every time.

Neen gets to look after Debro.

'Keep her safe.'

He salutes, dips into his jacket and pulls out a small automatic. 'Ma'am. Do you know how to use one of these?'

Taking the Colt, Debro unlocks it, jacks a round into its breech and returns it to safety, before tucking the side arm into her belt. She should have dropped the clip and counted her rounds, but it's still impressive.

She's certainly impressed him.

'I'm sorry,' she says. 'I didn't get your name?'

'Neen,' he replies. 'Sergeant Neen. This is my sister Shil.'

'Senator Wildeside,' Shil says.

'Debro, please.'

It's a strange meeting, two ex-militia grunts and the head of one of Farlight's greatest trading families, but no stranger than my first meeting with Debro on a prison shuttle. And we live in a strange galaxy that gets stranger by the day.

Neen leads Debro towards an arch.

He asks something of a Wolf Brigade lieutenant who looks in surprise at Debro, then shrugs and nods to battlements above. The next I see of them, Debro's added a pulse rifle to her weapons collection and Neen is showing her how to work the pre-charge lever.

'The mother he never had,' Shil says bitterly.

'Thought that was you?'

Tears fill her eyes and I grip her shoulders until the crying is done. It takes three sobs, two breaths and an angry shake of her head before she's pushing me away. 'And I still fucking hate you,' she says.

'That's, hate you, *sir*.'

I take the SIG from Sergeant Toro, whose eyes widen when it purrs obscenely and shivers in my grip.

'Ignore it,' I say.

'That's not kind,' the SIG says. It scans what's going on beyond the walls and burns a third of a battery pack as it works the odds. 'Particularly,' it adds, 'as you'll all be needing me to save your lives later.'

'That bad?'

'Been in worse.'

'What happened?' Aptitude asks it.

'I survived,' the SIG says cheerfully. 'Your grandfather didn't.'

Sergeant Toro tells the colonel that General Luc is on the H-pad, then hesitates on the edge of saying something else and says it anyway. 'You'll find he's otherwise engaged, sir . . .'

Standing right in the middle of the tower, his feet apart and his hands on his hips, General Luc barks out orders, in between scanning the sky and the valley with field-glasses. And, in between barking orders and scanning the sky, he grins. The Wolf was born for this.

'Sir,' I say.

'I'm busy.' He barely glances in my direction.

'Won't make any difference.'

Lowering his binoculars, he says, 'Didn't take you for a defeatist.'

'Didn't take you for someone to throw his brigade away.'

Snow-blasted grey eyes look at me and it's like staring into a cold wind as it scrapes over the ice sheet of some prison planet. I have no real idea how old the general is or what he has seen. I don't doubt this man has eaten human flesh.

So have I.

At least, I think she was human.

Birth separates us. Money separates us. Rank, power, privilege . . . But right now those things don't matter. In the things that do, we're alike. As he nods, I know he's coming to realize that.

'Sir,' I say, 'where are the bombers?'

The first thing you do with a defensive position is pound the fuck out of it. You destroy its occupants' will to fight. If we're not being bombed there's a reason and I know what it is. Leona told me, I was just too stupid to realize.

'No bombers,' the Wolf agrees. So I ask his permission to speak freely.

'Quickly would make more sense.'

Our rockets have destroyed half a dozen copters at most. As I watch, a goat tit on the walls lets rip, and another four rockets head skywards. An explosion of chaff sends three after false targets and the fourth misses, only to be blinded by more chaff as it loops back for a second run.

If the U/Free haven't helped the Thomassi with their defences, then their luck is extraordinary. We're already fighting a losing battle.

Most of the heavy copters are dropping their cargo, and the first new-model Tuskers are grinding their way up the spiral. I can almost taste the static of their engines and the slap of their tracks.

'Sven,' my SIG says. 'You might want—'

'Down,' I order. When Aptitude doesn't move, I grab her wrist and drag her to the deck. Vijay follows after. Not sure where Debro and Neen are, but he'd better be keeping her safe.

'Stay down,' I shout, when the colonel raises his head. 'Sir.'

Banking, one of the combat copters screams over the H-pad, its guns spinning as bullets slap across our deck, churning up bitumen and cutting a mortar man in two. Small-arms fire follows it into the distance, and it chaffs the only rocket to come close.

'Fuck,' Aptitude says.

The deck around us is a mess of spilt blood, crouching men and spent cases from the copter's chain gun.

'I imagine,' the SIG says, 'it'll be back for more.'

'Sir,' I tell General Luc, 'you must take Colonel Vijay through the gate.'

The Wolf goes utterly still.

'What gate would that be?' he asks finally.

His words are so quiet only I can hear them. General Luc's fingers are round the handle of his pistol, and he's already flicked safety. Vijay Jaxx fidgets behind me, as the SIG switches clips with an over-loud click.

'Of course,' I say, 'we'll need the key.'

The general's eyes widen at that. Slowly, so he can follow my movements, I undo the top two buttons on my shirt and tug free my dog tags.

'Where did you get that?'

'From a friend.'

The general laughs sourly. 'Any other surprises?'

Battle is raging above us. It sounds as if the Wolf Brigade are using up their entire stock of missiles; but sometimes there's no point saving ammunition for later, and I think we understand this is one of those times.

All the same, raging battle or not, I move slowly as I dip my hand into my jacket pocket and extract the planet buster, its top still open.

'Fuck,' General Luc says.

The first time I've heard him swear.

'Sven,' Colonel Vijay says, 'you might want to disarm that.'

At his suggestion, I flip the lid shut, twist the enamel ring below the button and stand down the planet buster.

'I take it you were planning to withdraw your parole?'

When I nod, the Wolf smiles.

Only three people on this planet know how a buster works, and two of them have forgotten, that's what Leona told me. It involves what General Luc's hex gate and the U/Free's ships involve. A folding of space so things that exist on one plane exist on another as well. Or, in the case of my planet buster, stop existing at all.

'Took it from the Uplifted,' I say, in answer to his next question.

'Never reported it?'

'Kept it as an insurance policy.'

A simplification of the last few months of my life.

'Sir,' I say, 'Paper doesn't know this exists. So it must be the hex gate that stops them bombing the shit out of us.'

A dozen questions fight for air time. The first out of General Luc's mouth is, 'What's Paper Osamu got to do with this?'

'We were lovers, sir.'

Behind me, Shil stiffens.

'You and the U/Free ambassador?' General Luc's disbelief is clear.

'She has odd tastes.'

'Obviously . . .'

'Sir, most U/Free don't know this is happening, because it isn't officially. The few that do know have it worked out to the last bait and switch and box of glass beads.'

'Don't like them, do you?'

'They think we're savages.' I shrug. 'OK, so they're right. All the same, this is wrong and those aren't Thomassi's forces out there.'

'Those are X39s. Octovian planes.'

'Yes,' I say. 'Octovian planes carrying Uplifted elite.'

The general considers my words. Then shakes his head so fiercely grey hair swirls around his shoulders. 'Even Thomassi,' he says. 'Even Sebastian Thomassi wouldn't . . .'

'You think he was given a choice?'

For the first time since we met, I have the Wolf's absolute attention. Missiles scream overhead and tanks growl their way round the mountain, while a spew of 'chutes drop from gliders like lines of falling piss.

None of that matters for him.

'Why not?' he demands.

'Because the U/Free will trick Thomassi as they tricked OctoV. They plan to fold us into the Enlightened, and nothing that Sebastian Thomassi, Colonel Vijay or you can do will change that. Unless we leave here now.'

He shakes his head, less forcefully.

Even if he wasn't in on the planning – or was, and simply didn't join in the attack – he knew about Thomassi's plot to take down General Jaxx. He would know, he tells himself. Surely, he would know if the United Free were behind this?

I see doubt enter his grey eyes.

General Luc blinks. 'What are you?'

'Sven Tveskoeg, Lieutenant, Obsidian Cross, second class.'

My salute is abrupt enough to amuse Colonel Nswor and Major Whipple, who hover at the edge of our group.

'Recently appointed ADC to OctoV's chosen successor, His Imperial Majesty Vijay Jaxx, Duke of Farlight and new ruler of the Octovian Empire. To who you and your brigade owe loyalty.'

'*Whom,*' Aptitude says.

Her voice is as clear as the note of a bell.

Chapter 55

IT TAKES ALMOST TWO HOURS TO ACTIVATE THE HEX GATE.
Well, thirty minutes to activate it and one and a bit hours to rip
the gate free from where it's been for the last five hundred
years. Behind the picture of Major Wolf, which hides a
bricked-up doorway.

Behind the door is a small room, filled with rubble, then
another door, blocked in its turn. Major Wolf, Leona Zabo and
their AI, Calinda, really wanted to keep the gate hidden.

'If you're lying . . .'

General Luc glares at me.

I nod, to show I understand. He knows I'm not lying.

OctoV, our glorious leader, the never defeated, whose very
sweat was perfume to his subjects, told me that Colonel Jaxx
was to be the new emperor.

Well, Leona did. But there's no need to make things more
complicated than necessary.

The Wolf has me repeat the bit about OctoV several times.

So I do. OctoV's last order for the commander of his
personal guard was that he transfer the Wolf Brigade's loyalty to
the new emperor.

'He told you this when?'

'A while ago,' I tell General Luc.

I'm not about to say it was in the shadow of an oak tree, with OctoV's avatar wrapping her arms around my neck. Any more than I am about to say I put a round through her head on his orders. Leona will remain an Aux in General Luc's memory. If he remembers her at all.

Engineers with angle grinders and hammer drills cut their way through the first door and clear the rubble. Then they attack the final door, coughing at a cloud of dust thrown by burning stone and mortar.

'Almost there,' Major Whipple says.

'Cut carefully,' General Luc warns him.

The Wolf knows his sappers can cut fast or carefully. Doesn't stop him demanding they do both. There is a battle raging, he reminds them.

We know. Those barrier gates are slowing the tanks on the spiral. Halting them long enough for anti-tank weapons to rip off their tracks. But the last wave of gliders dropped infantry into the high valley just below the castle.

Those men are now climbing towards us.

They wear stealth camouflage, carry pulse rifles and move in tight formation. The only way we can see them is on screen, and we find them using a weird mix of radar, echo location and thermal tracking.

General Luc insists, and he may be right, that they are Octovian. Renegade Death's Head or elite squads drawn from the cream of Farlight militia. But the metalheads targeting our courtyard are Silver Fist.

They drop, we kill them before they can land, they drop some more. Rachel's doing her share. To be honest, she's doing more than her share. The Wolf Brigade snipers aren't happy with that, which works for me.

Maybe they'll improve their aim.

'Faster,' General Luc barks.

His sappers keep cutting. Occasionally they glance my way, wanting to know why a Death's Head lieutenant has their general's attention. Why they're ripping apart a hidden room while their oppos die on the walls.

When one of them hits metal, everyone freezes. The sapper steps back, as Major Whipple steps forward, then the major steps back for the general.

'Sir,' I say. 'Let me.'

'At last,' the SIG says. 'He does something useful.'

Pistons hiss and braided hoses flex as my fingers grip stone.

Mortar crumbles and a scab of wall breaks free to reveal honeycombed bomb-shielding. Whoever hid the gate wanted it safe from damage.

A second later, the rest of the shielding tears away, and then I'm staggering under its weight, sappers scattering as I turn to rest it against a wall. One of them tries to move it and fails, raising his eyebrows.

Not sure what I expect.

Gold chasing? Weird carving, fist-sized chunks of memory diamond maybe? What I get is a door-sized hexagon on a simple stand. As the Wolf wipes away dust, ceramic gleams like bone beneath.

'Sir,' I say. 'We should get this upstairs.'

He looks round the little room, the rubble of its bricked door and the sheet of bombproofing against the wall. 'We can fetch Vijay down.'

His lips twist into a smile.

'I suppose Lady Aptitude goes too?'

'And Senator Wildeside. Me, my team, you. Everyone . . . We all go,' I add. 'There's no point otherwise.'

The Wolf sighs. 'Why you?' he asks.

That's the question really bothering him.

Why did our glorious leader choose me? 'Because I'm stupid enough to obey orders, sir.'

The feeds are full of events on Farlight. A glorious revolution is taking place. The corrupt regime of OctoV is crumbling as the poor and dispossessed rise against his brutal rule. The latest news is that OctoV has killed himself in his palace.

We see a vista of Farlight city.

A single shot is heard. They've given it too much echo. A real shot would be flatter, much more matter of fact. But the U/Free are keeping the news simple. We're barbarians, after all. Subtle isn't what they're selling.

'You've changed,' Debro says, when I say this.

'We all have.'

And we're going to change more, she must know that.

According to the feed, Prince Thomassi has asked the Enlightened for help in quelling the last few outposts of resistance. That would be us. As is their way, the U/Free will send observers to ensure the rules of civilized warfare are obeyed.

A map on screen shows our planet.

We're a tiny red dot. The rest of the planet is a peaceful blue. High over the Wolf's Lair are comm sats and news drones. We're being watched, and the viewing figures along the bottom say our audience is increasing.

Up on the walls General Luc has ten men. Some on belt-feds. Others fire rockets or mortars as fast as their launch mechanisms can handle. Needless to say, that's one sergeant, one corporal, a lance jack and seven troopers.

They're loaded for bear.

Pulse rifles across their backs, double holsters at their hips, knives in both boots, and grenades around their waists. Every semi AI and self-loading armament is up there. Doesn't matter what they hit at this stage. So long as they make a noise and keep the enemy occupied.

'Sven.'

'Sir?'

Vijay sighs. 'You don't need to salute every time.'

'You're the emperor.'

'Yes,' he says. 'I've been meaning to mention that.' His face screws into a look of deep worry. 'Is it true?' he asks. 'OctoV really said I was to replace him?'

'Yes, sir. That was the plan.'

We stand in General Luc's hall. Battle honours hang from the walls. Oil paintings of past campaigns mix with portraits of OctoV. In most, the emperor wears a green cavalry tunic.

In one, a Wolf Brigade jacket, with a pelt tossed over the shoulder.

I think I can see the faintest shadow of breasts. And then I decide I can't. Although it's hard to miss the softness of those hips.

Most of the Wolf Brigade have gone ahead to prepare for Vijay's arrival. Marching in pairs to the gate, they vanish as they step through. Only Aptitude, Debro and the Aux remain with the new emperor.

Plus those troopers on the walls.

They'll die, because that is their job. Make a noise, look like twenty times their number, make every rocket, grenade and round count and leave this world like men when the moment comes.

Turning to Neen, I ask, 'You understand your duties?'

'Sir, yes, sir.'

He recites the list back to me.

These are the new rules. 'Protect the emperor first, Aptitude second, her mother third. Die if necessary.'

I slap him on the shoulder. Neen looks surprised, then steps back and grins.

For a second he's the floppy-haired farm boy I met outside Ilseville. 'Never thought we'd get this far, sir.'

'Nor me. Thought I'd be replacing you months back.'

His grin widens.

Hugging his sister, he checks that Ajac's clip is full, Iona carries medical supplies and food, and Rachel has her rifle ready. Then he salutes Vijay.

'Sven goes first, sir. You go next. We follow . . .'

None of us knows what we'll find on the other side. The hex has ten thousand settings, according to General Luc. Who knows which one Leona chose?

Chapter 56

'YOU KNOW WHAT A SINGULARITY IS?'

Do I look like someone who knows what a singularity is? More to the point, do I look like someone that gives a fuck?

Pulling the pin from a grenade, I lob it high and hit the dirt, before rolling into a crater filled with stinking gas. Weak gravity hangs my grenade at the top of its arc, before dropping it over a broken wall. Regolith rains down in slow motion. Not sure there was anyone to kill. But the bang makes me feel better.

Choking on the gas, I crawl free and Leona's voice follows. Of course it does, it comes from the SIG-37. OctoV's avatar is making her final speech.

At least, I hope it's final. It's muddling as fuck to have your side arm switch personalities. Worse still, when everyone around you is being massacred.

'Do something useful,' I suggest.

'Like what?'

'Tell me where the fuck we are. Better still, tell me how to get to somewhere else . . .'

The bitch laughs.

'Sven,' she says. 'Take a look around you. What do you see?'

What does it think I see? A violet sky and the ruined, ruptured surface of a planetoid mined half bare for the water frozen under its dirt.

'Fuck all.'

Not a star in sight. A couple of ghostly smudges, but that's it. The air is cold enough to hurt when we breathe, and so thin the deepest breath scrapes barely enough oxygen.

General Luc is dead and Colonel Nswor, so is Major Whipple, and the captain whose jaw I broke, and the boy who showed me to the H-pad to meet Aptitude. I don't know his name, but then I don't know most of the frozen corpses around me.

It would be easier – and a fuck of a lot quicker – to count the living.

The Wolf Brigade never retreats. The Death's Head would rather die than surrender a single step. The Legion dies where it stands. The boasts infest my head like song lyrics as I find myself putting them to the test.

Vijay suggests we scavenge ammo.

If we do, he says, we'll have enough to prevent our attackers from uncoupling their mining ship from this planetoid.

Our new emperor's lie doesn't even convince himself.

At our back is a low run of stonefoam buildings with broken roofs. An explosion blew out the windows, bent girders and ripped the walls like paper. Judging from the ice dust in drifts against the walls it happened a long time ago.

Inside the biggest hangar is a machine that cracks water into oxygen. That hangar was where we came out.

'Who opened fire first?'

'Does it matter?'

Aptitude shakes her head. 'Just wondering.'

'Neen,' I bark.

'Sir?' he snaps me a ragged salute.

'Get her out of here now. Fifty paces back . . .'

My sergeant disappears with a protesting Aptitude in tow.

Slamming a fresh power pack into his pulse rifle, Ajac levers the pre-charge, waits two seconds for a diode to turn green and sticks his head over a wall, aiming for a rusting buggy that carries cutting equipment for the ship's anchor wires.

Oxygen tanks explode with a satisfying bang.

'Good shot,' Rachel says.

She is half immersed in purple gas, her Z93z wrapped in a strip of grey cloth to camouflage it as she hugs the ground near a break in Ajac's wall. An arse, broad shoulders, red hair, a rifle. She's killing our new enemy with grim determination.

You wouldn't think a mining ship was that dangerous. But this one is the size of a small city and armed with the kind of laser intended for cutting asteroids in half and freeing mile-square blocks of ice from planetoids like this.

It's been making short work of us.

'Singularity,' repeats the SIG. 'You know what that is?'

'Of course I fucking don't.'

'Know why it matters?'

'No, I don't.' Still, I'm pretty certain Leona's ghost intends to tell me.

Realizing her power pack is empty, Shil reaches for another and discovers she hasn't got one. So she grabs a Kemzin from the dirt, drops out its empty clip, and rifles its owner's body for more rounds.

Cartridges splash into a puddle of gas around her knees, making swirls in its purple surface as they fall. Her clip blips out in seconds.

Oxygen starvation makes her breathless; the cold wind purples her skin, unless that's the thin air again. Somewhere in the last half hour she has lost her helmet, her flak jacket, her pack and her scowl.

Her grin is altogether more terrifying.

The ghost of OctoV, once guardian of the true faith, is preaching heresy. This is no stranger than most of the things to happen today. So I say nothing and keep listening, although I steal ammunition from a corpse as I do, and swap my cracked helmet for an unbroken one.

'A few of you decided to become us. A few of us decided to be you. One of me decided not to be me. So it became someone else.'

'Who?'

'This me,' she says. 'As opposed to that me.' She means Gareisis, the hundred-braid, because once OctoV and he were parts of the same. Leona's ghost sounds sad.

'Vijay is the answer,' she says.

Anything else makes no sense. I just don't know what the question is. Since Leona's ghost claims not to know either, I'm going to have to work it out for myself.

'Sven . . .'

Vijay is calling me.

Turning round, I see what he's pointing at.

A spear of stars juts at forty-five degrees into the sky behind us and climbs and climbs, until it becomes a fat slash of stars and planets and local clusters that keeps climbing as our planetoid turns.

'Worth it, to see that,' he says.

Stir milk into coffee and you get a dip surrounded by milky legs that blend into rings. That's our galaxy we're looking at. We're on the outer edge of the outermost ring, looking in. 'Not over yet, sir.'

'Why? You got an idea?'

'A few . . .' Well, one actually.

'Need help?'

'No, sir.'

'Carry on then.'

Permission given, he retreats to where Aptitude waits, ten paces behind us, her face raw with cold and oxygen starvation. Neen's glance says he knows it's supposed to be fifty paces, but what can he do?

The oxygen is too thin, the wind savage and there's nothing to eat come morning but corpses. That might do for what's left of the Wolf Brigade, might do for me if it came to it. But Debro would rather starve, and so would Aptitude. And so, I suspect, would our new emperor.

'Clear me a comms channel to the captain.'

Diodes do a fancy dance as Leona's ghost leaves off preaching heresy and begins to flirt her way through the mining ship's security routines. *Pretty please*, I hear her say. *Promises, promises.* And then, *Got you.*

'Talk to the AI instead,' she suggests.

'Why?'

'Might as well start at the top.'

Taking the planet buster from around my neck, I flip the lid and turn the enamel band to prime its core. Then I hold it up, so the SIG can lenz it through to the ship. When that's done, I broadcast my message.

If the ship leaves, we will die. Since we will die, I have no hesitation in taking the AI with me. Even if the ship frees its anchors, it cannot outrun the explosion. The AI, the ship and its crew will be ripped to small pieces.

If anything remains of them at all.

All we ask is passage to the nearest planet. Since we have gold, we can offer to pay our way. Alternatively, we can all die. But that seems wasteful.

'Sven,' Leona's ghost says when I'm done, 'that was almost thoughtful.'

It takes five minutes for the firing to stop. And then a long hatch in the ship's belly drops, and a buggy bounces down the ramp. For a second it hesitates in the shadow of the ramp. But when no shots are fired, it comes towards us.

Ginal Ord is first officer on the *Heart of Darkness*, an independent but licensed mining ship, registered out of Finmu, capital of this arc of the halo. She is authorized by her captain to negotiate.

Her voice in our helmets asks who represents us.

By now Vijay stands beside me, as do most of the others. Shil still won't meet my eyes, which is to be expected. Debro waits, purple-skinned but refusing to show how cold she is. Neen and Iona stand shoulder to shoulder. While Aptitude watches Vijay, whose gaze flicks from the approaching buggy to where the Wolf Brigade lieutenant who talked to me about parole has troopers stripping valuables from the dead.

'Do we really have gold, Sven?'

I nod towards the lieutenant. 'He does, sir.'

Vijay smiles a tired smile. 'You realize,' he says, 'it's usual for senior officers to have captains or above as their ADCs?'

'Yes, sir . . .'

'Better get Neen to find you some new pips.'

Takes me a moment to work out what he means.

And then Neen grins as he hacks the rank badges from a dead captain and Iona fumbles with frozen fingers for her needle and thread, while the buggy draws to a halt and opens its glass pod to release a woman in a cheap exoskeleton.

'Sir,' I say, 'what do you think of their ship?'

'Well,' Vijay replies, 'it's large.'

That's one way of describing it. Imagine that a mad sculptor soldered together every rusting rocket and ruined hangar from the Emsworth landing fields to make a steel slum, then bolted on gun turrets armed with industrial lasers, sprayed the whole thing red and welded his handiwork to massive boosters.

'Do you want it?'
'*Sven* . . .'
'Just a thought, sir.'